Alex Andre

AS & WHEN

The E Apocrypha

Book 2

Disclaimer

All characters and events appearing in this work are fictional.

Any resemblance to real persons, living, dead, or yet to be born, is purely coincidental.

To L—for putting up with my obsessions, celebrating my highs, and carrying me through my lows.

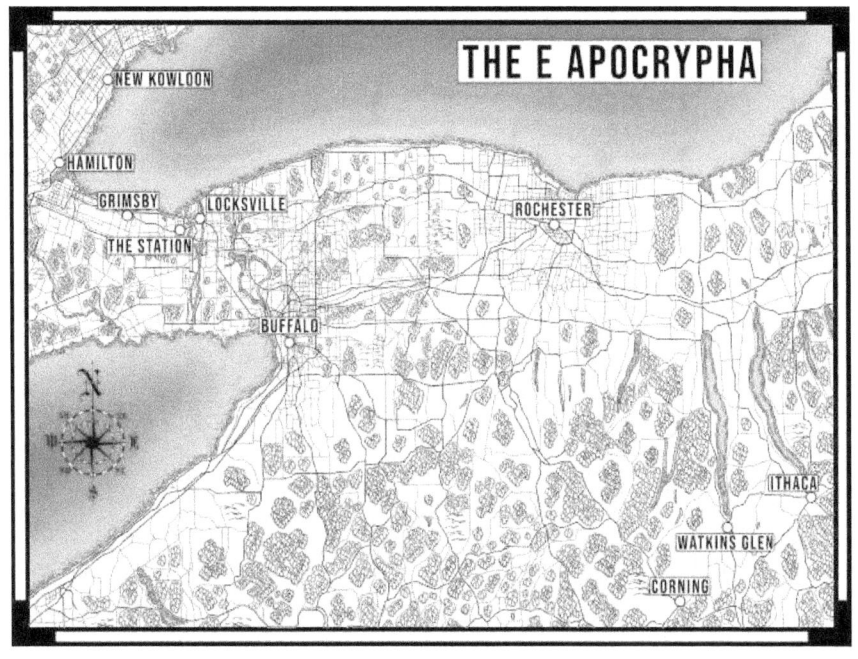

Map by Oscar Paludi "Exoniensis"

Part 1

THE BOOK

OF BO

Chapter 1

Locksville, Eight Years Ago

September 14, 34 PE

Fog. A blessing and a curse. A friend and a foe. *Foe-g*. Concealing. Deceiving. Unreliable.

As if they had a mind of their own, the bands and tatters of the milky vapors drifted through the grove, across the clearing ahead, and into the orchard.

Bo dug his boots' toes into the fir-needle covered ground. Again. As good a time as any. *Go! No, wait...*

He should have sprung from his hideout and dashed forward ten minutes ago. Or fifteen. Fog, the damn trickster, kept teasing him. One moment, a thick cloud enveloped the entire world. The next, exposed Bo and the tree he was crouching behind, making him feel naked, without as much as a light breeze to touch the hair on the back of his head.

A crack of a branch sent shivers down Bo's neck. He pressed himself tighter into the tree. Merge. Blend. Become a part of the scenery. *Fog, you bastard!* Dampening the sounds, fooling his sense of direction. Someone was out there. An animal? A bird? Birds don't break branches.

A blow between his shoulder blades ripped Bo from his tree and sent him three feet forward onto the wet grass. A deafening heartbeat or two later, before he could climb onto his feet, a heavy weight on his back pressed him into the ground.

"Why were you following us?!" A ferocious whisper in his ear.

"I wasn't!" Bo's vigorous objection turned into a mumble, with grass and mud filling his mouth. He wriggled, flailing his arms, but his attacker did not yield.

"Get off him, Marc, you're hurting him!" Another voice, thinner but insistent.

The weight on Bo's ribs lingered for another moment, then retreated, allowing him to lift his head, spit out the grass, and take a gasping breath.

"I—" He forgot what he was about to say. The most heavenly face floated before him, framed by the fog. Not beautiful, but... It wasn't scowling or angry. It didn't show disdain or pity. Nothing of the sort Bo had grown used to. It was compassionate. And yes, cute too. Enormous eyes the color of evening sky, dirty blond hair in two thick braids, and a mouth open with curiosity.

"Who are you?" the girl asked, crouching. "You here to steal apples too?"

"Bo. I'm Bo."

"*Bo*?" Her lips formed a comical ring, blowing a strand of her hair aside. "What kind of name is Bo?"

He frowned. "*My* kind. And I don't *steal*. I *take*. Who in the Seven Hells are you?"

"None of your business!" The invisible attacker cuffed him on the nape.

Bo growled and sent an elbow back and upward without looking. It connected. He rolled onto his back and found a howling, cursing boy above him. A few years older, bigger, nurturing his jaw, and promising revenge with a cold-steel stare. In one word, trouble. Bo was about to get his ass kicked.

"Stop it! Both of you!" The girl's agitated whisper gave Bo a pause. "Someone will hear! Is that what you want?"

Bo and the other boy looked at her, then at each other.

"*Now* who's the adult here?" Her crooked grin made her companion's cheeks redden. An echo of a previous argument, obviously.

She stepped closer to Bo and offered a hand. "I'm Aileen." Bo used her hand to pull himself up... She stood half a head taller than him. Her laughing eyes helped him swallow the awkward lump in his throat.

"How old are you, Bo?"

Lie? What for? "Ten."

"Awesome! I'm ten, too! And this is Marc, he's fourteen. Very serious, but not very smart." She snickered.

"Marc," said the boy, unnecessarily, rolling his eyes. "This little brat's brother. So, you weren't following us?"

"Didn't even know you were around. You shouldn't be here. This is *my* orchard."

"*Your* orchard?" Aileen's brows crept up. "You mean, your family's? Then why were you skulking?"

"Huh? Did you fall on your head?" The words slipped from Bo's tongue.

"Hey, talk nice!" Marc shifted, raising his fists.

If only Bo had someone as protective of him... "Everybody knows One-eyed Jeev's land is mine by the Deal!" He clamped his jaws and braced himself for the bigger boy's asskicking.

"The Deal?" The uncertainty of Marc's tone ruined his aggressive posture.

"Duh. Wait, you don't know the Deal?"

Aileen shook her head. Marc avoided Bo's eyes.

Bo gawked. "Where are you from?"

"Here," said Aileen. "We're from here."

"Locksville?" How come Bo had never seen them before?

"Locksville!" Marc jutted his chin and pushed his chest out.

"But you don't live in the streets."

"We—" Marc's voice faltered. "We do now," he finished firmly.

Huge beads of tears welled in Aileen's eyes. She shuddered and buried her face in her brother's jacket. "Our parents died last week." Her words were barely audible.

Marc pulled her into a hug. "Our house burned down," he hissed through his clenched teeth, over Aileen's head. "They didn't make it. We're on our own now." He paused. His features hardened, sharp cheekbones bulging out. "Tell me about the Deal."

Bo's mind was already slipping away. The fire. Charred bodies. Blackness swept into the world, reducing it to two swiftly narrowing circles... Until everything was gone.

Bo opened his eyes. Bright blue sky far, far above. Treetops, glowing in the oblique morning sunlight. No fog. He was on the ground.

Two faces leaning over him, one worried, another frowning. Ah, right. Aileen and... Mack? No, Marc. The Deal-breakers.

Something lifted off Bo's lips. What was Marc's hand doing there?

"You won't scream anymore?" asked the older boy.

"Anymore?" Bo's parched throat protested against speaking. Shit. Not again.

"You were screeching like a cat when somebody stepped on its tail." Aileen's wide eyes sparkled in the sun.

"How would you know?" Bo rasped. "You step on cats' tails often?"

A faint smile touched her lips. "Will you be okay? What happened?"

"My parents..." The blackness once more crept into his vision. Bo violently shook his head, slapped himself on the ear so hard it rang, and focused on that smile. "They died too. Two years ago."

Aileen's lips began quivering.

"No!" Bo's cry was too loud, but he couldn't care less. "Please, keep smiling! I... I feel better when you do."

She exchanged uncertain glances with her brother. Marc nodded. The forced grimace she produced was so awkward Bo couldn't help but laugh. Marc joined in. The wrinkles in the corners of Aileen's eyes straightened out, and her smile turned genuine.

Bo sighed. "Sorry. This happens to me, sometimes. When I talk about... *that.* Or some other things."

"The Deal?" Marc changed the subject.

Good. No more inconvenient questions from his sister. "Ah. Yes. Last year, all of us living in the streets, we had a *con-ven-shun.*" The word had refused to settle in Bo's head. Each time, he had to dig into his memory to rebuild it. The first part, *con*, made sense. But the rest... Oh, well. "Divided the zones, so we don't hit one place too often. I got Jeev's orchard."

"A-ha." Marc scratched his temple. "How do *we* get a zone?"

Bo met his eyes. "You don't. Didn't you hear what I said? It's all divided already." He sat up.

Marc ground his teeth. "And if we go and take what we want?"

Then you're stupid. Bo didn't say that out loud. "Then Uncle will send Streeters to beat the shit out of you. And after that, you won't be allowed to set foot in Locksville ever again."

"So... what can we do? What do we eat?" Aileen's horror was written plainly on her face.

Bo dropped his eyes. "I'll share my zone with you," he blurted before thinking it through. Stupid. But this girl... Why couldn't he resist her?

Marc clasped his shoulder. "Thank you. But I still want to talk to whoever's in charge of the streets."

"You— Okay, fine. I'll introduce you."

"Great. Now, can we go *take* some apples?"

Bo scanned the surroundings. No fog. No fog! "No!" His voice dropped to a whisper. "The fog's all gone. Jeev will see us."

"But I'm hungry, Bo." Aileen's shaky, mewling voice had him wrapped around her finger. "Had nothing to eat in a day. I want an apple. Or five."

Bo rolled his eyes, glimpsing Marc's understanding grin. Apparently, a lot of eye-rolling happened around this girl.

"Fine." Bo got his bearings. In bright sunlight, the place looked different from its fogged self. "This way."

"You, there!"

Bo almost jumped out of his boots. Shit! Jeev! "Scoot!"

He grabbed his half-full bag of apples, clasped Aileen's wrist with his other hand, and rushed through the orchard, ducking to squeeze between the trees. Marc followed on their heels with a deafening rustle. Everyone and their dog must have heard them already.

"I'm gonna fuckin' shoot you dead, little assholes!" Jeev's words rang closer than Bo had hoped. The sound of a racked shotgun made his skin crawl. Scrawny as he was, he felt a giant bull's eye painted on his back.

"Run!" he panted, pulling Aileen so hard her feet barely touched the ground. "Faster!"

The fence appeared behind the last row of apple trees. Almost there.

Bo launched the bag to the other side, threw his jacket over the barbed wire coils crowning the obstacle, and pushed the girl up. She scuttled like a lizard, clutching at the chain link cells. He interlaced his fingers and bent his knees. "Step in!" he growled at Marc. Marc didn't need to be asked twice. Holding the heavy boy's foot, Bo grunted and heaved him up. Marc grabbed the top of the fence, pulled himself, rolled over Bo's jacket, and jumped off. Bo climbed up after him...

"Ima kill you, thieving piece of shit!" sounded right below him.

Bo froze, straddling the fence. This was it. End of the road. At least Aileen and Marc would be safe, taking cover across the clearing. Bo closed his eyes, waiting for a shot.

Instead, a savage blow landed on his right thigh. Searing pain exploded on impact and filled the universe. Bo toppled over. A scream tore his throat apart. His pants caught in the barbed wire and he slammed into the fence, hanging upside down. He was too dazed to react, to protect his face with his hands.

The fence wires cut into his cheek and nose. Behind the splotches in his teary eyes and the square chain link cells, Jeev's face floated not a foot away. His one good eye studied Bo like an annoying bug. But all Bo could see was the disgusting empty socket where the other eye had been, in an angry shade of red.

"What am I gonna do with you?" Jeev scratched his gray stubble with his gun's stock. "Wouldn't be fair to shoot you trussed like this, and with that broken leg, you ain't gonna be much of a runner. Hm."

The words came from far away, beyond the shrieking of the pain in Bo's leg, echoing in nauseating waves through his body.

Jeev straightened up. "Sorry, kid. There's still a lesson to be taught here. Nothing personal, eh?" He pulled his shotgun back.

The last thing Bo saw was the butt of the gun swung into his face.

Chapter 2

Corning

October 2, 42 PE

Bo pushed away the branches and scanned the approach one last time.

Tick breathed over his shoulder.

They'd watched the perimeter for an hour and still hadn't seen a single guard. That made sense: why spend precious personnel on guarding something so useless? Yes, the Lords of Watkins took pride—a disproportionate amount of it—in owning such an unusual place. Beyond that, no one gave half a damn about the Museum of Glass. Well, not exactly. *Someone* gave enough of a damn to commission Locksville Streeters to do the grab and run job. Enough of a damn to attach to the contract a price tag so high that not only had Aileen accepted it, she also persuaded Bo to personally take care of it.

"This place is enormous!" Tick whispered. "Do you know where it is, whatever we're after?"

Bo half-nodded, half-shrugged. "Kind of."

"'Kind of'? And that's—"

"Shut up, Tick. I don't want to be here any more than you. You know how I hate travel—"

"No kidding. Everyone knows how you hate to travel. And, mind you, you talked my ears off about that."

Bo winced. That was true. "You brought me here. Thank you for that. Bring me back, and I'll thank you again. Right now, let me do my job, okay?"

"Sure, boss. Whatever you say."

Tick was making fun of him. As usual.

Bo studied the oddly shaped building. Why on Earth would anyone desire those useless trinkets this much? Who might that be? Aileen had mentioned a middleman... He grunted. Whoever the client, the job wasn't going to do itself. Bo rose from the bushes and hobbled toward the curving wall.

The upper floor overhang provided relative privacy. Bo attached a suction cup to the window, held his breath, and pulled the glass cutter's arm, drawing a perfect circle. The scraping of the diamond on the glass *was* quiet, must have been, had always been... But the silence of the windless night made it earsplitting, giving him goosebumps. Bo flattened himself against the glass wall and slowly exhaled. Seconds passed. No one came running or raised an alarm.

Bo lowered the round cut out into the grass.

Hopping over the windowsill with style would've been nice. Instead, Bo pulled himself through the newly made two-foot hole, as elegantly—or not—as his damn lame leg allowed. Inside, he fetched the hand-drawn map from his pocket and squinted to discern the scribbles in the faint moonlight. The building's irregular shape made it easy to orient oneself. A-ha. That way.

At first, Bo tiptoed through the halls, clearing each corner. After a while of not encountering a single living soul, he grew bold. He strolled on, periodically stopping to marvel at one intricate showpiece or another. Vases with swirly frozen smoke. Miniature bottles, red and green, painted with golden patterns. Jewelry, and jewelry boxes—all looking so expensive he could probably buy half the City of Locksville and have spare change left. If he could find a buyer insane enough to pay real coin for pointless trinkets. The possibilities were endless, but... *Concentrate*. He wasn't there to ransack the place. He had a very particular order to fulfill.

Bo continued past immense compositions of irregular shapes suspended from the ceiling in a circle wider than his arm span. As if someone had spilled molten glass and it solidified in the air, never reaching the floor. The full moon's pale light seeping through the tall windows rendered the exhibits otherworldly. Human hands produced *that*? No way. Impossible, even before the E.

The last turn, and... Seven bloody Hells! The colorful marine creatures on display were striking in their lifelike precision. Creepy. Unreal. Bo's boot squeaked against the floor as he stopped dead in his tracks. He took a cautious breath to ensure he was still surrounded by air—and not water.

He shook himself out of the reverie, opened his duffle bag, and laid out the packaging material. Lots of it. Baby blankets, woolen rags, small down-filled pillows.

Bo tentatively reached for a bizarre many-legged beast—or not legs? Did underwater crawlers have legs? Whatever those were. His hand jerked back. The figurine was cool and smooth, and too gentle to withstand a human touch, for sure. Or was it? Some amazing artist had made it, once upon a time. Someone else had put it on display here. Which meant it could be handled.

Bo gingerly picked up the creature with the tips of two fingers, turned to place it on a wad of rags, and... *Crack*. The sound echoed between the display cabinets. The millipede—if it was that—snapped in two, leaving the head in Bo's hand. He reacted fast enough to catch the body in mid-air, breaking off a few of the maybe-legs. Oh, no. His throat tightened, and tears swelled in his eyes. The irreversibility of the loss overwhelmed him. His carelessness had deprived the world of something unique that would never come to be again. Shit. Shit-shit-shit.

Bo stared at the forever ruined creature. Sorry, buddy. He placed it aside, to be packed separately. No sense in leaving it there. He'd have a sad souvenir of this day. Symbolic, in a way; broken like he was. Must be more careful with the next ones, or Aileen would snap *his* head off.

Mindfully, rethinking every movement, Bo proceeded to pack other exhibits. He'd got so immersed in the process, he lost all track of time. When the last, twelfth piece, wrapped in countless layers of padding, found a new cozy home in the bowels of Bo's duffel bag, murky pre-dawn had already painted the skies behind the windows in light gray. Damn. It wasn't supposed to take that long. They'd planned to leave the Museum behind under the cover of darkness. Bo consulted the map one last time, confirming his path out. Retracing his steps all the way to the cut window was going to take another twenty minutes. Tick was guaranteed to be less than thrilled. Bo sighed. Caution called to take the long route, but with no one around, he might as well leave the building like a normal, decent human being he'd never been.

Bo headed for the main entrance and, quietly whistling a lighthearted tune, crossed the narrow pedestrian bridge. The two men stepping out of the trees appeared as surprised as him.

October 3, 42 PE

"Howdy, gents!" Bo waved a hand at the newcomers and greeted them with his best toothless smile. Not the time for self-conscious, tight-lipped grins. Let the missing teeth he'd lost to that shotgun stock as a kid charm the locals. Or show them his harmlessness, whichever worked. "How're you this nice early morning?"

The men—members of some kind of military force, or just highway-men?—exchanged puzzled glances.

"Who are you? And what are you doin' here?" asked the older, heavier-built, more senior-looking one. His hand slid to the handle of the pistol on his belt. Metal plates sewn onto his jacket clanked. So, guards. Robbers wouldn't have cared about Bo's business at the Museum. They would've just killed him and taken his loot.

"Me?" Bo snorted, suggesting the very question was utterly ridiculous. He continued walking at a tangent from the guards.

"Yes, you."

"What, nobody told you?" Bo's legs kept carrying him on. If only they'd allowed him to walk without a limp... People with physical disabilities always raised suspicions.

"Told us what? I said, stop!"

The steps behind Bo accelerated. With no chance of outrunning anyone but a drunken turtle, he obeyed. Bullshitting his way out was the only card left to play.

"The Lord of Watkins won't be happy to hear about this!" Bo jutted his chin out, channeling his most lofty arrogance. "No, he won't be happy at all!"

Thin ice. Should've at least found out their damn Lord's name.

The guards stopped a few steps away. The younger, carrying a saber instead of a gun, examined Bo with a suspicious squint. The older man's face stretched in a carnivorous grin.

Uh-oh.

"Won't be happy *at all*," drawled the senior guard. Bo's own words, ominous when thrown back at him, made the hairs on his neck stand on their ends. "Countess Anna will not be amused to hear someone thinks she's a *he*."

Shit. Things were going further south, fast. How could he be so stupidly careless? Should have known better. Should have remembered: bad stuff happens when you travel.

A heavy hand clasped Bo's shoulder. He flinched.

"Is he giving you trouble, soldiers?" The guards straightened. The younger one twitched to salute, reconsidering at the last moment. Tick's authoritative voice and chiseled face tended to produce such an effect. "Let me handle this petty thief. I'll make sure everything he took returns to its rightful place."

Tick dragged Bo back toward the Museum's entrance. Bo, quick on his feet—figuratively, if not literally—played along. "Sir, no, please don't!"

The older guard cleared his throat. "Um, excuse me?"

Tick stopped, turned, and considered the man benevolently. "Yes, soldier?"

Bo pulled his head into his shoulders and twisted his face into a whiny grimace. He aimed to look like a cat held by its scruff, having been caught peeing in its master's boot.

The guard stepped forward, his eyes narrowed. "I'm sorry, who are you?"

"Someone who's here to ensure Countess Anna's treasures stay hers!" Tick shot back. "Who are *you*?"

"Sarge Beaverton." Another step. "And your name is...?"

"Follow me, sarge." Tick conspiratorially lowered his voice and pulled Bo to the Museum doors again. "I'll tell you inside."

Shouldn't they be escaping into the forest instead? With bitter yearning, Bo tracked the dark tree line over his shoulder until the doors closed behind him. He opened his mouth, but Tick's hand shoved him aside.

Bo's teeth clattered as he sprawled on the dusty floor, protecting the precious bag from impact. Behind his back, hacking, yelping, and dull impact sounds announced the one thing Bo hated more than travel: violence. He lay, waiting it out, careful not to look. Tick didn't need his help. They both were better off if Bo didn't interfere.

"Boss," Tick said high above him a minute later. Not even out of breath.

Bo sat. Both guards stirred on the floor, dazed, bound, and gagged. Damn, Tick was good! Even with the edge provided by the closed quarters, tackling two armed, strong, and likely trained opponents like that must've been challenging. And he'd ensured this happened out of sight, in case these two weren't alone. Smart—for muscle!

Tick did not pause to bask in well-deserved pride. Fists on his hips, he stared Bo down. "Seriously, boss, what's wrong with you? What gave you the idea you could dance through the main doors right into the street?"

An excellent question. Bo shrunk under Tick's unblinking gaze. He'd got sloppy, lulled by the quiet night without a soul to disturb his peace. "My bad, man. Won't happen again."

"Damn right it won't! It's not only *your* neck on the block. Next time, I'm not letting you out of sight." Tick's simmering subsided. "Okay, let's try this once more." He peeked through the doors and signaled to Bo to follow.

They tiptoed halfway across the bridge when a chain of five people parted from the forest and greeted them with drawn bows. Tick hung his head and raised his hands. Bo gingerly put down the bag and followed suit. Well, shit.

"You promised to tell me your name." The sergeant's mouth curved in a sarcastic smile. His shrewd, understanding eyes pierced Tick's.

Despite being tied to a tree, Tick beamed back, defiantly exposing teeth red with the blood from his broken lips in an unsettling display, evoking vampire tales.

The sergeant didn't flinch. "You're a first-class fighter, mystery man. Strong. Fast. Bold. I respect that. Unfortunately..." He sighed, studied his fingernails, and met Tick's eyes again.

That *unfortunately* tied Bo's guts into a knot. His heart skipped a beat.

"This scrawny cripple"—the guard tilted his head toward Bo—"is clearly a thief. Had you stayed hidden, fighter, we would've only roughed up your buddy a little. Not too bad, considering his affliction. We aren't savages here, you know. But no, you had to intervene. To humiliate me, Her Ladyship's Master-at-Arms, in front of my men. *That* cannot go unpunished. Sorry."

In one step, he closed the distance to Tick and calmly slid a knife across his throat.

"No!" The air whooshed out of Bo's lungs with the cry. His chest constricted, leaving him breathless. Tears gushed from his eyes, blurring the image of Tick sagging on his restraints with his head hanging down and to a side.

Bo thrashed against the ropes holding him to a tree, with the rough bark scraping his back, and the world blessedly turned dark.

"You're a strange little fellow."

The disembodied voice bore no malice, only perplexity.

Bo opened his eyes. He was on the ground. The sergeant squatted nearby. Bo turned away from the murderer and... peered straight at Tick's lifeless form. He groaned. His body convulsed, arching like a bow.

Beaverton's bark, "Rivera, hide the bloody corpse already!" split the air as Bo was blacking out again.

No one close by. Good. Bo pushed himself off the ground. *Pushed.* He stared at his hands. Unbound, unlike his legs. He sat up. Her Ladyship's seven guards had assembled around a campfire twenty steps away, speaking and laughing as if nothing horrible had just happened.

Bo closed his eyes and groaned. Tick, dead. Aileen's mission, failed. His future, gloomy. All because of his recklessness.

The smells wafting from the fire made Bo's stomach growl. The irresistible drive to sink his teeth into something pushed the unwelcome—but inevitable—thoughts to the back of his head. *Gwrrr*, twisted the all-consuming emptiness in his belly. Ravenous, as always, after an *episode*.

"Hey!" Bo yelled. *No more of that*, objected his aching throat. So, he'd been screeching again. Okay, one last shout. "If you ain't gonna kill me, gimme something to eat!"

The sergeant nodded at a soldier. The man grumbled, climbed to his feet, splashed a ladle from the pot into a tin bowl, and trudged toward Bo. Bo tracked the progress of the bowl, painfully slow for his sucking hunger. The dish halted several steps short, slumping lower and lower, spilling its coveted content. Bo's uncomprehending gaze traveled up from the lost chow... and discovered an arrow that had pierced the food-bearer's neck.

A commotion erupted around the fire, but Bo refused to watch. Three seizures in a row would be too much; he'd be sore for days.

None of this would have happened back home. Why had he let Aileen convince him to go? He'd never left Locksville before. "Tick will keep you safe." And that smile. Bo would have agreed to anything for that smile. He had.

Bo pushed his face into the fallen leaves, clean at the top and slimy closer to the ground. He squeezed his eyes shut, covered his ears with his palms, and emptied his mind. Whatever was happening would have to happen without his active participation, or even awareness. He'd already seen one death too many for a day. Hopefully, there would still be stew left in the pot by the time the violence had run its course.

Someone nudged his shoulder. "Tag. You're 'it'."

Bo craned his head and peeked with one eye. A uniformed soldier armed with a bow towered above him, cracking a smile. Not quite condescending... Lenient, maybe. His fatigues differed in color from those of Beaverton's men.

Bo rolled over and sat, hugging his knees. "I was playing hide-and-seek."

"Wrong game, then." The soldier unsheathed a knife.

Bo froze. The events had been unfolding too quickly to catch up. If he was going to die, so be it. At least, he won't have to bear the burden of responsibility for Tick's...

The soldier bent down and cut the rope tying Bo's ankles.

Oh. Okay.

Bo scanned the clearing. Other soldiers milled around, rummaging through pieces of captured equipment. A circle of small mounds surrounded the fire. Not dead people! Mounds of... rags. Yes, that. Mounds of rags that deserved to die.

His vision did not darken.

"By the way, thanks for screaming, pal." Great, now the soldier was mocking him. "You helped us locate these buggers. We've been searching all over the place."

"Why?" What an odd conversation to have over seven dead bodies. Eight, counting Tick. Shit.

"Seriously? Don't you know who we are?"

"N-no." Was he supposed to? "Sir," he added as an afterthought.

"You're not from around here, are you?" The soldier squinted.

Which answer would work better? Nobody liked strangers. But these people had attacked the locals, so being *from around here* didn't seem to offer much protection.

"No, sir."

"I'd ask where you're from, but I don't care. His Excellency Terrence the Second, Lord of Ithaca, has tasked Cayuga Rifles—that's us—with teaching a lesson to Watkins and that usurper whore Anna. Which we did. Spectacularly, if I say so myself. By the looks of it, pal, you were their prisoner. Which makes you our ally. The enemy of my enemy, you know, all that. What did you do to upset them?"

Might as well tell the truth. "Stole a few trinkets from the Museum." Bo raised his eyes to gauge his savior's reaction.

"Did you, now?" The soldier appeared amused. "Awesome! A cherry on top, as insults to Anna go. Okay, we're going to take off. Need a ride?"

"East?"

"Yup."

Not at all where he needed to go. Two-hundred-odd kilometers, north-west-bound, awaited him. Through unfamiliar, lawless, rough terrain. A week, if the cart and the horse were still where he and Tick had hidden them. And if not? What if it snowed?

Alone. Far from home. From friends. From Aileen. No way he'd make it back on his own. Oh, Tick...

Coldness spread down Bo's limbs. He shivered. "Um. Sir, how many people do you have?"

"Ten."

"What if Lady Anna—"

"The usurper whore."

"Yes. What if the usurper sends a larger force after you?"

"By the time she finds out what happened here, we'll be home with a few jugs of beer."

Bo let his weasel brain carry him away. "But do you want her to know this was His Excellency's lesson? She may retaliate, and your people would die. Wouldn't it be better to leave her guessing? Suspecting everyone around? Ruining trusted relationships? Flinching at her own shadow?" Convincing himself was a surefire way to convince others, and he loved his own ideas.

The soldier's eyes lit up. His lips parted. He was already hooked. "For a thief, you sure can talk, little pal. Spill it, what's on your mind?"

"Travel north, toward Rochester. The Watkiners won't expect that, will they? Turn east there. Head home on the far side of Cayuga Lake."

"Clever. Why?"

"Why what?"

"Why would you help our cause? And don't sell me any 'thanks for saving my life' bullshit, eh?"

Bo shut his mouth, already opened to sell exactly that. Fine. Time for honesty.

"Because coming north with you would take me closer to home. Safely."

The soldier—or likely the officer—examined Bo's innocent expression and nodded. "Let's go."

"I need to get my cart from the other side of the Museum. And my duffel bag, from somewhere around here. And... something to eat."

The officer rewarded him with a guarded smile. "*Now* I know you're telling the truth. No one fakes hunger."

October 5, 42 PE

"This is it, pal. We turn east here. Sure you don't want to come with us? His Excellency can use someone as crafty as you."

Commander Reiner of the Cayuga Rifles had shown himself sharp enough not to expect a positive answer. Which made his offer all the more endearing.

Bo gave him a guilty smile. "I may take you up on this invitation one day, Commander. But now I must—"

"Finish your job, I get it."

"Any chance to tempt you with a slight detour further west?"

"As much as I enjoy your company, pal... Your scheme has already cost us four extra days."

He leaned to Bo and whispered, "And if we cross paths with Buffs, things may turn dicey."

"Oh?"

"Yeah." Reiner chuckled. "They don't look kindly at our alliance with Rochester."

That made for an interesting map. And explained a lot. "Let me guess. The Watkiners side with Buffalo?"

The Commander's eyes grew a fraction wider. "Aren't you a shrewd little kid?"

Bo humbly looked at his feet. "Me? Not at all. Buffs and Roches—those are shrewd."

"How do you mean?"

"Don't you see, Commander? They're playing you off each other. I bet you ten coins the rest of the Finger Lakes lords split their allegiances roughly half and half. Am I right?"

Reiner's dark gaze pierced Bo. All the confirmation Bo needed.

"You know too much for a common thief," the Ithacan said, all his benevolence melted away.

"Know? I had no idea." Bo spread his arms. "You just confirmed my guess."

But the connection they had shared was already severed. Before, he'd been a harmless oddity, rewarding to save at no extra cost. Suddenly, Bo revealed himself as a player from a different field. Hide-and-seek, not tag.

He sighed. So be it.

"How do I find you in Locksville?" Ah. Reiner did figure him out.

Bo smiled. "You don't."

The Commander reprovingly tilted his head, and Bo relented. He owed this man his life, after all. "When in Locksville, ask for me in the streets. I'll find you myself."

Reiner pursed his lips. "Figures. Cheers, pal. You take care of yourself, eh?"

Chapter 3

Locksville

October 7, 42 PE

The cart rolled onto the bridge. Bo pulled the reins.

Last time he'd crossed it—in the opposite direction—it had looked different. *Everything* had looked different. Everything *had been* different.

Nine days ago, Tick had been driving, effortlessly navigating the zigzagging path between the barricades.

Nine days ago, Tick was alive.

Bo bit his lip. What was done was done. Almost home now.

Rainbow Bridge, the last obstacle. A narrow winding passage between rusty car skeletons, meant to prevent any attacking force from rushing either side, presented an insurmountable challenge for Bo's lackluster driving skills. He sighed, and let the horse do its job. For the last few days, the chestnut mare had taken Bo where he needed, with minimal direction from his side.

Halfway across, the sound of the hooves against the pavement changed. He craned his neck, looking back. *Ah, that spot.* Wooden planks covered a hole blown in the bridge years ago. One day, they'd rot enough to drop someone all the way down, into the churning river. Bo's stomach sunk at the springiness under his cart, but then he was back on a solid surface. *Here's to never crossing bridges again.* He shivered. *Scrap that. Here's to never traveling again.*

The road widened, running into a wall of fortifications up-armored with random pieces of metal and concrete; the Customs booths, all but one closed.

"Bo." The Customs officer acknowledged him with barely suppressed curiosity.

"Jerome." Nice to dispel someone's boredom. Even nicer not to be asked questions he wouldn't be forthcoming to answer.

Curt nods, and he was through, leaving the roar of the Falls behind. The Customs did not interfere with the Streeters; the Streeters did not interfere with the Customs. Live and let live.

Bo had once asked the Uncle—way back, before Aileen had succeeded him—why the Customs were so lenient toward them. If the Customs personified the law, and the Streeters operated outside it...

"Not *outside*, Bo. *Beside* it," Uncle Stanley had said, tilting his head. "Feel the difference?"

Bo hadn't understood shit then, but nodded knowingly. It all came to him later, when he grasped the full picture of the elegant complementary structure the two powers of Locksville comprised.

That unshakable balance Bo had known for most of his life wavered only once. Following Uncle Stanley's disappearance, all Seven Hells broke loose. Power tolerated no vacuum, and the void created by his absence sucked in rogues of all stripes. Nasty stuff swept over Locksville, spilling from its underworld onto the surface. The Troubles. The *good*, institutional Locksville shuddered, calling in the Counter Insurgency Unit to patrol the streets. All commerce halted—legal and *extra*legal—until the future Aunt Aileen stepped in, reestablishing the order and weeding out dissent with an iron fist. The fiercest, hardest, most ruthless seventeen-year-old Locksville had ever seen. A girl. The most important girl in Bo's life. And he? He had settled for being her best friend. And the consigliere.

Echoes of his horse's hooves pulled him back into the present. The tunnel, already? He must've day-dreamed through the last kilometers.

Good to be home. Save for the need to explain Tick's absence to Aileen.

"Shit, Tick..." Did he say that out loud? Bo looked up at the picturesque clouds drifting lazily across the perfectly blue fall sky. "Sorry, man, wherever you are. I'm so, so, *so* sorry."

Tick did not answer. Typical. With nothing better to do, his tenacity, which had earned him his nickname, could be concentrated on tormenting Bo's conscience now. As with everything Tick did—*had* done—he did it well. Smuggler. Wilderness guide. Enforcer, when called for. Bo's friend; one of the oldest. "Shit, Tick."

———

"Afternoon, boss. Welcome back."

"Hey, Goose. Take care of the horse and the cart, will you?" Bo passed the reins to the massive guy.

"Sure thing." Goose helped Bo off the driver's seat. "Where's Tick?"

Bo winced. Aileen had to hear this first. He grabbed his duffle bag and rushed into the Warehouse, pulling his leg with a louder than usual shuffle. Every step bringing him closer to Aileen made the need to see her more unbearable. Stupid leg.

The labyrinth of storage partitions—familiar, yet oddly changed, ever so imperceptibly, in Bo's absence. Or it was Bo who'd changed. Like best friends whose paths had diverged, each now carrying the baggage and the scars acquired apart. Like Bo and Marc.

Sounds echoed in the hollow space under the metal roof high above. Streeters went about their business, as if everything was normal; as if Bo hadn't entered the building, harboring the horrible news; as if Tick was coming back.

Past the guardroom, through the reception. Ignoring Fox, who sprung up behind his desk, Bo pushed the door handle...

"Boss." Something in Fox's voice made Bo freeze. "She's not there, boss."

Bo's muscles spasmed, protesting his attempt to move. With a dizzying struggle, he turned until his eyes met Fox's.

"Where. Is. She." The *wrongness* in Fox's contorted, panicked face made speech excruciatingly difficult.

"Th-that's the thing, b-boss..." Fox. Stuttering. *No. Leen!* "N-nobody's seen her."

Bo forced the viscous fog out of his head, regaining control of his voice. "How long?"

"Two days. We've been looking everywhere!"

"'We'? Who else knows about this?"

"No one. The Small Council. Me. You. That's it."

"Keep it that way. Last thing we need is another round of the Troubles. Oscar?"

"In his office."

Bo hobbled to the other end of the reception room. Oscar jerked, alarmed by the creaking door, met Bo's questioning stare, and dejectedly shook his head.

"Shit." Weakness overtook Bo's shaking knees, and he dropped into the guest chair.

"Yes, Bo. Deep shit."

If Aileen had not designated her Second as the Acting Uncle, that meant... Bo leaned his elbows on his knees and rubbed his cheeks. That meant she had not known she was leaving.

Bo forcefully exhaled and straightened up.

"Here's what everyone needs to hear, Oscar. Aileen is traveling. On a secret mission. Yes, important, secret mission, okay? So secret, no one knew she'd left you to be her Acting. Until now."

"Until now? What has changed… supposedly?"

"Now *I* have returned, and made her orders public, alright?"

Oscar inclined his head, struggling to catch up. A reliable guy, just not too quick-witted.

Bo frowned. "Not a single person can know she's missing, understand? Or you'll get such a shitstorm on your hands, the Troubles would look like a stroll along the Canal."

"And you? What are you going to do?"

"What do you think? Someone's got to go looking for her, right?"

Lost in his thoughts, Bo strode toward the White House. His limp became less noticeable when he didn't concentrate on it. Or so Aileen had told him. *Leen. What are you up to?*

Aunt Aileen did not have to report her movements to anyone, naturally, but most of the time still did. Basic operational security, and she was far beyond basic. The few times she hadn't, she'd nominated Oscar as Acting Uncle before leaving. Something so urgent had come up she'd had no time for that? A remote possibility. The only remaining alternative… *Okay, stop avoiding the obvious. Taken.*

After leaving Oscar's office, Bo had questioned Fox about suspicious activity in his absence. Fox had scratched his head and mentioned a couple of Buffs caught snooping around the Warehouse the day before. Nothing overtly hostile, not enough to justify breaking a few fingers to get honest answers. They'd been shown out not too gently. The whole affair left a foul taste in Bo's mouth. One thing was obvious: they weren't the ones who'd taken Aileen, or they wouldn't have been looking for her. Who, then?

A pair of military boots, firmly planted on the cracked concrete, entered Bo's field of vision and he stopped. He'd been doing this again—walking without looking. Bo's gaze climbed up and found a young soldier attached to the boots.

The soldier looked Bo up and down and graced him with an unfriendly "State your business."

The corporal on the other side of the White House's massive front door punched his subordinate in the shoulder. "Are you out of your fucking mind, dimwit? It's Bo!"

The soldier's cheeks paled. "Sorry, sir. Go ahead, sir." He shuffled aside, opening the door for Bo and ushering him in.

Bo ignored the rookie, acknowledged the corporal, and entered the grand foyer. In Marc's absence, only one person in Locksville could be of potential help: his boss. The mysterious, all-knowing Head of the Intelligence Service. Bo had no reason to frequent Locksville's Government Headquarters and needed a moment to get his bearings. *Ah, there.* He headed for the carpeted steps.

The assistant perked up, but Bo left him no time to intercept him, marching straight to the office door and pushing it open without knocking.

"Ah, Bo." Weinberg beamed, not skipping a beat, as if he'd been expecting this visitor, waved his assistant away, and invited Bo to sit.

Bo eyed the infamously torturous guest armchair and remained standing. His lips curved down. What an abomination. He should get one.

Weinberg grinned, rose, and brought a spare wooden chair from the corner. Having fulfilled his hospitality duties, he settled again behind his desk and aimed a mute question at Bo.

Bo reciprocated with what he hoped was an inquisitive stare. Weinberg did not yield. Relenting, Bo squeezed out, "Aileen."

Weinberg perked up. "What about her?"

"Shit. So you don't know."

"Know what? You're getting me worried."

"Makes two of us."

"Enough. Start talking."

"I've just returned from... traveling. She's been gone for two days, Dave, and nobody knows shit."

Weinberg's brows crept closer together. Bo had his attention. Or triggered his displeasure at being addressed by his first name. Or both.

"And you came to me because..."

"Who else would I come to?" Bo snapped. "Marc is not around, and you're 'the man who knows everything', no? Well, tell me what you know."

The silence stretched while Weinberg rubbed his eyes. When his hand came down, he looked a few years older. His true age, forty or even more. Ancient.

"Leave Marc to me. It's... complicated. As for Aileen, I haven't heard anything out of the ordinary. I can tell you I didn't give her any business. How are the matters on your end? Are you in control of the situation?"

"If you're worried about new Troubles, don't be. I deputized Oscar. He isn't Aileen, but he can run a tight ship. Our end will be fine."

They stared at each other. Weinberg, obviously calculating if he could trust Bo's assurances. Bo... Something in Weinberg's words scratched at the edge of his consciousness. *Wait, what?*

"Didn't give her any business?" Bo's soft words crawled like a hissing snake across the host's desk.

Weinberg sighed. "I figured it's time for you to find out. Especially, considering the circumstances."

Bo ran both palms through his hair. Not a squeak from Aileen about this. Hadn't she trusted him?

"Don't beat yourself up, Bo. It was strictly 'need to know'. I could benefit from, let's put it this way, running an occasional errand on the quiet side. Not through the official channels. Plausible deniability."

"Of course. It's a two-way street. How could I be so blind?"

"I've always admired your sharpness, Bo."

"Spare me." Bo sneered.

"As you wish. But be careful with your analogies. This isn't a two-way street. *I* don't run errands for the Streeters. You need me more than I need you."

"Yeah. Right."

Weinberg's eyes narrowed as he leaned against his chair. "Got something to say? By all means, don't hold back."

Bo gave Weinberg a thin, tight-lipped smile. The kind that made people question his motives, or upgrade their estimates of the danger he presented. "Oh, you need us more than we need you, Dave. Our sort of activities are inevitable. It's better to keep those handled by a known faction with established ties. The devil you know." Bo pointed at himself with a thumb. "The alternative? Everlasting Troubles."

Weinberg listened to Bo's heated monologue, resting his chin in his hand. "I can never keep up with how fast you kids grow up," he murmured.

Bo flushed. He was the second most powerful man in Locksville's second most powerful structure! *Kids*?! Then again, Weinberg was the first in *the* most powerful structure. And had been forever. Might as well call them kids.

"Don't get angry, Bo." Weinberg's voice was soft and... caring? "That was a compliment."

Was this how loving parents spoke to their children? Must be nice... Bo pulled himself together. "So, what do we do? Where can she be?"

"What happened to Uncle Stanley?"

Bo's breath caught in his throat. The conversation was taking a far grimmer turn than he'd hoped. He shook his head, not meeting Dave's gaze.

"Don't know? Neither do I," admitted Weinberg. "All I have is indirect, *third*-hand intel. There's a possibility it was The Station's doing."

Bo raised his eyes. Blood vacated his face. His stomach turned. "To destabilize Locksville."

Weinberg pointed at him with both index fingers. "Bingo. Worked well, wouldn't you say?"

"Holy shit. Aileen—" Shivers ran down Bo's neck. His hands trembled. *Oh, crap. Not another seizure. Not now.*

Weinberg brought up a hand in a warning. "Hold your horses. The Station is the least likely party to be involved this time. Marc—"

"What's he got to do with anything?"

"Told you, it's complicated. Marc is running The Station now."

Bo leaned forward. "He *what*?!"

"Yeah, hard to wrap your mind around. This isn't public knowledge yet, keep it under your hat, eh? To make matters more challenging, he and I aren't on the best of terms these days."

Bo suppressed another *what?* ready to slip from his tongue.

Weinberg pinched his chin between a thumb and a finger. "Go there. See Marc. If he'd extracted Aileen to keep her safe from me... it's all good. And if not, he's got a few former Inquisitors sticking around. They may know something, if this was his predecessor's plan."

"*Go*?" That came out sour.

"What's the matter? You said you travel now. Take Tick with you."

"Tick's dead."

"Oh. How?"

Bo clenched his teeth. "Irrelevant."

"Sorry. I'll give you a man of mine. For security."

"For security." Bo allowed his skepticism to surface.

"Rajan!" Weinberg yelled. "Come here!" Then added, quieter, barely audibly, "Bo. Tell Marc, whatever our disagreements, I'd never hurt Aileen. She's like a daughter to me."

⸻

Whoa. What a brute! Twice Bo's size. The man nearly scraped the door jambs with his shoulders.

"Yes, boss?"

Hold on. The slumping posture, the eyes seeking approval. A strongman? Definitely. But not a fighter. Too docile.

Weinberg pointed. "This here is Bo. You'll accompany him to The Station, to see Marc."

Rajan's taciturn face soured.

Weinberg's voice grew brusquer. "Bo and I are looking for Marc Novak's sister."

Bo's newfound bodyguard met his commander's stare with a flagrantly insubordinate glower. "Is she a traitor too?"

In a blink, Bo found his hand clutching Rajan's shirt. His other palm gripped his pocket knife. "No one. Speaks. Like that. About. Aunt Aileen. Apologize, or I'll cut your junk off." Rajan couldn't know Bo was all bark, no bite... Or was he? His hiss half-scared even himself.

Rajan didn't twitch a muscle, but his gray skin paled.

"That's enough." Weinberg's level remark pierced the crimson bubble of Bo's anger. Bo released his grip and stepped back.

Rajan tracked him until Bo was seated again. "*Scuse*. No disrespect."

"Play nice, children." Weinberg's dead-serious expression did not match his jocular words. "You, no name-calling. You, no poking holes in my men."

"Why send me, boss?"

"Bo is nonviolent."

Rajan's eyebrow crept up a smidge, but Weinberg ignored that. "He won't stand a chance in an open fight."

"Neither will he," Bo shot back begrudgingly.

Weinberg's grin broke the tension. "I keep forgetting how sharp you are."

Bo accepted the compliment with a curt nod, without breaking eye contact.

Weinberg spread his arms. "You've got me. I need Rajan at The Station to see what's cooking. I'll get a CIU detail to accompany you two there tomorrow morning. Satisfied?"

"For now."

"Don't push it, Bo." And just like that, they weren't equals anymore, no matter how much Bo wished to believe the opposite.

"What happened between Marc and him?" Bo nodded at Rajan.

"He'd saved Marc's life. They used to be friends, but had a nasty falling out."

Jealousy pricked between Bo's ribs. Since Marc's enlistment five years ago, he'd had his own circles. He and Bo weren't as close as they had been, growing further apart. And yet, the mention of Marc's friends who weren't him still stung. Not nearly as badly as Aileen's lover boys, but palpably enough.

"Marc," Weinberg continued, "how should I put it, made a *questionable* choice."

"Fu—" Rajan caught Bo's belligerent, inviting stare and closed his mouth.

"Yeah." Weinberg chuckled. "Rajan had personal reasons to disapprove. Has to do with his employment history at The Station."

Marc, running The Station; this guy, hating it. An easy equation to solve. The rest he'd find out from Marc himself.

Bo rose from his seat. "I'll wait for him"—a quick glance at Rajan—"at the Warehouse tomorrow morning. Alone. Your CIU goons won't find the welcome very warm."

Chapter 4

The Station

October 8, 42 PE

Bo's discomfort caused by the four silent Counter Insurgency Unit operatives was inexplicable. Riding their horses at the unhurried pace of Bo's cart, surveying the surroundings, and not sparing Bo a glance, they gave him no logical reason to fear them. Their guns were pointed away from him. And yet... The itch in the back of Bo's neck was a painful reminder: the CIU perceived the Streeters as pests, and themselves as wolfhounds. Little more than a handful of people were privy to the backroom alliance forged by Aileen, Marc, and Weinberg to curb the Troubles. The rest had seen the CIU's brutal crackdown, and didn't differentiate between the Streeters and the rest of the underworld. Locksville's best ensuring the safety of a Streeter? The four soldiers must have been as acutely aware as Bo of how unnatural this situation was.

The CIU was also responsible for pulling Marc away from Bo. That old wound had never healed, still festering when reminded of. Had Marc not enlisted, blinded by the promise of purpose and belonging, they would still have been close. Like brothers. And with Marc around, maybe Aileen would not have gone missing...

Rajan's quietness did nothing to ease Bo's anxiety. Not that Bo was eager to get him talking, but the damn silence ruffled his feathers, disrupted only by the clacking of the hooves and the creaking of their cart's wheels.

Weinberg's man, on the contrary, appeared content with his detached sulking.

Bo gave up. "So, you saved Marc's life, eh?"

"M-hum." Rajan didn't grace him with a look.

Bo waited for a continuation. None followed. Not much of a chatterer, huh? "Tell me more."

Rajan shrugged. "Slavers caught him. Tortured. Me, broke him out. Brought to Weinberg."

Ooh. So many words at once.

But Rajan wasn't done yet. "All lie."

"Come again?"

Rajan didn't answer for a while, chewing on his lip. "Marc, he worked with Inquisitor. Lied to me. Lied to Weinberg." Rajan turned to Bo and enunciated, "Fucking traitor." His almost-black eyes stared Bo down with an open challenge.

Marc, you cunning son of a bitch. There *had* to be nuances. Marc could be wily, clever, secretive. But a traitor? No way. Obviously, Bo wasn't getting the full story from this guy. Even if Rajan knew the full story—which was not too likely.

Marc was his own man now. Had been for a long time. Not a Streeter. Allegedly, not even a Locksviller anymore—a Stationer, no less! But he still was, and forever would be, a sworn older brother to Bo. Marc's reputation mattered.

Weinberg had asked not to poke holes in his man. Bo held Rajan's gaze, keeping his hands crossed.

When Rajan broke eye contact, Bo pointed into the distance on his side of the road. "What do you see there?"

Rajan studied the wild thicket. "Nothing."

"Exactly. Know what used to be there?"

Rajan didn't respond.

"See, this had been an orchard once. Belonged to a guy named Jeev. One-eyed Jeev. The guy who caused this,"—Bo pointed at his misshapen hip—"and this." He stretched his lips, demonstrating the missing teeth, and letting Rajan take the new information in. "Could've killed me, but didn't. Breaking my leg was a shitty thing to do, granted. I would've starved to death, if not for Marc and Aileen. But you know what? I wasn't mad at Jeev. Not *too* mad, anyway. The man was guarding his property, after all, and was in his full right. Guess what Marc did."

Rajan mutely waited. Bo's oratory talents were wasted on this listener.

"Marc went back the next night and burned Jeev's fucking house down, that's what. Jeev never recovered. Died a year later. Marc was fourteen."

Another chance for Rajan to react. Another blank stare instead.

Bo sighed. "Marc is many things. But a traitor he is not."

There. He said everything he needed. Whatever Rajan made of that was his gain. Or loss. Bo had done enough talking to last him until they arrived. Modeling Marc's motives based on limited knowledge was way more interesting than persuading this mule. And it helped keep Bo's mind off worrying about Aileen.

The leading CIU riders passed through a copse and stopped.

"This is it." Lieutenant Maxwell turned his horse. "From here on, The Station's territory." Under Bo's questioning look, the officer sneered. "We aren't wanted there. Courtesy of *former* Lieutenant Novak."

Marc had better made new friends. Because, as it turned out, his old ones were turning away from him in droves.

"Thanks for the escort, LT. I'm sure we'll be safe from here on."

The lieutenant gave Bo the stink eye. "Of course. Honor among thieves and all."

Bo urged his mare on, avoiding an unnecessary confrontation, but pulled the reins twenty meters down the road, taking in the view.

The Station. How come he'd never visited Locksville's nearest neighbor, not even to observe it from a distance? Sure, every self-respecting Locksviller made a point of despising Stationers, but Bo wasn't prone to *that* kind of self-righteousness. Must be the subconscious fear of violence associated with the slavers.

The sprawling compound in front of them surpassed everything Bo could have imagined—if he'd cared to dedicate The Station a thought. Fascinating and ugly, menacing and complex. Tall fences, barbed wire, watchtowers. Railroads entering from three directions. The nerve center of a sprawling trade network and a bastion of the Faith. The home of vicious Inquisitors and heartless supervisors. The prison for branded lifers and indentured workers. And Marc was now running *that*?!

He'd missed his opportunity to observe all that first-hand, because under Marc the Station was *guaranteed* to be a different place. Marc would never stand for slavery, or the ass-backward Faith. *Right?*

Bo took a deep breath and let the horse advance.

At the gate, a local sergeant didn't move from the road as Bo's cart approached and came to a stop.

His "Yes?" artfully conveyed a mix of boredom and annoyance, without a hint of curiosity or welcome.

"We're here to see Marc Novak." Bo maintained a level tone.

"Is he expecting you?"

"No."

"Then turn around and go the way you came. Mister Novak is a busy man."

"Tell him Bo's here." Before the soldier could brush him off, Bo raised a finger. "If you don't, I promise he'll have your hide."

Blood left the sergeant's face, and he threw a furtive glance to the roadside. Bo's eyes followed, coming to rest on... something. Something vaguely resembling a human figure. On a spike. Oh, shit.

He convulsed and slid off the cart. His vision obligingly darkened.

"Bo. Bo!"

Someone was shaking him by the shoulder. Bo peeked. As his focus returned, a vague shape transformed into Marc's familiar face. Familiar but different: harder, sharper. Older.

"There you are." The face smiled, shedding some age. "When they told me there's some weirdo who asked for me and went into a seizure, I couldn't believe my ears."

Marc offered a hand, helping Bo climb onto shaky feet. Rajan, the sergeant, and several soldiers observed suspiciously.

Bo checked around. A jail cell? That's where they'd taken him? Not a welcoming bunch, those guards.

Marc embraced Bo for longer than a simple greeting required. "*So* good to see you, bro," he whispered into Bo's ear. "It's been too long. You've got no idea how happy I am to be in the company of someone from my *normal* life. You still get hungry after your attacks? Let's get you something to eat."

Marc started walking, pulling Bo by his hand, but Bo stood still, jerking Marc around. Blood rushed through his ears.

"What?" Marc's smile dissolved.

"Aileen's not here, is she?" The numbness spread from Bo's soul to his tongue.

"What are you talking about?!" Marc grabbed Bo's shoulders and shook him like a rag doll. Bo did not resist, letting his arms dangle.

Aileen was not there. Taken, and not by Marc.

His hope had been hanging by a thread that snapped. His world crumbled. His life lost any meaning or purpose.

Marc saw Bo's face, stopped his attempts to reach through, and briefly hugged him again.

"Come," he muttered, plucking Bo and leading him out the jail doors.

Bo's reality shattered into insignificant images. A broken window with curved shards of glass, splitting the universe into distorted fragments. The Station should have awed him, but didn't. The trains should have spiked his interest, but failed. Marc's splendid office should have impressed him, but left him indifferent.

Marc guided Bo to a chair and gently prodded him down. He opened a closet behind his desk—that must have been *his* desk, right?—and after some clinking turned back with two half-full crystal glasses.

He slid one toward Bo and flopped down to his seat. "Drink."

Bo obediently upended his glass. Nothing. No taste, no bite.

Marc gulped down his, grunted, and thumped it on the desktop. "Speak."

The word dropped heavily between them. It oozed impatience, reluctance, anguish, and Seven Hells knew what else.

"She's gone, Marc." The sounds rolled out of Bo's throat, as if in a foreign language. No, not a language. Gravel, crunching underfoot. "Disappeared. Three days ago." An infinity.

"And you thought she'd be here." Marc's voice was as dead as Bo's own.

"Weinberg did."

Marc slowly nodded. His face, all sharp edges, was carved from stone; his eyes—cold granite.

"He would. Unless he's lying."

"I don't think—"

"If Weinberg *wants* to lie about something, you'll never know!"

Did Marc just raise his voice? At him? They *had* grown apart, hadn't they?

Bo stared straight into Marc's dead eyes. "Weinberg wasn't lying," he said with a forcefulness born of conviction—and offense.

Marc deflated, and his face came to life again, softening and sagging. "Sorry, Bo, I... I've been dealing with a lot here. Too much, frankly. And now this."

For many years, Marc had been the one to pick up Bo. To lift his spirits. To help him cope. The only older sibling he'd ever had, or at least remembered. And now he needed Bo's support; that much was evident. Not the time to break down. Leen... No! Aileen was not dead! *Pull yourself together!* Bo's spine straightened up. Crispy, ringing clarity swept through his head. The broken window into the world mended, regaining transparency.

Bo's three quick claps startled Marc. "Concentrate!"

Marc smiled, meekly and guiltily.

Bo didn't let him wallow in self-pity. "It wasn't Weinberg's attempt to control you, and it wasn't you snatching her away from Weinberg. Who else?"

A vertical line split Marc's brow. "The exiled Inquisitors? Unlikely. Too little time for them to sniff out I have a sister, and to plan a clean abduction. Besides, they would've announced themselves by now, one way or another."

Bo involuntarily flinched at that *another*. No.

"Dave suspects The Station had been behind Uncle Stanley's disappearance." Keeping his tone neutral demanded all of Bo's willpower.

"Does he?" Marc rubbed the bridge of his nose. "That would've been Khalifa."

"Who?"

"The Station's former Chief Inquisitor. The Kowloonese have him now. They won't allow him such scheming. Unless he'd pre-planned everything... Wait. Fuck me."

"What?" Lagging in understanding. Bo's most hated state.

"Clever bastards."

"What?!" Bo was on his feet, looming over Marc. "Who?"

"The Golden fucking Dragons, of course!" Marc's fist slammed into the desk, sending his glass rolling on its side.

"Everything okay, Mister Novak?" A strange man peeked into the office. A bushy, well-groomed beard; a thick stylish mustache; an odd headdress. And a hand on a dagger. "I heard yelling."

The man considered Bo and, having classified him as a non-threat, returned his attention to Marc.

"Nothing is okay, Jihan." Bo would have withered under the dark look Marc gave the stranger.

Jihan remained nonplussed. "Anything I can help with?"

"I'll let you know."

Jihan correctly decoded the implied *piss off* and retreated, softly shutting the door.

"My 'bodyguard'." Marc sketched air quotes. "Courtesy of—" He expectantly stared at Bo.

"New Kowloon."

"You know it."

Marc jumped to his feet and paced his office, muttering obscenities. A caged wild animal would have looked tamer. Bo patiently waited.

"They all want me to be their puppet, bro. Khalifa believes he'd shaped me into who I am. Weinberg thinks I owe him for the broken loyalty. Kowloonese insinuate dancing to their tune is in my best interest."

Step, another, third. "They can all go fuck themselves, bro."

Step, another, third. "My loyalty is to The Station now. I will not be manipulated."

Step, another. "New Kowloon stands to gain—or lose—the most. And this is how they play their hand?!"

"You can't know for sure if it's them."

"No. But if I find it is... I'll scrap all our trade agreements. I'll sabotage their ships. I'll steal their customers. I'll... Fuck, if a single hair falls off Aileen's head,

I'll tear down their bloody Hive with my own hands, container by fucking container!"

Marc stopped in the middle of the office; flushed, puffing, with flaring nostrils and bulging eyes of a madman.

Bo waited. This time, he was going to be the responsible adult. "Finished?"

Marc exhaled noisily and sat down, resting his palms on the desk. "Yeah. Whom else am I gonna vent to?"

Bo squeezed Marc's forearm. "We'll figure this out, bro. Together. Like we always did in the good ol' days, yes?"

"Damn, I've missed you, Bo. How long has it been?"

"Too long. But I'm here now."

Marc pressed his eyes shut, twisting his face. A different man opened them. Calm, composed. Deadly dangerous. "I cannot go. Too much is still up in the air. The Station would crumble if I leave now, and everything I've done would be for nothing. God Almighty and the Seven Hells are my witnesses: nothing is more important to me than Aileen, you know that, but—"

"But you've got responsibilities now." Bo voiced his own burdens.

Marc held Bo's eyes. "You've grown, little brother. I... I'm sorry I wasn't around to see that, Bo."

Marc's words touched the innermost cords of Bo's soul. Those whose existence he'd admitted to no one, not even himself. He'd waited to hear this for years, diligently denying the need. But being chastised for his absence in Bo's and Aileen's lives for five years was the last thing Marc needed in his current state. *That* conversation would have to be postponed. Maybe for another five years, or twenty-five. As long as Aileen would be there, Bo could wait.

"You did what you had to do, bro." Nobody had warned Bo that being an adult could be so difficult. But Marc's soft, grateful smile was all the reward Bo needed. "I'll go, Marc, don't sweat it. The Kowloonese *will* talk... and regret, if there's a reason. But you provide the transportation, okay? You're the Supreme Stationer now, or whatever your title is."

Marc chuckled. "I'm an Interim Executive Vice-Nobody." He stayed silent for a few seconds. "I know what a sacrifice this is for you, bro. How you hate traveling."

Travel. Bo's abdominal muscles tightened. He forced a smile. "For Aileen."

Marc stepped closer. "She's lucky to have you, Bo. Not sure the little brat deserves your devotion."

"That's for me to decide."

"Oh, you've decided eight years ago. Everybody knows. She's the only one with the blind spot."

Bo bit his lip. Marc was bang-on, of course. But said aloud, his words stung unbearably.

Marc must have realized he'd hit a nerve. "But I've got just the transportation you need. Something that'll blow the Kowloonese minds." He was already heading for the door. "Come with me."

Chapter 5

Vineland

October 8, 42 PE

"It's all your fault, moron! You've over-tightened the valve!"

"Idiot! It was under-tightened and leaking!"

The two Railroad Marshals had been at it for the better part of an hour. None of their jargon made sense to Bo, but one thing was clear: something in the engine had blown up, and until it got fixed or replaced, the train would not move an inch.

The train. A self-propelled machine, ugly as the Seven Hells and beautiful in what it symbolized.

The crudeness of the contraption's assembly was obvious, without knowing the first thing about engineering. It featured a patchwork of parts that must have belonged to scores of unrelated pre-E machines. It stank worse than a skunk. The thick black smoke it emitted brought tears to Bo's eyes and made his throat so rough he coughed for half an hour after accidentally inhaling it once.

On the other hand, it was a working engine—something the world hadn't seen in decades. An engine powerful enough to move itself *and* a passenger car. Not a curiosity, but a useful tool. Freaking awesome!

But the Marshals made a mistake, like a baby learning about the world through a painful trial-and-error process. Alas, no adults were in sight to help the baby back on its feet, bandage its scraped knee, and move on.

Another obstacle. Another delay. And nothing in Bo's power to do about that.

What were his options? Marc had been right: riding up to New Kowloon on a magnificent engine-drawn train would be a statement impossible to ignore. A message from Marc that would open not only the Great Hive's gates, but its inner doors, too. For now, though, Bo was stranded.

A shadow fell over him. Bo looked up. The same sergeant responsible for *welcoming* Bo to The Station had been assigned to guard the train, whether as a reward or as a punishment. Knowing Marc, the latter explanation fit better.

The sergeant ostentatiously raised his eyes to the skies and produced a long sigh.

"Till these jokers figure this mess out... Looks like we'll be spending the night here. Karim!"

One of the soldiers patrolling around the stalled train stopped.

The sergeant pointed to the nearby forest. "Go get some firewood."

Bo stumbled to his feet. "I'll go too. Nothing better to do here."

He had to occupy himself with something, even as mechanical as gathering wood. Otherwise, the excruciatingly slow crawl of time was guaranteed to drive him insane.

Each turn of the train's iron wheels taking him closer to Aileen, had helped him to hold it together. For her, he'd shirked his responsibilities to the Streeters. He'd ventured outside Locksville, engaging in travels he had dreaded since... *then*. He'd exposed himself to violence and death, at a cost of more seizures in a week than he'd had in years. All because without her, the world meant nothing. *She* was his world.

Stuck, useless, idle—he was going to fall apart.

"Don't hurt yourself in the forest," the sergeant said to his back. "Like, break a leg, or something. Your safety is our number one priority. Mister Novak's orders."

Bo waved a hand and limped on in a futile attempt to catch up with Karim.

The first shots caught him a hundred paces into the bush.

Bo dropped his armful of dry branches and crouched behind it, turning his head to understand where the gunfire was coming from. The forest made the task difficult, breaking and echoing the sound, but left little doubt the general direction was the train.

Bo was creeping toward the tree line when an arm clamped on the back of his neck and pushed him down. Soft moss muffled Bo's yelp.

"What do you think you're doing?" Karim's urgent whisper warmed Bo's ear.

"What do you think *you* are doing?" Bo turned his head to squint at the soldier.

"Keeping you safe, sir."

"Let go of me." Bo infused the growl with all the authority his awkward position allowed.

"No can do, sir. Mister Novak's orders."

"Okay, I get it. He's scared the Seven Hells out of you. But let's be real: can I outrun anyone?"

A brief pause, and the hand lifted. Karim kneeled and peeked from behind a tree.

"What do you see?" Bo whispered into his tense back. "What's going on there?"

The Stationer did not respond for a long time.

"Karim?"

The soldier half-turned, unclenching his jaws. "Nothing good, sir."

Long minutes later, the gunfire's intensity died down. The last few shots rang, punctuating the fighting. In the ensuing silence, nature reclaimed its reign. The birds' chirping returned, and the leaves above resumed their rustling, seemingly interrupted by the rude human affront.

Bo sat up. Karim faced him, squatting and leaning with his back against the tree. "Please don't look, sir."

"Beg your pardon?"

"Mister Novak had warned us. If you see violence or death, you may go into a fit. And scream, loudly. Disclosing our location to the enemy, and that would be a disaster."

Typical Marc. So overprotective... when around.

"The enemy?"

"By the green armbands, looks like the Zealots of the True Faith."

The Faith? Zealots? Like in the half-legendary stories of the Five Points' Crusades, suppressed by Locksville long before Bo was even born? These crazy fanatics were still around?! "Oh shit. Of course. The engine." Nothing could have drawn the Zealots' sacred wrath more than this ultimate abomination.

"They're setting it on fire as we speak, sir."

Bo squeezed the sides of his head between his hands. How was he to get to Aileen now? No, no, no. This could not be happening. "Our people?" Yes, *our*.

"All dead, sir." Karim's voice remained remarkably level.

"Would..." Should he ask? Ah, Hells, what did that matter now? "If you'd joined the fight, would that have made a difference? If you hadn't had to babysit me?"

Karim didn't flinch. "Unlikely, sir. We were outnumbered three to one." He raised his head, jutting the chin. "They gave a fine fight. Took over half the attackers with them."

"I'm sorry about your teammates, Karim."

"Thank you, sir."

"What do we do now?"

"Wait for the Zealots to leave, return to The Station on foot."

"How far are we?"

Karim chewed on his lip. "Twenty kilometers, give or take. Will you be able to walk that far, sir?"

Bo grimaced. "In three days. If you carry me half the way." Damned leg. Jeev, the cruel son of a bitch, must be laughing in his grave.

Karim's thick eyebrows pulled down.

Sympathy. Bo looked away. He needed no stupid sympathy. He needed a functioning leg. And a means to reach New Kowloon, quickly.

"I can make a travois..." Karim sounded unsure of his own idea.

Bo barked a mirthless laugh. "Hells, no. But..." He slouched and called up the map from his memory. "We must be close to Grimsby."

"Five-six kilometers, yes. What of it, sir?"

Bo straightened up. "That's where we're going."

"Sir?"

"I'm not going back. I'll charter a boat at the port. Take me there, then you're free to return home. But first... Are the Zealots gone yet?"

Karim checked. "I believe so, sir."

"Did they burn the whole train, or only the engine?"

Karim peeked again. "The passenger cart is charred, but still standing."

Bo *should* have cared about the train—the shining pinnacle of engineering in this day and age. He *should* have cared about its crew: the Marshals with their irreplaceable knowledge, the gruff sergeant and his guards. Those were genuine tragedies; on a different scale, yet both beyond Bo's selfish wants and needs.

The thoughts were remote, as if someone else's, stranded in the back of his head by pure accident. They faded behind the red, all-consuming anger at the dumb Zealots for interfering with his mission, erecting another obstacle on his road to Aileen.

"I need my baggage."

Karim rose to his feet. If he had any misgivings about Bo's priorities, he kept them to himself. "I'll bring it. Please wait here, sir. Is there much? How will I recognize it?"

Bo chuckled. "One black duffel bag. I travel light. But careful, eh? Its content is fragile. And precious."

"Yes, sir. I'll be right back."

Karim raised his rifle to a low ready, scanned the field, and stepped cautiously into the open.

Bo didn't look. If something were to happen to Karim, he'd hear. But Marc was right. It would be better if Bo didn't *see*.

He may have sent the man to his death if the enemies lingered around. But there was no way he'd leave without the Corning loot. Ridiculous, superstitious idea had taken hold of him. Aileen had tasked Bo with retrieving those trinkets. For him to complete his mission, he had to bring the glass creatures back to her. Until that happened, nothing bad could happen to Aileen. Would not. Should not. Or else he had already failed. And he would never fail Aileen. Sure, not how cause-and-effect worked... So what? Screw the cause and fuck the effect! He would not rest until he saw Aileen twiddling that seahorse with the same awe it had inspired in him the first time he'd seen it.

A branch crunched. Bo gasped.

"Is this it, sir?"

Bo zeroed in on the bag first. "Yes. Thank you." Karim was expendable; the bag was not. But his sigh of relief applied to the safe return of both.

The soldier's combat vest bristled with spare magazines, some smeared with blood. He pulled a pistol from a holster and proffered it to Bo.

Bo shook his head. "I don't do guns, Karim. If it comes to that, I'll stick to my pocket knife." He climbed to his feet.

The chilly air portended the encroaching evening. A gust of wind brought an acrid scent of burned wood, paint... and of something else that made Bo's innards twist.

Not to look. Not to smell. Not to think. Not to go back.

Only forward.

Chapter 6

Grimsby

October 8, 42 PE

Bo pushed the heavy wooden door open and recoiled, assaulted by a pungent wave of stench rushing past him to escape the tavern. Old unwashed sweat with sour undertones of cheap wine. Classy. He took a deep breath of the chilly outside air and dove in.

The hum of the conversations died down. All the faces in the dining hall turned to him, ghoulish in the dull yellow oil lamp light, animated only by the dancing red gleam from the fireplace.

Karim stepped over the threshold behind Bo. His rifle's safety clicked deafeningly in the evaluating silence. Bo reached back, pushing the gun's barrel down. He hobbled to the bar and struggled up a tall stool.

"A pint of your best for me," he said, loud enough for everyone in the establishment to hear. "A shot of your strongest for my friend—" Bo turned to face the inimical audience. "And a refill on me for whoever brings Lichen here in the next twenty minutes."

The oppressive cloud of malevolence dissipated as quickly as it had formed with Bo's dramatic entry. Avarice took its place. Three locals rushed to the door, pushing each other out of the way.

"One." Bo's sharp word halted the competitors. He randomly pointed. "You."

Bo's nominee gleamed victoriously and vanished outside. His disappointed rivals shuffled back to their table.

Conversations gradually picked up again.

The innkeeper wiped the bar with a towel that had known better days, placed a clay mug with a bubbling foam head in front of Bo, and a chipped shot glass before Karim.

"How will you be paying?" he asked, holding onto both containers.

Bo's coins clinked on the counter, drawing greedy glances from the nearby patrons. Under Karim's heavy stare, they returned to mind their own business, faking disinterest.

Bo raised his cup. Karim mirrored his gesture. The fallen required no words.

Bo sipped his beer. It had been a long hike. Karim would have made it in an hour. With Bo in tow, it had taken three. The sun had already set by the time they reached this stinking pit... But the brew proved decent.

"Lichen?" asked Karim. "An odd name."

"Got some sort of skin disease. All covered in spots in different colors. Hence the nickname."

"Ah. How do you know him?"

"A business acquaintance of mine, let's put it that way."

"And what exactly *is* your business?"

The door creaked, saving Bo from having to invent innocent-sounding half-truths. Lichen walked in, followed by the beaming messenger. The innkeeper topped up the eager guy's mug. Bo tossed another coin.

Lichen lowered himself onto a stool by Bo's side with dignity.

"Couldn't believe that scallywag until I saw you with my own eyes. Thought you don't travel, Bo. To what do we owe the pleasure?"

Another mug materialized before the old smuggler. Bo reached into his waist pouch, but Lichen's gesture stopped him.

"Thanks, Bo, my credit is good here. Isn't it, Charles?" Lichen peeked at the innkeeper from under heavy eyelids.

The proprietor produced a smile, as obliging as it was forced.

Bo shrugged. "I need a ride to New Kowloon."

Lichen sipped his drink and closed his eyes, whether savoring the beer or concealing his reaction. "Something's afoot." He studied the content of his mug with the level of attention it hardly deserved. "Suddenly, there's lots of traffic to New Kowloon. Mostly Locksvillers, some weird others too."

Bo didn't bite. "Can you take me or not?"

"Someone's extra snappy today..."

Bo pursed his lips.

"Would if I could, Bo." Lichen waved his tankard, sending gobs of foam through the air. "You know how much I appreciate your business. Unfortunately, Farley has carved a monopoly on transporting Locksvillers. Something to do with Weinberg."

Bo's mug stopped halfway to his mouth.

"Farley? With Weinberg?"

"I know, right? Unbelievable. And yet... You'll have to talk to him."

Lichen raised his voice. "Stay the night here. Charles will arrange a room."

Another meaningful glance, another fake smile. "Of course, Lichen."

"I'll tell Farley to find you in the morning." The smuggler's mug bumped into Bo's.

Bo didn't drink up. "I need to go *now*."

Lichen choked and snorted his beer. "You can't be serious. Even Farley, deranged as he is, won't cross the lake in the dark. Forget about it and enjoy your brew. Now, tell me how you've got a Stationer bodyguard."

October 9, 42 PE

No. No. No-no-no-no-no. But Leen! Yes, but... no. Coward! Sack up, dip-stick!

The queasiness in his gut rose in a tidal wave, sweeping aside the remnants of Bo's dignity. He leaned over the gunnel and heaved, noisily and painfully.

A shadow of a taunting smile touched Farley's lips.

"We haven't even sailed yet. A few too many beers last night?"

Bo swished a mouthful of water from a bottle and spat overboard.

The day had barely begun, and he was already exhausted.

"I..." How could he explain it to this seasoned sailor, who'd probably spent more time on the water than on land? "I can't be on the lake."

Farley's brow creased. "Sea sickness?"

Bo shook his head. And not just the head. His entire body was trembling.

The conflicting needs tore him apart.

On one hand, Aileen. On the other, his whole miserable life. The life of fear, of trauma, of memories he'd worked hard to suppress yet had regularly triggered. The improbable life of a crime syndicate advisor who pathetically succumbed to seizures, blacking out and screeching each time he was exposed to violence.

He wasn't going to tell Farley about *that* day on the lake. The day which had ruined his life forever; twisted him irreparably on the inside, long before Jeev had mutilated his leg and his face. About sailing with his parents to a new beginning. About the boat being boarded by pirates. About hiding under a pile of fishing nets, witnessing his mom gang-raped, then slaughtered along with his dad and the crew. About their desperate cries that would forever reverberate in his ears. About grasping onto a piece of flotsam for hours after the boat had been put to torch. About having resigned to a cold and lonesome death in the depths of the vast expanse of water, before another boat picked him up. About losing everything but his first name in the foreign city with an odd name,

Locksville. About having the cruelty of the world imprinted on him since the age of eight.

Bo said nothing, but Farley read enough in his pained stare. The captain's face hardened. His eyes seemingly got darker, deeper set.

"I see." He put a comforting hand on Bo's shoulder. "Climb back to the pier, Bo, and wait for me there. I've an idea."

Bo sat, hugging his shins and resting his chin on his knees.

Farley's silent boy was tying up and covering the sails.

The Great Hive towered on the distant shore, clearly visible in the crisp late fall air. Close enough to see, too far to reach. And the accursed, hated, impassable lake in between. If only he could be magically transported straight to New Kowloon...

The pier boards underneath creaked. Bo turned toward the steps.

Farley was approaching, pulling an odd dingy by a rope. His lopsided smile, goofy and devious at once, held promise.

Bo stared at him blankly. A cruel joke? Bo might have shown weakness, but the old smuggler should have known better. With Weinberg as Farley's newly found patron or not, Bo was plenty influential to bankrupt and shut down any illicit business this side of the lake.

"Know what this is?" Farley seemed intent on playing the game.

Bo continued staring him down.

"Right. How would ya? This, Bo, is a mo-tor-boat!"

Still failing to elicit a reaction, he explained. "A boat with an engine. Needs no sail. Goes so fast you'll shit your pants."

He toned down his excitement and grew serious. "No one would catch up with us on the water. Ya hear me? Does *that* make ya feel any better?"

It did. Not that going faster would reconcile him with the lake, but... this was enough to tip the scales. The side with Aileen rushed down, throwing Bo's fears into the air and scattering them to the four winds.

He jumped to his feet.

No time to waste.

"Sweet!" Bo had to shout for the words to reach Farley through the roaring of the wind in their ears and the high-pitched whine of the engine.

An involuntary smile found its way onto his lips. The *impunity* of fast travel. The invincibility. The sense of being untouchable by all evil. He... could get used to this. Maybe the blame lay not entirely with the lake.

"Told ya, no?" Farley grinned, too.

"Where did you steal this treasure?"

"It's Weinberg's."

No way. "He *gave* it to you?"

Farley's smirk twisted to one side. "Well... Not as such."

Bo's eyes opened wide. "Don't tell me you lifted it from him! Even you aren't that reckless!"

Farley cackled. "Say, he lost it. And I found it. Finders—keepers, no?"

Bo shook his head. "Farley, you're madder than I thought. But hey, it's your funeral."

Farley barked a laugh and laid a dashingly sharp turn, raising a tall wake and forcing Bo to grab for the gunnels, then throttled the engine and let the boat drift to New Kowloon's pier.

"There ya go." He threw a looped rope around a cleat and pulled. "Tell Weinberg Farley's always happy to help. But better don't mention the boat."

"What makes you think I talk to Weinberg?"

Farley tilted his head and squinted at him.

Bo drawled, "Fine. Thanks for the ride, eh?"

"Any time, Bo. Any time."

Bo awkwardly climbed up onto the deserted pier. He hadn't expected a welcome party, but... Not a person in sight, even a sentry? Strange. The Kowloonese must've been all cooped up for the winter already.

Farley passed him the duffel bag, and Bo limped toward the quay. Step by clumsy step, closer to Aileen. If she was there. She had to be! Because if not...

Chapter 7

New Kowloon

October 9, 42 PE

Insignificant. The one thing Bo had never been treated as.

For as long as he remembered, he'd meant *something*. Good or bad; impressive or pitiful; someone to fear or to control. The Kowloonese functionaries gifted him a whole new experience: of being a bothersome annoyance, a pebble in a boot. An experience he could do without perfectly well, so close to Aileen—and unable to breach this final wall.

"What do you want?"

"To speak with a Golden Dragon. Shang Ka Yi or Tam Wai Lam."

"What's your business?"

"Can't tell you."

"Wait here."

The same exchange, word to word, had already repeated four times, getting Bo nowhere. Something had to give, and it sure wasn't him.

"Stop!" Bo reached forward with his hand and lifted his behind from the hard chair.

The official—obviously, a low-ranking bureaucrat—paused on the room's brink. His posture showed how aggravated he was by such familiarity. The guard at the door shifted too, glaring at Bo.

Bo leaned back and folded his arms. Enough. Time to change the dynamics and reclaim the initiative. "I am from Locksville. Here on behalf of Captain Weinberg and Marc Novak," Bo said in his most authoritative tone. Technically, none of these statements was a lie. "If these names don't ring a bell for you, check with the Golden Dragons. I guarantee they'd mean a lot to them."

Add a moderately disdainful sneer for maximal effect, and... there. A seed of doubt.

The bureaucrat's face lost its arrogant indifference. Bo's practiced veneer stayed impeccable. He'd stared down much haughtier challengers throughout his career.

The official deflated, shedding his luster. "I will inform the Golden Dragons right away, sir. Won't be long." He left at a rapid gate, shy of running.

Bo crossed his legs and peered at the guard, to show him who was the boss in the room. As an exercise, and to pass the time. The soldier withstood the pressure better than the civilian, but eventually looked away.

The bureaucrat reentered and bowed subserviently. "Please follow me, sir, if you would. The Golden Dragon's office is this way."

Bo rose from the uncomfortable seat with a creak in his spine, picked up his duffel bag, and winked to the appalled guard. None of the locals sensed his tension.

***

"The mysterious envoy from Weinberg *and* Novak." The woman's expression was manifestly mocking. "Who might you be?"

The man at her side, to the contrary, maintained a flawlessly neutral face, with a tinge of artfully crafted goodwill. Nice. A good interrogator and a bad interrogator. Bo and Aileen had occasionally employed the technique, with similar roles.

Oh, Leen... He quashed the dull heartache.

Marc had given him the names of the two Dragons most likely to be involved, but somehow omitted the curious detail that one of them was a woman. Never mind. She wanted to intimidate him? He was going to break the pattern.

"Bo."

The Dragons waited for him to continue. When he didn't, the woman raised an eyebrow. "Bo... what?"

He'd be happy to know too... "Just Bo." No honorifics. Chew on that, Dragon.

She didn't bat an eyelash. A worthy opponent. "Hm, okay. Why are you here, *Bo*?" The Dragon intoned his name as if it were an oddity. Or as if she didn't believe it was real.

Bo squarely met her eyes. *Don't blink.* "To retrieve Aileen Novak."

Not a muscle twitched in her face. "Who?"

Do-doom. Do-doom. Frantic heartbeat filled Bo's ears. Was the Dragon intent on denying New Kowloon's involvement, or... was Aileen really not there? *Stay strong.* The worst time to crumble.

"Aileen Novak," Bo repeated levelly. "Marc Novak's sister."

The Dragons exchanged cryptic glances.

"What makes you think she's here?" The man spoke. "Is that Weinberg's idea?"

"No, Marc's."

"Huh. And why—"

Something in Bo's head snapped. The last strand holding him together. He could not bear not knowing anymore. "Just tell me if you have her!" His yell reverberated through the chamber, leaving it eerily silent after the echoes died.

Coldness spread through Bo's chest, clamping his windpipe with an icy claw. He may have just ruined his chances of finding out anything.

"You realize you're talking to the Golden Dragons of New Kowloon's High Council, don't you?"

Bo's skin shrunk into goosebumps at the woman's hiss. They were going to kick him out on his ass. The worst part? He'd still have no clue of Aileen's whereabouts.

"Golden Dragon," the man, Shang Ka Yi, murmured, "look at him."

Of course. Bo's unimpressive stature, bowed leg, and toothless mouth would sooner predispose to pity, not rage. Bo would take anything, including pity, as long as...

The man's next words rekindled the almost snuffed flame of Bo's hope. It flared with a whoosh.

"Don't you see how much he cares about her?" He leaned toward her ear and whispered something.

The woman cast her eyes down, studying her hands neatly folded on the desk.

Bo held his breath.

Tam Wai Lam glanced back at him, her expression unreadable. "She's here." The Dragon rose, pushing back the heavy chair. "I'll bring her in."

Bo exhaled noisily and met Shang Ka Yi's gaze. A guarded, understanding smile shattered the man's professionally inscrutable mask. Bo smiled back, sagging as the tension gradually released him.

"Thank you," he whispered. "I owe you."

"You owe me nothing except your friendship. And maybe information."

Whatever that meant, it didn't matter. Bo would have sold his soul to the last devil in the Seven Hells if that had brought him an inch closer to Aileen. Information? A small price to pay.

Tam Wai Lam was absent for too long. An irrational worry started getting hold of Bo. Shang Ka Yi was getting antsy too, glancing at the door more and more often. So did Bo.

And yet, when the door opened, Bo gasped.

Tam Wai Lam stepped in... Alone.

Until this moment, he had been afraid to believe, but believed nonetheless. That everything was going to be alright. That Aileen would come in, melt him with her smile, and...

Tam Wai Lam walked straight to Shang Ka Yi, bent, and whispered into his ear.

Shang Ka Yi's eyes met Bo's, and he frowned. Bo's heart sank, fluttering at the bottom of his stomach. "What...?" he rasped. "Where...?"

Tam Wai Lam finally turned her attention to him. "Miss Novak is nowhere to be found. We're still searching. The Hive is vast."

Bo's queasy knees buckled, refusing to support him any longer, and he dropped to all fours. He stared at the floor, fighting back the nausea. The sticky emptiness in his head smelled of ash. He slowly raised his eyes. The desk between them suddenly looked like a barricade meant to protect the two Dragons. "If—" His voice broke. He started over. Unadulterated malice spilled from his mouth and washed the room, scorching everything in its way and carrying his words to their destination. "If anything happens to her..."

The Dragons flinched.

Part 2

THE BOOK

OF AILEEN

Chapter 8

Locksville, Five Years Ago

May 29, 37 PE

The prickling pain below her ribs grew too insistent to be ignored. Aileen slowed down, checked over her shoulder, and almost tripped on her own feet. She stopped, leaning with her arm against the wall, clutching at her right side with the other hand, and forcing rasping breaths through her parched throat. Quick and shallow, they made no difference at all, failing to satisfy the urgent demand of her feverishly beating heart. Long-distance runs, definitely not her thing.

Marc's heavy steps approached. He had fallen behind, carrying the bulk of their loot. His puffing was as strained as Aileen's. Tick followed closely on his heels, dragging Bo. His concentrated beet-red face stood in stark contrast to Bo's paleness. Bo did his best to not hinder Tick, jumping on his good leg and keeping the lame one bent. Determined not to give up, as always, but recognizing that stubbornness alone wouldn't carry him through this chase. His eyelids were drooping, and he was about to faint any moment.

The pursuers cleared the street corner thirty meters behind them.

Aileen bit her lip. Her crew didn't take that much, hardly enough to make a dent in those merchants' stock. Why wouldn't they let her and her friends be?

The two men didn't appear to share her opinion. Exhaustion had slowed down their steps too, but they weren't giving up.

The chances of escape narrowed by a second.

"Drop the bags!" Aileen shouted to Marc. *Wanted* to shout, but produced only a coarse whisper.

Her brother's uncomprehending stare brought blood to her cheeks. How could he not understand?! "We can't get away like this! Give them their stupid stuff back, and help Tick carry Bo!"

To Marc's credit, he didn't argue. He threw the bags to the ground, lent Bo his shoulder, and the three picked up the pace past her.

Aileen pushed herself from the wall and settled into a heavy jog. Her feet thudded against the pavement, sending shocks through her knees and up her spine.

Marc and Tick, with Bo dangling between them, disappeared behind the next corner. Before turning, Aileen glanced back, to make sure the pursuers had quit, satisfied with reclaiming their property... Her breath caught. The two men passed by the bags without slowing their pace, and less than ten steps separated them from her.

"Leen!" Marc yelled. "Hurry!"

All four of them going to jail would be a waste.

"Go." Aileen waved her hand. "Go."

"Leen!" Marc's desperation brought tears to her eyes, but she slowly shook her head and stepped into the middle of the street, raising her arms and waiting for the grim pursuers to approach.

A thirteen-year-old girl could expect a certain leniency. Unlike Marc, who at his seventeen would be tried as an adult, or Tick, who'd had run-ins with the law and would face its full brunt as a repeat offender. And Bo? He'd had his share of suffering.

<hr />

July 2, 37 PE

Aileen grimaced. Disgusting, but she wasn't in charge of the menu. The only meal for the day. She had to eat.

She licked the spoon and scratched another line with its handle on the brick wall. Thirty-two. Thirty-two days she'd been rotting in this cell. Not even five weeks—out of the twenty-six of her sentence. Half a fucking year. Less than what Marc or Tick would've been given, but way beyond what she'd hoped for. Maybe she should've let them take the fall for that bust. She hadn't even planned to join in, it had been her brother who'd convinced her to tag along. *For her training*, right.

This was a resentment day. A day to blame everyone and everything for her misery. Unlike the yearning days, when she was ready to forgive her brother,

her crew, even the judge and the vengeful merchants—if only that would get her out of this hole.

Once she was out, she'd never allow herself to be locked up again. Never.

Aileen picked up the book. Nothing better to do, anyway, or she would've gone stir-crazy. What would she do when the jail library ran out? She'd already tore through—fifteen? Twenty? She should've kept track, same as she did with days.

"Novak, you've got a visitor."

Visitor? Aileen scrambled to her feet, tracking the warden's progress by the clinking of his keys. Since when were the inmates allowed visitations? And who would—

"Marc!" she exhaled, pressing her face to the bars.

His smile couldn't conceal the pain lurking in the corners of his eyes at the sight of her. "Hey, kid." His hand brushed against her cheek, and Aileen melted. Sweat dripped down her forehead and her eyes teared as she clutched her brother's wrists through the gaps between the bars. She forgot all the speeches she'd rehearsed endlessly, scalding and loving, depending on the day. She was never letting go of him. "Get me out of here."

"That's what I'm here for."

"What?" she squeaked.

This was what she wanted. What she asked for. What she prayed for, despite not believing in gods. And yet, Marc's words made no sense. She had twenty-one weeks and three days more to spend behind these bars. Her brother had never been fond of cruel jokes, not with her. So...

Marc brought his lips as close to her ear as the barrier between them allowed. "I traded you in."

"For what?" she whispered as quietly.

"For myself, of course. I signed up with the CIU."

"CIU?! You can't! They're the worst!"

"Actually... Okay, that's a longer conversation. For another time and place."

Aileen shook her head. She'd sacrificed her freedom to keep Marc out of trouble. He couldn't give up his, despite her belligerent blame-game on the resentment days. She released his arms and stepped back, swallowing her tears. "I can't let you do that."

"Sis, it's already done, and that may be for the best for both of us. I... I've never told you, but I'm getting tired of this Streeters life. You, Bo—you thrive on it, but me? Not my calling. The CIU offers me another chance."

"For what?"

"To become something Mom and Dad would've wanted me to be."

He could have sucker-punched her instead. The implication that their parents would not have approved of *her* career choice left Aileen gasping for air, unable to utter a word. Marc probably didn't even mean it like that, but at that moment, something inside her died. An invisible wall rose between them, more impenetrable than the bars of her jail cell. This was nothing less than treason. Her brother, her only family, her rock and strength, the one immutable part of the ever-changing world, just stepped away, leaving behind a gaping emptiness. Her gratitude for securing her release came dramatically short of bridging it. She could accept his flipping to the other side. Marc had his reasons, and who was she to judge him for doing what he thought was right? But he should not have hurled those words at her.

Aileen closed her eyes. "Let's go," she said to the stranger oddly wearing her brother's face.

Chapter 9

Locksville

October 5, 42 PE

For a moment, Aileen managed to straddle the divide between reality and illusion. She refused to let go of the dream, mildly unsettling but sweetly sexy, struggled to catch it by its tail and pull herself back in. Teetering on the brink of awareness, she almost succeeded, but her internal alarm rudely yanked her to the other side. Something in her immediate vicinity was off. She tensed and cracked her eyes open a smidge.

"Sorry for disturbing your sleep, Miss Novak." A calm, soft, unfamiliar voice. Male. She turned toward it. A silhouette, clearly visible against the pale moonlight in the window. A self-confident, top-notch pro, or a rank amateur. Judging by the serenity of his voice, the former was a safer bet.

Her sleepiness dissipated in an instant. An assassin? She made it as if to stretch, reaching under her pillow. Crap. Her handgun wasn't there, and the knife sheath lay empty.

"Sorry about that too, Miss Novak." The bastard sounded amused. "Reasonable precautions."

If he'd planned to kill her, she'd be dead already. If he were a slaver, or wanted to assault her in her bed, he would've gagged and bound her while she was asleep. Why wake her up? To gloat? Stupid. Besides, she wasn't a random girl in the street to be grabbed and trafficked. The intruder knew her name. This was targeted.

A wave of angry heat rolled through Aileen's chest and neck, reaching her cheeks, expunging the initial sticky fear. "What is the meaning of this?" she asked, redirecting her rage into icy disdain to let him know he didn't scare her.

"My profound apologies, Miss Novak. Do not be alarmed, we are here to ensure your safety."

We? She jerked her head to the other side. The shadows by the door concealed another figure.

"I am perfectly safe here," she growled. The absurdity of that statement wasn't lost on her, but what else was there to say?

"With us here, you are, Miss Novak." Yes, definitely amused. Smug son of a bitch.

"There are guards right behind this door. What if I call them?" *Shut up. You're pathetic.*

"That would be unfortunate. For them, I mean. They're no match for us. *We* are the ones inside your room, aren't we?"

A valid point. Aileen relented. "Who are you? And why are you convinced I need your protection?"

"Ajinder Singh, Miss, at your service."

"Singh?" The name rang a bell. "Singh. As in, West Sauga Clan Singh?"

"Precisely, Miss. Impressive! I must say, you're handling this far better than I'd expected."

"Fuck you, and fuck your expectations," Aileen grumbled without conviction, more out of residual annoyance. "What in the Seven flaming Hells are you doing in my room, Ajinder Singh?" She pulled up, leaning against the headboard, and wrapped herself in the blanket. Not for warmth or modesty, but to protect her personal space.

"Do you know where your brother is, Miss Novak?"

"Marc?" she blurted, inanely, and was grateful for his silence. Could've asked if she had any other brothers. Well, there was Bo, but... *Stop.* "No, I've got no bloody idea where he is. What did he get himself into this time, and how am I a part of that?"

"Marc Novak, Miss, is at The Station now."

Odd, but whatever. "Uh, okay, and...?"

"He's *running* The Station." Ajinder let that sink in.

Aileen beat back the *what?!* ready to escape her lips. Then swallowed a few other remarks, processing the cascading implications. "I see," she said. "One last question: who sent *you*? Not West Sauga, for sure. Clans have the balls, but not the interest in controlling The Station."

"Once again, Miss Novak... I was told you're good, but never imagined you'd be *this* good." The dark figure inclined its head.

Way to keep his cool. She could use someone like him... "Cut the crap. Who?"

"Golden Dragon Tam Wai Lam, Miss." Apparently, the guy wasn't easily offended.

"The Kowloonese? Of course." Aileen pressed her eyes closed and pinched the bridge of her nose. Such bad timing! Then again, was there ever a suitable timing for being abducted? She raised her head. "Who's the competition?"

"Beg your pardon?"

"Besides the Dragon, what other assholes want a piece of me?" Her irritation grew, and that suited her well.

"That's above my paygrade, Miss. And if I may, I'd advise against using such language referring to a Golden Dragon."

Aileen had had enough. "Know what? Fuck. You." She leaned forward and spit the words, enunciating each. Dark and dirty, they weren't meaningless cussing. She *wanted* to wound him, to make each syllable land as a ringing slap on his masked cheeks. "Fuck your Dragon. And fuck your cheesy compliments. Now, take your flunky and get the *fuck* outta my bedroom." She pointed at the window, the most probable way they'd snuck in. "I am capable of taking care of my safety. Crawl back up your Dragon's ass and pass my thanks for the warning."

Ajinder did not move. He clasped his hands behind his back and rolled from heels to toes. "Sorry, Miss Novak, no can do. Orders."

"Are you deaf? Or dumb?" Her furious whisper pitched higher. "Which part of 'I am not coming with you' did you not understand?"

"Miss Novak." Traces of suppressed temper finally flashed in the intruder's timbre. "I'm not sure you fully grasp the situation. Let me explain."

"Get."

"I am—"

"The fuck."

"—to deliver—"

"Out."

"—you to New Kowloon," Ajinder continued, as if she didn't interrupt him, "safe and sound. But not necessarily conscious. It would give me absolutely no pleasure—"

She threw her blanket at him and followed closely behind it, unleashing a barrage of furious kicks and punches... none of which connected. The empty blanket settled on the floor. She slowed down to scan the darkness for the sneaky bastard. A pair of arms clamped around her, pinning her hands to her sides. She opened her mouth to call for help...

"Bloodbath," a soft voice breathed into her ear, sending instant chills down her nerves and stopping her shout cold in her throat. "Call them, and it would be a bloodbath. Do you understand?"

She nodded, slowly.

"I really, *really* don't want to hurt anyone, Miss Novak. Neither you, nor your guards. But I will if I have to. Do not test me. Pretty please."

This ludicrous plea was the last drop. Aileen sagged, accepting her defeat. Ajinder guided her to sit back on her bed. She pressed her palms to her face, tired and out of options. She couldn't allow her team to get hurt. She was their Aunt. They were *her* people. *Her* responsibility.

The intruder—captor!—towered above her, so uncomfortably close that the heat radiating from him warmed her cheek; the sharp smell of his sweat tingled her nostrils. He cleared his throat. "Sorry about—"

"For fuck's sake, stop apologizing already." The sound of her own hoarse voice startled her. "I need to notify my Second I'll be leaving."

"You can't, Miss."

"The Hells I can't."

"The—"

"If you apologize or mention your orders one more time, I will slap you," she snapped, quietly and ferociously.

Instead, he said, "The Streeters will manage, Miss Novak. They always do."

He had *that* right.

"Okay." She stood up. "I'm gonna change. Can't travel in my sweats. Turn away."

"S— afraid I can't. Mustn't let you out of my sight. You can change later, on the boat."

Aileen peered with a challenge into the black-masked face and unhurriedly pulled her top off. Ajinder hastily looked away, as did his accomplice at the door.

"There. Was that so hard?"

The two led her out of the window and down a winding path over the roofs. She'd have to lambast the watch commanders for screwing up the Warehouse security this badly. When she's back. *If* she's back.

Chapter 10

New Kowloon

October 5, 42 PE

"Lemme get this straight—"

"Golden Dragon."

"I am not a Golden Dragon."

"*I* am."

Aileen glared at the woman in front of her. Tam Wai Lam held her ground, curving her pale lips. Oh, how much Aileen craved to wipe that smirk off the Dragon's face... But the realist in her prevailed. In all likelihood, her first sharp movement would have been her last. As in, forever last. Her anger wasn't worth dying for. But it was more than worth sharing.

"Lemme get this straight, *Golden Dragon*." The mocking should have compensated for her yielding to the title. "You send your lackeys"—she glanced at Ajinder's unreadable face; a very handsome unreadable face—"to abduct me from my home. Supposedly, so that no one else can grab me to leverage Marc."

"That about sums it up, Miss Novak."

"To use me yourself?"

"I have no such plans."

"Really. Like I'm gonna believe *that*."

"Golden Dragon."

Aileen took in a hissing breath, planted her palms on the desk between them, and leaned forward. "Nope." She smacked her lips. "Not happening." She sat back, crossing her legs and hooking one elbow over her chair's backrest. "Gonna force me?"

The hostess tilted her head to her shoulder. "And, say, if I were to call you *Aunt* Aileen, would you return the courtesy?"

Aileen sneered. "When the Seven Hells freeze over."

The Golden Dragon's smile grew wider. She turned to Ajinder. "I like her. She'll fit right in. Do you like her, Mister Singh?"

Ajinder responded with an almost imperceptible shrug. His cheeks, what was visible of them over his well-groomed beard, darkened a shade.

"I think he likes you too, Miss Novak," Tam Wai Lam narrated.

Aileen met Ajinder's gaze. His blush deepened, running all the way up to his headdress. A turban, yes, that's what they called those. Maybe the Dragon was right. Maybe he did like her. That changed nothing: the son of a bitch had abducted her!

She allowed a broad grin to settle on her face... And wiped it off abruptly, glaring at the Dragon with narrowed eyes. Back home, this trick could bring the scariest scumbags to their feet, standing to attention. The promise of her wrath usually sufficed, rarely requiring actual punitive actions.

Ajinder's face grew longer. Worry flickered in his eyes. The Golden Dragon, to the contrary, leaned back with a satisfied nod. "I can see how you've pulled off this Aunt stint, Aileen. May I call you Aileen?"

"As if I can prevent you." Aileen's grumble was almost perfunctory. The Dragon's compliment left her undeniably pleased. "So, what am I, a prisoner? A hostage?"

"'Protective custody' would be an accurate description." Tam Wai Lam's expression remained undecipherable. "You're free to roam the Great Hive, but do not attempt to leave it."

"If you're so concerned with my well-being, why not escort me to Marc? He'd keep me safer than anyone."

"That's where you're mistaken. I don't doubt he'd *want to*, but the situation at The Station is extremely volatile. His own safety is still very much in question. The Hive is the safest place for you right now."

"And keeping me on a short leash conveniently allows you to pull Marc's strings. However you spin this, your actions look blatantly self-serving."

"Aileen, Marc doesn't know you're here. Nor should he. I'm sure you realize this is not how blackmail works."

"No, this isn't. This is how denial of resources works."

The Dragon peered back at her. "You keep surprising me. That doesn't happen often. To your point, yes. Is that wrong, though, if we deny it from our, uh, *competitors*, without taking advantage ourselves?"

"Practically, knights in shining armor."

"No. A stabilizing force in the region."

"Yeah? Tell me again how stabilizing my abduction is for Locksville."

"I hear you've made the Streeters a far more robust organization than it used to be under your predecessor. They'll weather this. Your disappearance may cost Weinberg a few gray hairs, but that's a price I'm prepared to pay."

"Of course. You're prepared to have everyone else pay the price, as long as you get your way."

Tam Wai Lam smirked. "You make this sound nasty. As if you aren't the same."

Aileen ground her teeth. In the heat of the argument, she'd painted herself into a corner. The Dragon was right, but she would never hear Aileen admit that! Time to change the subject.

"Who are those mysterious *competitors* you're so concerned about? And how is stashing me away going to help Marc?"

"Now, *that's* the right question. In short, everyone trading with The Station, or contracting them to move their goods. From Rochester and Buffalo all the way to Michigan and Ohio. Take your pick. The moment they learn about the transition of power at The Station, they'd search for an angle to improve their standing. To extract concessions from Mister Novak before the status quo is reaffirmed. And you're your brother's most obvious pressure point."

"How would they even know we're related?"

"Oh, believe me, the moment someone becomes a prominent figure on this chessboard, their private lives are scrutinized to the smallest detail. It's been a week since Mister Novak ascended to power. The more remote players may not have heard of his exploits yet, but it's only a matter of time. I'm staying ahead of the curve."

"And how do *you* know? Even I didn't."

"New Kowloon and Locksville were closely involved in the change at The Station."

"Did you say *Locksville*?"

"Weinberg and the CIU," divulged the Golden Dragon.

Aileen pursed her lips. That old fox. Could've warned her, as Marc's sister, at least. "So, I'm simply a pawn."

"Not a pawn. A rook, I'd say."

"Still, a piece on the chessboard."

"As am I." Tam Wai Lam held Aileen's accusatory stare. "We all are."

"I bet you fancy yourself the white queen."

A line furrowed the Golden Dragon's smooth brow. "I am not the villain in this story, Aileen. Stop acting like a petulant child."

Blood rushed to Aileen's face. She opened her mouth to retort, but the Dragon did not wait. "You're so much more than that."

Was that a praise or a jab?

Tam Wai Lam paused, but Aileen stayed mute.

"Are you trying to hurt my feelings? Many have tried, with stronger venom than you'll ever have." The tiny wrinkles in the corners of Tam Wai Lam's eyes made the words sound more ominous than they must have been meant.

Wonder where their bodies have been dumped.

Another pause. "Are you justified in being angry? Absolutely. Will lashing out lead you anywhere? You know it won't. My suggestion, take some time off. Vent your frustrations on Mister Singh."

The subject of her proposal stirred and arched an eyebrow, but kept his comments to himself. Not just muscles and a handsome face, eh?

"When you calm down enough to see the broader picture, we'll talk again. This is nothing but a minor storm. Once it blows over, you can go home. Or to The Station. Or—" A meaningful smile stretched Tam Wai Lam's lips, hinting at something bigger.

"Or?"

The Dragon rose. "Or stay here. I can offer you the world. With your potential, I have full confidence you'll *own* it."

Aileen, speechless for once, watched her nod and leave the room with an enviably straight back.

Ajinder approached.

"What was that about?" Aileen asked, looking up at him.

He shrugged and offered a hand. Aileen frowned at it.

"May I take you to the dojo, Miss Novak?"

"The *dojo*." Turned out, men could still intrigue her.

Ajinder's mustache shifted, hiding his grin. "What better place to vent your frustrations?"

Aileen leaped to her feet with a predatory leer, ignoring his hand. "Lead the way."

She was going to beat the crap out of *someone*. The day was shaping up to not be all bad.

Realistically, Aileen didn't excel in this whole martial arts thing. Never had. Thus, she hadn't planned to spar, hoping instead to simply make a certain bearded mercenary hurt. Alas, the idea of standing still and taking the beating apparently hadn't crossed Ajinder's mind. Knocking him out, as a way to atone for her unspent anger and despondency, proved an unattainable goal. He lithely danced around Aileen, effortlessly parrying her every attack, deflecting her clumsy, ineffectual blows with his leather vambraces and shin guards, or absorbing them with his stone-hard thighs. To make her humiliation worse, the condescending bastard semaphored his half-hearted counterattacks well in advance. This wasn't what she'd been promised. This was the opposite of venting.

"Stop that!" she grumbled, out of breath. Her cheeks and ears burned from exertion and embarrassment.

Ajinder gave her the courtesy of not asking what she wanted him to stop. Aileen didn't register his attack. The shock in her ribs bent her in two.

Her abductor scampered to her side, putting an arm around her shoulders and leaning in to peek into her face. "Are you okay?" The concern in his voice sounded genuine. "I'm so sorry."

Aileen took a tentative breath. Then another one. That was going to leave a bruise, but nothing seemed to be broken.

She steeled herself, shutting the pain out, and sprang up. Her gloved fist connected with Ajinder's chin in a perfect uppercut. He staggered two steps back.

"I warned you to stop apologizing," Aileen rasped, holding on to the source of throbbing radiating in her side. The price was worth the opportunity.

Ajinder touched his jaw and moved it from side to side. His wicked grin spoiled her hidden triumph.

"You aren't much of a fighter, are you?" an inflectionless voice inquired behind her.

Aileen swung around. Her righteous fury was about to boil over in a few choice words, but the oddness of the girl she faced threw her off.

With the stranger's weird hairdo, part shaven, part braided, and her self-confident posture, Aileen would have pegged her for a rebel—but her emotionless features did not fit the image. She was a full head shorter than Aileen, and younger... Or was she? The ache, settled behind her eyes, aged her, and not graciously.

Aileen had seen such tortured eyes. Bo. Bo! Crap! He'd return from Corning and wouldn't find her. That... That'd be a mess.

She frowned. "I'm more of a fighter than you'll ever know. Just not in *this* way." Her indignation returned. She was an Aunt! Her name was used to scare Locksville's little children and grown-ups alike! She didn't need to justify herself before this freak.

Aileen turned back to Ajinder. "What are you so happy about?" She stepped closer, winding for another punch. Ajinder's smile didn't waver.

"Miss Novak, meet Park Yun-mi."

Aileen charged, ignoring the introduction. Ajinder angled a few inches back, dodging her fist and still looking behind her.

"You have to *want* to cause harm," said the girl. "Look."

A blur of motion. A foot, hooked behind Ajinder's legs. A palm, meeting his sternum with an audible thwack. Ajinder, tearing through the air and—*thud!*—landing on his back. The girl, kneeling on his arm with a lightning-fast strike at his throat. Her hand, halting a hair's width from his skin.

Silence fell over the dojo with everyone's attention on the girl.

"See?" She easily pushed to her feet, disregarding the gawkers. "Do it like you mean it." Her face remained expressionless. She neither bragged nor gloated. "But never use your fists. Without gloves, you'll break your knuckles, leaving your hand less than useless."

Aileen did not respond. She needed no bloody lessons from a snot-nosed upstart. She fought her battles with her wits, not her fists... or whatever.

"Ajinder said 'Novak'." The unabashed girl studied Aileen's face. "Marc's wife?"

"Wife?!" Aileen choked on the absurdity of the assumption. "Hells, no! Sister." She narrowed her eyes. "And how do *you* know Marc? You aren't his type."

"Met him here a week ago."

"Wait. Marc was *here*?" What other information had the Golden Dragon withheld?

The revelation pushed clobbering Ajinder way down Aileen's priorities list. She needed time to analyze and adjust her picture of the world. Of her place in it. Bo would have been helpful...

She began pulling her protective gear off. "Aji, take me to my room. Or cell, or hole in the ground, whatever they've got for me."

Ajinder grimaced. "The Golden Dragon made it clear you aren't a prisoner, Miss Novak."

"Um-hum."

He sighed and shook his head.

Aileen waited for him to start rolling his wrist wraps. When both his hands were sufficiently entangled, she slid forward and hit him in the chest with the heel of her palm. She channeled all the penned-up chagrin of the day, and fear—yes, there had been fear—through the point of impact.

With a startled squawk, Ajinder stumbled back, searching for footing, but snagged against the mat. He jerked his hands to flail for balance. The wraps didn't let him. He sent Aileen a pleading look and... *thud.*

Now, *this* was fun. *This* was venting. Aileen allowed herself a thin smile and turned to the strange girl. "Something like that?"

"Something like that," she said without a hint of humor. What was wrong with her? "But faster. And you forgot to trip him."

Aileen's smile died. "He did a fine job of that all on his own." She turned her back to the killjoy and approached Ajinder. Lying on the mats, he tracked her without attempting to get up.

"This would be a splendid opportunity to kick me, Miss Novak," he said. "Just not in the head, please. Oh, and... avoid the groin, if you'd be so kind."

Perfect deadpan delivery. Crap. Why did her abductor have to be so damn likable?

Aileen contemplated. "Huh. Now, *there's* an idea..."

Ajinder's legs flew too fast, sweeping her off her feet. She spent much more time airborne than seemed reasonable. The ceiling floated by, with lights and pipes snaking across. She took a full breath in... and only then had the air knocked out of her lungs by the floor. She lay, waiting for the world to regain its normal brightness, before carefully turning her head and meeting Ajinder's laughing eyes.

"Have you vented enough for today, Miss Novak?"

She lowered her eyelids. The bastard was having an inexcusable amount of fun. Unexpectedly, so was she.

Chapter 11

New Kowloon

October 6, 42 PE

Late last evening, she'd been too exhausted to let all the questions bother her. Not that they hadn't tried, but she needed her strength and flatly brushed them away. She had mechanically pushed down some chow and crashed into the bed, passing out before gathering the willpower to undress. At around four, her eyes had flipped wide-open in the stuffy darkness, and refused to close again. This time, for a change, her sleep was disrupted not by an intruder but by an overwhelming sense of unease.

Aileen sat up. A foreign smell tickled her nostrils. Of many—too many!—people, unfamiliar food, and something else. Oily, or greasy... *Machinery, that's what.* Her bare feet caught a distant vibration reverberating through the floor. *New Kowloon.*

Aileen fumbled, lighting a lamp on her third attempt. Its dancing, deceiving shadows left a lot to the imagination, but what little was visible did not shout, "*Prison!*" Narrow and long, her room was obviously the inside of a shipping container, one of the Hive's building blocks. Wooden planks covered the walls, hiding the metal and dissipating the warm light of the lamp. The bed she was in, wide enough for two to sleep in without too much discomfort, and a small bathroom partition occupied the far end from the door; a small table with two chairs sat in the middle. Not quite luxurious, but so much better than Locksville's jail she'd had the dubious pleasure of enjoying the only time she'd got caught. She'd take *this* over that pigeonhole with a sagging cot, a crumbling, lousy straw mattress, and a fetid bucket in the corner. When was it, four, five years ago? Ah, good times. She'd deliberately let the pursuers catch her while her crew made good on their escape. When she returned after only a month in the slammer, she discovered that the word of her selfless sacrifice had traveled. The Streeters had noticed.

A deep sigh escaped Aileen's chest.

The Streeters. Last time an Uncle had disappeared, too much nasty stuff had followed. Now, with her gone, would Oscar, an unimaginative but solid and reliable Second, have what it takes to lead? Bo would ensure things ran smoothly once he was back. Poor guy, how would he handle the travel? More protective of Aileen than Marc, he'd turn mountains to find her. But this was such a clean extraction, he'd have nothing to work with.

Marc. Running The Station. Crazy! How did *that* happen? What could make him flip again, this time on Weinberg himself? Since he'd enlisted, and especially after she'd become an Aunt, they hadn't been as huge a part of each other's lives as before. She'd been so angry with him at first, but had eventually forgiven him. For him, though, she had been, was, and would always remain his Little Sis. If there was any constant in her life, this was it. Once he learned about her disappearance, he'd go off his rocker.

Then there was Weinberg, who would not look kindly at her disappearance right under his nose. Such trespassing was guaranteed to rustle his feathers. Huh. He sure had eyes in New Kowloon. If she made herself seen and heard, word would reach Locksville. Wai Lam had not limited Aileen's movements around the Hive. A goodwill gesture? Whatever. Given the circumstances of her arrival at New Kowloon, Aileen wasn't under any obligation not to abuse this supposed hospitality. She was going to make the most of that arrogant woman's carelessness.

Not much, but better than nothing.

Oh, and that Dragon's phrase about giving Aileen the world—what could that possibly mean? Nah, empty promises to lull Aileen into compliance. Screw that.

Aileen rubbed her puffy cheeks. A minor miracle they haven't peeled off yet. Her eyes burned, as if full of hot sand.

A soft knock yanked her out of her hazy stupor.

Aileen slid off the bed, plodded to the entrance, hesitated a moment, and pushed the handle. The door opened a crack, unlocked. Indeed, not a prison cell, but she still was confined to the building. She peeked into the hallway. Ajinder. Aileen stepped aside and let him in.

She shut the door, shuffled past him, and plopped into a chair. Ajinder shifted from foot to foot, watching her rest her elbows on the table and lean into her palms with her jaw. Aileen raised her brows. "What? Here to snatch me again? Found a higher bidder?"

Ajinder puffed. "I saw the light under your door. Wanted to check if everything was okay." His voice pitched up. Angry? Offended? Not so thick-skinned after all, ha?

Aileen cocked her head to the side.

He lowered his eyes. And his voice. "I know, sounds stupid, right? Considering."

Aileen smirked. "The stupidest I've heard in days. Still, sweet of you to ask. Do you check on everyone you abduct?"

The faint light of the stingy lamp did nothing to conceal his blushing.

"Only the coarse ones."

Nice save, but he wasn't getting off the hook so easily. "You happened to walk past my door in the wee hours of the night."

"In fact, I did!" Ajinder threw his head up. "My room is just down—" He shut his eyes, took a deep breath, closed the distance to the table and sat across from her. "Can we please not do this?"

Aileen fixed him with the coldest of her gazes. "I don't remember inviting you to sit."

"Aileen—"

She frowned. "Miss Novak."

"Aileen," he repeated forcefully, "you may be a big shot in Locksville—"

"Why, thank you."

"—but we are not in Locksville."

"Whose fault is that?"

"Intimidation won't work on me—"

"Won't it?" It sure did, if he felt the need to bring it up.

"—because I know I can kick your ass."

"Wow. Way to impress the girl."

"A-a-and we are doing this again."

"Yup."

"Aileen, I came to apologize." He paused, allowing her to respond.

Aileen shrugged. "For what? It was a job. You did it well. Hear, hear. Attaboy. Now go abduct someone else."

Ajinder winced. "We don't do abductions."

Yeah, except when you do. "We?"

"The Singh brothers. Our family is in the personal protection business. That's what the Golden Dragon had hired us for. To keep you safe."

"Aha."

"Obviously, you don't see it that way. I... can understand why. And feel terrible about that. So, there."

The fatigue rolled over Aileen like a boulder. All other sensations—the anger, the anxiety—took a step back, letting the tiredness fill her veins with liquid lead. She dropped her forehead onto her hands, folded on the edge of the table. "What do you want me to say, Ajinder Singh, personal protector?" she asked into the floor, quietly, in little more than a whisper. "You want my forgiveness? Fine. Have it. Now what?"

No answer came.

She strained to pull her head up, propping her chin on her palms again. Ajinder's expression was comically helpless. Aileen mobilized the last dregs of energy to lean back and cross her arms over her chest. "Out of words? Didn't expect such an easy victory?"

He hung his head.

"Still not intimidated?"

Ajinder remained silent.

"Okay, want to redeem yourself? Take me back to Locksville. Or at least to The Station... if Marc really is there."

"He is. My brothers are there, guarding him."

"Same way you're *guarding* me?"

"You know I can't do what you're asking of me."

Was worth a try. "Then your apology is nothing but hot air. Remember what I told you yesterday?"

"Which part?"

"Get. The fuck. Out."

He stared back. A scolded pup, with tragic eyes and the corners of his lips drawn down.

Aileen rose, pushing her chair back with a screech. "Just go."

She shambled toward her bed, crawled between the sheets, and turned her back to him. So empty and alone. "You owe me two nights' sleep now," she mumbled into her pillow.

Hope spiked—against her best judgement, contrary to any logic, and in blatant contradiction to her own harsh words—that he'd see through her boisterous façade. That he'd slip under the blanket behind her. That his arms would wrap around her... Stupid, yes. Irrational, yes. But so needed.

She held her breath, listening, not daring to peek. She could say, "Are you coming or not?" That would have done it. She didn't.

A moving chair. Silence. A sigh. Quiet retreating steps. Door, firmly closed. Crap.

She played her role too well. She *was* too intimidating. Too stubborn. Too much an Aunt, not enough Aileen.

Sleep. Sweet, sweet sleep. It enveloped her with its soft tentacles, refusing to let go, but... The knock on the door repeated. *That's* what it was. Seriously? For fuck's sake, could a girl get one—one!—uninterrupted night of rest?

"Oh, come in, already!" she groaned.

Ajinder, of course. Aileen pulled her legs under her, settling on her knees and wrapping herself in the blanket.

Without looking her way, he strutted to the table and lowered a tray onto it. Dishes clanked. Her stomach eagerly growled.

"It's past nine. The cafeteria was closing, and I figured you'd be a danger to the Hive if forced to go hungry till lunchtime." Ajinder studied the steaming food, painstakingly avoiding looking at her.

How cute. "Aw, thank you." For once, Aileen had no snarky comments.

He finally acknowledged her with a dark, distant gaze. "Goodbye, Miss Novak. I am leaving on an assignment. No, not another abduction."

Severe features, austerely set lips. Way too serious, not joking or sarcastic. Had she hurt him that badly? After what he'd done, he deserved every bit of her derision. But what *had* he done? All signs indicated he'd really meant to keep her safe.

"The Golden Dragon is now aware of my displeasure with your situation."

Couldn't have been an easy conversation for him. Aileen mustered her kindest tone. "Where are you going?"

Her kindest wasn't kind enough; she hadn't practiced it in a while.

"Can't say." A stone mask. "For my client's security."

"When will you be back?"

"Three-four days." His cheek twitched. "Why ask? What does it matter to you?"

Ah, there. She'd been a total ass with him, but he had not completely given up on her yet.

She climbed out of the bed and plodded to him, securing the blanket on her shoulders with one hand. Her barefoot steps tapped on the floor.

He waited for her to approach, keeping a straight face, but her trained eye discerned what a struggle that was. She stopped close. Close enough to hear his breath quickening. Too close. They were the same height. Somehow, Aileen hadn't noticed this detail until now. She caressed his cheek with the back of her hand and was rewarded with a gasp.

"I'm sorry," she mouthed.

He read her lips and surprised her with a crooked smile. "Ah, so you *are* allowed to apologize?"

Aileen burst into giggling. Then wrapped her arms around his waist and lowered her head onto his shoulder. "You're a good man, Ajinder Singh," she murmured.

The blanket slid to the floor, but that was okay. He was warm, and solid, and much more comforting anyway.

He hesitated only a second before returning a hug.

Neither of them spoke or moved.

Why was it that in the past, she'd been drawn exclusively to bad boys? Maybe she hadn't encountered decent men due to the nature of her business; or had, but paid them no heed, enamored with rowdy swagger. As a result, she'd been burned a few too many times. Several of those relationships—before she'd become an Aunt—had been borderline abusive. None ended well. She'd concluded that no man existed worthy of her attention and buried herself in work.

And now, here was Ajinder, with his subtle but undeniable charm. Neither a smooth rascal, nor a goodie two-shoes. An old-school gentleman, adorable in his need to do right by everyone, yet witty and not taking himself too seriously.

Her tastes must have changed as she matured. This could be a good idea, or a terrible one. Only one way to find out...

Aileen lifted her head and took the plunge. "How soon do you have to leave?"

"I may have an hour. Why?"

Their faces were an inch apart, their noses almost touching. His velvety irises were dark, the pupils—dilated, deep, and asking.

Aileen broke out of his embrace and stepped back. She pulled her sweatshirt off and shook her head, letting her unruly hair spread over her shoulders. This time, Ajinder did not avert his gaze.

"Your food will get cold."

Seriously? Aileen rolled her eyes. "*I* am going back to bed now, with or without you. Your choice."

His exasperated sigh almost made her chortle. "When you put it like that..."

———

Aileen nestled her ear in the small depression between Ajinder's shoulder and the impressive pecs, twirling a lock of curly black hair on his chest. His finger climbed the steep slope between her waist and her thighs, and continued down her leg. On its way back, it slid across her belly. She twitched. "Hey! Tickler." His hand retreated, settling on the small of her back.

"Better?"

Aileen pressed tighter into him. "Perfect."

The silence that followed was not in the least awkward. It said everything Aileen wanted to say—and to hear. Ajinder's body radiated warmth, beyond merely physical. In his arms, she was *safe*. Even away from home. Even though he was the one who dragged her to this strange place. When he hugged her like that, nothing could harm her. She basked in this sensation, drifting away.

"Yes."

Her eyes fluttered open. "Hm?"

"I'm answering your next question. If I sleep with all the women I abduct."

She bit him playfully. "Am I that predictable?"

"You? Predictable? Ha, a good one. I'd never use these words in one sentence. No, just sounded like something you *might* ask. And no."

Aileen patiently waited for him to explain.

"No, I don't have another woman."

"And that's something I might ask, too?"

"Hells, no. You're too proud for that. But it's something you might have *pondered*. And worried about while I'm gone. And schemed to extract the answer from me in devilishly insidious ways."

"A little presumptive, no, Aji? This"—her fingernail ran down his abs—"was wonderful, I'll give you that, but what gave you the idea I'd give a damn about your other women?"

"You may fool yourself, but you won't fool me."

"No?"

"No. I can tell you're possessive and can't suffer competition. A fiercely territorial creature."

"A fierce creature, am I?"

"In a good way." His hug tightened. "Promise me one thing."

"Uh-oh." Aileen kept smiling, but a cold snake of doubt slithered under her breastbone. Clammy memories of her exes' outlandish demands and ugly jealousy flashed before her eyes. *Not again.* Was this another mistake she'd come to regret?

"Promise you won't run away before I return."

Aileen exhaled. Ajinder *was* different. Good different. "Why, so we can run away together?"

He tensed under her cheek.

Crap. Her big mouth. She brushed a hand over his ribs. "Sorry. A stupid joke. Didn't mean to jab you." Damn. She'd apologized twice in the last hour—more than she normally did in a month. His bottomless eyes made her too soft. But Aileen wasn't prepared to make *that* commitment.

Ajinder awaited her response. She needed an out. "All I can promise is that if someone else kidnaps me, I won't sleep with him."

"Ew. Crude, even by your standards."

"You think? Maybe." She pushed away and rolled onto her belly, propping herself on her elbows. His eyes flicked from her face to her breasts and failed to return.

She snickered. "Like what you see?" Another way to end the uncomfortable conversation.

"I like all of you, Aileen. What I see, and what I don't. Your twisted mind. Your venomous tongue. And yes, your boobs are to die for." He reached to touch her, but she batted his hand away.

"You'll be late."

"Screw that. Screw them all. I quit. I'll stay here with you all day."

"You can't. When you take me home to your clan and I, a merry little housewife, start popping one baby after another for you, who would put bread on the table? Go, go." She shoved him until he rolled off the bed, laughing.

His head reappeared above the mattress edge. "Housewife?"

She tossed a pillow at him.

When he was fully dressed and finished wrapping his turban, Aileen picked up her blanket, threw it over her back again like a cape, and joined Ajinder at the door. He put his warm, dry hands on her naked hips, grunted, and firmly pushed her away. Shaking his head, he sucked in a sharp breath. "Don't come any closer, woman, or I'll never leave."

She bent forward, as did he, across the invisible divide. Their lips touched. He turned away. "Take the food back to the kitchens. Tell them you're the Golden Dragon's guest. They'll cook a personal meal for you."

"Good. I'm ravenous."

In the doorway, he glanced back with a gentle, understanding smile. She winked and bit her tongue. Not to wish him safe travels; not to bid him to be careful out there; not to ask him to come back soon.

What was happening? *That*, these words—it wasn't her. Not Aunt Aileen, the tough arbiter of Locksville Streeters, feared by many and respected by all, used to herding grown-up men all day, every day. Not the independent young woman who picked any partners she wanted, and dumped them as easily on a whim.

She kept standing there after the door had closed behind Ajinder, clinging to the image of his smile. The smile freely given to her.

Until the scandalized grumbling in her guts reminded her of the cold breakfast.

Chapter 12

New Kowloon

October 6, 42 PE

Absurdly colossal, the Great Hive lived up to its name. Shipping containers stacked fifteen levels high formed a rectangular monstrosity around the inner compound that hosted auxiliary buildings. With her stomach satisfyingly heavy, and nothing but free time on her hands, Aileen had been traipsing the complex's walkways for an hour, up and down the stairs, turning randomly wherever her feet took her—and still had not completed a single full circle. Out of idle curiosity, she set out to find how many containers wide each side of the structure comprised, but even that answer eluded her.

Some hallways were strictly utilitarian, nothing but metal surfaces echoing hollowly and unkindly under Aileen's feet. Others assaulted her aesthetic taste with the garish opulence of their thick red carpets, gold-painted walls, carvings, and statues.

She ought to have been impressed. The Hive was a marvel of modern engineering; a towering, in-your-face reminder—as if anyone could forget—of New Kowloon's might, prosperity, and technological superiority. It was impossible not to compare it to the best Locksville offered, and that comparison was decidedly not in her home's favor. The Hive's sheer scale, the thoughtfulness of its design... The electric lights and central heating, for crying out loud! It dwarfed the ancient canal locks, let alone the White House she'd used to consider pretty grand. And the Streeters' Warehouse? Merely a den of a provincial, inconsequential organization. Whose leader could be snatched away and locked up, neither because of something she had done nor due to what she was—but for having the wrong last name.

Her spite had resurfaced with Ajinder's departure, and dulled the Hive's splendor. If its power was used to deny Aileen her freedom of will, it deserved to be sneered at. Occasional spikes of rage at the injustice broke through her lip-curling revulsion, and she barely restrained herself from kicking an innocent ancient vase or smashing a glass cabinet.

And crowds, those suffocating crowds—everywhere. She'd already seen more people than she'd met in Locksville in a week. At first, they all seemed similar. Deadly serious, unsmiling faces; uniforms, differing only in colors. Like bees, milling around with a singular purposefulness. Whoever had come up with the name Hive was spot-on. Worker bees, soldier bees... And the freakin' Dragon for the queen.

The Kowloonese she'd encountered made a show of paying her no attention, but gave her a wide berth. She caught sideways glances when they thought she wasn't looking. So much for merging in and losing the tail she surely had. Fat chance. A lone foreigner half a head taller than an average Kowloonese, with her distinct blond hair, had to be an attention magnet.

Let them gawk. Aileen swallowed her discomfort and pulled her chin higher, staring at the passersby—presumably rudely by the Hive's standards. A devious smile stretched her lips.

If the locals' curiosity matched a fraction of what an average Locksviller harbored, the rumors were guaranteed to have made rounds already. Eventually, those would reach Weinberg's ears, and then... Okay, that might take time. She'd better manage her expectations. For now, why not use the Dragon's carte blanche to get the lay of the land? And the layout of the Hive, while at it. One day, Aileen may need not to break out, but to smuggle something in. Fate, the Great Fickle Bitch, worked in mysterious ways.

The so far unrestricted access practically invited her to challenge its boundaries. This *was* an odd abduction. Back in Locksville, if she'd roamed the White House like this, she would've been stopped and questioned a few times already. Here, the security guards looked through her with glassy eyes, not once inquiring about her business. Aileen climbed to the top floor where, logically, all the dignitaries would be holed up.

As she cleared the last flight of stairs, two black-uniformed guards, who could be twins, blocked her way. "Restricted area," one barked.

"Why?" An opportunity to push the limits of her "freedom".

Neither of the soldiers responded. Their unmoving eyes bored into her chin.

"Where would I find Golden Dragon Tam Wai Lam?"

Silence.

Aileen smirked. "Fine. Tell her I said 'hi'." She wasn't looking for a confrontation... yet. There was plenty to explore before that.

The twelfth floor gifted her a hidden jewel. A tiny round table with a single chair nestled in a strangely deserted corner where the two outer walls converged. Enormous floor-to-ceiling windows faced south and east. Aileen approached, and her breath caught. Under the menacing dark skies, heavy gray waves rolled across the lake. The shoreline curved into the distance, luring the eye further and further away, until... *there*. Locksville should be somewhere around there. Home, unseen but calling.

Glued to the window, Aileen lowered herself into the chair. She could drink in this astonishing view forever. And she did, losing track of time. The waves, in their eternal onslaught on the land, raced against the storm clouds. Furious lightning bolts hammered the earth in the distance. South of Rochester, where Bo should be.

A thin splinter of worry pricked her heart.

Bo would be fine. Tick wouldn't let anything bad happen to him. Between those two, they've got enough brain and brawn to stay out of trouble.

"You've found my favorite spot."

Aileen didn't recognize the male voice, but refused to take her eyes off the view. "It's perfect. I am surprised there's no lineup to spend a minute here."

"People of New Kowloon generally keep themselves busy. No time for lounging. Or so they want me to believe."

"You must be some kind of head honcho."

"That's one way to put it."

Aileen deigned to glance over her shoulder. Nothing special, a typical middle-aged Kowloonese. Average height, medium build, round face, neatly cropped straight black hair. Only his laughing eyes stood out, underscoring the overall aura of self-confidence. Not a uniformed drone.

"Sized up and classified." He chuckled, drawing another, longer look from Aileen. "But still cannot compete against the spectacle outside. Kudos, Miss Novak, you've got your priorities straight."

Not too subtle. "Is this when I'm supposed to ask who you are?"

"But you aren't inclined to."

"I..." She feigned a frown, as if gauging her interest. "I register a minor spike of curiosity. Borderline negligible."

The man smirked.

Interesting. Not full of himself. Has a sense of humor. Not *just* a head honcho; top brass. The armed duo looming discreetly further down the corridor confirmed her assessment. "Golden Dragon?"

"Very good, Miss Novak." The man inclined his head without breaking eye contact. "Golden Dragon Shang Ka Yi."

"Am I expected to bow?"

"As you wish. I don't really care."

"How progressive. Okay, what's your game, Golden Dragon? Unless you've come to claim your favorite spot, of course."

"Would you yield it?"

"No."

"That's what I thought. Its magic outranks authority."

"Noted. In that case, I'll make it my quarters."

"I'll arrange for another chair. You can't hog the view all for yourself."

"I'll trade you *this* chair for a ride to Locksville. No, eh? What *can* I offer you for an edge over Tam Wai Lam?"

"Miss Novak." The reproachful tone said it all. She hung her head. "*No one gets an edge over Tam Wai Lam,*" continued the Dragon. "Not you, not I."

Weren't these Councilors supposed to be at each other's throats all day long?

Meeting her unconvinced look, he spread his arms. "I'm her husband."

Damn. Aileen closed her eyes. A trap, and she walked straight into it. "Why are you here, Golden Dragon? To gloat?"

"Heavens forbid, Miss Novak. My wife speaks highly of you, and that is not a common occurrence. I hoped to form my own impression."

"Have you?"

"I have. Apologies for distracting you. Occupy the chair for as long as you'd like." He turned to leave.

"Hey, Shang."

His implacable features showed nothing but polite attention when he faced her again, but his tensing neck betrayed how offensive her familiarity was. Awesome. That was intentional.

"Tell her I still think she's a cunt."

Aileen expected outrage, whether manifested through icy disdain or an angry rebuff; an indignant slap, or a night in a solitary cell. One reaction to her provocation she did not expect was a thin smile.

"Thank you, Miss Novak. I'll pass your message verbatim. I'm sure she'll see it as a compliment." He saluted Aileen with another curt bob of his head and left her with her jaw dropped.

Rarely had Aileen been outmatched this badly.

The distant thunderstorm had shifted toward Locksville. A symbolic harbinger of the fresh Troubles?

She stared into the limitless volume outside, not seeing it. The memories flooded her from—how long ago had it been? Almost two years. How time flies.

The day after Uncle Stanley's disappearance was the first time she had feared for her life. Ever. Locksville being Locksville, its underworld shunned violence. You could steal, swindle, or smuggle—but violent crime had always been a taboo. Until that day. She didn't know who had broken this unspoken rule first, but once the blood had been spilled, the floodgates were opened.

Streeters had never been a single band. Rather, a loose confederation with common interests, delimited sectors, and an arbitration mechanism: the Uncle—or the Aunt—to oversee adherence to the Treaty and to mediate disputes. With that person gone, all the grievances, old and fresh, came to a head. Competing factions suddenly recalled erstwhile insults and rushed to claim retributions, reshaping their domains while no one was watching. No, bodies did not pile up in the streets, nor did blood run down the gutters. But the word traveled, of scores settled; of people disappearing; of knives drawn—and used. Unfamiliar faces started showing up; foreigners, not bound by Locksville's norms and conventions. They brought with them barbarity, such as Locksville had not remembered since the E. Armed robbery, home invasions, rape, and murder. Locksville shuddered.

Aileen, Bo, Tick, and Fox, along with half a dozen crewmates, had barricaded themselves in a warehouse—the one to eventually become *the* Warehouse.

On the fourth day, Marc knocked on their door, grim-faced and exhausted. "The CIU is blind," he said, rubbing the dark bags under his eyes. "We only react. That'll never stop this shitstorm." He looked around at the sullen listeners. Kids. They were all just kids. "And you don't have the muscle."

"Weinberg," breathed out Bo, always the sharpest.

"Weinberg." Marc snapped his fingers and nodded. "Coordinate through him. And remember, I was never here, you didn't see me. This was your idea. A grassroot initiative. Concerned citizens. Got it?"

And it worked. By gods, it worked! Aileen and her crew forgot about sleep. Day and night, they'd been convincing, and cajoling, and threatening, and collecting intel... Until the ghostly quiet shrouded Locksville. All local teams had fallen in line. The foreigners had been eradicated by the now all-seeing and omnipresent CIU, or took the hint and turned tail. And the Streeters' emergency assembly unanimously voted Aileen in as the new Aunt.

She closed her eyes.

Last time, an entirely different hand had been dealt. Uncle Stanley, a pillar of the community, a landmark, had had no need for a strong Second. The one he'd had—a glorified secretary—fled the moment things went pear-shaped, never to be seen again. And just like that, everything had disintegrated.

Aileen had learned her lesson. She'd invested tons of time and effort into building a robust organization that could function without her. *That* was what responsible leaders did. Not hogging all the power and knowledge to themselves. Not cowering in their den, surrounded by guards yet still fearing a coup by a strong contender they had groomed. Instead, finding people who'd be prepared to fill the void, if worse came to worst. Oscar was solid enough to hold the fort, but... Aileen wasn't ready to step down. Her legacy? It could wait. *Should* wait.

She loved being an Aunt. Not because of the authority—although that gave her a kick, too—but because of the meaning this role provided. She'd been the right person for the job; nothing could beat that in satisfaction. Yet, here she was, useless, yanked away for a reason unrelated to her being an Aunt. To be a piece in someone else's game? No. Not a pawn, nor a rook. Not even a queen. She was a *player*. Tam Wai Lam had offered her the world? Whatever that meant, Aileen didn't need it. All she wanted was to get back to her Locksville, to have her Locksville's back.

Staying would mean admitting defeat. Never!

And actually... Nothing was holding her. Aileen jolted upright, struck by this realization.

Back home, Aji, the sweet bastard, had leveraged her into obedience by threatening her crew. He took her to the waiting boat, which she couldn't escape, and straight to the Hive. But now, no one held any power to control her. And if they thought they could keep her confined—well...

Aileen indulged herself with a carnivorous grin.

The Dragons were in for a rude awakening.

Chapter 13

New Kowloon

October 6, 42 PE

"I hoped I'd find you here." Aileen dished out a prerequisite amount of positivity. Positivity she could scarcely spare, but beggars couldn't be choosers. Her injured, sour ego would have to suck it up.

The odd girl's smooth, complex combat routine continued uninterrupted. "*Fss, fss,*" she pushed her breath out through her teeth with each punch, accompanied by sharp snaps of her sleeves.

Aileen pursed her lips and waited, scraping the bottom of her patience's deepest reservoir.

The furious "*hee-ya!*" signaling the final blow sent panicking echoes scattering around the cavernous dojo, empty at this time of day.

The hairs on the back of Aileen's neck stood on their ends. Wouldn't want to be on the receiving end of *that*.

"Why were you looking for me, Novak's sister?" The girl finally acknowledged Aileen's presence. Her face showed neither surprise nor irritation. Not as much as mild interest. Nothing.

Aileen counted to five, sifting through her readily available stock of expletives and discarding them all as counterproductive.

She used the silent pause to analyze the girl's features. After yesterday's sparring, Ajinder had mentioned she was an outsider too, a Korean from the City. Aileen strained to discern any facial differences from the Chinese she'd seen. The eyes? The nose? The jaw shape? Possibly, but she'd have to see more of those Koreans to generalize. For now, she gave up. The important part was that the girl wasn't a Kowloonese. A "flaw" that could—and should—be exploited.

"The name's Aileen. And you're Park... Yenmu?"

"Park Yun-mi." The Korean didn't bat an eye. "What is it, Aileen?"

No small talk or pleasantries? Aileen shrugged. Fine by her. "Just wanted to chat. We both are foreigners in the Hive, and may have common interests..." She let the unfinished phrase hang, allowing Park Yun-mi to unpack her meaning and pick up where she'd left.

The girl's dark, unsmiling eyes mesmerized Aileen. They reached deep into her soul, and in that instant the futility of her subterfuge became painfully obvious, before any words were spoken.

"I understand you aren't here willfully." For the first time, Park Yun-mi showed emotion. Not the one Aileen had hoped for.

Aileen winced, raising her hand to stop the girl. "Don't you dare pity me. If you won't help, just say so."

Park Yun-mi calmly withstood Aileen's glare. "I won't help."

Aileen clenched her teeth and turned to leave. A dead end. Bummer.

"Wai Lam means well."

Whatever feelings suffused the voice behind Aileen's back, they ran deep. She froze, returned her attention to Park Yun-mi, and barely recognized her. The impermeable mask had melted away, leaving a mix of sorrow, affection, and stubbornness. Standing before Aileen was a child, a little girl; hurt, yet hopeful. Eager to convert a neophyte to her cause.

"She really does!" Yun-mi reinforced her conviction with a firm dip of her head. "I'm loyal to the Golden Dragon, Aileen, and I won't help you escape. But that's the thing: you don't have to! She's the best patron anyone can wish for." A frown furrowed her forehead. "And trust me, you wouldn't want her as your enemy."

"I *don't need* a patron. I *am* a patron." Aileen squinted. "What makes you think I asked for your help against *her*?"

The girl's lips stretched into a reproving line. "Your underestimation is insulting."

"I" —Aileen sighed—"apologize." She met Yun-mi's scrutinizing gaze. "You're going to tell her about this conversation, aren't you?"

"You know I am."

"Then why are you still talking to me, as if you care?"

"I don't want you to get into trouble."

"Why?"

Yun-mi hesitated. Her eyes wandered aside before finding Aileen's again. "First, I sympathize with your plight. I was captured once too, not long ago."

Aileen's eyebrows crept up. "By the Dragon?"

"What?" The girl indignantly shook her head. "Of course not! By... someone else. I killed him."

Aileen whistled. "Okay, that's... Color me impressed. And the second reason?"

A hint of a knowing smile. "Because Ajinder likes you. That's enough of a recommendation for me."

A bittersweet sadness uncoiled in Aileen's chest at the mention of his name. She hadn't paid attention to it before, but it must've settled there since his departure earlier that morning. How odd.

Come to think about it, Yun-mi's smile could be patronizing. And the bile spreading in Aileen's guts was suspiciously similar to jealousy. What the...

"Ajinder, huh?" Aileen tilted her head. "A romantic interest of yours, is he?"

This time, she caught the transformation of Yun-mi's face. It sank, as if she'd lost the faculty of all her facial muscles at once. The pain Aileen had seen there before resurfaced behind the girl's glassy eyes. Yun-mi's lower lip trembled. She bit it and looked away. When she turned back to Aileen, she'd regained full control, wearing the same mask as when they'd first met.

"I don't have romantic interests," Park Yun-mi, older and remote again, stated in a dull voice.

The tips of Aileen's ears burned. Her stupid, girlish jab had cost her the bond they might have established a minute ago.

"Look, I'm sorry if what I said disturbed you." Aileen raised her palms pacifyingly. "Did you lose someone close?"

"None of your business!"

Aileen flinched at the fierce hiss, but took Yun-mi's thin wrists into her hands.

What happened next was too fast to notice.

The girl's arms disappeared from Aileen's hold, and the force of two sledgehammers shoved at her chest. With her legs up in the air, her shoulder blades hit the mat. Something in her spine cracked, and the daylight flickered.

Park Yun-mi's stern face invaded Aileen's shockingly narrow field of vision. "Don't you dare pity me."

The little piece of shit was quoting Aileen's own words. Fuckin' A.

There was good news too: Aileen's legs obeyed her. Not a given, considering her painful landing. She struggled to her feet with a percussive groan. The girl observed without offering help.

"That was uncalled for," Aileen grumbled, tugging at her disheveled clothes.

Park Yun-mi mulishly stared into the floor.

Aileen flashed a lopsided smile. "Looks like I may have *over*estimated you, after all. Let's talk again when you grow up."

Her stomach sank in anticipation of another attack, but Park Yun-mi didn't take the bait. Only the skin over her sharp cheekbones grew a shade darker.

Outside, Aileen leaned against the dojo's door, deflated. This had been her single viable lead. And what a spectacular, unmitigated disaster it had unraveled into.

The Golden Dragon Tam Wai Lam was, undoubtedly, a smart woman. She must have known Aileen would try every vector of escape. The fact the Dragon hadn't found it necessary to restrict Aileen's movement around the Hive spoke volumes. Wai Lam had been confident Aileen would fail. This could be a subtle, sophisticated mental torture, intended to break Aileen's spirit, or just calculated arrogance.

Aileen pushed herself upright, squared her sore shoulders, and pulled her chin up.

She wasn't giving the Dragon the satisfaction of breaking her. She'd find her way out, if only to flip the bird to that all-powerful woman. Even if the Dragon was as moody and vengeful as her punk protégé, whose muted sobs carried from the other side of the dojo door.

While she'd been wasting her time on the stubborn Korean, the view outside the twelfth-floor window had changed. The lake, the sky, the entire *volume* of the world had disappeared as if it had never existed. As if Aileen had dreamed it up. Low clouds had moved in, enveloping New Kowloon in a depressingly gray drizzle. The twirls of water mist suspended in the air shifted constantly, like milky bowels of an enormous, nightmarish creature. A Leviathan. Which made her... what, the Biblical Jonah?

Aileen stared until it became impossible to tell if the weather front was moving, or the Hive sailed, cleaving the murky sea, with her at the bow.

Droplets accumulated on the glass, desperately clinging to its smooth surface until they could hold no more. They dove, head first, to their death, clawing at their hapless relatives, and dragging them along into the abyss.

A gust of wind aimed a sheet of rain at Aileen, splattering it against the window. She recoiled and gasped, woken from her semi-meditative state, and shook her head. *It's stupid water. Stop assigning sentiments to inanimate objects.*

She stretched, yawning, and cringed at the protestations of her back and shoulders.

Park Yun-mi, that little bitch! What a powder keg. Against all odds, Aileen's blurry reflection in the darkened window smiled. They'd talk again—not as potential accomplices, but... Like it or not, as kindred spirits. They had too much in common to waste this connection.

Poor girl. Ajinder would know what had happened to her.

The bittersweet feeling returned.

No. Oh, Hells, no! Fuck me. She was getting attached.

The abject horror wiped off the reflection's smile.

Uncles and Aunts didn't marry. Uncles and Aunts didn't have children. They owed their singular loyalty and undivided attention to the Streeters. Not to mention that their significant others and progenies would make for perfect pressure points… Much like she was for Marc, as it turned out. *That* lesson Aileen was unlikely to forget.

Her time with Ajinder was never intended to be anything beyond a fling. A pleasurable, comforting, fun—but necessarily meaningless—experiment with a suave, ridiculously handsome guy. Same as with her past transient passions, but with less drama.

Another reason to flee the Hive, and soon: to avoid the inevitably awkward conversation with Ajinder. And, if she were to be completely honest with herself, to cauterize this yearning to see him again. Before it developed into something bigger; something she would be unable to control.

The series of gong sounds reverberating all over the Hive provided a welcome distraction. Dinner time.

Trying to force a creative solution was pointless. Aileen's brain didn't work that way. Her best ideas materialized randomly, triggered by unknowable stimuli. Maybe downing some food would invite one.

Aileen rose and joined the throng of the worker bees, which had filled the Hive's passages with the hum of conversations. More trickled from the tributary corridors, merging into the flow.

Whether the word of her presence had traveled enough and she ceased being a fresh oddity, or the locals couldn't be brought to care as much after a long day of work, but they didn't bother creating the same empty bubble around her as they had in the morning. People stepped on her heels and bumped elbows with her, same as with each other. A few apologized, most didn't. And the chatter, the incessant chatter! As if they all spoke at once, and no one listened. Of course, that wasn't true. The hollow acoustics of the metal corridors must have contributed to the illusion. Not like she was going to learn something useful from the drones' blather, anyway.

"… mule… goods…"

Aileen's brain, attuned to the subjects of her professional interest, filtered these words. She surreptitiously glanced to her left. The two men of an indeterminate age, dressed in similar dark-blue coveralls, evidently didn't mean for their conversation to be overheard. One of them caught Aileen's eyes before she could fake bored disinterest. Damn it. He leaned to his partner, whispered, and dragged him by the elbow into a side corridor. The human torrent carried Aileen on. Struggling against the traffic would attract unwanted attention, and by the time she returned to the junction, they'd be long gone. Worst of all, no way she'd be able to identify them among hundreds of similarly clad workers.

None of that mattered.

Somehow, the artificial light in the hallway became brighter, the stale air—fresher, and the buzzing of the human swarm lost its annoyance. Aileen's head cleared. Her heart rate picked up, celebrating the breakthrough.

Of course! How could she *not* think of that?

New Kowloon, a large-scale and rigidly governed commercial enterprise, with its notoriously convoluted system of tariffs, customs, and taxation, *ought* to have had a clandestine smuggling operation. Human nature, no way around that. Enticing them to cooperate would be a breeze. Now, it all came down to a technicality: flushing them out. How difficult could that be?

Chapter 14

New Kowloon

October 6, 42 PE

Waiting. Marc had always excelled at it. Aileen? It drove her mad. Unfortunately, it represented a significant part of her game, and she'd learned to embrace the suck. Not letting her foot tap impatiently; restraining her fingers from drumming on the table; preventing the corner of her mouth from twitching with each jerky movement of the clock's second hand. No one would know what a toll exercising such control took.

She'd sent her feelers out. The ball was not in her court.

An hour earlier, Aileen had entered the busy cafeteria. In the late morning, when she'd followed Ajinder's advice to demand her Dragon guest's meal, the place had been empty. This time over, she stumbled into the tail of a long queue. Yet, contrary to her pessimistic expectations, the waiting didn't take forever. The Hive's food court logistics were polished to perfection, and within less than fifteen minutes, Aileen was standing with a tray full of steaming chow, searching for an unoccupied spot. In the end, she wedged between two locals at a table that provided her the best view of the mess hall. Her neighbors muttered—no doubt, something unflattering, but luckily unintelligible—yet gave her the space and ignored her from that point on. That served Aileen just as well. With their dull-green uniforms, they weren't of particular interest to her. She scanned the diner for clumps of dark blue, the warehouse staff. Because, naturally, where else would any self-respecting smugglers be based, if not in an intimate proximity to the wares.

Seven long tables hosted blue coveralls.

Aileen discarded the dead-eyed majority. Tired, disinterested in anything or anyone, these perfect laborers ingested their food mechanically, with the same practiced efficiency they must've performed their jobs.

Two groups warranted a second, longer look. One comprised boisterous youngsters, brash and loud, stretching the thin line between a lively social gathering and disorderly conduct. The other—their complete opposite, mature and composed. Frowning at their rowdy colleagues, but not intervening. Definitely the ones in charge. Of what? That remained to be seen.

If they finished and left before her, she'd lose them until tomorrow.

Aileen wolfed down her dinner, swallowing half-chewed mouthfuls without tasting, and rose. The route to the dirty dishes' rack could reasonably include the passage between the two tables of interest without raising undue suspicion. Her approach aroused the younger audience's attention; the jerks stared shamelessly at her chest.

She deliberately bumped her foot into a bench, sending the empty plates flying from her tray. The clinking of the utensils against the tiled floor brought the chatter around to an abrupt halt. In the ensuing silence, with dozens of curious and judgmental eyes on her, Aileen mumbled a humble apology and stooped to clean up her mess. One young man hurried to help. The rest focused on her ass. The hum gradually returned to its pre-accident level.

Her enterprising helper placed the last utensil on her tray. "What's your name, beautiful stranger?"

Aileen looked up with perfect indifference. The cocky clown, confident in his game, winked and grinned.

"Aunt Aileen of Locksville Streeters," she enunciated. "And I want a word with whoever's in charge of *things* here."

Her admirer caught a sideways glance from the leaders' table. His smile died, and he melted away.

The *adult*'s gaze, a smidge too cold, slid over Aileen and returned to his counterpart. They continued their subdued conversation, but Aileen had gotten all the confirmation she needed. He'd stopped chewing when she had introduced herself. He'd leaned his ear a fraction of an angle toward her. He'd *heard*, and her words weren't empty sounds to him.

Unsure where to wait to be contacted, Aileen drifted up and down the Hive, until she wandered to "her" spot on the twelfth-floor corner. Why not?

She had to be under constant surveillance, but her minders weren't too bad at their job. The place looked as deserted as ever.

The *outside* had changed again. Aileen caught the last traces of a faint, colorless sunset. It petered out, swallowed by the low cloud cover, and the darkness claimed its rightful place, dispelled only by a precious few spots of dull, ineffectual light.

Aileen didn't hate the night. Half of the Streeters' activities took place under its blessed cloak. But this view, it was... wrong. Sad. Reeking of hopelessness.

Before having discovered this vantage point, she'd never been exposed to so much *space*. Never realized how sparsely the human beings populated it. She'd seen old, pre-E night pictures of the area, showing dense, uninterrupted swaths of glow. What a far cry...

The blindingly empty darkness slowed the passage of time to a crawl.

Don't tap your foot. Don't drum your fingers.

The corridors behind her were too devoid of people. Unnaturally so for the crowded Hive. The Dragons must've redirected all traffic away. To make her feel like a true VIP? Or to prevent her from talking to anyone else? *Whoever the fuck cares?* Sitting there wouldn't get her a meeting with the Kowloonese smugglers.

No. Aileen swung to her feet. She wasn't letting Tam Wai Lam outplay her once more.

The few running footfalls and a glimpse of movement in her peripheral vision were all the warning Aileen had been given before someone slammed into her from a side passage, sending them both skidding across the floor. Aileen reacted on reflex, tucking her head in, but her shoulder connected with the far wall. Pain flared. She gasped.

"What the actual fuck?!" Aileen disentangled her arms and legs from the other person's and strained to push off the heavy body stirring on top of her. "New eyes, twatwaffle? Pull your head out of your ass and watch where you're going!"

The weight lifted. Ah, a familiar face. The playboy from the diner.

Aileen cringed and batted away his arm that rested, as if accidentally, across her breasts. "Next time, buy a girl a drink before you fuck her up, asshat."

The prick climbed off, authentically portraying his deepest regret. "Oh, Miss, I'm so, so sorry! Please forgive my clumsiness!" He offered her both hands.

Something fishy was going on. Aileen frowned one last time and allowed him to pull her to her feet.

"Are you alright, Miss?" He held one of her hands for an extra second, before letting go... and leaving a piece of paper clutched in it. Smooth little jerk.

"I'm fine." Aileen played along, rubbing her shoulder with the other hand. She didn't need to simulate grumpiness. "Get lost, shit for brains."

The messenger bowed, hiding a smirk, and scurried away.

Aileen thrust her hands deep into her pant pockets, depositing the mystery note away from the gawkers' prying eyes.

Few things in her recent memory had been as difficult as keeping a straight face and maintaining a leisurely stroll all the way to her room.

Aileen closed the door and scanned the walls. Were they watching her? Not the Dragons themselves—although, given their deviousness, this couldn't be ruled out completely—but their trusty minions. Nothing too obvious caught her eye. *Figures.* The Kowloonese were obsessed with subtlety. If the room had any peepholes, those would be skillfully integrated into innocuous design elements.

Had they watched her antics with Ajinder, too? Must've been quite a performance.

"Screw you, perverts!" Aileen flipped both middle fingers and turned a full circle. "Enjoy *this*, fucking turdburgers!"

She retreated into the narrow bathroom, the only place with plain, unadorned surfaces and an exterior wall. Her hands shook, and it took two tries to fish the crumpled note out of her pocket. Aileen sat on the toilet, leaning forward to obstruct the scrap of paper from as many directions as possible, in case someone *was* watching her even there.

"8:30 2nd floor women's bathrooms"

Torn between exhilaration and anxiety, waiting for her pulse to stop thumping in her ears, she methodically ripped the scribbles into lentil-sized bits and flushed them down.

Okay. This is good, this is what you wanted—a meeting. Breathe.

Aileen sucked in one hissing breath, another, and unclenched her teeth. Her fists unfolded. Her neck, taut as a bowstring, relaxed.

There, much better. Things were in motion again. She was going home. In less than half an hour, she'd be making the arrangements.

Public bathrooms, huh? Evidently, not every unit in the Hive had its own. Hers *was* a VIP one, after all.

Aileen surveyed the place. Stalls on one side, washing stations with dull, warped mirrors on the other, and two rows of showers further in. All conspicuously empty, save for a single person awaiting Aileen: the dark-blue coverall in charge, the adult she'd seen in the diner. A man in the women's bathroom. The Dragons didn't hold the monopolistic sway to send the Hive denizens the other way.

Aileen nodded. "Nice touch. My tail is male, and wouldn't follow me in here, eh?"

The host inclined his head, hiding his face behind his long, well-groomed gray hair. "You are sharp, Aunt Aileen of Locksville Streeters. Though you should know that you've been followed not by one, nor two, but three of Wu's men. Which means we have little time before they start getting suspicious. What is it you wanted to discuss?"

An overt compliment and a thinly veiled snub in one sentence. And no introduction. This was going to be tough.

Aileen narrowed her eyes. "You know who I am." An unnecessary question.

"Yes." An equally unnecessary affirmation.

"Do you know why I'm here?"

The delay in the man's response was hardly noticeable. "'Here' as in the Hive, or as in this women's bathroom?"

"Both." She would not make it any easier for him.

A smile touched the corners of his thin, pale lips. Aileen reciprocated. Her cheeks warmed. Ah, the rush of a nice battle of wits!

"I know your arrival wasn't exactly voluntary, but the secret of 'why' is too closely guarded. As for the purpose of this meeting, that's precisely my question. Enlighten me, please."

Aileen killed her smile and stared into her counterpart's unreadable little eyes. "I want you to smuggle me out. To The Station, or better yet, to Locksville."

The man stroked his short beard. "In exchange for?"

Aileen had expected this turn of conversation and rattled off her proposals. "Full collaboration between your operation and the Streeters. Representation of your interests in our region. Preferential treatment of your shipments to and from New Kowloon. Fifteen percent discount."

"Twenty-five."

"Twenty."

"Acceptable." The local paused. "We would be happy to help..."

Would? This couldn't bode well. Counter conditions?

"There's one hiccup."

There it was. Aileen pursed her lips, projecting displeasure.

The man apologetically spread his arms. "All commercial travel from the Hive has been suspended for the winter."

Something in Aileen's belly turned upside down. She didn't let herself lose focus, forcing her spine to keep upright. Aunt Aileen could take a blow in stride. She wasn't letting this man see her despair.

"Thank you for your time, Warehouse Master." Maybe not his exact title, but had to be close enough. "And for taking the risk." She extended her hand.

He shook it without hesitation. "I look forward to revisiting this subject closer to the springtime. Sorry I couldn't be of more help at the moment. Please reach out if there's anything, ah, *local* I can assist with. Denny will be your contact."

"Denny?"

"My nephew. You've met. He delivered the invite."

"Oh." Fan-fucking-tastic. Nepotism at its best, and she'd have to deal with the brazen rug rat drooling over her curves.

There was nothing left to say. Stuck in New Kowloon for the next six months. The mental image of the place burning to the ground, with the Dragons wriggling inside, warmed her heart. If only the Hive wasn't made of so much metal...

Aileen flushed the nearest toilet, splashed water onto her hands over a sink to lend veracity to her visit, and left without looking back.

The most alluring course of action was to crawl into her bed, snuggle in her blanket, and pupate till the spring. But before that, she had to walk the blasted building some more, so that mysterious Wu's agents wouldn't second guess her strange trip to a public bathroom.

Chapter 15

New Kowloon

October 7, 42 PE

Aileen had spent the last hour in the cafeteria. Well past the end of breakfast time, but no one had approached to kick her out. A few other tables were still occupied, the one behind her by a group of foreigners, too.

She hunched over her tray, struggling to force the meal down. The Kowloonese cooks had made it rich and flavorful, but in her current state, it tasted bland. Poor food, subjected to the wrath of her merciless fork in the confines of the plate, had nowhere to run. Same as her.

She couldn't afford to give up. There *had* to be a way to escape. Alas, the ideas she'd brainstormed, crazy as they might be, had not panned out. It all came down to transportation, and there was none. Caravans—over for the winter. Ships, the same.

With no guarantee he'd learn of her whereabouts before the seasonal travel ban was over, Weinberg's quick intervention was unlikely.

If she tried to walk out, she'd be stopped; Tam Wai Lam had said as much. Even if she'd succeeded in sneaking out, what would she do? Hide in the City? She knew no one there, and no one knew her. No clan would have any incentive to take her in. She could hike to The Station... Alone? Right. She'd never make it past Hamilton, and ending up in the emir's harem wouldn't be the worst-case scenario.

Time was running out, before Ajinder's return would make her getaway improbable and, worse, awkward.

The cards were stacked against Aileen, while Tam Wai Lam held a full house.

Aileen chewed on a cold clump of disgustingly greasy noodles. Might as well have the follow-up conversation with Wai Lam. Ask her about that offer of the world. Not as enticing as freedom—and the oh-so-sweet perspective of giving the Dragons a middle finger salute—but the intriguing hook held a vague promise.

She sighed. Fine. She'd seek an audience in the afternoon.

"This is a disaster waiting to happen! No supervisors? Insane!" Someone was so riled up, Aileen's wandering attention switched to the emotional conversation at the next table.

"Yeah, Novak has no clue what these actions may lead to." Another voice, more thoughtful than agitated.

Aileen stiffened. How could they not know she was right there, listening in? *Wait.* The strangers were referring to Marc!

"Granted, with only workers and no lifers," continued the second speaker, "it isn't as bad. They volunteered to work for money, and shouldn't make much fuss."

"Not on my watch," the third, deeper voice joined in, with a vicious subtext. All three laughed. "Don't you worry, Farook. In four days, we're back in Buffalo, the charter is over, and the train is all yours to return to The Station. Who knows, maybe by then Khalifa will show up and everything will revert to normal."

"From your mouth, Morris, and into God's ears!" Three cups clinked in a toast.

Aileen sat still. Train. Buffalo. The Station. Marc. She leaned forward, resuming the torture of her lunch, careful not to disclose her interest in the conversation. Fighting the superstitious fear of spooking away this unexpected chance.

She listened to every word, all the while polishing her plan. She had till the train's departure in the morning. Plenty of time to get ready, with the Warehouse Master's help.

"So-o-o..." Denny playfully wiggled his eyebrows.

Aileen hated being wedged between him and the wall, but had resolved to tolerate the creep for the sake of facilitating her imminent escape.

"My uncle suggested a cover for us: I'm hitting on you, and you're swept off your feet. Totes believable, am I right?"

His hand brushed against her thigh, and Aileen's best intentions went out the window.

She gripped his little finger and twisted it upward. One of the few self-defense techniques she'd mastered to an acceptable level.

"Ouch, ouch! My hand!" Denny danced on one foot, trying to find a point of balance where it would hurt the least. His howls pitched higher as she increased pressure.

Aileen leaned into his face, distorted by pain. "Listen carefully, boy. I'm way out of your league. So-o-o." She wiggled her eyebrows, imitating him. "Here's the *updated* cover story. You keep hitting on me, because you're a shithead, and never learn. And I keep blowing you off, because that's far more believable. Do we have an understanding, douchebag?"

Denny, having lost his luster, quickly nodded. "Yes, yes. Let go of my hand!"

Aileen didn't. Instead, she curled the rest of his fingers further in with her other hand. He collapsed to his knees, rasping, "P-please…"

Should she make the pleading puppy cry? Nah, that'd take the lesson too far. She needed the Big Boss's nephew tamed, not broken.

Aileen fixed his bulged eyes with a menacing stare and whispered, "If you *ever* dare touch me again, I'll break your pretty little fingers in so many places, your hand will only be useful as a soft wipe for your ass. Got it, charmer?"

"Got it."

His manifest dejection dramatically improved Aileen's mood. She released his palm, pulled him up, and patted him on the shoulder.

Several passersby slowed down.

"Everything's fine here!" Aileen waved. Her bright, toothy smile scared them more than eased their concerns. Whatever the case, they hurried on.

She returned her attention to Denny and found him smiling at her. Not the sleazy sort; genuine, adoring. "You're so… You're amazing, Aunt Aileen!"

Without that lady killer mask on, the kid sounded almost normal. Maybe he still wasn't rotten through and through.

"Now, where were we?" Aileen hid her embarrassment with cheerfulness. "What did your uncle say?"

Denny's face fell, and Aileen's heart skipped a beat. *Shit. Now what?*

"Sorry to bring the bad news. He won't help." The unfortunate go-between nervously gauged Aileen's reaction, with his hands prudently hidden behind his back.

Aileen grimaced, rubbing her eyes. "Why? What's his excuse this time?" She kept her voice level. The kid was just a messenger. No reason to take her frustration out on him.

His face reflected inner struggle until he came to a decision. "Don't bother with Uncle's explanations. They're bullshit, anyway. The truth is, he's afraid of Wu, and of the Golden Dragon." Denny squared his jaw. "But I am not. My crew will help you."

Holy smoking Seven Hells. Careful now. "Why?" she asked again, but suavely.

"Because it's time for a change. Time for the young blood to take over from the old farts. To try fresh approaches. To stop kowtowing to the Dragons."

Unbelievable. The kid saw himself as a revolutionary!

"Because," he added shyly, "I want to help you."

"I appreciate it, Denny." Aileen cautiously chose her next words. "Do you expect anything in return?"

Sparkles of humor flashed in his dark eyes. "Nothing *like that*, Aunt Aileen. I am not dense. You'd refuse, I'd call everything off, you'd be mad at me, we'd become enemies. And I'd rather count you among my friends. My offer is simple. Give me whatever you've promised my uncle, but exclusively for my crew."

"Deal," Aileen shot back as soon as he finished. She didn't need to think this through before answering. After his uncle's refusal, this was better than anything she could've hoped for. Even with no guarantee he'd deliver. Even if, later, he'd get cold feet from playing on the adults' field and lose his nerve. Even if his lust and alpha pride had overcome this noble act of tolerating her rejection. All that could still happen, but this was a *chance*.

"*Denny*." She tilted her head. "Not a Kowloonese name, is it?"

"No. It isn't my given name. I chose it myself."

"You did?"

"Yes. My generation is fed up with those stupid ancient traditions."

"Huh. And your uncle has accepted that?"

The question hit home. His contented smile broadened.

"I didn't give him a choice."

Hubris. Did he realize what he was up against? Challenging his uncle was a stretch, but could be within his power. The Golden Dragon? Tam Wai Lam would eat him for breakfast. And Aileen was pitting him against such a force.

She stomped out her doubts. Denny made his own decisions. That these decisions aligned with her interests, was a lucky coincidence. He was a means to an end, nothing more. What happened to him after she was on her way home was of no consequence. And if he survived, all the better; she'd have a trade partner in New Kowloon.

Aileen rewarded him with her least malevolent smile. "Good for you. Okay, you have the list of what I need and know where I must be by tomorrow morning. Make it happen."

Chapter 16

Outside New Kowloon

October 8, 42 PE

The tiniest detail could make or break the most elaborate plot. Hers had been extremely elaborate, accounting for everything... Almost everything.

Denny had come through. His strikingly intricate plan had involved cross-dressing, a double with blonde-dyed hair, and his crew running theatrical interference to distract Aileen's minders. At the crack of dawn, she was led through service passages to the loading bay, and given a bundle of equipment: a winter jacket, a warm hat, a pair of boots, and two pairs of coveralls. All according to her "shopping list". Excessive, but she didn't want to freeze at night. She'd been provided with enough food to sustain her for a week, had two flasks of water, and a portable light. The one aspect she hadn't thought through was a bathroom. Or, rather, its absence. The need to use one was gaining urgency by the minute.

Aileen had never been on a train before. She'd imagined a luxurious interior, in the best traditions of pre-E comfort. That possibly held true for the passenger car occupied by the two Buffs and the Stationer. But she had snuck into the cargo boxcar, filthy and full of thin dust left by the coal it had delivered to New Kowloon. Yet, despite the unpresentable state of her travel arrangement, she couldn't bring herself to empty her bowels inside. To shit where she slept, like a pig? No way!

It was getting dark outside, and the train had stopped for the night. Through the torturously long day, Aileen had been too anxious for eating, and consumed her water sparingly. Even so, she wouldn't be able to hold it in for much longer.

The haulers made their improvised camp, attaching a large tarp to "her" car. They lit a fire and cooked dinner, all in unnerving silence. A few quiet words uttered now and then, and the whiffs of smoke and flavor drifting through the slits in the boxcar's walls were all the signs of their presence. Thirty overworked, unhappy men could unleash despicable abuse on a lone young woman if they'd discovered her there, on a dark night in the middle of nowhere. Aileen shuddered. Under all the layers of warm clothing, goosebumps covered her skin. She'd never been so vulnerable. In Locksville, she'd grown accustomed to her crew always being around to ensure her physical safety. Now, they were hundreds of miles away. Her name likely meant nothing to the haulers, thus lacking its usual intimidating weight. A gun could've served as a deterrent, if she had one. She'd put it on her shopping list, but Denny's logistics had come short in this department.

Aileen's stomach muscles clenched as a wave of animalistic fear washed over. Not a pig!

She slid the car's heavy door, inch by painful inch, cringing in anticipation of an inevitable creak that would give her away. The door, blessed be, did not betray her. Aileen slipped out through the foot-wide opening on the side facing away from the haulers' camp and tiptoed into the bush.

With the primary goal of her foray completed, she allowed herself to relish the moment. The motionless forest; the sprinkling of stars above, between the naked branches of skeletal treetops; the clean air, cold but refreshing, free from the ubiquitous coal particles that must've filled her every crevice. Most of all, the freedom. No strangers telling her what she could and could not do. No fabulous but suffocating Hive. Once home, she'd sleep in a tent for a while, until she stopped associating solid walls with confinement.

"Beautiful night, *sí*?"

She flinched, but collected herself. Aunt Aileen, not a fragile damsel! "Yes, it's nice."

"I'm Paul. Wanna join us for dinner?"

Aileen hesitated. The cat—she—was out of the bag. Hiding wasn't an option anymore. She could run, and would probably succeed, but then what? In the bleak starlight, she assessed the man from the corner of her eye. Burly, tall; a shaggy beard, covering his face up to the eyes; a knitted hat and frayed, patched clothes. A posture of a strong but tired man. Of a relaxed man, not one preparing to attack.

Paul misinterpreted her silence. "Good food we got there. Timmy bought beef from Chinese. Hot stew, *perfecto* for such night. You welcome to it, Miss. Musta been a long day in that boxcar."

Shit. They knew she was there all along. And did nothing. Odd. Did this mean they weren't a threat? And... what kind of rapist would extol the menu?

Aileen nodded decisively, as much to herself as to the man. "Thank you, Paul, I'd be delighted. Let me grab something first."

He helped her up onto the train and caught her when she leaped back with an armful of Kowloonese supplies. She was a thief, not a freeloader.

No one jumped her when they entered the circle of light, nor questioned her presence. A folding chair promptly materialized in front of her by the fire. A steaming bowl with a wooden spoon pleasantly warmed her hands. A patch-work quilt was offered to her; grimy and lousy, but... She gratefully allowed Paul to wrap her legs in it. The foodstuffs she donated were taken to the improvised kitchen without a word. She brought gifts and accepted hospitality, and that was that. Everything was as it should have been. *Perfecto*, indeed. Aileen could never have imagined such a sense of belonging in a company of rough, terse haulers. They enjoyed the quiet rest. And she enjoyed it with them, mesmerized by the crackling fire, relieved of the pressures of the day, savoring the warmth in her stomach. Everything was going to be alright...

"What in the Seven Hells?!" The shout jolted Aileen out of her happy trance. She looked around, zeroing in on a figure standing on the passenger car platform. The voice belonged to that Stationer, what was his name? Farook. "You're salaried employees now, but that doesn't mean you can bring along a whore! Outrage! I'll have you all fined for this! I'll dock your pay!"

"She ain't no whore, Master Farook." Paul spoke flatly, but the undertones of veiled resentment were there alright.

Aileen rose, regretting the loss of the quilt's warmness. "I'm a stowaway. Need a ride to Locksville. Can pay you there."

While Farook considered her with a scowl, two other men joined him, stepping out through the door. The Buffs. One older and slick, probably a trader. The other, with a hard face and an evaluating squint of his eyes, obviously a security man. Ah, that would be Morris.

"Come here," he barked.

Aileen obeyed. She would've preferred staying with the friendly haulers, but these three ran the show. No way around dealing with them now. Fine. She'd dealt with worse.

"Hells, you're filthy." The Buff wrinkled his nose as she approached.

Aileen didn't have a mirror, but her face couldn't have fared much better than her clothes and hands smeared in coal streaks.

Her eyes found Paul. "Thank you, this was great." He nodded, and she climbed up the short ladder.

The inside of the passenger car was every bit as rich as she'd pictured, and then some. Antique furniture, soft cots and loveseats, artwork and sconces on the walls, and lots of golden paint gleaming in the light.

The two Buffs sat at the table where their interrupted dinner had been waiting. Farook remained standing.

"What's your name?" he asked, frowning.

"Cinderella."

The Buff trader chortled, but Farook pursed his lips. "Cheeky, ha? This is a cargo train. No passengers. How would you like being dropped off in Hamilton?"

"The emir is not your typical Prince Charming, Cinderella, but I'm sure you'll come around to enjoy his hospitality... eventually." Morris reveled in being a dick. Noted.

Aileen ignored him, looking straight at Farook. "You're a businessman. I can pay. What's the problem? Name your price."

Avarice lit the trader's eyes. Ah. *That* type. "No one at The Station needs to know," she pushed to seal the deal. "Keep the full amount, or share it with your friends here." There; trapped.

"Do you have the money?"

Aileen chuckled. "So you can rob me *and* sell me to the emir? No, you'll get paid in Locksville."

"We don't stop in Locksville, smartass. The Station, then Buffalo. Take it or leave it."

"The Station, have it your way. Marc will—" *Shit.*

Farook's eyes widened. The two Buffs' glances snapped to her. Morris left the table and circled around Aileen.

"Marc, eh? Locksville, eh?" He brought a lamp closer to her face.

She squinted and turned away from the blinding light.

"I am not too good at math, but one plus one equals Aileen Novak. Right, Cinderella?"

Aileen darted to the exit, but someone grabbed her hair and yanked it back. Sharp pain pierced her scalp, and she smashed into the hard floor. The impact beat the air out of her lungs. Dazed, she tried to call Paul, but Morris was already on top of her, pinning her arms with his knees and gagging her with a rag. Resisting, she swung her head from side to side, but a heavy slap left her ears ringing and her mouth filling with the taste of blood.

"Hey!" snarled her assailant. "Behave!" The second slap followed, emphasizing the message and sending her head in the opposite direction. Tears welled in her eyes—from the powerlessness, not the pain. Stupid, stupid! Such a dumb mistake!

Morris unceremoniously rolled her over and tied her hands behind her back. "You're coming with us to Buffalo, Princess!" he growled. "Free ride, imagine that!"

"Uh, Morris?" bleated Farook. "What are you doing?"

"Say another word and I'll gag you too," snarled the Buff. "You won't as much as chirp when we pass through The Station, or I'll kill you *and* your family. Do I make myself clear, birdie?"

The Stationer panted. Well, fuck. No help there.

Morris rose. "On your feet, Princess."

Aileen dragged her knees under her and stood awkwardly. Morris grabbed her chin. "Now, listen—" She bit his palm over the gag. "Ow!" He jerked his hand away and slapped her again with the other. "You bitch!"

The image of Park Yun-mi in the Hive's dojo floated before Aileen's eyes. *You have to want to cause harm.* Oh, she very much did! But with her hands tied... She bent and rushed forward to ram Morris with her shoulder. He sidestepped, and Aileen's forehead slammed into an unyielding edge of the table. White blinding pain exploded in her skull. Before she could regain her bearings, the Buff weighed on her, pinning her upper body to the tabletop. A fist pounded on her kidney. The gag muffled her howl. A fine china plate cracked under Aileen's cheek.

"Morris, that's enough." The Buffalo trader sounded unamused. "Stop it."

"Piss off, Ricky. We need her alive, but that's about it. You hear, Princess? I can do this all day, so calm your tits. Or..."—He pushed his hips against hers—"I can fuck you raw in every single hole until you can't walk or talk. Would you like that?"

Aileen was too groggy and hurting to retort.

"That's what I thought." He smacked the back of her head and stepped aside.

Aileen slid off the table to the floor. Something hot and sticky crawled over her eyes and down her cheeks. Blood. Must've opened her forehead pretty badly, but there was too much pain everywhere to localize the gash.

"Farook, stop the fucking bleeding before she messes up your precious carpets." Morris sounded, above all, disgusted. "And for God's sake, clean her up."

Chapter 17

Somewhere

October 9, 42 PE

Sometime toward the morning, Aileen had settled beside her body, in a strange state with her mind detached from the aching shambles of her frail shell. Her head was a hot mess, pulsating with her heartbeat; a vessel full of viscous liquid, in which every sound boomed, resonating for hours. The one time she dared open her eyes, the weak light of night lamps sent blinding spikes deep into her brain. Her mouth and throat dried up around the gag, and she couldn't lick her broken lips. Those had crusted, and cracked any time she twitched a face muscle. Her arms had gone numb behind her a long time ago; she wasn't sure she still had them. She was hot, floating in a puddle of sweat. And her lower back hurt badly. She could not cope with all that, and left.

The two traders had cleaned her face up, bandaged her forehead, and transferred her onto a cot. After that, they went to sleep. When she was sure no one would hear or see, she cried. That didn't help. The time had come and gone, ebbing on and off. Sometimes it was there, and sometimes it wasn't, leaving black gaps in her memory.

The morning came.

Someone walked around. Someone gave commands. The train started moving, making her nauseous. Someone removed the gag and tried to feed her. She obediently swallowed the tasteless lumps and threw them up. Someone yelled. She would've covered her ears, but couldn't, because she had no hands. Instead, she squeezed her eyes shut. She should have used the opportunity to cry for help—but her parched throat would produce no sound. And... she was afraid. Park Yun-mi, the girl with the dead eyes, had been right. Aileen wasn't much of a fighter. A schemer, an organizer, a big mouth—yes. But not a fighter. She wasn't ready for more beatings, more pain. For Morris to carry out his terrifying threat. There was no doubt in her heart he wouldn't hesitate to do the vilest things to her.

"She's got a concussion, you idiot. A bad one. Happy?" someone snapped at someone else.

"Not my fault she head-butted the table!"

Aileen watched her body fold back onto the cot and curl into a ball.

"Look at her!" The first voice rose, angrier and louder. Could it be quieter? Please? "She's just a girl!"

"Not *just* a girl, Richard! She's Marc fucking Novak's sister! You realize what a goldmine this is?"

"Novak won't be happy when he learns about this, Morris." Another voice.

"Shut up, Farook, or I'll shut you the fuck up forever. I don't need Novak happy, only incentivized."

Marc. They were talking about Marc again. Marc would come to her aid. He always had. But now she had to rest...

She woke up—or came to—because something fundamental had changed in the world. The train, it had stopped.

Aileen looked around. Richard, the Buff trader, sat at the table, grim and angry, arms crossed over his chest. The other Buff, the asshole—she didn't want to even *think* of his name—put a handgun between the plates, staring meaningfully at Farook. The Stationer stood by the door, hesitating. He glanced at Asshole and averted his eyes. His gaze fell on Aileen. There was pity, and distaste, and loathing. But most of all, fear. He pushed his lips into a line, shook his head in resignation, and opened the door.

Fresh cold air burst into the overheated, stuffy car, along with a cacophony of voices. Outside, people were going about their business, talking, laughing, oblivious to her plight. Farook gave commands; something about detaching the cargo car and relieving half the hauler team. With a loud clang, the train jerked.

She thought she heard Marc's voice and recognized the top of his head in the opening behind Farook. Salvation... So close, yet so out of reach. She couldn't move. She couldn't shout. Dark despair overwhelmed her, suffusing every cell of her body. A wail of grief escaped her tormented throat, but all she heard was a muted moan.

And then the train was in motion again. Leaving behind Marc, her hopes, and her safety. Farook closed the door, cutting off the sounds of the free world, and meekly returned to the table without looking her way.

It was all her fault. Why couldn't she stay in New Kowloon? Warm, comfortable, fed. Pampered in every imaginable way. And safe, so fucking safe! She could have waited for Ajinder, and convinced him to take her home. After all, he'd accomplished the job the Kowloonese had hired him for. She could've offered him another job. With the way he looked at her... she would have bent his integrity enough. But no, she *had* to run, like a mulish child, to spite the Dragons. And then, she'd had it all backwards, fearing the wrong crowd. Those clean, rich, well-spoken passengers were the ones ruining her day, not the unwashed but hospitable haulers. She'd choose Paul over Asshole any day.

Richard came over and helped her sit. He raised his hands toward her head and she shied away, shutting her eyes. She hated herself for that fear, for the cowardly reaction, yet couldn't control it.

"Sorry, didn't mean to startle you."

Aileen peeked. The trader removed the rope keeping the gag in place, pulled the bloody rag out, and disgustedly threw it away. He wiped her face with a clean, wet cloth and untied her hands. Unable to move them, she let her arms hang helplessly at her sides. And then the torture began, with millions of hot needles digging into her palms as the circulation reclaimed her limbs. She buried her hands in her lap and folded in two over them, growling in pain. At least they won't see her tears.

"What on Earth are you up to, Ricky?" Asshole's voice grated on her ears.

"Go fuck yourself, vicious sadist!" the trader snarled back. "You've got your way, we're bringing her to the Union. But we don't have to be animals, alright?"

"You don't enjoy roughing up your women? Want to take her gently? Have at it!"

"For fuck's sake, LeClaire, you sick degenerate!" Richard spat on the carpet between them. "I've got a daughter her age!"

Asshole hooted a laugh.

Richard poured water into a tin mug and held it before Aileen. She nodded gratefully and wrapped her palms around it. Her arms shook violently, and she splashed half the content over her knees before bringing the mug to her lips. It chattered against her teeth and she had to bite the edge to make a gulp. Water dripped down her chin. She was pathetic. And miserable. She couldn't take it anymore.

The mug fell from her hands, its impact dulled by the carpet. Tears gushed down her cheeks. Richard stepped closer, letting her bury her contorted face in his shirt.

"Shh. It's okay." He patted her on the back. "Everything's going to be fine. Do as you're told, and you'll be home before you know it."

The words burned her like a brand. *Do as you're told.* The least Aileen thing ever. She still *was* Aileen, wasn't she? Hells, yeah! Aileen Novak—the Aunt, the sister, the worst enemy to have. She'd made a mistake, been caught off guard, and paid the price. But, like a cat, she always landed on her feet. This time would be no different if she played it smart. Let them think they broke her. She'd strike back when the time was right. When they least expected it.

She pushed away and rendered a wan smile. "Thank you, Richard. You must be a great dad. I wish I had a dad like you."

His face softened. "I try my best."

Score. One down, two to go.

Part 3

THE BOOK
OF AJINDER

Chapter 18

West Sauga, Four Years Ago

December 5, 38 PE

"Yes, brother." What else could he say?

Ajinder accepted the rifle from Jihan's hands. The chilling, aloof touch of its metal parts contrasted with the wooden stock's genial willingness to receive—and return—his warmth. The weapon had a character, if not its own will. Hopefully, they'd become friends, because Ajinder's life, as well as those of his brothers and clients, would depend on that.

Hello, Viper. It was... *had been* Bikram's habit to give names to inanimate objects. A quirk that could've seemed weird in someone else, but that was Bikram. He'd made it look adorable. He'd made *everything* look adorable. He was... *had been* the most charming Singh brother. Until he died.

Bikram. Dead. What a bizarre thought. His excruciating sickness over the past several months had done nothing to prepare Ajinder for its inevitable conclusion. Bikram, the most cheerful of his brothers, was supposed to live forever. Yet, the heft of his rifle in Ajinder's arms claimed the opposite. So heavy, and gaining more weight as the finality proliferated through Ajinder's muscles, tendons, and nerves. He couldn't drop it, that would've been sacrilegious, desecrating the memory of his brother. He squeezed the firearm with all his might, fusing the metal and the wood into the skin of his palms.

Ajinder was a tracker. The sniper role was reserved in the family business for the second oldest brother. Ajinder didn't ask for either title, but with Bikram gone, inherited both. If this was meant to be, he'd make the most of it.

He hugged Viper, mindless of the oil smudges it left on his white mourning clothes, and turned away from the gurdwara. The rest of the funeral could continue without him. He was going to pay his respects to Bikram by getting to know his brother's tool of the trade. The last link connecting them.

April 20, 39 PE

"Jihan! Stop dragging it out!" Ranbir all but vibrated with anticipation. "Spill it!"

Ajinder kept his cool. What was forgivable for a fifteen-year-old was below his station. He'd just celebrated his nineteenth birthday, and it would take more than Jihan's promise of big news to get him overtly excited. But it was a struggle.

Jihan's teacup hid his amused smirk. He took an extra-long, deliberately noisy sip, and relented. "Remember that job we did last fall for New Kowloon? Turns out, the Golden Dragon was thoroughly impressed. So much so, she decided to retain our services on a semi-permanent basis. The Singh family has got a contract with the Hive!"

The room erupted in cheers.

Ajinder joined in, toning down his enthusiasm to a level below his younger brothers'. He was the second oldest and had to act the part, hiding the all-too-childish delight bubbling in his chest. Only one concern clouded his celebratory mood. "What kind of missions are we talking about?" Ajinder held his breath.

Jihan raised his cup in the air, toasting the question. "Nothing you'd disapprove of. No raids, no ambushes. Personal protection only, the cleanest business there is."

"The most lucrative, too," said Preet, grinning from ear to ear.

"That's right." Jihan nodded. His inquisitive eyes gauged Ajinder's reaction.

Ajinder let the air quietly trickle out. Good. For a moment there... Never mind. They still were the good guys. Regardless of his nightmares, persistently trying to convince him otherwise since he and Viper had opened their score. His fingers habitually traced the rifle's smooth curves. *We are tools, you and I. Dangerous, efficient tools. But I can make sure we're only used to make the world a safer place.*

Chapter 19

New Kowloon

October 9, 42 PE

"Hey, wait up!" Ranbir caught up in a rattling of rapid footsteps. "What's the hurry?" he huffed, slightly out of breath.

Ajinder regarded him with a sidelong glance. "You're so out of shape."

"I'm not!" Ranbir bristled with indignation. "That's unfair! I'm carrying twice your load!"

"You're the youngest. And I'm on point."

"As I said, unfair."

"Fine. You want the point? You can have it next time. Now, stop whining and keep up."

"What's the rush? We're done with the job." Ranbir sprinted a few steps ahead and walked backward in front of Ajinder, scanning his face. "Aha! It's a girl, isn't it?"

Ajinder fought to keep a straight expression, and failed. A grin curved his lips. The tips of his ears warmed up.

"It *is* a girl!" Ranbir clapped. "You sly dawg! Who? Someone I know? A Kowloonese?"

Ajinder rolled his eyes. Ranbir's barrage of questions would not stop until he'd extracted an answer.

"No? Not Kowloonese? Then why are you racing to the Hive? Wa-a-ait a minute! Don't tell me it's Yun-mi! She can do *so* much better!"

Ajinder snickered. "Nope."

"*No*—not Yun-mi?" Ranbir tilted his head to the side. "Or *no*—she can't do better?" A tilt to the other side.

"Neither." The pup was having too much fun at his expense. "Stop this, I'm not telling you."

"But why? Are you ashamed? Is she ugly? Come on, give me *something*! Is it serious? Did you bring her a gift?"

Ajinder moved his head from side to side again, keeping his smile mysterious.

Ranbir stopped in his tracks, and Ajinder almost collided with him. "No," his little brother breathed out. All his joy evaporated. "No, tell me you didn't."

"What?" Ranbir's concern was contagious. Ajinder grew serious, too. "What're you talking about?"

Ranbir's face came close. "That woman we brought from Locksville? Is it her?" he whispered.

Ajinder, inexplicably uncomfortable, broke eye contact.

Ranbir slide-stepped back, turned away, and threw his hands up. "That's it!" he shouted to the skies. "My brother has officially lost his marbles!" He faced Ajinder again. His neck craned as if he tried to look deep into Ajinder's eyes. "For the love of everything that's holy, brother, what is *wrong* with you?"

Ajinder shrugged. "Why?" Ranbir's reaction was unpleasantly unexpected.

"Aji, you're supposed to be the smarter one, second only to Jihan the Wise. You don't see how bad this is? *I* see it, and *you* don't?"

Ajinder scowled and strode on, bumping Ranbir's shoulder and pushing the annoying kid out of the way.

"Really?" his brother cried from behind. "*Really*, Aji? How mature." He caught up again, and for a while walked alongside Ajinder in silence. His offended puffing quieted. "I can see why," he muttered. "Besides her looks, of course. She... She's a flame. Don't let her burn you. Remember, she's drawn the interest of the Dragon herself. Everything about her spells trouble. Be careful, is all I'm saying."

Ajinder placed a hand on his brother's shoulder. "Thanks, bud. You may yet become the third wisest in the family."

"*May*?"

"Yes, if you never speak of this again."

―――――――――――

In their corridor of the Hive, Ajinder stopped a few doors short of his room. Ranbir went on before noticing his absence. He turned, quizzically raising a brow.

"I..." Ajinder pointed at the door. "Need to check something." He blushed, hoping the dull hallway lights would conceal his awkwardness. His brother rewarded him with a wide smile and a wink, saluted, and continued to his own room.

Ajinder held his breath and delicately knocked on Aileen's door. He waited for ten infinitely long heartbeats. Not a sound inside. Should he try again? What if she was sleeping? Yes, it was around noon, but she didn't really have a schedule to follow. And he owed her two nights' sleep... He sucked his lip in, hiding a smile. He was in the mood to further grow his debt.

When an endlessly long wait after the second attempt yielded nothing, he headed for Tam Wai Lam's office. If anyone tracked Aileen's movements, it would be the Dragon.

The frenetic activity at the top floor of the Hive made him uneasy. The guards acknowledged him, and one looked like he was about to ask something, but held his tongue. Unusual, to say the least. In the doorway, Ajinder nearly ran into Mei Yan, the Golden Dragon's assistant. She squeaked and apologized. "Mister Singh, you're here! Excellent, the Golden Dragon was looking for you."

A bad feeling twisted his gut. And he was used to trusting those.

Mei Yan led him in. Shang Ka Yi was there, and some other guy, but what grabbed Ajinder's attention and refused to let it go was Tam Wai Lam's expression. Sad, embarrassed. Never had he seen her like that, nor imagined he would. He saw not a Golden Dragon, but a human. The striking difference tightened the knot in his stomach.

She faced him, and he drowned in her dark eyes. He knew before she opened her mouth. *Aileen.*

"Mister Singh. How timely."

"Is something wrong with Miss Novak, Golden Dragon?" When did speaking become so difficult? He had to force the sounds out.

"Very astute, Mister Singh. Miss Novak is missing."

"*Missing*, Golden Dragon?" The word made no sense. Ajinder squinted, as if that could improve his hearing.

"Missing, Mister Singh," Tam Wai Lam repeated emphatically. "Given your involvement in her initial adaptation here, we were hoping you'd have a clue on her whereabouts."

Ajinder closed his eyes, fighting back dizziness. "*We*?" He focused on the unfamiliar face. "Who's he, Golden Dragon?"

"Meet Bo, Mister Singh. From Locksville."

Ajinder tensed, but the Dragon had provided no sign she was planning to make him a scapegoat.

"He was very, uh, *persuasive* in his inquiry about Miss Novak," she said. "Golden Dragon Shang Ka Yi and I saw it right to let him meet her. Unfortunately, we are unable to locate Miss Novak anywhere in the Hive. You were among the last people to interact with her. Looking back, can you remember anything—anything at all—that would help interpret her intentions?"

Interact. One way to put it. Did the Dragon know? Never mind. He'd asked Aileen not to run. She had turned it into a joke, evading *that* promise. Ajinder's memory inconveniently rendered the circumstances of their conversation. Aileen, resting in the crook of his arm. His fingers, tracing the sweet curves of her body... A dull heartache brought him back.

"I'm afraid not, Golden Dragon. That was three days ago, a lot of time for someone as resourceful as Miss Novak."

"Three? Not four?"

"We... had a conversation on the morning of my departure." He caught a sharp, hostile glance from the Locksviller.

Tam Wai Lam inclined her head. "I see. Okay, here's my suggestion. Wu's people are canvassing the Hive to identify every person she had been in contact with. Neither of you would be particularly helpful with this effort, so how about you two check her room? See if you can glean something."

"Of course, Golden Dragon. But if you learn anything, may I ask you to let me know? I feel responsible for her safety."

"Sure." Tam Wai Lam, already occupied with other thoughts, waved her hand.

He bowed and headed to the door. The Locksviller picked up his duffel bag.

"You may leave your stuff here for safekeeping, Mister Bo," said Shang Ka Yi.

Sheer horror blinked in the little guy's face, and he clutched the bag tighter to his chest. "It goes wherever I go." His voice was thin, angry, and lisping.

The Golden Dragon remained nonplussed. "Suit yourself."

Ajinder led the foreigner back to Aileen's room. He had to pause a few times to wait for his hobbling companion to catch up. Instead of gratitude, the skinny brat burned him with a furious stare. "Okay, what?" Ajinder asked at the next stop. "What's your problem?"

The Locksviller approached, his limping painful to watch. "You said you feel responsible for Aileen's safety. Why?" That was not a question, but a demand for an answer.

"I was hired to extract Miss Novak to the safety of New Kowloon. And though that contract had been fulfilled—"

"You!" The Locksviller punched Ajinder on the nose. Ajinder did not bother dodging, letting the clumsy attack connect. Weak and inept, it did little harm. But it came from the heart.

Ajinder wiped the thin trickle of blood off his mustache. "I guess I deserved that... once. But try touching me again, and I'll end you." He looked up from his bloodied palm, and found the guy half-turned away, bent at his waist, clutching the staircase guardrail and trembling. "Hey," Ajinder put a hand on his forearm, "are you okay, man? I didn't mean it like that."

"Don't. Touch. Me." Snapping through the clattering teeth produced a comical effect rather than deterrence, but Ajinder pulled his arm away and waited patiently. In a minute, the shaking subsided. Turning, the guy glared. "I am not your worry."

What a weird kid. Kid? Yeah, Ranbir's age, give or take. "You've got it, champ. I couldn't care less. Coming?"

Without Aileen in it, her pointless room had no right to exist. Everything seemed to be the same as on the day he'd left, yet elusively different. As if a layer of invisible dust had settled on every surface, giving it the vibe of abandonment.

Ajinder's eye caught on familiar items. The blanket on her bed, tied in knots; the same blanket she'd put on as a cape so adorably. The sheets, preserving the shape of her body. Ajinder swallowed a lump in his throat. He shouldn't have left. Maybe Aileen still would have been here. Could've been his contour too on these bedsheets now. That was a stupid job, anyway. Little money, way too much protection. Ranbir would've safely delivered that Iron Dragon to Dixie Mall alone. Should not! Have! Left!

She's gone, she's gone, she's gone, mocked a dull echo in his empty skull. Why didn't she wait for him? For three days, the hope that she would had energized him.

No, this could not be right. This wasn't happening. Aileen was playing a practical joke to snub Wu and Tam Wai Lam, right? Right?

Purple anger brushed the denial away, blinding Ajinder for a second. How could she?! Didn't she care at all? He wasn't good enough for her, ha? His fists tightened, ready to smash something, or someone. He drew two painful breaths, and the fire in his chest receded before he could cause any permanent damage.

Another chance was all he needed. He won't make the same mistake, oh no. He'd never let her out of his sight...

He saw something he hadn't noticed before and suppressed a groan. "Aileen's sweats are gone. She's in the wind."

The Locksviller froze. "How do you know her sweats?" The kid slowly raised his eyes and bit his lower lip. "You two fucked, didn't you? Of course. You totally did."

Ajinder grabbed him by the shirt and lifted his light frame into the air. The prick angled his head back, away from the looming violence.

"Listen to me... Bo," Ajinder growled. "I don't know who you are, or what your deal is. But if you ever, *ever* talk like that about Aileen, I'll tear your head off and make a vase from your skull. You feel me, *partner*?"

Bo nodded, quickly and shallowly. Ajinder lowered him, smoothened his rumpled clothes, and swept imaginary grains of dust off where he'd held him.

"Are all Locksvillers so crude? We didn't *fuck*. We're two consenting adults who spent time together, to mutual enjoyment. For the record, I *like* her. A lot."

"Spare me those details. Please." Bo's hollow voice carried nothing but anguish. He sat on the bed, picked up Aileen's blanket, and twisted it in his hands with a thousand-yard stare.

"Bo? Who are you, really? What's your connection to Aileen?"

"The greatest of all questions, *partner*." Bo's face crinkled into a sour mask. "Who am I to her? A sworn brother, of a sort. The best friend, I suppose. Her consigliere."

"Her what?"

"Adviser."

"You? You're the Streeters' adviser?"

"Hard to believe, right?"

"And you care about her."

Bo buried his face in the blanket.

Awkward. Poor kid. Ajinder sat by his side and put a hand on his shoulder, but Bo shrugged it off. "I don't need your pity." His muffled words came dry and crispy.

"How did you know where to look for her?" Maybe changing the subject would make the situation a tad less uncomfortable.

"Long story." Bo faced Ajinder, calm and collected. For a change, his cold gray eyes did not try to burn Ajinder alive. "We won't find anything here. You're right, she ran. Let's hope this Wu comes up with more. Now... You sound serious about her. Which kind of makes us a family. A broken, dysfunctional family. May as well tell me your name."

"Bo!" The slippery man on the pier threw his arms wide in a warm and fake welcome. "Good thing I waited, eh?"

"Good thing, yes," Bo muttered, evading the non-committal embrace. He clumsily slid down to the boat's bow and put his ridiculous duffel bag at his feet.

"Captain Farley," Ajinder saluted with a hat tip.

Bo glanced between them. "You two know each other. Why am I not surprised?"

"Told ya, lotsa traffic back'n'forth." Farley grinned, sizing Ajinder up. "Remind me *your* name?"

"Ajinder, Cap."

"Whatever. Where to, Bo? Home?"

"Take us to Grimsby."

"Ah, up for some more of Charlie's brew?" Farley winked.

Bo remained singularly serious. "We'll need a pair of horses."

Ajinder lowered his rucksack and jumped into the rocking boat, waving his hands for balance. "Can you ride?"

A stubborn scowl split Bo's pale-green face. "I'll figure it out."

Ajinder looked around. No mast. Odd. "Are we paddling? Thought you said it's a quick trip."

"You'll see," Bo hissed through his squeezed teeth, clutching the gunnels so hard his knuckles turned white.

"Ya bet yer skinny ass it is!" Farley guffawed and ripped a cord.

"Whoa!" The headwind almost pulled Ajinder's turban off when the boat picked up speed, to the laborious whine of the engine. "Whom did you rob to get this *thing*?"

Farley smiled mysteriously.

"You said, 'traffic'," Ajinder shouted. "Who else, besides us?"

The captain theatrically shrugged. "Dunno, don' care. Ain't paid to ask questions."

"You mean, you're paid *to not ask* questions," said Bo.

Farley rolled his eyes. Ajinder studied the deformed little guy, squinting against the wind and the water spray. Definitely more to him than what met the eye. Must be interesting to chat with... when he wasn't acrimonious or worried.

Worried. No reason to be. Wu, the old bulldog, had delivered, as always. The head of the Hive's smuggling outfit and, coincidentally, one of Wu's most trustful agents, had reported he'd been approached by Aileen but refused to help. Everything pointed to her interest in the Buffalo-bound train that had left the Hive the day before. Apparently, a warehouse had issued Aileen work clothes. A low-level administrator at the shipping bay had recalled noticing a tall, blond foreigner snooping around. Wu had less confidence in those accounts, and hinted there could have been deeper issues in the Hive, but Ajinder didn't listen. Aileen was on that train, headed to The Station. Or to Locksville. Whatever her destination, she was going to be alright. He just needed to make sure of that. Out of professional courtesy, nothing else.

Ajinder leaned back, letting the wind play with his beard, and smiled. Ever since learning the details of Aileen's escape, he'd had to suppress a happy giggle. Would've been unprofessional for him to show Tam Wai Lam he'd been rooting against her scheme. Here, she wasn't around to judge him. With half a lake separating them, he could safely afford relieved laughter. Aileen, you wily vixen! You did it! Outplayed the Golden Dragon!

He met Bo's prickly stare. "Lighten up, fam! It's all good!"

The kid's lips stubbornly curled down. "I'll lighten up when I see her."

Ajinder shook his head.

And Farley pretended he wasn't listening.

Chapter 20

The Station

October 9, 42 PE

When Bo slid off the saddle for the fourth time, Ajinder sighed loudly enough for his horse to flick its ears. Farley too tsked skeptically. "Not gonna get very far like that, no, ya won't." The captain scratched his temple. "How 'bout we put ya 'cross yer friend's horse?"

"He isn't my friend," Bo muttered, obstinately pushing himself up in the stirrup. His mare threw its head up and snorted.

"See?" Farley's ability to suppress a smile was impressive. "Even the horse agrees. Give up."

Ajinder urged his mount closer. "Bo," he said in a low voice. "Stop. You'll hurt yourself."

Bo ignored him, continuing his futile attempts with an ever-deepening frown, until he stumbled and almost fell. With difficulty, he extracted his boot from the stirrup, cussing under the breath, and acknowledged Ajinder. "What? I am not gonna let you truss me like a saddlebag."

"No need. You can sit in front of me. Sideways, to spare your bad leg."

Bo did not respond, staring at his toes.

Ajinder looked at Farley. "Give us a moment, Cap, will you?"

The sailor saluted with a lopsided grin. "I'm off to Charlie's. Have fun, gents. Ya know where to find me, if ya ever need a ride, eh?" He tied the reins of Bo's horse to the fence and retired toward the tavern.

Ajinder waited for Farley to get outside the hearing range. "I could spur my horse and leave you behind in a cloud of dust. I'm not much of a rider myself, but ten coins says I'll be at The Station before dark. In fact, that's the most appealing option right now."

"Why don't you?" Bo asked his boots. "Why are you still here, annoying me with your jabbering?"

"Because Aileen would not appreciate me abandoning her capricious side-kick behind."

"I'm sure you'll find a way to console her."

"Dang! You're being vulgar again. Listen, I will not apologize for what I had with Aileen. I'm not even sure it meant as much to her as it did to me. If anything at all. But that isn't the point."

"And what is?" Bo glanced at him.

"That you're important to her. Stop being such a drama queen and climb up. Come on, what do you care about more: seeing Aileen, or what a random backcountry goatherder may think of you along the way?" Ajinder leaned down and extended a hand. "What's it gonna be?"

Bo pursed his lips and grabbed Ajinder's wrist, clinging to the duffel bag with his other arm.

———

Calling himself *not much* of a rider was generous. Ajinder's riding skills were worth crap. Better than Bo's—a low bar—but bad enough to make for a slow and arduous journey. The passenger kept sliding off, forcing Ajinder to pull him back up and unnerving the horse. Unsurprisingly, the sun wasn't in the mood to wait, and rolled down shortly after they'd passed the halfway point. At least, that's how far along Bo had claimed they were. In a regretful oversight, Ajinder hadn't brought a map. If it had been up to him, he would've ridden to the nearest railroad crossing and followed the tracks until running into The Station. But Bo had declared he knew a proper way, and Ajinder made the mistake of relying on the Locksviller's navigational skills. All went well while there still was light. Since the sunset, they'd had to retrace their steps twice already.

"Wait." Bo touched his chin, turning from side to side, squinting into the darkness, and almost sliding off the horse again.

"Um," Ajinder said, grabbing the guide by the scruff and adjusting his position.

"Shut up," Bo responded, quickly and nervously. "I know the way."

"So you keep saying. Take your time, I've got all night. Why are you jittery? Expecting trouble?"

"It's my job to expect trouble. Aren't you?"

"I always expect trouble. That's why I'm calm."

"Show-off."

"Jerk."

"Great talk. That way."

The waxing crescent moon lost the contest against the heavy cloud cover, providing occasional hints of its existence—but no light. The stars were scarcely a myth. In the west, the sky still stayed half a shade lighter with the memories of the dusk, but The Station lay to the east.

The road cleared a tree line, and several distant fires greeted the travelers. Ajinder halted the horse and pulled his rifle from behind his back. "Hold still," he said.

The fire filled the scope, but the darkness divulged no additional details.

Bo remained uncharacteristically quiet—and tense. As they rode closer, the fires rose. A mystery... or a bunch of watch towers.

"Well?" Bo relaxed and craned his neck. "I don't hear an apology."

"Ever been thrown off a horse?" Ajinder murmured suavely. There, civil.

"Ungrateful savage." Bo yelped and flailed at Ajinder's strong pat on the back. "Okay, okay, calm down, will you?"

"Who's there?" a surly, unwelcoming voice inquired, muffled by a massive gate.

Bo straightened up. "Karim? Is that you?"

The small wicket opened with a creak, and a brawny soldier stepped out with an oil lamp in one hand and a rifle in the other. Additional armed shapes waited inside.

"That was a quick trip, sir." Without asking, the soldier helped Bo off the horse.

"Don't get me started, Karim. Take us to Marc, please."

Karim regarded Ajinder for a moment and waved to the other guards. The gates cracked open, enough to let the horse through.

"Did you bring the engine back?" Bo asked in a low voice.

The soldier's nod was almost indistinguishable in the darkness. "Had to clear the tracks. There was a train scheduled to return from New Kowloon today."

Bo's head jerked up. "Did it?" he asked, with an edge. Ajinder held his breath.

"Yeah, around noon. Went on to Buffalo. Why?"

"Did... anyone arrive on it?" As much as Ajinder had tried to calm himself, he could not *not* ask. This was it, the moment of truth!

"Some traders, I presume."

"Passengers?"

"Not that I know of, sir."

Bo sharply inhaled. Ajinder could use rational reassurance, too. "Means nothing, Bo."

The kid's shuffling quickened. He almost fell through Marc's office door, gasping, "Aileen?"

Jihan's familiar bulk stepped forward. His eyes widened in recognition. "Ajinder? What are you—"

Ajinder jumped off the horse and threw the reins to Jihan. "Not now, brother." He rushed in after the kid.

One look at Bo's broken figure, leaning with his elbows and forehead against the wall, and Marc's ashen face, was enough. "Not here?" Ajinder slumped into a guest chair.

"Somebody, tell me what's going on," Marc wheezed out.

Bo shook his head, groaning. Ajinder closed his eyes and took a deep breath, waiting for his maniacally racing heart to slow down.

"Ajinder?" Jihan's basso rolled behind him.

Ajinder forced himself to look at Marc. "Aileen. She was supposed to be on the train that arrived from New Kowloon today." Or… if she outsmarted Wu… "Bo."

"M-m."

"What if she wanted everyone to *believe* she took that train?"

Bo pushed himself off the wall. "Deception." His sharp gaze pierced Ajinder.

"Sounds like her, right?"

"That'd be a perfectly Aileen thing to do. But then…" Bo hung his head. "We're back to square one. With no idea where she might be."

"Where else would she go? Not by water—Farley's boat was the only one there, I checked. Not by foot, I hope. Anyone she knows in the City?"

"Guys!" Marc's shout interrupted their rapid exchange. "You're making no sense. Start over. Was she at the Hive?"

"Yes," Ajinder and Bo replied together. The kid looked at him with annoyance, and Ajinder gestured, yielding.

"I knew it!" Marc slammed a fist into the desk. His face darkened. "This is war!"

"They did this to protect her!" Ajinder's reaction may have been too heated for a neutral observer. Marc's eyes narrowed.

"Not now!" snapped Bo. "Find Aileen first, settle the scores later."

Marc gnashed his teeth and remained silent.

"She escaped yesterday," Bo continued. "But the Kowloonese didn't find out until today, when I came knocking on their door. Wu's sources said she might be on that train."

"Could she continue straight to Locksville?" Ajinder dared to ask.

Marc's gloomy stare conveyed everything he thought about the suggestion. "The train spent half an hour at The Station. I was there. Old grudges aside, she would've at least said 'Hi'."

"Ask the haulers," said Jihan, who'd stayed silent to this point. "They notice more than they let on."

Marc tapped a finger on his desk. The ticking sound resonated in the quiet space. "Do it. Bring the Team Two foreman."

No one spoke in Jihan's absence. Marc locked his frown on Ajinder while his jowls moved, making no secret of his hostility.

Ajinder's brother returned with a burly bearded man in tow, presumably a hauler. The man started thoroughly wiping his boots on the doormat, but Marc had no patience for that. "Come in, Paul, come in!"

Paul removed his hat and bowed. "Good evening, Master Novak."

"Not a master! How many times do I have to tell you?" Marc sucked in a breath through his teeth. "Never mind. Tell me, was there a young woman on the train you hauled today?"

Paul looked around the room, uncomfortable with the amount of attention. "Yes, Ma— Mister Novak."

Ajinder, Bo, and Marc exhaled.

"She traveled in the empty boxcar," continued the hauler. "Last evening, I invited her to dinner. Seemed like a nice lady. Am I in trouble, sir?"

"No, Paul, you are not in trouble. Then what happened?"

"Nothing, sir. She ate. She liked the dinner. And then went into the passenger car with Master Farook and two other men. She said she'll pay for a ride to Locksville."

"Fuck me," said Marc.

"Shit," said Bo.

Ajinder said nothing. What was there to say?

"Maybe she didn't know I'm here?" asked Marc, of no one in particular.

"She did." Ajinder rubbed his eyes.

"What makes you so sure?" Marc's irritation grew with each word.

"Because I told her, okay?" Ajinder raised his voice too, squarely staring back.

"Knock it off, you two!" Bo's outburst rattled the windows. "I'm trying to think!" He paced the room, his limp all but disappearing.

Ajinder and Marc glowered at each other, but kept quiet. When Bo wasn't looking, Marc flipped a middle finger to Ajinder—and to Jihan behind him. Ajinder rolled his eyes.

"It's the Buffs." Bo stopped abruptly. "I guaran-fucking-tee it. For the exact same reason the Dragon wanted to hide her. Shit. Can we still catch up with them?"

Marc wetted his lips. "If they've parked in Locksville for the night."

"Any chance you've got another engine?"

"I've got one better for you. A carriage. With four horses, it's faster than any train. Khalifa, the self-aggrandizing bastard, had it built to impress the neighbors."

Ajinder slapped his knees, rose, and stepped to the exit. In the doorframe, he turned to Bo. "Are you coming?"

Marc stood too. "You're the one who shot Khalifa, no? Right in front of my fucking face. You've got a nerve setting foot at The Station! Why are you here? What's your involvement?"

Ajinder threw his head back in exasperation. "Do we have to do this now? Can we face off once Aileen's safe?"

Bo stepped in between them. "He's right, Marc. Seriously, lay off him. He seems to be a decent guy, and he cares about your sister. What more do you need?" He looked at Ajinder. "You didn't hear me say any of that, got it? *I* am still mad at you."

Ajinder nodded, hiding a stupid grin. The little Locksviller was okay. Annoying like all Seven Hells, but okay.

Marc chewed on his lips. "Fine. Your call. Ajinder, is it? You may find this useful." He reached under his desk and pulled up a machinegun.

Ajinder's brows crawled up.

Marc waved the questions off. "Long story. Know how to use it?"

"I've shot one, once or twice."

"Good. Just in case. Here's the ammo. Now, let's get you two into that carriage. I can't spare more than one fireteam. Make do, or get Weinberg to involve the CIU. Karim!"

On the porch, Ajinder embraced Jihan. "I know you have questions. I bet you've guessed the answers already. For you, the most important task right now is to convince Novak the Dragons acted in good faith. Because they did. Tam Wai Lam *really* wanted to keep Aileen safe."

"Understood. I'll deal with that. Regardless, I'm glad to see you, but why *are* you here?"

"The Golden Dragon had hired me to extract Aileen from Locksville. And then..."

"And then?"

And then? Why *was* he there? "She's very special, brother."

Was that all? Enough to send him on a wild chase? Yes! The *yessest* yes ever! She was crass, strong-willed, and used every chance to make fun of him. She was also sharp, bright, and warm under all those layers of invisible armor. Meeting her had split his life in two: the gray, trivial *before*, and the dizzyingly colorful *after*. He didn't need her to settle with him in the Clan lands, to pop babies and be a housewife. Being beside her was all he asked for. Would she let him? That was a million-coin question.

"She's important to me," he blurted, making this official. Now the Patriarch knew.

Jihan stroked his beard. "I see. Be careful, Aji. The playing field is changing. The rules are being rewritten. In times like these, no one counts the collateral damage. Don't become a part of it."

Ajinder squeezed Jihan's forearm. "What about me says 'collateral', brother?" A corner of his lips twitched.

Jihan patted him on the shoulder. "Nothing, Ajinder. Nothing at all."

Chapter 21

Locksville

October 10, 42 PE

Leaning forward, eyes bulging, shouting, "Faster! Faster!"—Bo looked possessed. Ajinder could not judge him. His own giddy elation with Aileen's escape had morphed into a dark brew of worry, despair, and self-blame. He jerked with every snap of the whip, yet the next one couldn't come soon enough.

At first, the carriage had departed The Station at a careful trot. The soldier holding the reins had stoically resisted Bo's calls to pick up speed until Karim pushed him aside and took over. Whatever connection the severe mustached corporal shared with Bo made him responsive to the Locksviller's pleas. A heated but hushed argument between the two Stationers ensued, cut short by Karim pulling the rank.

The mad race through the darkness was an exercise in tempting fate. In daylight, no sane coachman would have agreed to drive the horses so recklessly fast for fear of the ubiquitous potholes. In the pitch-black night, the threat they posed was still menacing—yet invisible. The possibility of a horse breaking a leg tickled Ajinder's nerves, but was, somehow, easier to ignore while the danger remained unseen. Especially from inside the carriage, where he and Bo clutched their soft, cushioned seats.

Ajinder counted off seconds. *Locksville is close to The Station. Only a short stretch. Locksville is close to The Station. Nearly there. Three quarters of the way, for sure. Locksville is close to The Station.* With enough luck...

A high-pitched, frightened scream of a horse tore the night. Other three joined in a discordant chorus. The carriage lurched and careened. It teetered precariously on two wheels and came crashing down onto Ajinder's side. The window shattered right in front of him, sending shards into his face and leaving him barely enough time to tuck in his head and protect it with his arms. Broken glass crunched underneath. Bo, all sharp elbows and knees, landed on top of him. For a moment, reality lost focus.

"Hey. You okay, man?" Someone pulled on his collar. "Ajinder?"

Why was he so groggy? Who knocked him out? He shook his head to get rid of the noise filling it. "What... What happened?" Whose voice was that? *His?* No way. "Where—"

"Bo, Singh, are you alright in there?" called someone from outside the dark box they were in.

"Peachy!" The voice originating near Ajinder trembled.

A sharp, deafening report of a nearby shot achieved what all Ajinder's meek attempts had failed to: before the echoes died, his mind shed the fog, and provided all the answers with instant clarity. Aileen! The train. The carriage. The crazy race through the darkness. The improbable luck... until it ran out. The shot! Who fired at whom? Were they ambushed?!

Ajinder pushed off his small companion—Bo, yes—and fumbled for his rifle. No, too dark. Must've been thrown around when the carriage was overturned. No time. A lighter rectangle above them amid the blackness; the second door, hanging ajar. He eased his knife in its sheath, pulled himself up through the opening, and peeked around. Trained to the darkness inside, his eyes needed no adjustment to the gray ambience. Karim's stocky, square figure stood with a pistol above a prone horse.

"Shit." Ajinder climbed out, offered a hand to Bo, and dragged him up.

"Shit," agreed the little guy.

"Yeah," said the corporal, "had to shoot it. Zarif's leg is broken."

"Whose?" asked Bo.

"My brother's." One of Karim's soldiers responded from behind the carriage. "Thrown off by the crash. Because of you, crippled fucker! *Faster, faster!*" he mocked.

"Private, belay!" Karim's voice rose with an implied threat. "That was my decision. *I* am responsible. Now, hold that tongue, or—"

The sound of many hooves stomping on the road was unmistakable. It died down a hundred paces away. "CIU!" roared someone authoritative. "Drop your weapons and identify yourselves!"

Ajinder's imagination readily conjured a bunch of well-trained fighters dismounting and spreading stealthily through the trees, enveloping the trespassers. That was what he would have done in their place.

"Huh," muttered Karim, "you're gonna have to do the explaining, sir."

Bo sat on the edge of the carriage roof. Or a wall? "Lieutenant Maxwell? Is that you?"

"Who's asking?"

"It's Bo, Lieutenant. With a few soldiers from The Station and... a friend. We could use your help here."

"Who fired?" The officer didn't sound intimidating anymore, only cautious.

"Had to put down a maimed horse." Karim, somber at better times, was outright grim.

A many-legged shadow came down the road and split into four separate outlines. One approached and whistled. "What a mess."

"Yeah, all part of a larger cluster fuck." Bo sighed. "Will you help us, or not?"

"An odd company, for a Streeter. Begs the question, what were you doing here in the small hours of the night?"

"Maxwell, we—"

"That's *Lieutenant* Maxwell for you."

"Dammit, Lieutenant, we're in a hurry. Weinberg will answer all your questions. Now, would you *please* call your men to push this thing upright?" He patted the conveyance he was sitting on. "We really need to get going."

"Cheeky little clown," the officer grumbled. "If Weinberg doesn't corroborate your story, you and I will have another chat." Then louder, "Alright, boys, let's get this wreck back on its wheels!"

His soldiers hurried forward.

"Ajinder," said Bo, sliding to the ground with the grace of a three-legged dog, "are you drooling or bleeding? Dripping all over my fucking back."

With three nervous horses, two bent wheels, Zarif's leg in an improvised splint, and his brother muttering non-stop profanities under his breath, Bo did not risk objecting to a slower pace. Ajinder, his cut arm bandaged and hanging in a sling, kept quiet, too. His only consolation was Viper, found unharmed and now resting between his knees. Their mounted CIU escort warned Karim of especially large depressions in the road. Besides that, no one spoke. The lieutenant had tried to probe Bo for answers once more and gave up.

"There," shouted a CIU scout, pointing. "Your train!"

Bo jumped out of the still moving carriage, mindless of his physical limitations, and rushed toward the railcar. Ajinder and Karim overtook him. After the night's darkness, the predawn supplied enough light to see the car and the adjacent haulers' camp.

Karim ran up the stairs first and banged his fist on the door. Ajinder followed closely and, without slowing down, rushed past the corporal. The kicked-in door crashed against furniture inside. "Aileen?" he called, circling the interior. "Aileen!"

Someone stirred in a bed. "What... Who are you?" The voice was greasy with sleep and quavering with fear.

"Farook?" Karim lit a lamp and loomed over the trader. "Where are they?"

"H-who?"

With his good hand, Ajinder grabbed the plump Stationer by his collar, pulled him out of the bed, and slammed him into the wall. Farook's teeth clinked, as did the dishes in the cupboards.

"Aileen Novak," growled Ajinder. "Where is she? And the Buffs?"

"I... I..."

Ajinder slapped the wriggling worm. Not too hard; the sling limited his movements. Another clink of glass on glass.

"Start talking, or my friend will cut you into ribbons," Bo whispered under Ajinder's elbow.

"You aren't helping." Karim pushed them both aside, guided the shaking trader to sit back on the bed, and offered him a glass of water. "Farook," he said calmly, "talk. What happened after you left The Station yesterday? Where's the woman?"

"They... They took her." The trader sputtered and broke into sobbing. "They threatened me! They threatened my family! There was nothing I could do!"

Bo wound up for a punch. Ajinder held him back by his elbows. "Let him speak."

"Took her where?" asked Karim with exemplary patience.

"We crossed into Buffalo territory... late evening... They left with the Union soldiers... Sent me back... with a message for Novak."

"Let me guess." Bo oozed venom. "Cut the tariffs, or else?"

Farook stared back, glazed-eyed. "How did you—"

"M-motherfucker." Bo turned away and punched the wall. He hissed and bent, clutching his fist to his chest.

Ajinder did not comment.

"You sleazy piece of dogshit," said Karim in the same fatherly tone as before, patting Farook on the shoulder. "Your train was parked at The Station for an hour. An hour! And you said nothing? Warned no one?"

"They—"

"They wouldn't have done a thing. What, shoot you? In The Station's railyard? That'd be the end of them. They may be scheming assholes, but sure aren't suicidal."

Farook hung his head. "Easy for you to say. Morris had a gun to my back."

"Morris?" asked Bo, straightening up. "LeClaire?"

The trader sniffed and bobbed his head.

"You know the guy?" asked Ajinder.

"M-motherfucker," repeated Bo, this time swinging his fist through the air. "Of course, I know the guy! Only Buffalo Union's Deputy Security Supervisor."

Oppressive silence stretched, disrupted by the trader's sobs and Bo's heaving breath.

"Can we take on him?" Ajinder sent his tentative question tiptoeing across the car.

"'We'?" The kid had perfected the art of reveling in bitterness. "You and what army?"

"The Station's?" Karim raised his head.

"Not funny, Karim. Marc's hold on The Station must be precarious as it is. An all-out war with Buffalo? Nah, no way. Never mind the tiny detail that the Union's military is, what, four or five times stronger than yours? Plus, half the warlords to the south are their vassals."

"So"—Ajinder spread his arms—"what do we do? Surrender to their blackmail and hope for the best?"

Bo frowned. "Hells, no! I wouldn't trust that fucker as far as I could throw him!" He nodded decisively. "Okay. Karim, lead the train back at first light. Update Marc. Take Zarif and his brother home."

Karim didn't move. "Will you be safe, sir?"

"Come on, man. This is my turf. Besides, Maxwell won't let me out of his sight, for better or for worse. Oh, and this sack of shit"—he scowled at Farook—"is coming with us."

"Coming with us... *where*?" Ajinder gagged on the sour blackness inside him, threatening to spill out.

"To Weinberg, naturally. He'll find a few strings to pull."

Ajinder shrugged. "As bad a plan as any."

Chapter 22

Locksville

October 11, 42 PE

The carriage stopped. "White House, the last station!" called Maxwell from out front. Careful not to get cut again on the remaining shards of glass, Ajinder pushed the door. It resisted, creaked, giving way, and fell off, hitting the ground with a startling clatter. He almost stumbled after it.

"That ought to wake up the neighborhood," chuckled the lieutenant. "Come, boys."

Ajinder's head cleared. Almost falling would do that. Combined with the deafening bang and the fresh, chilly air.

After leaving the train, he'd sunk into a semi-conscious state. Through the day before and most of the night, he'd been functioning on hype and grit. Swinging from hope to worry and back, he had kept going... until he hit a wall of powerlessness. The impact sent him spiraling down into a dark place. A short ride to the White House provided the much-needed respite to his mind, but his heart continued its fall into the bottomless pit of self-flagellation and worst-case scenarios.

The dawn diluted the murky grayness with a tinge of pink, signaling the end of the infinitely long night. But despair clung to Ajinder, smothering him with a film of cold, clammy sweat.

Bo blundered out of the carriage, pulled out his duffel bag, and stopped at Ajinder's side. "You look like you've been to Seven Hells and back."

Ajinder scoffed. "The pot calling the kettle black." A wrinkled forehead, bags under his eyes, and a scowl affixed to Bo's gaunt face aged him gracelessly. But the ever-present fire still blazed inside the little man, stoked angrier than ever.

On his previous visit, Ajinder had taken pains to stay away from the city center, so this was his first sighting of the White House. Surprisingly, it lived up to its name. Locksville's administrative complex sported immaculately painted walls. Ajinder had never given it much thought, but somehow had always believed the moniker was a figure of speech; an obscure historical reference to another famous government building.

A CIU operative led a handcuffed Farook away and around the corner. Bo followed Maxwell in through the main entrance. Ajinder trailed behind. Was he to expect trouble? *Meh, whatever.*

"Captain, do you ever sleep?" The lieutenant's booming basso echoed through the empty hallways.

"Waste of time," responded a vaguely familiar voice.

Ajinder wearily crossed the office threshold and stayed near the exit. Force of habit.

"Bo," said Weinberg, "nothing?"

Bo shook his head and stared meaningfully at the CIU officer.

Weinberg invoked a polite smile. "That'll be all, Lieutenant."

Maxwell saluted and hesitated, no doubt struggling with the unanswered questions.

"Stick around," Bo rasped, claiming a chair in the corner. "Your services may yet be required."

Maxwell frowned and sent a questioning look to Weinberg. The captain examined Bo and slowly nodded. The lieutenant sighed and squeezed past Ajinder. Subordination wasn't too fashionable here.

Captain Weinberg shifted his focus to Ajinder. "I know you. We've met in New Kowloon. You're one of the Singh brothers... Uh, Ajinder?"

"Yes, sir." Under different circumstances, the captain's attention would have made Ajinder uncomfortable, but in his current state, it failed to stir him.

"This is beyond peculiar, but we'll get to that. Bo, what are you waiting for? Talk."

"It wasn't Marc."

Weinberg's squinted gaze flicked to Ajinder and back. "The Dragons?"

"Yes, Tam Wai Lam." Bo's voice held only fatigue, without a hint of disapproval.

Weinberg rolled his eyes. "That woman... She'll be the end of me one day. And? She didn't let you see Aileen?"

"She would have, but Aileen had escaped."

Weinberg clapped. "That's my girl!" His grin melted away against Bo's unchanged, grievous expression.

My girl? Ajinder perked up. What relations could the Head of the Intelligence Service have with the Streeters' Aunt? Aileen, his agent, like New Kowloon smugglers' boss for Wu? Not in a thousand years!

"She snuck onto the train leaving the Hive."

"Then... Is she at The Station, with Marc?"

"Two Buffs were on that train, returning home." Bo's voice trailed into a coarse whisper. "They recognized her. Took her to the Union tonight. The worst part? It was LeClaire himself."

By the time Bo finished, Weinberg's expression matched his. Haggard face, old eyes, and the same downward crescent of the mouth. He rubbed his cheeks. "This is bad. This is really, really bad."

"We missed them by mere hours," Ajinder added, a tad apologetically.

Weinberg fixed him with an unblinking regard. "And why are *you* here, Ajinder Singh?"

That question, again.

"He—" Bo started explaining, but Ajinder stopped him with a sharp gesture. It was his mess to pay for. He met the notorious captain's eyes. "I had extracted Aileen from here." Screw the consequences.

"He's in love with her," Bo announced grumpily, depriving Ajinder of this self-sacrificial opportunity. "Kinda makes him family."

"Oh." Weinberg's hard stare softened. He touched his chin. "I've heard about this bizarre tradition, when the groom is expected to steal the bride before the wedding, to prove his prowess. Didn't know West Sauga practices it."

"We don't, sir." Ajinder refused to look away. "I did this under the Golden Dragon's orders, for Miss Novak's safety. Everything else"—he blinked, perturbed by the public discussion of his feelings—"happened later. I apologize for my gross disregard of Locksville's sovereignty, sir."

"Um-hum." The corner of Weinberg's mouth twitched. "You may as well sit, Mister Singh. I don't foresee any need for your hasty retreat through that door."

Ajinder stiffly walked to the single unoccupied seat—a low, broad armchair—and sank into it. The intense scrutiny from both Locksvillers gave him goosebumps. "What?" he asked, too crisply, looking from Weinberg to Bo and back.

The captain's brow crept up. "You appear comfortable."

Huh? Ajinder squeezed his eyes shut and shook his head. Comprehension continued eluding him. "Excuse me? Should I not?"

Weinberg leaned back. "Can you believe this, Bo?"

Bo examined Ajinder as if seeing him for the first time. His chin almost touched his chest. "Are you truly comfortable?"

"Y-yes." What was all this about?

"Get outta here." Bo turned to Weinberg, gesturing at Ajinder. "He's comfortable."

Rage did not befit a true warrior. Ajinder had been taught the value of level-headedness from an early age. He'd never exploded. This time, he came close. Anger rolled from his stomach up, settling behind the bridge of his nose. "What is wrong with you two? Discussing my comfort instead of planning Aileen's release? Yes, I'm comfortable, okay? Can we move on now?" Swearing did not befit a warrior either, but how exhilarating it would have been...

Weinberg saluted him. "At least one person in this room has got his priorities straight. You are right to call us out on our digression, Mister Singh. It's just... Care guessing how many people have found this armchair comfortable? Indulge me, please."

The question made no sense. The soft, cozy, enveloping chair was fine. Ajinder shrugged. "All of them?"

The Locksvillers exchanged puzzled looks. "Two," said the captain. "Only two people, ever. A certain grumpy jerk from Five Points and..." He paused for dramatic effect. "Aileen. Her secret is to climb in with her feet."

Ajinder's fingertips tenderly stroked the armrest. Illogical, yes. It couldn't have held her smell or warmth, but the silly act was the closest substitute to touching the real her. He caught the other two men watching him. Bo quickly averted his gaze. Weinberg sighed. Ajinder blushed. "Why do you have it, if it's so bad?" he asked, to cover his embarrassment.

"I get interesting guests in this room sometimes, Mister Singh. What they are prepared to tell me may be of value, but I am often more interested in what they are less willing to disclose. That part is easier to fish out when they're struggling with physical discomfort but are too proud to admit it."

"Sounds too elaborate. Don't you have a torture chamber or something?"

Captain Weinberg smiled beatifically. "Of course. Both approaches have their merits. But now we really are digressing. The problem is,"—he grew serious again, and the swift transition made Ajinder skip a breath—"there's nothing I can do right away. I've got eyes and ears in the Union, naturally, but they're more of, uh, informers, not proper agents. It will take time to activate them and get anything meaningful back. Two-three days, minimum."

Bo's hand slid over his eyes, as if the lights in the room had become painfully bright. His voice crackled when he asked, "What's your read on LeClaire?"

Weinberg pinched his ear. "He's a total, phenomenal ass. Full of himself and drunk on his power. But stupid he is not; he won't do anything... *irreversible*. The main issue I see, he's got no incentive to release Aileen even if Marc yields to his demands. In fact, keeping her and extracting further concessions is his most logical play. Now, you said there were *two* Buffs on that train. Who was the second? Or will we need to question your Stationer?"

"Some guy named Richard. Means anything to you?"

"No last name?"

"No."

"Hm. Only one Richard I can think of, Maynard—a senior trader. If it's him, that's good news. I hear he's a level-headed man. Pretty decent, for a Buff."

"That sounds like him, based on Farook's retelling. Problem is, he doesn't call the shots."

"Obviously. When LeClaire is involved, no one else ever calls the shots." Weinberg placed his palms on his desk. "Alright, boys. It's safe to assume Aileen is in no immediate danger. Give me a little time, and we'll figure something out. You both are understandably anxious, but try to get some rest." He waited until his guests begrudgingly acceded. "Oh, and Bo?"

"Yes, Dave, I'll check on Oscar."

"Thank you. I've heard nothing from or about the Streeters—which is a great sign—but still."

Ajinder and Bo stood up.

The captain raised a finger. "One last thought..."

"What?" Bo didn't hide his exasperation.

"You may want to ask Mister Singh to point out the holes in your security. There *are* holes, if he was able to pull his stunt with no one the wiser."

Bo met Ajinder's eyes. Ajinder spread his arms with a shrug, accepting the obligation. "Anything for my family."

———————

Oscar scratched his head. "Told you, the roofs are a vulnerability point."

"You said nothing of the sort!" Fox exploded. "Don't put this on me! This was your screw-up just as much as mine!"

Both glared at Ajinder.

"How did you come up with this route?" asked Bo, surveying the Warehouse roof.

Whatever their business acumen, as far as security was concerned, this outfit reeked of amateurism. Anyone with even one eye would have found a dozen glaring holes. That, of course, was not something to share out loud. "We observed your day and nighttime guard routine."

"Hells, rub it in, won't ya!" Fox smacked his fist into his hand.

"*We?*" Bo cocked his head. "How many of you were here?"

"Twenty-eight."

"Wha—" Fox's jaw dropped.

"I'm kidding." Ajinder half-closed his eyes. Patience. These were Aileen's people, which put them on the same side. "Just my brother and I."

"Oh." Fox snapped his mouth shut.

Same side, yes? Here's to hoping he'd never need to abduct any of the Streeters again. "Map out all the ingress and egress pathways. Obvious, less obvious, and seemingly impossible. Exercise attacks and incursions, force on force. Randomly alternate guard schedules: shift times, detail sizes, post locations, patrol routes. Lay an occasional ambush and make the practice known." Ajinder paused. All three Locksvillers were unabashedly gawking at him. "That should be enough to get you started." He smiled shyly. Not to rub it in, eh?

"Hey, boss?"

All the heads turned to the hatch behind them.

"What?" Bo and Oscar barked at once, and exchanged glum looks.

"Sorry, Oscar, I meant Bo," mumbled the head in the opening. "There's Weinberg's man downstairs, asking for you and your guest." The messenger shot a curious glance at Ajinder and quickly averted his eyes.

"Thanks, Goose. Tell him we'll be with him shortly."

"Sure thing, boss." The head bobbed and disappeared. The hatch door slammed shut with a ringing bang.

Bo turned to his two companions. "None of what you've heard here leaves this roof. Fox, I want a plan for implementing Ajinder's advice by sundown. Start with the schedules. Oscar, work out a long-term upgrade. Agreed?"

Both nodded.

Groaning, Bo pulled up the rusty, squeaky door, climbed three rungs down, and stopped. "Ajinder is untouchable. Don't get any ideas."

Fox scowled. Oscar glowered.

Bo raised his voice. "Are we clear?"

"What do you think it is?" Ajinder asked. Obviously, Bo wouldn't know any more than him, but the silent waiting had become beyond unbearable. Ajinder had already gone through every conceivable and inconceivable scenario that could lead Captain Weinberg to summon them hours after sending them away.

Bo rewarded Ajinder with a dirty look and returned to hypnotizing Weinberg's door. His good foot kept its rapid tapping on the floorboards.

Steps inside the office brought Ajinder to his feet before the door opened. Weinberg beckoned. "Come in, guys."

Maintaining a respectable pace took a lot of effort. Bo cared nothing about his image and shuffled on with such unexpected agility, he nearly bumped into the captain.

Weinberg hurried to clear the way, letting the little guy in. "Sorry, folks, if my invite gave you false hopes," he said, closing the door behind Ajinder. "Still no news about Aileen, but... We have a visitor."

"Golden Dragon." Ajinder bowed.

Shang Ka Yi nodded back.

"Look what the cat dragged in. Here to apologize?" Bo claimed a chair, crossing his legs and arms. His irascible stare had zero effect on the Kowloonese.

A cryptic smile touched Weinberg's lips. "Are you, Golden Dragon? Your lovely wife has snubbed me twice in as many weeks."

Ajinder's patron kept his face. "She isn't your biggest fan either, Captain, but that's immaterial to our discussion." He met Bo's eyes, and the impudent Locksviller broke the contact. "Gentlemen, my wife and I attribute utmost importance to New Kowloon's relationships with The Station and Locksville. We are not entirely happy with the way events have unfolded and are willing to go the distance to mend your trust. Having learned about Miss Novak's current predicament, I rushed here to extend an offer of help."

"Haven't you helped enough already?" Bo muttered.

"Mister Bo, need I remind you how much I sympathize?"

Bo's cheeks reddened. "And I *am* grateful, Golden Dragon." Whoa. Did the little prick just thank another person? "But what *can* you do? Hire Ajinder again, to fetch Aileen from Buffalo?"

Ajinder ground his teeth. As if he hadn't considered this himself, over and over again! Buffs would hold her at a secret location, under heavy guard. Not exactly the same as extracting an unsuspecting target from her own bedroom.

"In a way, Mister Bo." Shang Ka Yi inclined his head with dignity.

Judging by their frozen figures, neither Weinberg nor Bo expected such a turn of conversation any more than Ajinder himself.

The Golden Dragon relished the effect of his words for another second or two. "I'm here with my flagship, and a perfectly legitimate excuse to visit our Buffalo Mission: to wrap up the trade affairs for the winter. That's your way in. I'll provide a distraction, one that the Buffs will find impossible to ignore. Use that opportunity to grab LeClaire. From there, I'm sure you'll know how to proceed." Shang Ka Yi's grin took a predatory flavor.

"Distraction?" asked Ajinder. "How will we know it worked?"

"Trust me, you won't miss it. No one in Buffalo will. Also, we'll be in touch." The Kowloonese dropped his arm behind his chair and placed a small suitcase on Weinberg's desk.

"The radio?" Childish excitement swept through Ajinder, despite the gravity of the situation. Weinberg nodded.

"The what?" Bo straightened up. "Am I the only one without a clue?"

"One word of caution." Shang Ka Yi grew serious. "That distraction *absolutely* cannot be traced back to me. I'll be nowhere near when it all goes down, and won't be able to pick you up. You'll be on your own from that point on."

Ajinder squared his shoulders, faking confidence. "I'll manage."

Bo stood up. "*We*'ll manage. Dave, I'll need every Buffalo map you can scrounge. No help from the CIU, I presume?"

"Sorry, kid, we cannot afford to be implicated either. Neighborly relations and all. But you'll get your maps."

Bo solemnly nodded. "Figures. I'll gather a team." He bent to pick up his bag and paused. "Wait." He straightened up. "Buffs are, above everything, merchants. Can't we buy Aileen out?"

Shang Ka Yi perked up. "Got anything concrete in mind?"

Bo lifted his duffel bag. "Someone in Buffalo had offered an extra hefty contract to snatch these. *A lot* of money."

"And *these* are...?"

"Sea creatures from the Museum of Glass."

The Golden Dragon's eyelids drooped, as did the corners of his lips. "What an unfortunate serendipity. Sorry to disappoint you, Mister Bo, that was my contract." He waved his hand dismissively. "It's meaningless now. Those figurines were meant for our *former* Chairman Chang."

"So, I traveled for nothing. Tick *died* for nothing."

"I'll honor the terms of the contract, of course, if that's of any consolation."

"No." Bo's response was immediate, resolute, and final. "I'm keeping them. As a welcome home gift for Aileen. When do we leave, Golden Dragon?"

"At first light tomorrow."

Chapter 23

Buffalo

October 12, 42 PE

Ajinder squeezed the button on the side of the mysterious device and waited a few seconds. Was it okay to proceed? It gave no sign. He brought it up close to his lips and murmured, "We're in position."

The radio spewed crackling and wheezing noise, and a distorted, unrecognizable voice said, "Stand by."

"That's it?" Ajinder turned to Bo, who lay nearby on the flat roof and observed the Buffalo Public Safety Directorate through binoculars. As if he wasn't curious at all about the piece of prehistoric tech.

"What did you expect?" asked Bo without interrupting his reconnaissance.

Ajinder twisted the fragile oddity in his hands. "Don't know. More than two words, for sure."

"You sent the message, they've got it."

"I guess. Anything unusual in the building?"

"Why would there be? For the Buffs, it's just another day... so far."

Ajinder stuffed the radio into his vest pouch. "What do you think the distraction will be?" he asked, scanning one window after another through his rifle's scope.

"What's with all the questions? Nervous? Aren't you the calm one, always expecting trouble?"

"Touché." Ajinder chuckled—involuntarily, in an unexpected reprieve from the pre-action tension.

The flash behind his back was so bright, its reflection in the Directorate's windows momentarily blinded him. The second sun bloomed in the west, competing with the drowsy late-fall midmorning light. The shock wave arrived a fraction of a second later, blowing loose debris off the roof, rattling the few structures still attached, and shattering glass downstairs. Ajinder ducked and covered his head, waiting out the booming sound of the explosion as it rolled over, echoing in the streets below.

"Holy cow!" Did he shout? The ringing in his ears made it difficult to judge. He glanced back. A column of thick black smoke was climbing lazily from the Harbourfront warehouses, billowing into a giant mushroom. Angry flames licked its base. That ought to have taken a lot of explosives.

Bo's lips folded into an O shape, producing a whistle that remained unheard. "Your Dragon friend doesn't fuss around." His high-pitched voice came from afar. "Difficult to miss, as promised." He returned his attention to the building across the street, reminding Ajinder to do the same.

A nauseating whine of a crank siren rose from the depths of the Public Safety Directorate. Its main entrance's tall double doors flipped open and disgorged the inhabitants, in singles and groups, until a large crowd assembled outside. Several energetic people, presumably the officers, organized the personnel into teams and led them toward the port lands. Only a few stragglers were left behind, milling aimlessly around.

"Let's roll, folks!" Ajinder called, helping Bo to his feet and winking at Fox, who held the door. "Party time!"

Broken tree branches strewed the cracked pavement. Waiting for Bo to limp closer, Ajinder picked up a thicker one and cleared the few shards still clinging doggedly to the window frame. One bandaged arm was enough. "See? Didn't need your glass cutter, after all."

The northern wall of the Directorate's imposing, eight-story brownstone building faced an eerily deserted side street. No one was around to notice the intruders snaking their way to the nearest blown out window. Bo; Waffles, a sketchy, nondescript character of the sort you better not turn your back to; Pogo, a tall, stick-thin, awkward looking but nimble teenager; Pinky, a bear of a man, effortlessly lugging Marc's machinegun; and Fox, closing the file, the wiliest of the bunch, second only to Bo. What an odd company. Supposedly, the most capable among Aileen's own crew, because once Bo had announced the purpose of the raid, there had been no shortage of volunteers. And none of them harbored warm feelings toward Ajinder. Never mind. They were there for Aileen, and only that counted.

Ajinder took the point through empty hallways and stairs. He was stalking past the third-floor door when it swung open, almost hitting his shoulder. A local burst into the staircase and froze, squinting into the barrel of Ajinder's handgun. Ajinder jerked him from the doorway, slammed him into the wall, and stole a quick glance into the corridor beyond. No one. Good. He nodded to Waffles, who pushed the door closed.

Ajinder retrieved the interloper's pistol from its holster and shoved it into the back of his own waistband. He patted the man down for hidden weapons while observing his face. Pupils dilated, mouth shut, hands up. Paled, but hasn't lost his nerve. Caught up fast. Not a paper-pusher. "Name, rank, position?"

When no response came, Ajinder reproachfully cocked his head to the side. The prisoner dropped his gaze. "Lieutenant Scott Dawson, National Guard, Staff Secretary."

Ajinder rewarded him with a tiny nod. "We have no bone to pick with you, Lieutenant. We're here on a... uh... personal business. Don't try to be a hero, and"—his eyes darted to the wedding band on the officer's finger—"your wife will get to see you tonight. Deal?"

"Deal," Dawson answered with his lips only, jaws tightly shut.

"You'll forgive us some precautions, yes?" Ajinder turned to Pogo. "Tie his hands and gag him."

"Hey—"

Ajinder raised an eyebrow and lined up his handgun with the lieutenant's forehead. "Problem?"

"No, sir." Dawson shook his head, breaking eye contact. "No problem at all."

"Great. If so, you wouldn't mind showing us the way to LeClaire's office, would you?"

At the sixth-floor staircase, Dawson mumbled, "Ee-a-hea" and pointed to the door with his eyes. "We are here," he repeated once Pogo removed the gag.

"I am disappointed, Lieutenant." Ajinder waved to Pogo. The tall kid replaced the bandage across the officer's mouth, ignoring his protestations.

"What's wrong?" Pinky's basso echoed up and down the stairs.

Ajinder sighed. "Lieutenant Dawson wants to die a hero. The Deputy Supervisor's office is on the eighth floor. *This* door would lead us straight into the Guard barracks."

The butt of Waffles' rifle sank into the officer's stomach. The Buff folded in two and dropped to his knees. Bo's sharp gesture stopped Waffles from striking the back of the prisoner's head. "No killing if we can help it." The kid didn't let the bloodlust blind him. Kudos. There *was* more to him than bluster and acrimony.

Ajinder stalked up, clearing the next flights of stairs. Eighth floor. The nerve center of the Directorate. Ajinder cracked the door a smidge, kneeled, and stuck a small mirror on a folding handle through the gap, low above the carpet. A few seconds to study the space on the other side, then withdraw. "An antechamber, one inner door, two armed guards," he narrated softly for the ragtag team of Locksvillers breathing into his back.

"Anti-what?" whispered Pogo.

"A waiting room," Fox translated for him.

"Fox," said Ajinder, "you and I rush them. Try to overwhelm and subdue quietly, without opening fire. But if push comes to shove... you know."

Fox snarled, uncannily resembling his carnivorous namesake. "I know."

"Pogo, on my three, throw the door open. I go in first, take out the left one. Fox, after me, the one on the right is yours. Clear?" Both nodded. "One..."

A loud bang reverberated in the hollow space. Dawson, half a flight below, kicked the ringing guardrail post with his boot, again and again. Valiant moron. Pinky's fist to the side of the head sent him rolling down.

"Two, three!" Ajinder sped up his count. Pogo looked at him confusedly, crumpling his sock hat. "Now!" Ajinder barked. The guy flinched, the door disappeared, and Ajinder jumped in. The two guards, alarmed by the noise, had covered half the distance to the entrance. All the better, less time for them to react. He dove under the rising muzzle of a gun and swept the soldier off his feet. At the edge of his vision, Fox's jumping kick sent the other guard crashing into a reception desk. "Subdue, not kill," he reminded the Locksviller, squeezing the struggling guard in a chokehold.

"Piss off," growled Fox.

"Fox!" Bo's sharp call turned both their heads. "You will take every word coming out of Ajinder's mouth as gospel, and follow it to a T, clear?"

Fox dropped his eyes. "Yes, boss." A sideways glance at Ajinder. "Sorry, man."

The palatial office behind the inner door met the assault team with stifling emptiness. "Not here, eh?" Bo stated the obvious, entering behind Ajinder. "Very well, we'll wait as planned."

———

Not knowing when the slow, meaningless passage of time would abruptly morph into life-or-death action had always been the toughest part of waiting. Maintaining peak alertness for hours was not humanly possible, but falling into a thoughtless apathy would be a crime against his longevity... and with it, the mission.

Ajinder settled in an armchair by the miraculously intact window, facing the door and holding his handgun in one hand. His rifle stood nearby, leaning against his knee.

Pinky dragged in the still unconscious Dawson, dropped him in the corner onto the two passed-out guards, and claimed the office owner's antique chair. The machinegun ended up on the desktop, foreign to the setting and sending a clear message to anyone entering the room.

Pogo and Waffles, dressed in the guards' uniforms, took positions outside the door. Their utterly non-military postures and loosely fitting garments left them little chance of fooling someone—assuming that someone would spare them a look. "Would the arrogant asshole acknowledge simple guards?" Bo asked. "I bet ten coins he doesn't know their names." That line of thought had merit, and if the masquerade could provide an extra edge, why not?

Bo himself, accompanied by Fox, browsed the files in a long shelving unit behind the desk. Most he discarded to the floor, but a few found their way into his backpack. "Uh," he said, or "Hm," or "Huh." Or even, "I bet Weinberg would love to see *this*."

And Ajinder simply waited, alert but careful not to pass the threshold of frazzling tension. Everything was going to be alright. LeClaire would come, succumb to their overwhelming argumentation, take them to Aileen, and promptly let them be on their way back home. That last part of the plan was a little fuzzy, but... They'd make it work.

Despite his preparedness, mental and tactical, when the staircase door creaked in the antechamber, Ajinder jolted. Keeping the inner door closed was critical to maintaining the dress-up charade, at the expense of not knowing what went on outside the office. He strained his hearing. Footfalls and muted voices.

The heavy, leather-covered door opened, and two men strolled in, oblivious to the fake guards behind them.

"... whose negligence this— What a— Guards!" The older man jerked to retreat. The door slammed into his face. His younger companion, similarly dressed in civilian, scanned the room with the unmistakable expression of someone used to having the last word. *Don't. Don't.* The young man's hand darted to his holster, as Ajinder knew it would. Damn.

The unfortunate gunslinger's knees buckled while the thundering shot's echoes still bounced around the enclosed space. A neat, round hole decorated the bridge of his nose. The red stain behind him began its slow descent down the faded wallpaper.

"Hello, LeClaire," Bo flatly greeted the first Buff.

So this was *him*. Face, speckled with blood droplets, paler than paper. And knotted brows. Scared and angry at the same time.

"Ah, Novak's cripple sidekick," LeClaire spewed. "And her pathetic menagerie." He paused on Ajinder. "And you, raghead? A hired gun?"

Ajinder stood and holstered his pistol. His stomach turned, but he clenched his jaws. For Aileen. An image of her face, half-hidden by her flowing hair, with a roguish twinkle in her eye, pushed all else to the fringes. Including the weak pangs of conscience at the abhorrence of what he was about to do. It needed to be done. No one else would. Locksvillers? Kids with guns; thieves with an aversion to violence. And in this place and time, extreme violence was called for.

Staring straight into his eyes, he sauntered up to LeClaire. A contemptuous *what are you gonna do?* grimace twisted the man's mouth downward. Before anyone could react, Ajinder grabbed the man's right wrist and thrust his knife through it. The wall panel gave out a thud, muffled by the pinned hand. A moment later, the window rattled with the Buff's howl.

Ajinder squeezed LeClaire's throat and whispered, "Me? Just someone upset with your treatment of Miss Novak. Someone you didn't know you should not have upset. Now you do." The murkiness of pain and confusion filled the Buff's eyes, but Ajinder's grip on his neck didn't allow him to sag. "I thought I'd skip the threatening. Why waste time convincing you we should be taken seriously? For your sake, I hope this little demonstration is enough. Now, where is she?"

"You'll never find her!" Hysterical notes distorted the Buff's strangled voice.

Ajinder shook his head. "I was told you're some kind of local mastermind. How come you still aren't getting it? We are not here to search. We're here to convince *you* to take us to her. Think you're brave? Think again. There are many, many ways to inflict extreme yet non-lethal pain." He leaned closer, still holding LeClaire's eyes with his. "Everybody breaks," he added softly, faking a genial smile and wiggling his knife. "Everybody."

The Buff gasped, shivered, and resignedly closed his eyes. "I'll take you to her," he wheezed out.

"No monkey business?" Bo's voice trembled. So did his hands. Anger? Fear? On his own, the Locksviller would never have achieved the needed level of intimidation, try as he may. Ajinder's blade stuck through the Deputy Super- visor's palm made it an altogether different story.

"Can you...?" LeClaire slanted his eyes toward his impaled hand.

Ajinder yanked his knife out, extracting another growl of pain, wiped it on the Buff's shirt, and sheathed it. He stepped back, fished a rolled bandage out of his vest, and tossed it to LeClaire. The Buff scrambled to catch it with his left hand and missed. He kneeled, picked the roll, and proceeded to clumsily wrap it around his mutilated palm. Blood suffused the bandage, but a few additional wraps stopped the dripping. Panting, LeClaire struggled to tie down the end; no one offered to help. Ajinder caught Fox's appreciative gaze. Fox noticed and tipped an imaginary hat.

Ajinder slung his rifle behind his back, unholstering his pistol again. "Where to?" he asked.

LeClaire's shifty eyes refused to meet his. "The jail, of course. The basement level."

"You threw her *in jail*?!" Bo hissed, stepping closer and balling his fists.

Ajinder held him back. "Save your breath. Let's go."

He yanked LeClaire to his feet by the scruff, wrapped the crook of his elbow around the prisoner's throat, and pressed the handgun to his temple. "Lead the way, Deputy Supervisor. Oh, and, as Miss Novak's *sidekick* put so aptly, no monkey business, eh?"

Chapter 24

Buffalo

October 12, 42 PE

The pair of jailers in the basement were too easy to subdue. Pinky and Waffles herded them with half-hearted jabs into an empty cell and locked the door.

"Well?" Ajinder peered at LeClaire.

"All the way to the end."

The further they advanced down the corridor, the more jittery the captive grew. Had his fear finally outmatched the anger? Or... crap.

Ajinder stopped dead in his tracks and dragged LeClaire by the neck into a deserted cell. The Supervisor yelped and thrashed. Ajinder released him, only to deliver a backhand blow across the face that sent the man rolling on the concrete floor. Ajinder's heart beat steadily, at an elevated rate usual for combat, but with no spikes hinting at Aileen's close presence. Maybe it was his intuition.

"What's going on?" Urgency lowered Bo's voice.

Ajinder peeked into the corridor. "Aileen?" Nothing. Not even an echo. "Aileen!" he called louder. Still no response. He turned to the Buff cowering in the corner, nurturing his hand.

"She's not here." No question mark was required at the end of Ajinder's statement. He already knew the answer.

"Nope." A defiant smile stretched LeClaire's face.

"It's a trap."

"Yep. Thank you for voluntarily walking into my jail."

"You don't strike me as suicidal, LeClaire. Slick, clever—yes. Cunning? Maybe. But you're too narcissistic for self-sacrifice. You'd sell your mother to save your life. So, what gives?"

The Buff's smile morphed into a cornered wolf's grin. "You left me no choice, smartass."

Ajinder's nails bit into his palms. He'd never thought a plan could be *too good* to work.

"We can walk out the same way." Fox nervously squeezed his shotgun. "Who's to keep us here?"

"You'll find out soon enough."

"You're awfully smug for someone surrounded by six angry men," Waffles said, cracking his knuckles.

"Shut up, everyone." Bo leveled a heavy stare at the enemy. "Where is she?"

Aileen needed Ajinder's help, but he continued failing her. A dark cloud enveloped him, extinguishing all emotion and leaving cold, calculating logic. He dragged his knife against its sheath to produce a menacing rasp. "I'll start with an eye. What do you say, Bo?"

"Reasonably non-lethal. I knew a guy back in the day, One-eyed Jeev. He'd managed. An ugly motherfucker who broke my leg. Not as much of an asshole as this one here, though. Go ahead, make my day."

LeClaire's smile faded. "Now, wait a second—"

Ajinder was on top of him; the tip of his blade drew blood from the Buff's eyelid. "You think I'm joking?" He increased the pressure. "You think those are empty threats? Ask your hand."

"Okay, okay!" The Buff's cry flounced about the cell. "I'll tell you."

"M-hm." Ajinder didn't move the knife.

"I shipped her out to the countryside, for safekeeping." The words came gushing out. "I knew..."

"Yes?"

"I knew her brother would send someone to get her back, so I hid her away."

Ajinder sighed. "Countryside—where?"

LeClaire bit his broken lip, sucking the blood. Ajinder moved the blade, cutting deeper into the skin.

"Stop! I... If I tell you, you'll kill me. Let me take you to her myself."

"If you don't tell us, we'll kill you too, but slower. In the end, you'll wish you'd taken a quicker way out." Ajinder shrugged. "Your choice."

"Wait," said Bo. "I know. One of the Finger Lakes warlord domains, yes?"

The Buff's other eye widened.

"Aha." Bo nodded. "Springwater? Watkins?"

LeClaire jerked and grew still.

"Watkins." Bo's morose grimace dropped the temperature in the cell by a degree or two. "Lady Anna, huh? Well, fuck me sideways."

Ajinder glanced at him. "Someone you know?"

"It's complicated." Bo pressed his lips into a thin white line.

The prisoner started shaking. Ajinder withdrew the knife and slapped him. "Calm down. You get to live until we're out of here. Disarm your trap, whatever it is. Once we're in the clear, we *may* yet let you go."

"But—" Fox met Bo's gloomy frown and shut his mouth.

"Your last chance, Deputy Supervisor," Ajinder continued, as if uninterrupted. "Don't screw it up."

"This is Lieutenant Dawson of the Buffalo National Guard!" a bull-horn-amplified voice roared from the guard post. "Release Supervisor LeClaire and lay down your weapons!"

"Your trap?" Ajinder asked. A smile crept onto the Buff's bleeding lips.

"We can still kill you," said Bo.

"And never walk out of here alive." Smugness returned to LeClaire's face.

"Debatable." Ajinder shrugged. "We've got enough firepower to decimate your National Guard."

"Maybe. But they hold the choke point."

"Call them off."

"They won't listen. Standard operating procedure."

"Use him as a human shield," suggested Pinky.

"They'll shoot me, then you." The son of a bitch had an answer to everything. Well, damn.

Ajinder peeked behind the jamb and hurried to retreat inside. Bullets whizzed by. Frightened cries from other cells filled the corridor. Pogo sank to the floor, quivering and hugging his knees. Bo patted him on the head, causing the sock hat to slide onto Pogo's eyes. "Pogo's here to pick locks, not to shoot or get shot at," he responded to Ajinder's unasked question.

Ajinder smiled at the poor guy, hopefully encouragingly. "I gather none of you are gunfighters, yet here you all are. For Aileen." He pointed at LeClaire. "Pinky, knock him out."

"Gladly, boss."

Boss?

Bo, too, raised his eyebrows.

Ajinder turned the radio on. "Can you hear me?" The device remained quiet, save for low-level crackling. Ajinder depressed the button again. "Hello? Anyone?"

The longer the team looked at the unresponsive radio, the longer their faces grew. Until a voice cut in. "Go ahead. What's your status?"

Ajinder looked around at his worried but resolute men. "We've got a situation here. They've pinned us down in the Directorate basement."

"And the target?"

Ajinder ground his teeth. "Not here. In Watkins, presumably."

The silence crackled. The voice returned. "I'm with our mutual friend here." The Dragon must be back in Locksville, with Weinberg. "Turns out, The Station is full of surprises. Relief is on the way. May take a couple of hours. Stand by. Keep the radio on."

———————

Yet again, time crawled with the unwillingness of a snail drowned in molasses. At first, the Guardsmen had shown initiative. Fox, keeping the watch by the door with Ajinder's mirror, had caught their sneaky encroachment and met them with a generous buckshot dispensation. His potshots had left three soldiers dead or agonizing, with the rest hastily retreating. Later, the besieging force tried to rush the team. Half a belt of machinegun fire convinced them to reconsider, with five more bodies bleeding on the floor.

"Dawson!" bellowed Ajinder. "How many more will you sacrifice for this asshole? He isn't worth a single life!"

"Lay down your weapons and come out with your hands up!"

Ajinder hung his head. What a stubborn mule. He took a lungful of air. "Lieutenant... Scott! I told you, we've got no scores to settle with you or your men! We came for LeClaire, we've got him, there's no need to spill any more blood!"

"We don't negotiate with terrorists!"

"Terrorists?!" Pinky exploded. "Us?!" He leaned out of the door and sprayed the approaches with another burst of automatic fire.

"Hey!" Ajinder punched him in the stone-hard shoulder. "Stop this!"

Pinky took his finger off the trigger and stared at Ajinder. "But—"

"Conserve the ammo!" *Meathead* almost slipped his tongue.

"Uh, yes, boss. Sorry, boss. It's just, he called—"

"I heard that too, Pinky. It's unfortunate they see it that way, but shooting at them won't improve their opinion of us. Look at it from their point of view: we set off an explosion that cost the city half its windows, raided the Directorate, and took a hostage."

"Uh." Pogo scratched his neck. "So... we *are* terrorists?"

Great. Self-doubt, just what they needed. Ajinder mobilized all his persuasive power. "Of course not! We're here to free Aileen. No cause is nobler than that! *We* know this, they don't. Any collateral damage is on him." He pointed at the still unconscious form of LeClaire.

Convinced or not, none of his companions broached the subject again in the ensuing hours of viscous waiting, sprinkled with occasional chit-chat.

To break the depressing silence, Ajinder asked, "I've got to know, what's with all the nicknames?"

"It's a Streeters' thing," said Fox. Was there a challenge? Or just the pride of belonging to something bigger?

"Clearly. I get 'Fox'. I *think* I get 'Pinky'." Ajinder brought up his little finger. Pinky's joyous grin confirmed his theory. "But Pogo? Waffles?"

"It's confidential." Pogo blushed. "End of discussion." The rest of the Locksvillers giggled. Ajinder shrugged.

"And Waffles," said Fox, "once ate twenty waffles in one sitting. Made him famous. Was shitting squares for a week."

How imaginative... not. But it wasn't Ajinder's place to judge. These had been leading questions, anyway, giving him a segue to the more interesting exploration. "Awesome. And Bo?" He fixed the little Locksviller with an inquisitive stare.

Bo didn't flinch. "My real name. The only name I know. Odd enough that I don't need a nickname."

Odd enough indeed. Perhaps, a subject for a deeper—and more private—conversation, some other time. "What about Oscar? His actual name too?"

"Nope." Fox frowned, not hiding his dislike of his provisionary chief. "One day, he discovered the phonetic alphabet. Drove everyone crazy. His name starts with an O, so..."

"Right." It all fit the pattern. "And Aileen? Is that her real name?"

"Oh, yeah." Fox grew serious.

"She's plenty unique," said Bo quietly. "Aileen, there's only one."

The others nodded thoughtfully.

Yes. Oh, yes. Double, triple meaning. Uncountable meanings, and only one Aileen. Control the face. Ajinder looked into the corner, away from the Locksvillers...

... and met LeClaire's puffy eyes, groggy but awake. The man who'd taken Aileen from him, abused her, treated her as if she wasn't a person. Black hatred, such as he'd never experienced, rushed through his veins, boiling his blood, turning it into pure venom. In an instant, he was on his feet. In the next, the tip of his boot swung into the Buff's ribs. And again. And again. And then into the face, the disgusting face with the mouth opened in a mute cry. The mouth that personified all the evil in the world. The gaping gate to the Seven Hells that needed to be sealed forever. Yes. Yes.

Shouts at the limits of his hearing, beyond the booming pulse and the roaring rage, barely reached him. Several pairs of arms struggled to pull him away. He cursed them and fought back. He was on a mission to expunge evil, didn't they understand?!

His detractors prevailed. He lay on the floor, face down, immobilized by the weight of two or three people on top of him. "Easy, brother, easy," someone whispered into his ear. He turned toward the voice and found a familiar face. Bo, with tears standing in his eyes.

"Let me go," Ajinder asked levelly, back in the cell, back in the present. Bo looked up and waved a hand. With a grunt, the weight lifted off Ajinder's back. He pulled his arms and legs under him and sat. Pinky helped him up. Ajinder glanced at the corner where a pile of rags groaned and whimpered. *He* did *that*? He'd been prepared to kill that man, to stomp him to death. He would have, had he not been stopped. The worst part? Not a shade of regret. Another wave washed over him, this time—shame. What he'd done was wrong. Was supposed to be. Must have been. Yet he was still ready to do it again. "I needed him to bleed." The words rolled off his tongue of their own volition. He had to explain his actions; first and foremost, to himself. "I needed him hurting, concussed, puking his guts out, like she was. I needed him to pay for what he did to Aileen."

Bo put a hand on his shoulder. Pinky patted Ajinder's back, followed by Waffles and Pogo. In the doorway, Fox tipped his imaginary hat again.

"Ho ho, someone's sweet on Novak," the corner croaked. "A nice piece of ass, she is. Should've taken a sample when I had a chance."

Four sets of boots stepped toward LeClaire in unison. "Stop!" barked Bo. "He's provoking you to end him. He wants the easy way out. He won't get it, understood? I've got better plans for him."

"Hello there." A new voice, coming out of the thin air, startled everyone. "Hello?"

The radio! Ajinder fumbled to get it out. "Yes, we're listening!"

"Your ride is here."

Bo pried the device from Ajinder's hand. "Karim? You again?"

"Push the button on the side," Ajinder whispered.

Bo nodded and repeated, "Karim?"

"Yes, sir."

"Where are you?"

"Railroad tracks, a hundred meters west of the Directorate, give or take. We'll lay suppressive fire for you. And folks? I'd keep my head down, if I were you."

Ajinder and Bo exchanged puzzled looks. "I guess we'll find out shortly." Bo giggled nervously.

Ajinder took a deep breath to collect his disheveled thoughts. "Alright, boys. Here's the plan. Pinky, load a fresh belt. Go prone. On my signal, light them up. I'll pick off any heads that pop up. Then we rush them. Fox, that's your opportunity to shine. Blast away, but be mindful of our backs, eh? Waffles, take out the garbage." He pointed over his shoulder at LeClaire. "And Pogo, you keep Bo safe. Get ready." He watched the team take their places. With some training...

Upstairs, mayhem erupted. The sounds penetrated the concrete ceiling of the jail. Crashing, falling, breaking. Impacts, so many impacts. Dust powdered Ajinder's shoulders. Yells at the guard post related confusion and arguing.

Ajinder warily extracted a grenade from its pouch.

"What's that?" Pinky's curiosity trumped everything.

"A last-ditch measure, pal." Ajinder produced a crooked, cheerless smile. *And a year's worth of wages to buy me a ticket to the Seven Hells.* "Cover your ears!" He exhaled, pulled the pin out, and hurled the small, harmless-looking ball toward the exit. *Two. Three. Four.* The blast rocked the building. Bits and pieces of *something* blew past the cell entrance. More dust and plaster poured down. Ajinder's ears, though covered at the time of the explosion, rang. He tapped Pinky's shoulder. "Now!"

The big guy pushed the machinegun barrel into the corridor and opened fire. Ajinder peeked out above him, uncomfortably leaning his rifle on his bandaged hand. The guard post, now painted in red and white, filled the scope. A movement. A gun. Squeeze the trigger. Bang. Reload. More movement. Viper bucked in his hands again. Reload. Clear. Clear. "Clear! Okay, boys, let's go! Fox, rack that shotty! Go, go!"

Dawson lay amid the carnage and the rubble. Eviscerated, staring lifelessly into the ceiling, his arm with the ring finger two meters away. Stupid. Stupid, stupid, stupid. And sad. Ajinder's stomach churned, threatening to rebel at the sight of the surreal devastation. He called up an image of Aileen. These soldiers had stood between him and her freedom. He'd given them plenty of chances. They'd made their choice.

He peeked into the staircase and recoiled under a barrage of bullets. One hit the jamb inches from his face, showering him with splinters.

"Have more of those kaboom-thingies?" Pinky asked enthusiastically.

"I wish." Ajinder winced, pulling a sliver of wood from his forehead. "Fox, take care of them."

The Locksviller didn't move. The blood left his cheeks. Under everyone's stares, he blushed as quickly, pressed his lips tight, and resolutely squeezed past Ajinder. Near the door, he paused once more, shouldered the shotgun, and took a few deep breaths. Then with an ear-splitting, high-pitched "A-a-a-a!" jumped, head-first, into the staircase. He shot and racked in quick succession. Then clicked and racked, having run out of shells. Then bent over, leaning on his knees, and dry-heaved. Only his heavy breathing and the cluttering of the enemy's gun, sliding down the stairs, interrupted the ringing silence. That, and the firefight one floor above. Fox straightened, reloaded the tube magazine with his shaking fingers, and started climbing up.

"Foxy, you beast!" Pinky rumbled. "Well done!"

"Don't call me that," Fox retorted, panting.

Pinky turned to Ajinder, and his face wrinkled with concern. "You're bleeding, boss."

Ajinder wiped his cheek. Red smeared the once white bandage on the back of his hand. "Meh. It's nothing."

"No, not that. Your arm."

Ajinder touched his left shoulder and jerked his hand away, hissing. When did that happen? The bullet that had grazed his muscle cauterized the wound. It bled a little, but hurt like a son-of-a-bitch. His gaze fell on Bo, thrashing on the floor. "Go, cover Fox!" He shoved Pinky into the stairwell and rushed back to Bo's side. "Is he hit?" he yelled at Pogo, who was violently retching.

"N-no." Pogo wiped traces of barf off his chin. "What, you don't know?"

"Know what? Speak!"

"Bo's got this... *thing*... He checks out when there are dead bodies around. Or violence."

"What?" Ajinder frowned and shook his head. This made no sense. Although... The small signs he'd kept discarding snapped into an explanation now. But shit, the timing, it couldn't be worse. "Grab his other hand!"

They climbed the stairs with Bo dangling between them, shaking and keening, eyes rolled up. Waffles trailed behind, dragging a semi-conscious LeClaire. Pogo gagged when they skirted the dead Buff stretched on the steps, with a bloody mess where his chest and jaw had been. Ajinder met the stare of the glassy eyes. *Sorry, man. This didn't need to happen.* Another body to feed his nightmares.

Pinky and Fox secured the ground level door, but no one was challenging them. The sounds of the firefight were coming from the main entrance.

"Who are they shooting at?" Ajinder asked.

Fox spread his arms. "My guess is as good as yours, boss. Must be those folks on the radio."

The radio! "Karim?" Ajinder called. "We'll be exiting through the north side. Don't shoot us."

"Hurry, sir," came the response, with a steady pounding of automatic fire and whining of ricochets in the background. "It's getting a bit too hot for comfort here."

Ajinder led the team out through the window they'd used to enter the building lifetimes ago. They took the street parallel to the one abutting the

Directorate's doors and came up on a railroad crossing two blocks to the west. "We're at the tracks," he updated the radio and checked on Bo. The kid grew quiet, but hadn't regained his senses yet. "Will come to you from the north."

"Stay where you are, sir. We'll pick you up."

"Uh, okay." Ajinder pointed to Fox, Pinky, and Waffles. "Protective perimeter." They didn't know the drill, but improvised well enough.

The railroad. Did the Stationers bring a train here? Under fire? The haulers would all be dead in under a minute! *The Station is full of surprises.*

A cloud of smoke rose above the buildings. Another distraction? The vibrating ground announced the approach of something heavy. Then came the sound. Ajinder held his breath. Nothing he was familiar with sounded like *that*. An enormous growling monstrosity showed up, puffing and fuming through a tall pipe. No haulers. Hitched to it was a railcar, all covered in metal plates with countless bullet impact pockmarks. Smoking machinegun barrels bristled from narrow slits. One of them issued a long burst until a building obscured the train from the Directorate.

The engine slowed down and stopped. A thick steel door opened in the side of the armored car. A wide white smile lit Karim's grimy face. "Well met, gentlemen. Hop on!"

"Pick up your jaw, lout," Bo muttered at Ajinder's side.

"Back to the land of the living?" Ajinder lifted the kid by the armpits and passed him on to Karim in an utterly undignified way.

"Get on, get on!" a frantic shout from inside the train whipped up the tension. "They're closing in!" Another burst of fire underscored the urgency.

Ajinder hauled balking LeClaire up, then helped the rest of his team. *His team*, yeah. Funny how they all came around to call him 'boss'. He climbed up last, wincing when his shot-up shoulder reminded him it required attention.

Karim grunted, shutting the heavy door and throwing the latch on, then turned and shook Ajinder's hand. "Well done, Mister Singh. One day, you'll be telling your children about this raid, and they'll think half of it is a tall tale."

"There's a thought. But to have children, I must first rescue their mother."

Chapter 25

Rochester

October 12, 42 PE

Ajinder sat up with a start, gasping for air. His heart pounded against his ribcage, desperate to break free. Sweat drenched his clothes, trickling down his back, inviting the night's chill while burning the wound on his bandaged shoulder. He stared into the darkness, seeing nothing. Had he gone blind?! Shadows shifted around him. Phew. *This* darkness was just a lack of light. And it *moved*, taking him with it. It shook, grunted, and squeaked. It had a heart of its own, enormously loud and powerfully beating. Oh. Right. The Station's armored, fire breathing train. Moving on its own, powered by an *engine*. What a time to be alive!

But the weird reality failed to offset the horror of his too vivid memories. The nightmares clung to him, refusing to let go. He'd been chain-dreaming. Dream after dream after dream, each worse than the other. As always after a kill. Over time, he'd grown to fear sleeping more than fighting. In a fight, what was the worst that could happen? He'd die. That would be a tragedy for his family and the Clan, but *he* wouldn't be there to care. His soul would shed its mortal shell, to be reincarnated in another one. Ajinder didn't seek death, yet had made his peace with its inevitability. His dreams were infinitely worse. He'd never killed without a reason, but they deprived him of any opportunity to rationalize his actions. His targets—vile as they'd been—had claimed their victimhood, and tugged at the strings of his conscience. They took their vengeance by weaponizing his dreams, stacking everything upside down and turning him into the villain.

"Murderer!" they'd clamor, parading their wounds, clawing at him, baring their teeth, chasing him down the endless labyrinths of the Seven Hells. And he would run like a coward, letting their accusations burn scorched holes through his back.

This time, Dawson was there too, holding his severed arm in the other hand, waving it in the air like a club, tripping on his own entrails. His nameless soldiers marched behind him, stern and determined, spraying blood in every direction. LeClaire's aide followed, plugging the hole in his forehead with his finger and unleashing an endless fusillade at Ajinder from a handgun.

With a shaking hand, Ajinder brought his canteen to his cracked lips and gulped the stale water to wet his parched throat. He was a warrior, a protector. He'd never taken an innocent life. All his kills had been good kills. Then why...?

"Damn, man," said Bo's disembodied voice nearby, "you slept, like, ten hours in a row."

Damn? Very apt. If his nightmares kept extending with the list of his kills, one day he simply wouldn't wake up. Ten hours! *Wait, what?*

"Ten hours? Where are we?"

"Approaching Rochester, I would hope."

"Rochester? We aren't returning to Locksville? To The Station?"

"Nope."

Pressure he hadn't noticed lifted off Ajinder's shoulders.

"Good." He sighed with relief. "Don't know why Rochester, of all places, but going back would've felt like defeat."

"I checked the maps. It's the closest we can get to the Finger Lakes by rail. There are other reasons too."

"Such as?"

"You'll see. If they pan out."

"I don't like the sound of that."

"We've got nothing to fear. This war machine we're in, it's a game changer. Unstoppable, until it runs out of fuel."

"Or ammo."

"Knowing Marc, he'd packed it with all the ammo and firepower he could scrounge at The Station. Say whatever you want about him, but he learns his lessons."

"What are you talking about?"

"This is The Station's *second* engine train. The first one was supposed to take me to New Kowloon. The Zealots burned it."

"Oh."

"Yeah. Karim had lost his entire team there."

"Not making the same mistake twice," confirmed the darkness in Karim's grim voice. "Their day will come. We'll purge that scourge, mark my words."

Ajinder shut his useless eyes. The world was changing. The Station's powered trains; Shang Ka Yi's self-propelled flagship; Farley's—or Weinberg's?—speedboat. Engines were making a comeback everywhere. There were rumors about a treasure trove of knowledge Yun-mi had brought to New Kowloon. The political landscape was shifting too, as Jihan had warned him. Over the winter, the Clan must reassess... pretty much, everything. But all that would have to wait to be processed. The change in *his* world left no space for anything else. His need to see Aileen grew overwhelming, clouded only by one question: would she feel the same?

<hr>

October 13, 42 PE

The train's wheels screeched, and it ground to a halt.

"Rochester, sir!" came a call from somewhere out front.

Karim lit a lamp and rose to his feet. Ajinder squinted, blinded by the light. "Now what?"

Bo shrugged. "Now we wait for the welcome party. It must be three in the morning. No chance they missed our arrival. I bet the entire city is up, scratching their heads, guessing *what* we are." He stood up and stretched. "Karim? Coming?"

Ajinder stayed inside, pushing his rifle's barrel through a porthole. He'd be more useful as the overwatch. At the squeal of the door hinges, soldiers around Ajinder came to life, checking their machineguns, scratching, yawning, farting, and exchanging single-syllable interjections. Hopefully, they had enough discipline drilled into them not to aim their weapons anywhere near their commander and the Locksviller. On second thought... "Gunners, I've got the meeting point, you cover the approaches. And don't forget the far side." Better safe than sorry.

His request was met with underbreath grumbling, but no one objected.

"What about us?" Pinky bassed into Ajinder's ear.

Ajinder recoiled and bumped his head against the metal wall. "Don't do that!"

"Do what?"

"Sneak up on me!"

"Sorry, boss. So?"

Ajinder sighed. "Nothing. Check your gear, take a piss, stay calm, and await instructions."

Before long, human shapes moved through the passage between the nearest warehouses. "Got company," announced Ajinder. "Platoon-sized. Hold your fire."

Karim's lamp created a small illuminated bubble amid the sea of blackness. Bo and Karim waited in its center. Two figures approached. One stepped into the light, the other stopped behind and to a side, on the border of the shadow. The weak lamp didn't lend enough lighting to distinguish the details of their faces, but their neutral, non-threatening postures were clear enough.

"Hello," said the one in the front. "What is this? Who are you?"

"Hello, uh, Lieutenant?" Bo waved, politely and a bit childishly.

"Captain Rockwell."

"Captain, I need to talk to Niem."

The officer stiffened. "Commander Nieminen does not look kindly on having his nighttime rest disturbed without a reasonable cause." In a less officious, almost quizzical tone, he added, "Gentlemen, you realize it is half past three, don't you?"

"Captain," replied Bo, matching the tone, "a combined Locksville-Station team has honored your city with its presence, having arrived on an engine-powered armored train. You realize that's enough of a reason any time of the day, don't you?"

Ajinder chuckled. Classical Bo.

The captain still hesitated. "Are you sure this can't wait till the morning?"

"We're on a clock, Captain. If nothing else wakes Commander up, tell him we've come here straight from Buffalo, bearing gifts from its ransacked Directorate."

The Roch saluted. "Very well, sir. I'll see what I can do." Even with the little light the lamp provided, his white-toothed grin was unmistakable.

"Gotta love it when he wraps them around his finger," snickered Fox on Ajinder's left.

"How?" breathed Pinky on his right. "How does he do it?"

"Audacity," said Ajinder. "And balls the size of your fist."

"Ah," Pinky came across uncharacteristically thoughtful, "that explains those baggy trousers."

Ajinder laughed into his mustache. These kids might yet grow on him.

An authoritative man marched brusquely into the light, trailed by Captain Rockwell. "This better be good. You are...?"

"Bo. Locksville Streeters."

Commander—that must have been him—nodded. "I've heard of you." His eyes lingered on Karim, then took in the train. "You've got my attention, Bo. What have you got for me, and what is it you want?"

Bo fished a stack of papers out of his backpack. "A token of our goodwill, Commander Nieminen." Karim picked up the lamp and brought it closer, shedding light on the documents.

The Roch unhurriedly ruffled through them. When he looked up, his face, now clearly visible, bore a perplexed expression. "This is quite unexpected, Bo. How did these files end up in your possession?"

"I helped myself to Deputy Supervisor LeClaire's archive."

"Did you, now? I wonder what he had to say about your taking such liberties."

"Nothing, Commander. He was otherwise preoccupied."

"It's all extraordinarily intriguing, Bo, and I've got many questions, including"—his eyes flicked to the train—"your use of this abomination. But first I have to ask: why bring these to me?"

"The enemy of my enemy—"

"Rochester Confederation and Buffalo Union are not enemies." A cunning smile undermined the stern tone of the officious rebuke.

"Of course not, Commander, apologies. Let me rephrase. The *rival* of my enemy is my natural partner. I need something from you."

"Go on."

"My team and I require transportation—ideally, with an escort—to Ithaca. And a letter to His Excellency Terrence the Second, requesting his assistance."

Nieminen took a moment before responding. "What kind of assistance might you need from him?"

Bo squared his shoulders. "A raid on Watkins Glen."

The Roch threw his mane back. "That's a big ask. You're obviously familiar with the alliances' disposition in that neck of the woods. Don't know how, but more credit to you." He waved the roll of papers in his hand. "This wasn't a mere gesture, after all."

"It certainly was, Commander. Now, if you're asking for adequate compensation, I've got a more sizable contribution to your cause. It's somewhat sensitive, though, so before we proceed, I've got to confirm: do you trust every single soldier in the cordon out there?"

"If I didn't know any better, I would've been offended, Bo. Or alarmed. But... Rockwell, send them one block back."

Bo turned to the train. "Pinky, bring our guest."

Pinky stomped to the far end of the car, returned with LeClaire in tow, and pushed him through the door. Pinky's "Oops!" coincided with a heavy thud of a body hitting the ground. He dragged the prisoner into the light, and the Roch's eyes widened with recognition. He opened his mouth and closed it, like a fish.

"Full disclosure, Commander," Bo said, "he's a little worse for wear, but still in good working condition. Perfectly tenderized to answer your questions."

"This," muttered Nieminen, "puts me in an extremely delicate situation, Bo."

Bo's laughter was the last sound Ajinder expected to hear. "That's why I suggested limiting the number of witnesses, Commander. The Buffs know only that The Station's retribution force had raided the Directorate and captured the Deputy Supervisor. No one would ever look for him here."

"Retribution, huh?"

"A long story, Commander, which I'm sure LeClaire would be happy to retell. For all I care, you're free to squeeze him for every bit of information, and make him disappear."

"You'll pay for this, you mangled little shit!" LeClaire must've regained enough lucidity to realize what was going on.

Pinky's fist connected with the Buff's ribs, and he choked on the rest of his tirade.

"A generous offer, Bo. I believe I've got a certain amount of retribution to exact myself." LeClaire shrunk under Nieminen's unsympathetic gaze. "You've got yourself a deal. Rockwell, see to it. I'll draft a letter for Terrence."

Fox pulled Bo into the car. "Holy smokes, Bo, that was pure awesomeness!"

"Yeah," added Ajinder, "pretty badass."

"What can I say?" Bo humbly cast his eyes down, but a grin split his face from ear to ear. "I'm damn good at this." He patted Karim's arm. "This was a fun ride, Karim. Pleasure as always. Safe travels home! Hope you've got enough fuel and ammo to get you there."

"Fuel—just barely, but ammo to spare."

"Something tells me Weinberg will be amenable to help. Say hello for me, would you? Oh, and if Shang Ka Yi is still there..." Bo sighed. "Pass him my thanks, too. He and his wife are off the hook."

"Said a mouse to a dragon," narrated Ajinder under his breath. Then, louder, "And Karim? Tell Marc we're going to get her. Come Hells or high water!"

Part 4

THE SECOND

BOOK

OF AILEEN

Chapter 26

Watkins Glen

October 12, 42 PE

The scenery outside the window changed too lethargically to provide a distraction. The soft swaying of the stagecoach and the rhythmical creaking of its springs had lulled Aileen into a bored apathy.

After leaving Buffalo with the dawn the day before, Richard and she had quickly exhausted all conversation topics. Frustratingly, Aileen had failed to push his buttons. The trader remained stern, refusing to engage in small talk, and impervious to flattery. Her subtle probing into his greediness had imploded, ruling out bribery, and his disapproving glare seared her for hinting at defection. She asked Richard to tell her about his daughter, hoping to establish a rapport she'd be able to broaden and exploit, but instead of lightening up, he turned away, sulking.

Aileen stared at him until he couldn't ignore her anymore.

"What?" His deep-set eyes flashed in the shadow of his brows.

Aileen furrowed her bandaged forehead. Her misery had cut through his armor before. If only she could reproduce the same conditions... without being beaten up or concussed. And without threats of rape. "Help me, Richard. Please." Her lips quivered, and voice broke perfectly.

The trader gnashed his teeth and leaned close to her. His dilated pupils brimmed with anger.

Aileen recoiled. She'd provoked a reaction alright, just not the reaction she needed.

"What do you want me to do?" he growled. "Ah? What? Take on our armed guards?" His thumb pointed through the window. "Put my family in danger? I've stood up for you once, and it cost me dearly." He took a few noisy, heaving breaths. "Stop trying to manipulate me. I've been doing this forever, long enough to forget the tricks you haven't even learned yet."

Aileen averted her eyes first. That was a resounding defeat. A complete fiasco. She shivered and drew her knees to her chest, pulling the sheep skin tighter around herself. Between the ubiquitous drafts and the chills in her soul, she couldn't stop shaking.

She was an impostor. How in the Seven fiery Hells had she become an Aunt? Worse yet, how had she persuaded herself she was legitimately worthy? On the heels of the Troubles, reeling from the shock, the Streeter factions had seen what they wanted to see. She'd been a young, energetic crew leader who'd worked miracles at a time of crisis. She'd carried no baggage: no allegiances, no feuds, no strings to pull. An ideal candidate to become a neutral mediator. After that, she had done her best to maintain the right image. The aura of her title, fueled by the solid legacy of her predecessor, had taken care of the rest. She'd been so convincing, she herself believed in her prowess and influence. Until now, when her eyes were forced open, painfully, to the fact she was nothing but *a sister of*. A self-important, boisterous fraud. Her skills, purportedly sufficient for the small, quiet pond of the Locksville Streeters' bubble, had proven woefully inadequate to the harsh, unimpressed outside world.

Aileen sobbed.

Richard groaned. "Again? Haven't we been through this?"

He couldn't know that this time it was for real.

Abducted—twice!—and abused, disenchanted and devastated. Away from the only home she'd known, from the few people who'd cared about her. Alone.

Anguish sneaked past her crumbling defenses and gripped her heart so ruthlessly, she gave in and burst into weeping.

"Hey. Hey, stop it." Richard frowned, helpless and taken aback. "Please don't. Aileen!"

But she was inconsolable, bawling, smearing tears and snot over her face.

In the afternoon, Aileen had quieted down. For the following day, they traveled in depressing silence—until meeting the two mounted Watkins guardsmen who joined her escort on its way to their capital.

Aileen had accepted the inevitable: their cavalcade was not turning back. Her next steps would have to be planned at the destination. Small, powerless steps those would be, commensurate to her puny abilities. But hey, better than sitting on her butt doing nothing. She could not abide *that*, no matter what.

"Watkins!" announced the local rider, his giddy shout full of pride—and relief. Understandable, if the best you've got is a bow and arrows against the three accompanying Buffs' automatic rifles and bullets. It wasn't supposed to be *against*, if she'd gotten the lay of those alliances correctly, but such disparity would make even a close ally uncomfortable.

Her understanding didn't earn the Watkiners any sympathy. They were to become her jailers, after all.

Aileen surveyed the settlement through the window. *This?* This god-forsaken backwater was her new home away from home? Where she would spend the winter? Oh, fuck. Well, at least it was picturesque.

Richard's scowl reflected her musings.

"Curb your enthusiasm, eh?" Aileen cackled mirthlessly.

The trader tried to stare her down, but this time was the first to break eye contact.

"Ah, guilty conscience." Aileen nodded with fake thoughtfulness.

He threw his head up, meeting her mocking regard. "You've got no idea what you're talking about, girl."

"No? I seem to vaguely remember you being present for my abduction. But," she shrugged, "I could be hallucinating. You know, concussion and all."

Red splotches covered Richard's face, but he stoically withstood her charge. "I spoke against that."

"Much good that did me."

"Much good that did *me*."

"Oh?"

"You know why I'm here?"

"To be my chaperone, I imagine."

"I was—" He snapped his mouth shut as the stagecoach came to a stop. "Never mind."

Gawkers poured out at the covered entrance to a sprawling four-story lakeside mansion. A handful of kids gathered across the road, pointing at the Buffs and their rifles. Rounded eyes, gaping mouths. Pure awe. Ah, the pastoral backcountry.

Aileen jumped out of the stagecoach. Richard followed, searching for someone in charge.

A ripple tore the crowd, and it parted into two uneven lines. A pompous man, dressed in a dizzying array of reds, yellows, and greens, marched down the middle with an air of utmost importance. "All hail Her Ladyship Anna, Countess of Great Watkins and Odessa, Baroness of Elmira, Protectress of Corning, Rightful Heiress to the Throne of Ithaca!" The butt of his staff hit the ground with a loud crack, and everyone around bent in deep bows. Everyone besides Aileen, Richard, and their Buffalo escort.

The herald's face darkened. He locked eyes with the trader and opened his mouth to bark at the impudent foreigners, but an energetic woman, in her late twenties or early thirties, emerged from the building and strode past him, punching him in the shoulder. "That's enough, Lawrence. Our guests are overflowing with the requisite awe and admiration. Aren't you, guests?" She graced them with a charming curving of her lips.

Her hair, black as a raven's wing, set off the woman's pale skin. A dark green dress, tasteful and undoubtedly expensive, complimented her figure. It also matched her eyes, inquisitive and teasing, which scanned the Buffs and paused on Aileen.

Aileen stuck out her tongue.

Lady Anna frowned dramatically, but her eyes laughed.

Under different circumstances, Aileen could have liked this countess. Unfortunately, the circumstances being what they were, the woman was an enemy combatant. She just didn't know that yet.

"Greetings from Buffalo, Your Ladyship." Richard's velvety baritone was irresistibly ingratiating, but he was an enemy, too. They all were. Every single one, to the last lousy kid lurking in the bushes.

"Buffalo, huh?"

"I am Senior Trader Maynard, the new Trade Representative at Your Ladyship's exalted Court."

"Exalted? You have a way with words, Senior Trader. Welcome to Watkins! Would this be your wife? Accompanying you to witness the widely famous wonders of our exalted Court?" She winked at Aileen.

Richard's face turned severe. "This is Miss... Newman, Your Ladyship. On behalf of the Government of Buffalo, I am humbly requesting Watkins County to grant her temporary asylum and protection."

Son of a bitch. Depriving her of everything, including her name. She'd make this straight, in good time.

The countess took another measure of Aileen. Aileen shook her head and mouthed a voiceless, "No." Last chance for the locals. Anna's frown grew genuine, and she returned her attention to the Buff. "Your arrival shows that the ties of friendship and respect between our nations are stronger than ever, Trader Maynard. I accept your request and look forward to expanding our cooperation. Please come in and enjoy our hospitality."

Aileen's eyelids slid down. Shit. The hard way it was.

Richard extended a hand to her. How gentlemanly. She stared at it as if it were a venomous snake.

"Don't make a scene." The Buff's insistent whisper was pathetic.

"Fuck off, Ricky," she murmured with her most enchanting smile. "I am not your daughter."

She could as well have slapped him. The Buff winced. Blood vacated his face, and his arm dropped limply. He turned away, facing the hostess. Good, that needed to be said. But the man had a point: introducing herself with a scandal wouldn't endear her to Anna's *exalted* court, and being an outcast would make it difficult to manipulate anyone.

Aileen boldly stepped in front of brooding Richard and inclined her head. "Your Ladyship." Let her think Aileen was more important than a Senior Trader.

The countess eyed her favorably and gestured to her retinue. "Marie, take Miss Newman to the Commodore suite. Make sure she's comfortable. Miss Newman, Marie is at your full disposal. Kate, you handle Mister Maynard's accommodations, suite 316. I'll see you both at dinner in... three hours? Yes, that should do." She ushered the guests inside. Richard dismissed the Buffalo escort and headed to the entrance. His maid followed with his suitcase.

"Excuse me, my lady..." Marie clutched her apron. "Where is your baggage?"

Aileen put her hands on her hips. "Yes, Trader Maynard, indeed, where is my baggage?"

"Uh." Richard's discomfited expression was heartwarming. "Miss Newman had to leave in a hurry. She traveled light. Perhaps Her Ladyship's household could lend her a change of clothes? We'll go shopping first thing tomorrow."

"Shopping?" Countess Anna snickered. "This isn't Buffalo, Senior Trader. Here, we have our clothes tailored. But not to worry, Miss Newman will want for nothing."

Her scrutinizing attention reminded Aileen she wasn't exactly dressed for court appearances, even by these boonies' standards. Or maybe especially by their standards. Shapeless dark-blue Kowloonese coveralls; thick plaid shirt, seedy and washed too many times; ugly work boots of an indeterminate color... Aileen had never cared for trendy looks. Her life as a Streeter had ensured a steady supply of higher-priority problems. Her clothes had to be functional and, preferably, clean. Anything beyond that was superfluous. She wasn't ashamed now either. But if she wanted to fit in, she had to look the part. Presentable, at least.

"Don't worry, sweetheart," the countess touched Aileen's sleeve, as if she'd read her mind. *Sweetheart.* Yikes. "You and I wear a similar size. At the dinner, you'll dazzle the audience with garments worthy of a queen! And we'll definitely need to do something about this god-awful headscarf."

Headscarf? Oh, crap. The bandage. If Countess Anna was serious, she was dumb as a rock, or... She wasn't. The mischief in the corners of her eyes was unmistakable. What a relief.

The two maids led the way up the stairs. At the third floor, Kate opened and held the door for Richard while Marie continued her ascent.

"Wait." The Buff froze at the landing. "Our rooms aren't nearby?"

"A man, staying on Her Ladyship's level?" His maid giggled and blushed. "That would be improper, sir."

With a concerned grimace, the trader watched Aileen eluding him. Moments before the next flight of stairs concealed her, she flipped him a finger. Childish, but those small joys were going to help preserve her sanity through the long, long winter. She didn't linger to observe his reaction.

An involuntary moan escaped Aileen.

If going home wasn't an option, this bathtub filled with scalding water was where she wanted to spend the rest of her life. The foam popped with a whisper too delicate to be real, tickling her senses and adding an extra dimension to the experience. Marie, murmuring a cheerful song under her breath, scrubbed Aileen's back, working around her bruises and abrasions.

"Tell me about life in Buffalo, my lady."

Damn it. Did every moment worth savoring have to be spoiled? "I wouldn't know where to begin. What do you want to know?"

"Oh, everything! I've never been to a city, my lady. Traveled to Odessa once, but I guess that doesn't count."

A reasonable assumption, judging by the fact Aileen had first heard the name half an hour ago, among Countess Anna's other titles.

"It's, ah, big. And disgusting. And full of ugly, greedy, untrustworthy people. You're lucky to have never been there, Marie."

"My lady?" The sponge stopped. "You're saying the most awful things. It can't be all that bad!"

"That has been my personal experience." Sweet vengeance, one poisoned mind at a time.

Marie resumed the scrubbing, but without the humming. "Your bruises," she asked after a while, "are they... from Buffalo? Is that why you fled?"

Better keep it simple. "Yes."

"Sorry to hear, my lady."

"Word of advice? Never trust a Buff, Marie."

"I'll keep that in mind, my lady. But... you're a Buff, too."

Smart girl. "I am not."

"Beg your pardon, my lady? How can that... You came with... Where *are* you from?"

Aileen smiled enigmatically. "Maybe I'll tell you later." Let the word spread. Let the backrooms buzz with speculations. Let Her Ladyship ask uncomfortable questions, and let Ricky wriggle like a worm in a frying pan. Aileen peered at Marie, challenging her to further inquiries which she'd flat-out refuse to answer.

Marie bit on the corner of her lip, twisting her asymmetric face even more. Neither beautiful nor homely, with medium-length wiry hair an indeterminate shade of brown, she would have been unremarkable—if not for the quick, curious eyes. Plus, any time she opened her mouth, Aileen found it difficult to resist her fleeting yet undeniable charm.

Marie's struggle with curiosity was impressively short. She put the sponge aside and took a comb. "Love your hair, my lady." Unremarkable, charming, *and* smart. Huh.

"Apologies, this may hurt a little." Marie examined the tips of Aileen's hair. "It's so tangled."

Yeah, no kidding. The events of the last couple of days hadn't facilitated her usual grooming habits. Coal dust, congealed blood...

All thoughts vanished from Aileen's head. The comb's teeth against her scalp touched something far deeper. The world span, and her luxury suite faded.

She was a little girl again; seven, maybe eight. Sitting in a shallow basin, scooping up lukewarm water with her cupped palms and splashing it on her goosebump-covered, skinny knees. "Mom, I'm cold!"

Mom kept working the comb. "Let me finish brushing your magnificent hair, and we'll be all done."

"But mom? Why can't I use the tub? I don't want to wash in this teeny-tiny bowl anymore. See? I don't fit into it! I've grown!"

"I'm sorry, honey. We'd need lots of water to fill the tub, and we don't have enough fuel to heat it up. Your brother washes in this basin just like you. Your father and I, too."

"Mommy?"

"Yes, pumpkin?"

"Who brushes your hair when you wash?"

"I brush it myself, love."

"May I do it next time?"

Mom's gentle smile brightened the cramped washroom more than the drowsy oil lamp ever could. "Of course, honey. So great to have another grown woman at home!"

Aileen giggled. Their home was the best. Even when they didn't have enough hot water. Because she had the best mom and the best dad, and even Marc, the annoying monster, could be not so bad sometimes.

"My lady?" The words, weak and distant, did not belong in her old washroom. "My lady? Are you alright?" Louder this time, the question pulled her away—from the shallow basin with the cold water, from the dim light of the sooty lamp; from mom; from home; from the happy childhood memory that she hadn't known she'd kept.

Aileen opened her eyes. Her cheeks were wet, and not from the bathwater.

"Why are you crying, my lady? Something I did? Or said?"

Aileen vehemently shook her head, blinking and swallowing the lump in her throat. "No, Marie, you did nothing wrong." Her voice wavered. "Please brush me some more."

"Of course, my lady, with pleasure!"

Aileen slid down into the spacious bathtub until the water, hot and deep, covered her up to her neck. Pampered like a fairytale princess. Awarded a breathtaking view of the narrow lake, stretching into the distance behind the glass doors and painted pink by the sunset rays. Called "my lady." About to dine with royalty. And yet... She would have given all this up in a heartbeat, to return to that dank and chilly washroom on the outskirts of Locksville.

Cinderella? Fuck, yeah, on her way to a royal ball! Aileen turned away from the mirror wall. "What do you think?" She twirled left and right, letting the hem lift off and wrap around her legs.

No response was necessary. Awe, with a smidgen of jealousy, was plainly written on Marie's face. "Breathtaking, my lady. All men will want you, and all women will hate you for that."

"Perfect."

Aileen examined her reflection from one side, from another—and liked what she saw. Her hair was collected into a crown-like French braid, running down one shoulder. A few slanted strands artfully covered the powdered patch on her forehead, hiding the cut and the angry bump. Lady Anna's purple dress had turned out to be the right length, but too wide at the waist and too narrow at the chest. The first problem had been solved in no time by a deft seamstress and a broad black leather belt. The second... Aileen had let Marie convince her it wasn't a problem. This resulted in the most revealing, risqué neckline Aileen had ever worn. A massive silver pendant ensured no one would miss that. She was hotter than the Seven Hells' scorching fires! And no glass slippers, phew.

Never lacking in men's interest, Aileen had taken it for granted. Going through extra motions to boost her appearances was a vain waste of time. She'd been perfectly fine with her cargo pants and hoodies. But this... this was a novel experience. A *woman* looked back from the mirror. Not an authoritative

Aunt. Not a tomboy Streeter. Nor a *sister*. A woman in her own right, with her womanhood brazenly weaponized. Likely overkill, but to Hells with that. She owed it to herself to test-fire it once.

Lady Anna's stance on geopolitics—and pretty much everything else—remained to be determined, and chances were, she'd soon climb to the top of Aileen's list of enemies. But at this moment, admiring the ravishing stranger in the mirror, Aileen was grateful to Her Ladyship for helping her discover *this* side of herself.

Now, what veneer should she wear?

Beam like a hick who's honored to be invited and happy to mingle with such a distinguished society? Too much, too fake. She had just arrived from a major metropolis. No one would buy into that act.

A slack, expressionless mask, to show how little she cared to be there? Rude. And scary. They might decide she was a psycho killer. Not necessarily a bad thing, but she hadn't begun building the bridges yet; too soon to burn them.

Aileen settled for a guarded smile. It hinted at mysterious knowledge she may or may not have. Perfect.

"Well, I'll be!"

Aileen spun around.

Lady Anna strolled into the room in a cloud of cloying perfume, followed by two haughty maids of honor. She wore an indigo dress similar to Aileen's but far more conservative, a shining tiara, and a good few pounds of other jewelry. "I knew there was more hidden under those hideous rags and grime. Isn't she a doll?" The countess leaned her ear to one of her followers.

"She is, Your Ladyship. An absolute doll." The woman's hostile squint starkly contrasted with her meek words.

Anna wiggled her finger in a circular motion. Aileen obeyed, completing a full turning.

"Stunning!" The countess clapped. "You're rocking this dress. I have to admit, Miss Newman, you're wearing it better than I ever have."

"Your Ladyship!" the second courtier objected, but the countess silenced her with a sharp gesture and a flicker of annoyance.

"Marie, you outdid yourself today. I am pleased." Anna nodded to Aileen's maid.

"Thank you, Your Ladyship." The girl bowed in a reverent curtsy.

"Lady Anna?" Aileen had to know. "This is beyond my wildest expectations. Why are you treating me so well?"

"The alliance with the Buffalo Union is the cornerstone of our foreign policy. Any guest from Buffalo is a guest of honor, and this is the least I can do." Was Anna's proclamation a bit too solemn? "Now leave us. All of you, scoot."

The three maids withdrew at the dismissive wave of the countess's hand. The door quietly closed.

Lady Anna crossed her arms over her chest. Her radiant smile morphed into an ironic one. "These hens already despise you. Imagine how much they'll hate you when they see their suitors drooling over you."

"Was that your plan all along?" Alone with the hostess, Aileen judged honorifics unnecessary. The countess didn't seem to mind. "To isolate me until you piece together Buffalo's play?"

Lady Anna's green eyes peered into Aileen's. Aileen met the scrutiny neutrally, even ambivalently. Her challenge had already been laid at the woman's feet.

Anna nodded. "Too astute. Who are you, Miss Newman? Who are you, really, and why are you here?"

"I cannot answer those questions yet."

"I'm trying to decide how to react to this." The countess brought a finger to her jaw. "I could say, 'How dare you!' Or even, 'I could make you.' But let's start with 'What needs to happen for your answer to change?'"

This woman was good. And, coincidentally, an absolute monarch of this strip of the land, with Aileen entirely at her mercy.

Aileen took Anna's hands in hers. The countess's brows arched, but Aileen ignored that. "I am grateful for your hospitality, Lady Anna. You extended it without knowing the first thing about me. I don't know how I can repay you for that."

"I'd barter for honesty," the hostess muttered, with that heavy irony again.

"I..." Aileen lost her train of thought.

"I can tell you aren't too experienced in this whole smarm thing. Skip that part. And, for your information, touching the sovereign is usually frowned upon. Deeply. Corporal punishment is not out of the question."

"Sorry." Aileen released Anna's hands and raised her open palms apologetically.

"That's okay. You couldn't know. Now you do. Moving on?"

Aileen was precipitously losing points, and the hostess could end this lopsided match in a knockout any moment. Aileen took a long breath in and out. "May I speak freely?"

Anna threw her arms in the air. "Took you long enough."

Aileen grimaced. "Looks like I'm going to spend the winter here—"

"You mean, you're stuck with me."

"Another way to put it. And I want us to be friends. Or whatever it is one can be with a sovereign." She checked the countess's reaction.

Anna actually laughed. "Go on."

"I can't tell anyone why I'm here. Not until I understand who's who."

"There's only one who's who in Watkins, and you're talking to her." All signs of fun vanished from Anna's features. She *was* the ruler of this place, and she did not like Aileen's implications.

Faux pas. Fuck. How did she always manage to ruin every promising connection? "Your Ladyship." Aileen bowed. "I'll tell you this: I am not here of my free will; I am not from Buffalo; and Newman is not my real name." She dared to look up.

"But you are someone important."

"Sort of."

"Don't worry, Sort-of-Important-Person, I'll take good care of you..."

"Aileen."

Anna's prickly glare softened. "Aileen. What can you tell me about Maynard's business here?"

"Ostensibly, to be my minder. Beyond that, no idea. Didn't he say he's a new Trade Representative?"

"Crock. There's no trade to speak of between Buffalo and the Finger Lakes. Spying, perhaps?"

Aileen shrugged. "Not impossible, but unlikely. He's too righteous. Would make an awful spy. This could be an exile, as a punishment."

"For what?"

"You'll have to ask him, Your Ladyship."

"Oh, I will."

That sounded ominous, but... Fuck him. Whatever trouble Maynard was in, he deserved it. Coward. Traitor.

Deep inside, at the edge of her consciousness, displeasure stirred, foreign and untimely. She was being unfair to Richard. He'd come to her aid on that train of horrors. He'd stood up for her—only once, but that was one time more than the others. She shouldn't have expected him to choose her over his family, safety, and future. But she wasn't prepared to forgive him yet. Maybe later, someday. This wasn't that day.

"Lady Anna, are we... good?"

The hostess wrapped an arm around Aileen's naked shoulders. "We're good, sweetheart. I'm still dying of curiosity, but will wait. Just one more thing." Her other hand lifted the silver pendant from Aileen's cleavage and twisted it playfully until the thick chain hugged Aileen's neck too snugly for comfort.

Anna stepped forward to catch Aileen's wide-open eyes. "*I* run the show here. You'll do well to remember that. We understand each other, yes?"

Aileen gingerly bobbed her head, as much as the tight chain's bite allowed.

"Good!" An angelic smile blossomed on the countess's face again. She released the pendant, adjusted it for a perfect fit between the tops of Aileen's breasts, smoothed out non-existent wrinkles on her dress, and looped an arm through Aileen's elbow. "Shall we, gorgeous? The court must be livid over our conspicuously extended absence."

Aileen, still processing what had just happened, docilely paced along, struggling to match the countess's wide, purposeful stride.

"Oh, and I can't wait to hear how you've earned that atrocious shiner on your forehead."

What a bitchy thing to say. Autocrat or not, Anna should not have played with Aileen's feelings, like a bored cat with a petrified mouse. As similar as the two of them were, Aileen leaned toward disliking her flamboyant benefactor. A Wicked Fairy Step-Godmother to Aileen's Cinderella, that's what Anna was.

Here's to hoping she won't force a fucking prince upon me.

Chapter 27

Watkins Glen

October 12, 42 PE

"Excuse me, please." Aileen rose, forcing a perfunctory smile. To her right, Lady Anna, blushed and plastered, paid no attention. Maynard, on her left, glowered, but even his comical despondency couldn't hold Aileen at the table. She picked up her skirt and stepped off the dais. With determination, a few calculated shoves, and judicious use of elbows, she weaved her way past the press of salacious guests and weary servants. She burst through the garden doors and hungrily swallowed the chilly, refreshing night air until her gasping breath settled. Far from midnight yet, but *her* spell was fading off.

Buzzed after the series of mandatory toasts lauding Lady Anna, Aileen had her inhibitions wearing dangerously thin. If she had to spend another minute at the suffocating feast, she would have fainted—or exploded. Or turned into a fucking pumpkin.

The density of the crowd filling the banquet hall was a contributing factor, but her distress was rooted mainly in the atmosphere.

She wasn't bothered by the men shamelessly ogling her; nor by the women, dowsing her with their no less predictable disdain. She'd been promised that, and the attention matched the expectations.

Her problem was with how rapidly the dinner party had devolved into a rowdy drunken mayhem. There were no princes. The cream of the local high society, however they fashioned themselves—nobility, yeomanry, militiamen—must have been engaged in a pervading conspiracy to embarrass the countess, competing for the title of the grossest swine. Aileen had no other explanation.

The tension was palpable in the air, as if the guests believed this was their last day on earth and rushed to grab and enjoy all they could reach before everything was taken away from them. Shouting matches and scuffles erupted more frequently with each upended cup of booze.

An exalted court, indeed. Aileen's finery wasn't an overkill; it was a waste of refined taste. An exquisitely sharp rapier, where a primitive bludgeoning weapon would do. She couldn't bear to be a part of that circus for a second longer.

The walls, doors, and windows of the building, overgrown with a lush tapestry of climbing vines, muffled the sickening pandemonium, shielding Aileen from the frenzy. The ringing in her ears subsided. Her stomach stopped churning.

She plodded to the waterfront, resting her eyes on the dark waves. Blessed breeze carried away the disgusting smells clinging to her hair, the contrived pretenses, the sticky attention—and with them, the last shreds of warmth. Aileen shivered, hugging her exposed shoulders. The wind succeeded where the humans had failed, making her feel half-naked. A moment later, a thick woolen shawl enveloped her.

Startled, Aileen sidestepped, but her maid's "There, my lady," put her at ease.

"Thanks, Marie, you're indispensable. Now, go back, report to the countess that I'm fine."

Marie didn't bat an eyelash. "Her Ladyship doesn't require such frequent updates. She's interested in the bigger picture. And you shouldn't be out here alone, my lady."

"Your lady won't be." The resonant swagger, no doubt aimed to be reassuring, was anything but.

Aileen rolled her eyes. The thousand-limbed monster seething in the cesspit did not let its prey slip away, sending its gooey tentacles after her.

Marie's annoyance mirrored Aileen's. "Miss Newman, Sergeant Armando, Watkins County's Master-at-Arms. Forgive him his lack of manners, he's only been doing this for a week."

Aileen reluctantly turned.

A short, broad man, with a handgun holster and a sword on his belt, stared Marie down. His lovingly groomed black hair framed a dark face with an aquiline nose and fell onto the red-yellow-green cloak. The same colors the pompous announcer, Lawrence, had worn earlier. Must be some heraldic shit.

Another man, thinner and older, with a shock of tousled gray hair and unkempt stubble along his jawline, dressed in similar but faded colors, observed the introduction with unmistakable ridicule. The three steps separating the men spoke volumes: no friendship was lost between these two.

The thin man bowed to Aileen with an artful flourish, swaying and almost losing his footing. "And I am Henry, the royal historian. Our spymaster won't acknowledge me, leaving me no choice but to introduce myself. She isn't fond of Armando either, but for different reasons." He leaned to Aileen. "Our freshly minted sarge considers himself irresistible. With his new uniform, more than ever. Miss Marie did not view his advances favorably." His loud, conspiratorial whisper reeked of alcohol.

Aileen wrinkled her nose. What useful information was being dumped on her, got lost in the overwhelming stench.

"Spymaster?" Her eyes slid from Henry to Armando and stopped on Marie. The maid frowned. At Henry.

How interesting. Aileen had her back scrubbed not by a common eavesdropper, but by the spymaster. Her little gambit worked; Lady Anna considered her a more important intelligence target than the senior trader. On second thought, she was worse off with such a level of attention. Maybe she should reinforce the idea that Maynard was there for nefarious purposes. She snickered, attracting everyone's looks. "Aren't you three charming? And why isn't Miss Spymaster fond of *you*, Henry?"

"Why, for fear of competition, of course!" The historian comically squared his shoulders. "I collect information, too!" He failed to maintain the serious posture for longer than one breath and bent over, giggling and chortling.

"Historian, huh? How much history does this, uh, *place* have?" Aileen scrambled for a neutral word.

"You'd be surprised, my lady, you'd be surprised." The drunkard wouldn't stop cackling.

Aileen switched her focus to the Master-at-Arms. "Sarge, I'll spare you the embarrassment. You've got no game here."

"We'll see about that." The pigheaded idiot winked.

Aileen exchanged understanding looks with Marie. "What happened to the previous Master-at-Arms? Was he so insistent, too? Did you bite his head off?"

Marie grew serious. "We lost him in an unfortunate incident."

"Incident?" Henry made a gurgling sound. "Got his entire team slaughtered like sheep. One hell of an incident, I'd say!"

"Shut up, you marinated toad!"

The spymaster's hiss achieved zero effect. Words kept rolling out of the historian's mouth. "And where? Not raiding. Not in a noble battle against the Ithacan renegades, oh no! A simple patrol in—"

"Shut! Up!" Armando's roar produced no better results.

"—Corning!"

Henry's mumbling and hooting continued, but Aileen wasn't listening anymore. She froze. Corning, a week ago. Around the time Bo was supposed to be there. Tick's handiwork? No, that couldn't be the case. A team of soldiers—too much, even for him.

Aileen coughed to clear the soreness spreading in her throat. "Who attacked them?"

The sergeant glanced at Marie. She nodded.

"We don't know," he said. "Whoever did it left no identifying marks. There was another fresh grave nearby, but not someone we know."

"Anything special ab-bout the b-body?" Aileen's lips went numb, defying her articulation.

Armando shrugged. "Nothing in particular. A guy. Why such an interest?"

Aileen shook her head, unable to speak, and turned her back to the locals. Not Bo, then. Tick? The lake provided no answers. If the body was Tick's, Bo stood no chance of making it home on his own. She killed them both.

"Leave me," she croaked, and stumbled.

Marie caught Aileen's arm, keeping her upright. "You heard Miss Newman," the fake maid snapped. Authoritative notes cut into her normally docile tone. "The lady is unwell. Quit shocking her with these gory details. Get lost, you two! Shoo, shoo!"

Aileen barely noticed the receding footsteps behind her back.

"Can you walk, my lady?" Marie caressed Aileen's temple, returning an unruly lock of hair to its proper place behind her ear. "Would you like me to take you to your room?"

Aileen did not respond. Pain, as real as physical, constricted her windpipe. She could hardly breathe, let alone speak.

Marie gently pulled her to the side. "Come, there's a bench."

Aileen obediently followed.

She was a failure. As a leader, as a friend. A pitiful schemer, and a pathetic boss. It had all been a game for her; she'd enjoyed playing it excitedly and recklessly. And now people have died. People closest to her. All her fault.

She sat, staring into the water. The lake reflected a perfect image of her state. Dark. Heavy. Uneasy. Like her, its waves came from far away, and threw themselves against the stony shore, desperately seeking atonement in self-destruction. The lake understood her and extended an invitation.

Tempting, so tempting. And why not? Must be nice there, under the surface. Quiet, worry-free. No crowds. No fighting. No running, to or from. Not a care. Drift along, let the currents carry you; or sink to the bottom and rest forever.

Aileen shifted her weight to stand, to walk down the pier and accept the beckoning lake's hospitality—

Marie's hand found hers and squeezed. She didn't offer words of reassurance, nor asked what was wrong, and Aileen was grateful for that. This simple touch anchored her to the land of the living. The living who could be brutal, vile, and ugly—but also supportive, warm... Loving.

A wave swept over Aileen, and the water had nothing to do with it. A wave of shame; black ink, staining her every pore. Walking into the lake was the easy way out. A cowardly, selfish way. Taking it would devastate Marc. Destroy Bo, if he was still alive. And then there was Ajinder.

Streeters needed their charismatic Aunt. Mark and Bo needed their sister. Ajinder... His needs were still fuzzy, but undeniable. And Aileen, what were her own desires? She needed a win. A victory, even a small one, to break this streak of bad luck, poor decisions, and painful defeats. Aji's hug would've been nice, too.

Aileen returned the squeeze. "Thank you."

"Don't mention it, my lady." Marie's voice rang with the feigned carelessness of a shallow maid.

Aileen checked her unperturbed profile, hardly recognizable in the dim moonlight. "How does this work? How do you reconcile being the spymaster and a maid?"

A sly smile curled Marie's lips. "Maid is my day job. Her Ladyship needs a few prompt, energetic girls to help with her routine. Information gathering is my hobby."

"Right." Aileen lowered her eyelids, letting Marie know she didn't believe a single word. "And those maids of honor?"

"High politics, I'm afraid. Daughters to noble families, you know. Cushy titles, inflated egos, fine food, unlimited drinks. Promoting them to the inner circle makes them easier to monitor."

"Lady Anna called them hens."

"Lady Anna doesn't mince words. She is not wrong."

"What does Lady Anna call me?" Alright, Aileen might not be as good as she'd pictured herself until recently, but she still couldn't resist a fine game of wits. Her energy surged, the rush of being alive, the rebound after brushing elbows with the afterworld.

"What do *you* call yourself?" Marie clearly enjoyed this game, too.

Aileen hesitated.

"Come on." Marie's hold on Aileen's hand tightened. "You know *my* secret now. Be fair, give me something."

Aileen stood to gain nothing from withholding this information. Might as well develop a credit of honesty. "Aileen. Aileen Novak from Locksville."

Marie shrugged. "Sorry. I gather your name is supposed to ring a bell in more civilized places. As I said, we here know little about the rest of the world. Our step-siblings across the marsh are who matter to us, if you know what I mean."

"The other warlords?"

"Yeah, especially the Ithacans."

"What's your beef with them?"

"You really don't know? Figures, I guess. Ugh, where do I begin?" Marie chewed on her lip. "Harry can prattle about this stuff until your ears curl, so if you want to learn more, find him and pour him a drink. But here's the gist. Terrence Harmon died five years ago, dividing his domain between his two sons. The eldest, Terrence the Second, got Ithaca. The younger, Count Jason, inherited Watkins. The thing is, they hadn't been on the best of terms even before the split. Siblings, am I right?" Marie winked.

Aileen frowned. Marc. Bo. They'd had their share of arguments, but fighting? *War*? Never.

Marie's grin faded. "Anyhow. Things turned ugly. Terrence claimed their royal father hadn't been in his right mind when drafting his will. He declared Jason's claim illegitimate and attacked us, to reunite the Harmon lands."

"I imagine he didn't succeed."

"My lady is very sharp. He didn't, but that hasn't stopped him from trying. His treaty with Rochester forced us to search Buffalo's patronage as a counter-weight. And so, here we are."

"Wait. Count Jason—"

"—met an untimely end, falling off his horse last summer."

"Aha." Aileen rubbed her chin. "Let me guess. This left Lady Anna, his grieving widow, next in line."

"Yes."

"And that horse accident..."

Marie brought her face so close to Aileen's, her breath tickled Aileen's skin. She took Aileen's other hand. "I'll pretend I didn't hear that. Please, my lady, never hint at what you just did. I enjoy your company, and it would be a shame to see your pretty head separated from that stunning body for high treason."

Aileen needed no further confirmation. She struck gold. The remaining question was how to use this information as leverage. That, and—

She looked at Marie's fingers, intertwined with hers. "Marie, are you flirting with me?"

An unsure smile wavered on the maid's lips. "What if I do? Is that so wrong?"

Whether her interest was genuine or a part of the spy act, Aileen didn't ask. Minutes ago, Marie had stopped her from passing the point of no return. For that alone, Aileen was prepared to give the spymaster the benefit of the doubt. She sighed, delicately tugging her hands free. "My life is plenty complicated as it is, Marie. Can we keep a clean snoop-target relationship?"

Marie cast her eyes down. "Sure. Would you still have me as your maid?"

Aileen stroked her arm. "I'd love that. Wouldn't trust anyone else to spy on me."

Marie assumed a cheerful façade. "Ready to retreat for the night, my lady?"

Aileen rose. "Your place or mine?" She couldn't resist.

Marie pulled her chin up. "Ow. Not funny, my lady. This will cost you."

"What?"

"How about the true reason you're here?"

Chapter 28

Watkins Glen

October 13, 42 PE

"I take it you did not enjoy last night's banquet?" The countess's teasing tone and amused expression did little to conceal her challenge.

"No, Your Ladyship. It was disgraceful."

A collective gasp escaped the hens of honor, clustered behind their sovereign's back. The background hum died, leaving the throne room ominously silent.

Aileen's abs contracted.

A frown brought Anna's brows close together. Anger flashed in her hooded eyes, and her stubbornly set jaw held a promise of swift and painful retribution. Aileen did not yield, and the countess's expression transformed into perplexed. "Some honesty in this room. How refreshing. Speak your mind, Miss, ah, *Newman*."

Aha. Naturally, Marie had appraised her boss about Aileen's lakeshore revelations. And Anna chose to keep that knowledge to herself; just as Aileen would have.

Aileen surveyed the room. Two dozen extra ears; a dozen extra mouths; half a dozen extra brains. Too many variables to account for. "Shouldn't we have this conversation in a more private setting, Lady Anna?"

The countess leaned back and crossed her arms at her chest. "I have no secrets from my court."

Aileen almost smirked, but Marie, vehemently shaking her head in the far corner, caught her eye. Aileen swallowed the *Don't you?* ready to leave her lips. "As you wish, Your Ladyship," she said instead, with a shallow bow. "The food was great. And the drinks... plentiful."

"But?"

"But the guests..." Aileen spread her arms with a shrug.

Scandalized murmurs flew behind Anna's back, cut short by her drawled "I see."

The countess sardonically looked Aileen up and down, reminding her she herself wasn't as sparkling as yesterday, but Aileen remained unmoved by the spite. This late morning, she wore a snug pair of denim pants and a black leather jacket over a simple white shirt. Not quite her favorite outfit, but a reasonable compromise between comfy and badass. Marie's taste had once again proven to be impeccable.

Anna sighed. "My dear girl." Ooh, the age card. Ouch. "Sure, our boondocks culture isn't as sophisticated as the civilized circles you're used to—"

"*So-phis*— I don't know that word, so I'm sure not *it*. Just an orphan from a poor suburb. But—"

"But"—Anna sharply cut in, irritated by the interruption—"your biggest mistake is thinking our guests were there to entertain *you*."

Aileen tilted her head, waiting to hear where this was going.

Satisfied she had Aileen's attention, the countess nodded. "You're awfully self-centered, Miss Newman. Understand, a sovereign's primary responsibility is to keep her subjects distracted from the negativity in their lives. Otherwise, they may grow unhappy, and that could lead to treasonous thoughts. So, last night, *you* were there to entertain *them*—my faithful lords, officers, militiamen. They're a rough, rowdy bunch, who don't mind a few scraped knuckles and bloodied noses. Fighters without a fighting spirit wouldn't be worth their upkeep, ha? But when they aren't fighting, I'd rather keep them in line not through threats and punishments, but by letting them drown their brains in booze and feast their eyes on your spectacular tits. And every time I say so, you'll parade those, smiling encouragingly at the last of my drunken pigs."

This made a disturbing amount of sense.

"I am not tits for hire, Lady Anna."

"You'll be what I say you are, sweetheart. If I send you to a whorehouse, you'll say, 'Yes, Lady Anna,' and spread your legs."

Blood rushed to Aileen's cheeks. "Buffalo—"

"—doesn't give a damn. All they care about is having you tucked away from the foreign eyes."

Ah, fuck. She'd loosened Maynard's tongue. So much for a guest of honor.

"Our alliance with Buffalo is strategically important," continued the woman, "and I'm happy to oblige. Beyond that—you're my toy, to play with as I wish."

Aileen's nostrils flared as she locked her incinerating gaze on the countess.

Anna slapped her throne's armrest. "Do not test my limits, girl! I've had people executed for lesser insubordination! I can't hang or disembowel you without breaking Buffalo's trust, but I *will* dispatch you to that brothel."

In Aileen's narrowed peripheral vision, Marie frantically patted the air, begging her to let it slide. She looked so silly...

And just like that, Aileen relaxed. This was not a hill to die on. Weinberg would have said, in one of their rare coaching sessions, "Pick your battles, kid."

She'd win by not engaging.

Aileen smiled. "Understood, Your Ladyship."

Lady Anna, caught off balance by the fluid shift in Aileen's attitude, eyed her suspiciously for another minute. Everyone else in the room held their breaths, besides the scruffy historian whose bulged, birdlike eyes sniggered back at Aileen. The bastard *understood*.

Aileen curtsied in an awkward rendition of an art she'd never practiced. "May I leave now, Lady Anna?" She was humility personified. Stifling a chuckle was harder than controlling her bladder after three mugs of beer.

The countess dismissed her with an imperious flick of her wrist.

Aileen backed away, shut the throne room door, leaned with her forehead against the far wall, and convulsed in silent laughter.

The door behind her creaked and softly closed again. Two sets of steps approached.

"My, what a shitshow."

Aileen turned to Henry. Their eyes met, and both bent over, giggling. Marie's dramatic, reproving sigh caused another bout. Finally, out of breath, Aileen straightened.

"I admit..." Henry held onto his heaving chest, gasping for air. "I under... estimated you, young lady. Your act is still... pretty rough, though. Not a threat to my illustrious court jester career."

"Jester? Didn't you say you're a royal historian?"

"I did, didn't I? Old habits die hard. Her Enlightened Ladyship isn't very fond of the past. Bringing it up is liable to trigger her head-chopping habits. Luckily for me, she appreciates my twisted sense of humor, or I would've been unemployed. Or dead. Most likely, both."

"Oh? You've got a sense of humor? Enough to be distinguished from your drunken antics?"

"Meow, young lady's got claws!"

"Look at the bright side: you wouldn't be sent to a whorehouse."

"That was a very hurtful comment! Why, you don't find me attractive?" Henry ran his palm through his hair, jerked up his chin, and barreled his chest.

Marie stomped her foot. "Will you two jokers stop? This is serious!"

Aileen put an arm around the historian-turned-jester's shoulders. His hand snaked behind her back, briefly venturing into the inappropriate territory but ultimately settling on her waist. His crooked smile mirrored Aileen's defiance.

Marie bit on her lip. "You act crazy! Like... like rabid wasps!"

Aileen and Henry exchanged puzzled looks.

"Rabid wasps?" Aileen pulled her head back. "Creepy."

"Vexing," agreed the historian. "Where did *that* come from?"

"Come on." Marie sniffed the air. "Neither of you is even drunk!"

"I am hungover! That counts, too."

The spymaster rolled her eyes at Henry's fake indignation. His next words, barely louder than a murmur, but harsh and lucid, sucker-punched her. "Why do you care?"

"I..." Marie stiffened.

"I get why you'd care about her." Henry's head bobbed toward Aileen. "She's such a sweet thing, who wouldn't? But me? You don't even like me. Never made a secret of that."

"Father, please..."

Aileen twisted out of Henry's hold, stepping aside. Now that she knew what to look for, the familial resemblance showed through. The same wide nose, similarly set eyes, protruding cheekbones... "Damn. Didn't see *that* coming." She left the *sweet thing* comment unanswered.

The historian shrugged. "Everyone knows. No one gives a hoot." He squinted slyly at Aileen. "To answer your next question, my darling daughter disapproves of my lifestyle and"—he lowered his voice to a dramatic whisper—"of my unenthusiastic mindset when it comes to Her Glorious Ladyship."

He grinned at Marie's concerned frown. "What? These walls have ears? So? The reports will end up delivered to you, anyway."

"Or to Armando, if I'm involved."

"You're such a killjoy." Henry threw his hands up in surrender. "Fine. I'll retreat to my archive. Anyone willing to join is welcome. Drinking alone is a sad affair."

Aileen stepped forward. "I'll tug along. Could use some booze to take off the edge."

"My lady!" Marie's eyes grew wide. "It's not even noon!"

"Not like I've got anything better to do, until my tits are called up to duty again, have I?"

Marie paled under Aileen's blazing glare.

"Hey, hey!" Henry grabbed Aileen's wrist and dragged her away. "Only court jesters get to torment my daughter. You've got a long road ahead, before you can take my place!"

"The same goes for criticizing the countess," he added in a low voice, once they were in the open air.

Henry led Aileen along the lakeshore. He didn't force a conversation, humming an unrecognizable tune and letting Aileen take in the surroundings.

They passed between two rows of boats on racks. Some showed signs of recent use and care. Others, more than a half, were in different stages of disrepair. A few stands rusted through and yielded to the weight of their cargo, spilling the vessels onto the ground. Quite a few looked abandoned, but only for years, not decades.

"How much population have you lost since the partition?"

Henry perked up. His melody concluded with an upbeat whistle. "Huh," he said. "About a third."

"Died in the wars?"

"Wars? Nah. We don't do wars, we raid."

"Even with Ithaca?"

"Especially with Ithaca. What, you think we meet in an open field, with battle formations, cavalry charges and all? We don't have the skill or the manpower, young lady. By the way, what should I call you? Not Miss Newman, I hope."

"Aileen is fine. So, how do you fight then?"

"Raiding, aren't you listening? Looting, pillaging. Ambushes. Nothing noble. The losses are negligible, rarely more than a few militiamen here and there. Maybe ten people in a particularly bad year. You can see why that debacle with the old Sarge Beaverton was such a disaster."

"What do you think happened there?"

"As a historian, I wish I knew, but suspect we'll never find out. As a cynical jester, I don't want to know."

"Explain. The jester part, yes?"

Henry glanced around and lowered his voice to a whisper. "Something's fishy about that story, that's all I can tell you."

"Hm." There'd be time enough to press Henry for answers. "So where did a third of your people go?"

The historian shrugged. "Some died. We've had a few years of poor harvests. Others left."

"To Ithaca?"

Henry did not respond for a hundred steps.

Did she offend him? Was he going to answer this, or any of her other inquiries already forming in her head?

"You're a clever girl, Aileen, in an analytical way. It pains me to admit, but your brain may even be more impressive than your tits. But you should learn which questions better remain unasked."

Aileen growled. "Okay, ground rules. First, stop calling me 'girl.' My age is not a factor. I'm a grown woman."

"I can see that."

Aileen poked the ancient playboy in the ribs. "Second, no more jokes about my tits; or"—she quickly added—"any other body parts."

"You're no fun."

"That's what your court gig is for."

"Harsh."

Aileen stopped. "Take it or leave it. I'm serious."

Henry bowed ceremoniously. "Your conditions are acceptable, my lady."

Aileen strolled past him, her head carried high and proud.

"Say, Henry," she put out the feelers when the historian caught up, "you would know: is there any, um, underworld here?"

"You mean, like the Seven Hells?"

Aileen pursed her lips.

Henry snickered. "Fine, fine, apologies, my lady. Just so I understand, you're asking about local rogues, petty thieves—"

"Smugglers. Mainly about smugglers."

The historian creased his eyebrows, examining her face, as if trying to decide if she was joking. "You *are* serious." He shook his head. "I bet I know why. If I'm right, it's better—"

"To skip to the point."

Henry sighed. "My dear Aileen, have you seen our fine town? How we live, what we do?" He gestured around.

Aileen obediently surveyed her surroundings. "Not enough to draw conclusions."

"Maybe. Probably. Don't let the countess's glitzy ball awe you. Watkins is dirt-poor. We live a not quite Stone-Age life, but barely early-Medieval. Whatever people produce here, it's to sustain ourselves. The *richer* folks trade their meager surplus at the regional Fair twice a year. There's nothing to smuggle, Aileen, in or out. Crime? The worst we see is Joe Schmoe punching John Doe in the eye for fooling around with his wife."

Damn it to the Seven Hells and back. *LeClaire, you devious asshole.*

"Aim!" hollered a hoarse voice nearby. "Loose!"

Aileen ducked at the strumming of a dozen bowstrings and the rustle of flying arrows.

Henry's soft chuckle made her blush. "Their aim may not be ideal, but you can be reasonably sure they won't miss their targets by *that* much."

Aileen climbed to her feet, patted off the dirt, and peeked around the corner of the nearby structure.

"Aim! Loose!"

A squat drill instructor paced behind the line of nine young men and two women, all shooting across the cleared parking lot at bales of straw fifty meters away. A wide building with a faded *WA M RT* sign sat on the far side of the lot.

"Behold, the mandatory weekly training of the brave men of Watkins Militia. Optional for the brave women."

"Why the sarcasm? They seem to be pretty good."

"You haven't seen the good archers yet. They train later in the afternoon. These are the green ones."

"If you say so. When is firearms training? I wouldn't mind sending some lead down the range."

"You're kidding, right?" Henry's shaggy brows formed two apostrophes. Seeing her incomprehension, he sighed. "You big city folks don't appreciate what you've got. The countess can count"—he giggled—"on her one perfectly manicured hand how many guns we have. One less now, with the loss of Beaverton's revolver."

"But why? Wasn't this area full of guns before the E?"

"Guns—yes, but the ammo had run out, eventually. And none of the big boys would sell us any, or even the reloading supplies."

"So—"

"So, bows and pole arms is what we fight with."

"Same with Ithaca?"

"Same. Terrence the First had run dry years before his death."

The store met them with a thick smell of dust and mildew. Henry confidently weaved his way through the aisles in the near darkness, dispelled by narrow columns of light penetrating through the broken roof high above. He tampered with a lock by touch and pulled open a large stainless-steel door.

Another beam of sunlight sneaked through a tiny barred window cut in the metal wall. It met a few glass bottles hanging from the ceiling; their hazy content dispersed it.

"What is this place?" Specks of dust floating through the sunbeam mesmerized Aileen. She looked away, allowing her eyes to adjust to the gloomy interior until she could glimpse the details.

"My inner sanctum!" The pride in Henry's voice was undeniable. "My treasure!"

"You mean those"—Aileen pointed at the shelves holding notebooks along one wall—"or those?" She gestured to a wine rack.

"Both!" Henry laughed happily.

"But a room made of metal? You built it?"

"Me? No! It's a commercial fridge in an old supermarket. I wanted a place that cannot be easily broken into... or burned."

"Fridge?"

"You know, like a cold room. But colder."

"Weird."

"Not at all. Not before the E."

"You remember that? How old were you?"

"Twelve. Old enough to remember—though sometimes I wonder if those memories haven't been an odd dream." The old man sank into thoughts, and Aileen did not disturb him.

Eventually, he shook himself up. "Look at me, what a disgrace. I promised a lady a drink when we get here, and haven't offered one yet. I'd understand if you've lost any respect for me."

"One needs to have something to lose it."

"Jeez, that hurts! Alright, cheeky grown woman with unmentionable parts, what's your poison?"

"Let's start with a beer."

"A prudent choice."

Aileen grabbed a bow-legged wooden stool. "Why didn't *you* escape to Ithaca?"

"Are you kidding? And risk moving the archive?"

"Tell me, Henry," she asked into his back between the clinking and pouring sounds, "what does your archive cover?"

"Everything, my dear." Henry turned, holding two mugs and beaming with pride. "Everything worth remembering since the establishment of House Harmon. Documents, maps, statistics, personal account transcripts—you name it."

"Wait, you mean from *before* the partition, too?"

"Naturally. You think His Lordship Terence the First had another historian? He'd kept my archive here, away from the prying eyes in the capital."

The absence of local smugglers called for a more creative, circuitous approach. Like taking Anna down before their inevitable clash cast Aileen to the next level of hell. The archive could hold the key to that. "Teach me."

"Teach you what? Our history? Why on earth would you want that, when you can just drink with me?" He set a mug on the table before Aileen.

"Because the countess isn't fond of the past."

"A rebel spirit, huh? I like it. You'll make a fine jester one day." Henry sipped his beer. "Anything specific you're interested in?"

Aileen exhaled. "Count Jason's death."

The historian choked and spit out his drink, spraying Aileen's face. She didn't move to wipe it off. He met her probing eyes over his beer mug. "Haven't your parents taught you not to play with fire?"

"I'm an orphan." A drop dripped off the tip of her nose.

"Uh. That explains a lot." Henry reached to the cupboard behind him, grabbed a crumpled, musty towel, and offered it to Aileen. "Why that particular episode of our history, if I may ask?"

"Your daughter has cautioned me that digging into this subject would earn me the gallows."

"And, of course, you saw that as an invitation."

"Of course. Now, I'm asking the royal historian, not the court jester: are *you* afraid of the fire?"

"Let me consult them both." Henry unhurriedly chugged his brew. "The historian says, what the hell, let's stoke it. And the jester is curious whose burial pyre it's going to be."

Chapter 29

Watkins Glen

October 15, 42 PE

Aileen cupped her ears with her hands, but the annoying scraping sounds penetrated through the imperfect barrier, dooming any attempt to concentrate on reading.

She slapped her palms against the table. "Henry, what the Hells? A sudden urge to mix a drink?"

Marie chortled.

The historian, wearing a tarnished apron, continued whipping something up in a metal bowl with a whisk. "I'll give you one more guess."

Aileen ran her fingers through her hair. "Is he always so annoying?"

Marie shook her head. "Normally, he's *more* annoying. Whatever you two do here, you've been a good influence."

Aileen pointed at Henry. "That's the *better* version of him? Fuckin' A."

Ding-ding-ding-ding-ding. The old man's whisk deliberately beat against the bowl's walls.

"Stop it!" Aileen cringed. "Fine, I don't know. You're neither a cook nor a baker, so not eggs, not dough. Tell me."

"Ink, my dear. I'm making ink. Charcoal ash, water, a drop of vinegar. Where do you think ink comes from? From milking black goats?"

"Frankly? No idea. We use pencils in Locksville."

"Pencils." Henry stopped working his whisk. "Forty years after the E, you still have enough?"

"Spot on, paper-stainer! There's a whole shipping container of them. Found in a warehouse and nationalized."

"Nationalized?"

"The government took it over."

"Thank you, dear, I know what 'nationalized' means. But why?"

"They distribute the pencils for free, 'to promote literacy and arts,' as they say."

"Damn. Does your government have an opening for a historian? Hells, I'd settle for a jester!"

Aileen's cheeks turned cold. "I'll be sure to ask, next time I'm in town." Her voice rang with icicles.

"Oh." The corners of Henry's mouth slid down. "Silly me. That was insensitive. How can I make it up to you? Beer? Rye?"

She couldn't be mad at him for too long. "If that's your way of making up to me, I'll never be sober again."

"Fair point. Marie, Miss Aileen becomes too irritable when hungry. Be a darling and fetch lunch for your lady. Bring something for me as well, while you're at it."

Marie's face hardened. She was about to object, but met Aileen's mocking stare. "Maid is your day job, you said? No need to watch me, I'm not going anywhere."

"I am more concerned with the poison he may pour into your ears." Her sigh left space for interpretation.

"I am deeply offended. My own daughter..." Henry wrung his hands.

"Fine, fine, I'm going." Marie sprang to her feet. "You both are intolerable. Why don't you marry and drive each other crazy?"

"Sure about that? That'd make me your stepmother." Aileen bared her teeth. The mental image held promise.

"Gah!" Marie slammed the door.

"There's a thought..." Henry's whisk made a slow, suggestive circle in the bowl. "I'm plenty virile still."

"Ew." Aileen threw an inkwell at him. "Don't want to know what that means, just... stop."

The historian dodged the projectile. "We've got half an hour, give or take. Let's not waste it."

"To be clear, we've switched the subject? Talking about history now, yes?"

A wry smile brightened Henry's face. "Alas, my dear."

Aileen pushed away one notebook and dragged another closer.

Marie had been impeding their research for the second day in a row, limiting their discussions to innocuous subjects of distant past, general philosophy, and brewing recipes. "A good maid follows her lady even into a monster's den," she had said the previous morning, trailing Aileen to Henry's hideout. Aileen and her co-conspirator stole every moment of Marie's brief absences to dig into what truly mattered: the late Count Jason's fatal incident. Her constant presence unnerved Aileen, but there was no simple way to get rid of the unwanted company without raising suspicions.

"Don't just sit there, grab another notebook," Aileen told her the day before, exasperated. "Maybe you'll find an anecdote or three to share at the court."

Marie's discomfort made Aileen regret the suggestion before the maid responded, "I can't read. The most bookish person in Harmon lands never found the time to teach his only child."

Henry shamefully lost the ensuing staring contest.

"I can read to you if you'd like," Aileen offered, to diffuse the awkward tension. That was a noble but, in retrospect, lame act. It had blocked the possibility of studying the *dangerous* volumes under the spymaster's nose.

This morning was only marginally better. Aileen's presence was the reason the old fridge room had not gone up in a fiery explosion of the unresolved issues between the father and daughter. Aileen felt partly responsible: without her, Marie wouldn't have had grounds to be in the same room with the disfavored historian. But bridging the divide between the two was rather low on Aileen's priorities list. She had a monarch to take down, and the precious minutes until the fake maid's return were running out faster than moonshine in the historian's cup.

"I've been thinking..." Henry's uncharacteristically contemplative tone distracted Aileen from trying to find where in the text she'd stopped last time. She tore her eyes off the page.

"We should check the missing persons reports from around the X Day." Henry nodded to himself, unwilling to mention Count Jason's death even with no one else present. "Mostly after, and maybe a couple of weeks before."

"M-m?"

"The countess is never shy about lopping off undesirable heads. What's a few lives against the greater cause of her steady rulership? Nothing. If she really had a hand in... you know... Her principal aim would've been to eliminate any possibility of, ah, *the deed* being traced back to her."

Aileen stroked her chin. "Your best idea, so far. Mixing ink does you good. Can you check this while I read something stupidly mundane for Marie?"

"Sure."

"Then we have a moment or two of privacy... I said, don't!" She pointed a warning finger at the grinning historian. "Tell me, how popular was Jason?"

"Eh. The folks here... They give little damn about who sits on the Big Chair, as long as the taxes aren't too high, and they get to keep most of their harvest. But the militia loved him. He didn't hide behind their backs, and spent more time in the barracks than in the throne room."

"And how does Anna compare?"

"You and your questions... Always the perilous ones. The peasants, I suppose, like her more. She provides entertainment."

"Beheading and disembowelment."

"As well as hanging, quartering, burning at the stake... And the list goes on."

"What an inventive, cruel bitch."

"Careful, my dear. You've just earned yourself an extra year in that whorehouse."

"Yikes. To think I liked her at first." Aileen shivered. "What about the militia?"

"With them, it's more complicated. They sure appreciate her booze, as you witnessed, and the display of your—" Henry snapped his mouth shut. "Never mind. Despite all that, their resentment runs deep. She doesn't mingle with them, never rides with them on a mission, and..."

"And?"

"She's a woman." The historian looked away. "It must be gnawing at them on the inside, taking orders from her. Most of her court are women, too. The Master-at-Arms and an old jester hardly make a difference."

"Never thought I'd see patriarchal values as a positive."

"Why positive? They'd play against you all the same."

"*Me?* What do *I* have to do with anything?"

Aileen shrunk under Henry's pitying stare. "My dear girl, who do you think is going to blow Jason's assassination wide open? Me? Armando? There's no one but you."

"I did not sign up for *any* of this," Aileen said in a small voice.

"Fine." Henry shrugged lightly, as if they were discussing her refusal to have another beer. "Forget everything I said." Humming, he shuffled to his wine rack, filled a glass, and raised it. "Long live the most merciful Countess Anna, the wisest ruler of Watkins and the rightful heiress to the Throne of Ithaca!"

Aileen buried her face in her palms, scared shitless and offended at the same time. She wanted to see Anna go down, just not in an open confrontation. Her accusations would have to be ironclad, and all she had were vague speculations. She had too much to lose if her challenge went pear-shaped. "Ithaca?" She hid her shame behind curiosity. "Is that a thing? For real?"

"It's a *claim*. Mainly there to spite Terrence. Unrealistic, unsubstantiated, unthinkable... at first. But you know how it is, even most outlandish lies, repeated uncontested often enough, start gaining credibility—"

He swallowed hard at an insistent knock on the door and Marie's muffled, "Can somebody open? My hands are full."

She entered carrying two large bags. "What did I miss?"

Nothing much. Just a foolish little conspiracy to commit treason that would cost us our heads. Or worse. Aileen pressed her lips hard together, ensuring those words didn't accidentally escape.

"Toasting to Her Ladyship's wisdom and longevity!" Henry demonstrated his glass with liquid sloshing at the bottom.

Marie pointedly noted Aileen's empty hands. "Making excuses for your day-drinking, as always. Some things never change." She stomped to the table and unpacked pots and dishes in front of her lady. Henry showed the first signs of anxiety when the content of the second bag continued piling up before Aileen. The last item to see the light was a quarter-loaf of bread, which Marie tossed at her father. He deftly caught it midair, turned this way and that, and returned a questioning look.

"Problems?" Marie put her fists on her hips.

The old man looked at his meagre ration, at Aileen's fragrant spread, and back at Marie.

The maid remained unmoved. "*You* aren't my lady. Reap what you sow."

Henry dumped the rest of his drink down his throat, bit into the bread, and settled at the far end of the table, staring at the scratched wood in front of him.

Marie sat across from Aileen and threw one leg over another, prepared to wait.

"Ahem." This feud was becoming annoying. "You've made your point, whatever it is. Now, I *command* you both to sit with me and share this meal." Aileen's hard stare made it clear she wasn't taking a 'no' for an answer.

The two moved closer, not looking in each other's direction; Henry—puffing, Marie—showing with her posture she was only conceding under duress and out of duty.

After a few minutes of silent chewing and Henry's repeated sighs, Aileen put her fork down. "Okay, enough. I don't know what your story is, and I don't care. This childish bickering has got to stop! You're making this too awkward for me. Sort this out elsewhere. Throw a few fists at each other, if that makes you feel better. But quit this moping already! 'Boo-hoo, my daddy doesn't love me!' 'Poor me, my daughter doesn't respect me!' You're two adults, act like it!" She took a long overdue breath.

"Your discomfort doesn't give you the right to speak like that, Aileen," Marie said in a dead tone. "Not everything is about you."

"Oh, no? Then why are you here? If this isn't about me, get the fuck out." Marie paled.

Henry cleared his throat. "She's right, Marie. Let's talk this through, once and for all. I don't love you. Never have. You've always been a burden. A disappointment. A daily reminder of your mother."

Marie's huge eyes glistened. She sobbed, put her hands over her mouth, stifling a cry, and rushed to the door, dropping her chair.

Aileen and Henry sat, unmoving, for a long time. The air in the room, all of a sudden stale and dusty, became difficult to inhale.

Aileen's heartbeat eventually slowed down, leaving enough breath for words. "You didn't have to do that."

Henry did not respond.

"I can tell you love your daughter, fiercely. Deep inside, she knows that, too."

Silence.

"It's impressive and disturbing that you'd make such a painful sacrifice to get her out of this room."

"Then let's not waste time on idle talk." The lines crossing the historian's face cut deeper. The jester spirit had vanished, leaving behind a sour old man. "Get that notebook, before she sends in a replacement."

Hours later, Aileen was ready to swear the hairs on her neck crawled on their own in horror. Lady Anna's insidious scheme was beautiful—in a perverted sort of way. The chain of conspirators, each introducing additional distance between the countess and her crime, had been methodically cut, link by bleeding link.

The only problem: Aileen couldn't prove *anything*. She banged her fist on the table. "Damn it to the Seven Hells!"

Henry, haggard and mirthless, looked up with a mute question.

"We need evidence! Witnesses! Or it's my word against hers, and I don't like those odds. We must talk to people. Perfect conspiracies don't exist. Someone must have seen or heard something, no way around that."

"You can't. Involve one more person, and that'll be the end of it. Of you. Of me."

"You're being dramatic. Surely—"

"I am not. We're a nation of snitches. Everyone spies on everyone. Marie on Armando, Armando on Marie. Both on the court. Wives on husbands, brothers on sisters, children on their parents. If you learn of a crime and don't report it, you'll share the punishment. See something, say something."

"Clever."

"Yes, keeps the populace in line. One citizen at a time."

"Shit."

"You don't say."

"Why haven't you ratted me out yet?"

"I'm a historian, remember? I know where such practices lead. In the end, only drunk jesters would be allowed to speak their mind. Don't want to see *that* happen here."

"So, what's our next step?"

Henry's wrinkled eyelids drooped all the way down. "Don't know about you, young lady, but I'm going to soothe my nerves with another glass of magic potion and turn in for the day."

Aileen decisively pushed away from the table. "Have fun. I'll be in my room. Will try to patch things up with Marie, maybe." She caught Henry's appreciative glance and walked out of the fridge.

At the supermarket doors, the oblique sunlight outlined a lone, broad-shouldered figure. Aileen tensed. Was she being arrested? Already? Doubtful. There'd be more guards.

"Wonderful evening, Miss Aileen."

A moment to put the name to the voice... Armando, the Master-at-Arms. Yikes.

"I was told I may find you here. I must admit, I didn't believe it until now. Why would a snazzy lady like yourself want to waste her time in the company of that drunken quack? Never mind, I'm here now to brighten your day."

The man was positively in love with his suave voice. What a disgusting prick.

Armando's arm casually wrapped around Aileen's shoulders. "How shall we spend the evening, hm? My place, perhaps? I had a box of vintage wine delivered today. You'll like it."

Aileen shook his arm off. "Stop. Right fucking now. I told you, I'm not interested. Leave."

"Ooh, not all lady-like, after all. Maybe a kiss would clean your dirty mouth..." He leaned in.

Aileen shoved him away. "I said, get lost, asshat!"

Armando crimped the lapel of her jacket in his massive fist and slapped her. "Just who do you think you are, huh?"

Another slap.

"No one rejects the Master-at-Arms!"

Slap.

Each slap numbed Aileen's mind, driving her deeper into a stupor. This was LeClaire's train, all over again. Her arms hung limply along her sides, paralyzed by clammy fear. Her innards clumped into a gelatinous clod.

"You put on the airs of someone important, but you're no one."

Slap.

"You hear me, snooty bitch? I know all about you."

He squashed her face between his vise-like fingers. "Look at me! I can do anything I want with you. Nobody cares. And I *will* do anything I want. With your crappy attitude, you'll be on your back in the whorehouse, spreading your legs just like Her Ladyship promised, in no time. I'm calling dibs." His other hand released her jacket and squeezed her groin. "I'll take the first sampling, while you're still clean and tight."

"Hey!" Echoes of the distant shout bounced around under the tall ceiling. Henry's hurried steps approached. "What are you *doing*?!"

"Taking what's rightfully mine!"

The historian stepped forward. "She's my apprentice. Let her go!"

"You're full of shit. Move along before I stir it inside you. Last warning, old fart."

"Lady Anna will hear of this!"

Armando grunted. "Sober, you're even dumber. *She* told me to break this wildling in."

Henry's punch achieved zero effect. The sarge's short hook, to the contrary, sent the old man to the floor in a heap.

"Fucking clown," Armando muttered. "Now, where were we?"

How could this nightmare be real? This *was* happening. To her. Unless...

In the boiling soup of Aileen's feverish brain, a cold, solid thought crystallized, scraping her skull with its sharp corners.

"Wait, not like this," she babbled. "Let me treat you." She sank to her knees and undid his belt buckle.

"I *knew* you were a whore, all along." His jeering grin widened as she pulled his pants down...

...and died when she snatched the handgun from his holster and pointed it at his chest.

Holding his petrified eyes with her vengeful glare, Aileen squeezed the trigger. *Click*. Nothing happened.

Armando roared. His fingers clamped around Aileen's neck. "You stupid, stupid bitch!" He didn't even bother disarming her.

As Aileen's vision darkened around the edges, she struggled to recall Marc's lessons. She fumbled around the bottom of the handle. The magazine was in. Empty chamber? Blindly, she pulled the slide back and released it.

Armando froze.

Aileen did not feel her finger curling back. The gun jerked in her hand, and a deafening ringing filled the world.

Armando's hand was ripped off her throat, burning her skin with deep scratches.

Aileen coughed, shaking her head to clear her vision and her ears. She climbed heavily onto her wobbly feet.

Detached, emotionless, she observed her attacker wriggling on the floor, his left hand trying to stem the blood gushing from his right shoulder. He probably growled, or howled, or wailed; Aileen's eyes showed her the maw of his mouth, but no sounds existed beyond the ringing cotton wool.

"Stupid whore, huh?" Oddly, Aileen *felt* the words forming in her chords but did not hear them. "Snooty bitch, huh?"

His eyes, white with pain and wide with dread, followed the muzzle of his gun. No, *her* gun. She gripped it properly, with both hands, and aimed. Straight at his nuts.

This time, even the thousand bells in her ears couldn't silence Armando's scream.

The stomping of many feet reverberated through the floor. People piled in through the doors and stopped dead in their tracks, blocking the entrance. Their shouts started filtering through the receding noise in Aileen's ears. "She shot the sarge! Armando, she shot Armando! And Henry!"

Henry? She didn't shoot Henry. What were they talking about? Ah, he was still on the ground, knocked out cold.

Two militiamen cut through the press and drew their bows, aiming at Aileen. "Drop the gun! Drop the gun or we'll shoot!"

The gun? Aileen glanced at her hands. She was still clutching it.

She shrugged and let it slide from her fingers.

The soldiers rushed forward, twisted her arms, and tied them behind her back. "Somebody check on the sarge!"

In a blink of an eye, an entire anthill was milling around her. The militiamen dragged her outside.

"He's dead, bled out!"

The news warmed Aileen's heart—making it the single warm object in the whole cold, dull universe.

The guards threw her to her knees beside an archery target butt. Aileen did not resist. The militiamen, joined by a few of their comrades, stepped forward, pushing the agitated onlookers away from her with their bows. All looking the same, the locals scowled, yelled, shook their fists in the air, spit at her, and obstructed the sun. That last part, somehow, was the worst.

The ebbing and flowing of the crowd's hum died down. The wall of grayness parted, and Lady Anna strolled through.

"Is this true?" she inquired, crossing her arms. "Did you kill my Master-at-Arms?"

Aileen's face went slack under the countess's furious frown. She had no defiance left in her, only indifference. "Yes, Your Ladyship."

"Then you'll die, too." Anna's growl extracted an excited howl from the crowd.

"He tried to rape me." Didn't her reasons hold any importance at all?

"Lies! Armando was a noble man!"

"Ask yourself, why else would I shoot his dick off?" If Aileen was going to die anyway, might as well drop the ludicrous honorifics.

"Did she?" the countess asked the senior guard.

The militiaman nodded. He kept a grave expression, but a twitch of his hand to cover his private parts gave away his horror.

"You're a sick, twisted brat. I'm sure he was only trying to charm you."

"Right. By calling me a whore, grabbing my pussy, slapping and choking me? Forgive me if I refused to be charmed."

"You—"

"He also bragged that *you* sent him to break me in."

A shocked murmur swept through the crowd.

Anna's scowl deepened. "Were you alone?"

"Henry tried to intervene, but your lapdog knocked him out."

"Then it's only your word. Who would believe such wild allegations?"

"I would. I heard him say that." Henry pushed through, and the gawkers shied away as if he were contagious. An angry purple bruise adorned his cheekbone.

"Not your best jest, fool." Anna glowered. "Save your breath." She raised her voice for all to hear. "This woman is guilty of murdering an officer of my court! She dies, here and now. Militia, tie her to the target and stuff her full of arrows!"

"Your Ladyship!" Marie gasped behind her. "The alliance with Buffalo! They need her alive!"

"Buffalo-schmuffalo. Some crimes cannot go unpunished! We'll deal with them next year. By the way..." Anna's eyes narrowed. "Where were you? You were supposed to be with her at all times. If you hadn't neglected your duties, Armando would still have been with us!"

Marie paled. Her red, puffy eyes widened.

A wicked smile curved the countess's lips. "There's an example to be made. Guards, tie her up, too! She's as guilty of the Master-at-Arms' death."

Something twisted in Aileen's guts. She'd already accepted her fate. This was the natural conclusion to the downward spiral of the events that had swiped her ten days ago. The one debacle she wouldn't be able to scheme, lie, or negotiate her way out of. Too bad, so sad. But Marie? Aileen's soul revolted against accepting the weight of her death, too.

This was the time to stand her ground. All or nothing. What was the worst they could do? Kill her twice?

She opened her mouth, and the words gushed like a mountain stream. Quiet at first, rapidly picking up volume—and determination.

"This woman you call 'Your Ladyship' is a cold-hearted murderer. A usurper. She killed her husband to take the throne and eliminated everyone connected to her plot."

A wave rippled through the surrounding faceless bodies. A huff, as if the throng took one collective breath.

Aileen addressed the militia, the noblemen, the commoners. She addressed Marie and Henry. She addressed everybody but Anna, whose weak attempts to interrupt her were swept aside by the force of Aileen's conviction.

"Treason! Gag her! Tear her tongue out!" Rage distorted the countess's features, but fear bounced in her eyes. And Aileen was not the only one to see that.

"Let her speak." The old militiaman's slow, deliberate words landed heavily among the murmurs of the crowd. The blood vacated Anna's cheeks. She didn't argue.

The guard turned to Aileen. "Those are serious accusations. Have you any proof?"

A promising beginning, but this was where things got sketchier. Aileen's insides thawed, and the faint whiff of *the game* tickled her nostrils.

"Remember Philip, Count Jason's groom?"

"Yes, what of him?" the guard drawled.

Aileen checked Anna's reaction. Pure hatred glared back. The countess's lips were pressed so tightly together they turned white. Good enough for Aileen, but the audience needed more than that.

"Count Jason died falling off his horse. No matter how you look at it, this was his groom's fault. Either gross negligence, or... intentional sabotage."

"So?" the guard prompted. "Where are you going with this?"

Aileen didn't need his prodding. She was on the roll. "You all know, the threshold for drawing the countess's ire is pretty low. Getting her husband killed should've earned Philip her close attention. Was he executed, or at least disciplined?"

"The word is, he fled to Ithaca, with the first wave of traitors."

"You mean, refugees. I know some have returned." Aileen projected her voice, making it carry across the packed parking lot. "Has anyone seen Philip in Ithaca?"

No answer came.

"What does this prove?" the guard asked, but the understanding had already changed his tone. Thoughtful, not grumpy anymore.

Aileen shrugged. "That he disappeared without a trace. Who would benefit from that?" A flimsy connection, but nobody pointed that out. "Three days later," she continued piling evidence, "Alan the Twiddler, your fellow militiaman, was killed in a drunken brawl. Fell on his own knife, poor guy. How is he related? He had guard duty at the royal stables the morning of Count Jason's untimely death."

The crowd murmured.

"You want more? Here goes. You all knew Sarge Beaverton. By all accounts, a decent man. He'd been heard having misgivings on the subject. Almost as if he'd had a hand in cleaning up that mess. Guess what: a week later, he's sent on an unusual, unnecessary patrol at Corning. No one had patrolled it, ever. So, why there? Simple: no witnesses of him walking into an ambush where his team was massacred. Somebody was waiting for them there. Somebody who knew they were coming."

Aileen threw this explosive charge and finally looked at Anna.

Sweat beaded the countess's forehead. She sensed the change in her subjects' mood, too, and fought to turn the tide. "None of that proves anything. Rumors. Hearsay. Bullshit. I am your sovereign, and I command you to execute this traitor immediately!" Her voice almost didn't tremble. The woman deserved respect, if not sympathy.

The militiaman did not move. "Everyone who heard Beaverton talking was on that patrol. Except me. I was ordered to go too, but my wife went into labor that day. I believe this lady."

"My cousin died in the ambush!" someone shouted.

"My dad was poisoned!" Another. "He investigated Count Jason's death!"

A dam had burst. More and more Watkiners recounted their brush with the conspiracy's aftershocks. On their own, each had been scared out of their minds to speak up; adding their voices to the chorus gave them courage.

On her knees, with her hands bound behind her back, Aileen floated above the scene. Sweat suffused her clothes, but she didn't care. She had won.

"Armando was boning the countess! Fact!"

Irrelevant to the subject, true or not, this revelation delivered the final blow. The invisible superiority bubble around Countess Anna collapsed. The crowd swept in, surrounding her.

"Tie up the countess," the senior militiaman ordered his people. "Lock her up. She'll stand trial for regicide and usurpation."

He bent behind Aileen, cut her ropes, and helped her up. She swayed, but he caught her and bobbed his head. "You did well, Lady Aileen. There'll be turmoil and confusion, but we won't need to live the lie anymore. Thank you. I'm Parsons, by the way. Jack Parsons. Looks like I'll be assuming the Master-at-Arms' position now. As for the next in the rulership line—"

"About that," a familiar voice announced over Aileen's shoulder, and she recoiled from the alcohol fumes. "Get me their attention, Jack."

Parsons considered Henry's request, skepticism written all over his sneering face. Aileen nodded, and the soldier yelled at the top of his lungs, "Listen up, everybody!"

Hundreds of faces turned in creepy synchronicity. Hundreds of mouths paused mid-phrase.

"Here's the thing," Henry giggled. "We need a new ruler. You must be wondering who that may be. Wonder no more, for I have the answer!"

His proclamation was met with muttering and a few catcalls.

The historian ignored those. "In the year 11 PE, His Lordship Terrence the First ascended to the throne. He cemented his laws in his 13 PE Codex—"

Aileen leaned to his ear. "Get to the point already! You're losing them."

Henry's naughty, meaningful smile rustled her feathers. What was the old joker up to?

"Paragraph seven stipulates"—the historian raised his voice to compete against the growing hum of the annoyed listeners—"that whoever overthrows the current ruler, inherits the throne."

As the crushing realization dawned on Aileen, Henry hurried to explain. "Doesn't matter if the previous ruler was deposed through a military action, single combat, or"—he turned and applauded Aileen—"in a battle of wits. Please join me in hailing our new ruler, Countess Aileen!"

Shocked silence hung over the parking lot. A second later, it erupted in a roar. The militiamen were not as fast as the civilians to accede, but followed Jack's lead when he took a knee before Aileen.

"Henry! What in the—" The ear-splitting noise swallowed Aileen's hiss. "Son of a bitch, you framed me! You knew all along, didn't you?"

The historian bowed humbly, pressing a hand to his heart.

"You'll pay for this." Oh, she'd think up some exquisitely fitting punishment for the old boozer.

Aileen faced the crowd. Shit. Was she supposed to say something? Words of gratitude? Encouragement? Promise not to be like her predecessor?

She waved her hand. The cheers swelled.

"Do I have to address them?" she whispered to Parsons.

"You're the sovereign, Lady Aileen. You don't *have* to do anything. But as your loyal Master-at-Arms, I would advise for it."

"Thanks." Aileen squeezed his shoulder. "Watkiners! It's been a wild day. I'm sure our royal historian will waste countless pages capturing its events."

Their laughter was pleasing. Maybe she'd prove to be a poor ruler, but her comedic talent was undeniable. Should she care if they liked her? That remained to be decided.

An ephemeral touch on her nose broke her musings. Then on her cheek, and her forehead. She tilted her head back. Snow. About time. Perfect.

"That's a hint," Aileen announced. "A new season, a new era. Go home, citizens, keep warm. And have a drink on me!" Whatever that meant. Did she have a treasury? Was she rich? Crap, she'd have to deal with budgets. No!

Her newly gained subjects cheered again; the press broke into individuals and groups, and streamed to the exits from the parking lot—turned archery range—turned execution grounds—turned coronation square. Parsons and three of his men formed a protective barrier around Aileen, pushing Henry outside, to her vengeful delight. One guard took off his jacket and held it over Aileen's head.

"Jack, do you think Anna has loyalists? Would they be a threat?"

Parsons scratched the back of his head. "Sorry, my lady, I am not privy to her court's inner workings. Given her, hm, *temper*, I don't expect her to have many friends. At least, the kind that won't turn their backs on her now, you know. But there may be a few. I'll sniff around and let you know, my lady. I'd be more worried about Terrence making a move once he learns of our changes."

"Thank you, Jack. Make the arrangements. Oh, and bring me that gun I used today, would you? I might keep it around, for the fond memories."

A guard behind her chuckled.

Aileen sharply turned to him. "Anything you want to say?"

"Only that I'm proud to serve you, Lady Aileen." His broad, white smile couldn't be more genuine.

Aileen relaxed. "Thank you, soldier."

Parsons reached under his jacket and offered Aileen the gun, handle first. She tucked it into her waistband.

"Jack," she said after a while.

"My lady?"

"I know the militia hadn't been very fond of taking orders from a woman. Am I going to face the same challenge?"

Parsons smacked his lips. "Permission to speak freely, my lady?"

"Go."

"There are women, and there are women. Nobody will mistake you for *her*. I, for one, have absolutely no issue being at your service, Lady Aileen. Others... Depends on the kind of leader you show yourself to be."

"Makes sense. Thank you for your honesty."

"I figured I'd use this chance to give you the truth, before you get used to the bootlicking, my lady."

"Me? Bootlicking?! Never."

"I pray you're right, my lady."

They entered the main compound and climbed to the top floor. Aileen stopped at her room's door, but Parsons went on down the hallway.

"Jack? This is me."

"Respectfully, you're mistaken, my lady. *That* is." He pointed at the countess's suite at the far end.

Aileen took a sharp breath.

She was a Countess now. A sole ruler of a small, backwater, contested, but independent state. Unreal! On top of having been beaten and almost raped, having shot a guy in the balls, and coming within a hair's width from being executed. A cold day in the Seven Hells? No, just another day in the life of Aileen Novak, an Aunt, a fugitive, a hostage, a sovereign. Well, fuck.

"Thank you, Jack."

"I'll take care of the security arrangements, my lady. Blessed night."

She leaned into the double doors, pushing them open, and found Marie waiting inside, bent in a deep curtsy, eyes on the carpet.

Conflicting emotions overwhelmed Aileen. "What are *you* doing here?"

"Your Ladyship..." Marie didn't dare look up. "If you would hear me out... For the sake of old times."

"Speak." Aileen recalled the recent conversation with Parsons and added, "Freely."

Marie straightened and met Aileen's eyes. "I am not happy about today's turn of events."

"Oh? Which part?"

Flustered, Marie gnashed her teeth. "Most of them."

"What happened to 'my lady'?"

Was that a flicker of annoyance?

"Lady Anna was my patron. She made me what I am. But I am ready to swear my allegiance to you, *my lady*."

Aileen arched her brow. "You're *ready*. What a relief." She stepped forward and grabbed the girl's scruff. "What makes you think," she whispered into Marie's ear, "I care about your allegiance?"

Marie tensed, not moving a muscle. "Your Ladyship will need a spymaster."

"Why should I believe a word from your mouth? For all I know, you were in on all Anna's plots, if not the actual mastermind behind them. Did you plan Jason's assassination? Helped eliminate the witnesses?"

"I did not!" Marie tried to push her head up, but Aileen forced it back down. "I had no part in that, Your Ladyship," Marie added, quieter and meeker. "She made me the spymaster on New Year's Eve."

"Great, so only Beaverton's team's blood is on you."

"I didn't know..." Marie's stifled whisper broke on a sob. "She asked me to pass a letter to Ithaca. I had no idea it would end like... that." She sought Aileen's eyes. "You have to believe me!"

Aileen scoffed. "My freshly minted Master-at-Arms advised me a few minutes ago that as a Countess, I don't *have to* anything."

"I am at your mercy—"

"You are. Answer me this: did you know Anna had ordered Armando to break me?"

Marie shook her head. "I didn't, I swear, on... on everything I hold dear!"

Aileen released her and stepped aside. "There's not a single thing of any importance that you knew about. You don't make a great spymaster, do you?" *Unless she's lying through her teeth.*

Marie sank to her hands and knees. "No, I don't."

"Why is this job so important to you?"

"A chance to become more than a simple chambermaid."

Aileen plumped into a chair and put her feet on the antique lacquered desk. "I'll tell you what. I could use a good maid. Let's start with that and see where it takes us. Leave the spying to others for the time being."

Marie rushed forward and kissed her hand.

"Stop it!" Aileen drew back, disgusted. "Never do this again."

"Thank you, my lady, thank—"

"If I ever get even the slightest suspicion you have a hidden agenda..." Aileen folded her fingers into a gun shape and pointed at Marie's head. "Poof."

Marie flinched and grew serious. Her spine straightened. The transformation from a groveling servant into a self-confident person was striking.

Aileen wrinkled her forehead. "This is more like Marie I know. What was all that pathetic act about?"

"I wanted to see what you're made of, Your Ladyship. What kind of ruler you may be."

"Damn, girl. Right now, I'm sorely tempted to have you flogged for playing games with me. Add that to your never-do-again list, understood?"

"Yes, my lady. Sorry, my lady. Never again, my lady."

Aileen tilted her head. "You're mocking me."

"I thought you liked to be called 'my lady'... my lady."

"Ten? Fifteen?"

"My lady?"

"Lashes. How many lashes you've just earned."

For once, Marie swallowed a response.

"That's better. Don't push it. Was *anything* you told me true?"

Marie solemnly nodded. "All of it, Lady Aileen." She didn't squirm under Aileen's scrutinizing stare.

"If I—"

"*All* of it, Lady Aileen," Marie repeated firmly.

Aileen rose. Her legs felt like wood. She stretched. Something cracked in her back. "Light the fireplace and take your leave. I'm off to bed now." An unfinished business gnawed at her at the edge of her mind. Oh. "Marie?"

"Yes, Lady Aileen?"

"I was on my way to see you when that sick fucker accosted me."

"What about, my lady?"

"To tell you your father loves you. Very much. More than anything. A ridiculous amount of love. He sucks at showing it, but that's the truth." There. Her debt was repaid.

Marie impetuously snuggled against Aileen and hugged her. "Thank you," she breathed. "I don't care how many lashes this earns me. I... I'm yours. Forever."

Aileen patted her back. This was the person who'd held the entire nation in fear of speaking out. *Fool me once...* The less you trust them, the closer you should keep them. Weinberg knew what he taught her... *Wait.* He'd kept her close, too.

Chapter 30

Watkins Glen

October 16, 42 PE

Opening her eyes felt like a chore. She didn't want to do chores. She didn't have to do chores... *Didn't have to!*

Aileen's eyes opened wide. She sat with a start.

Were yesterday's events real? Was *any* of it real? Maybe she had dreamed everything up—the abduction, the Hive, Ajinder, the train... She groped around in the darkness. No, this was not her bed in the Warehouse. Slick, smooth linens. Shit, so that's what silk was, slippery, cool to touch. She'd never seen real silk. She couldn't dream it up. This was the countess's bed. And she was in it. She was *it*, the countess.

Aileen slid off the tall mattress, trudged to a gray rectangle hinting at a window, and peeled the curtain aside. The light blinded her. She jerked her head away, squeezing her eyes shut. Then, still wincing, peeped through a narrow slit. The world was white and pure. No, the world still was ugly and full of shit like it had always been, but all that was covered by undisturbed snow that had continued overnight, hiding the mud and the wickedness.

Aileen turned to the room. Definitely not the Warehouse.

An enormous bed occupied the middle, wider than it was long, carved redwood with a canopy and all. *Armando was boning the countess*, came an unwanted recollection. Here, on this bed? Ew. First thing she'd ask Marie: to change—and burn!—the sheets, precious silk or not.

A matching desk and a dressing table, all probably pilfered from the same museum.

Two doors, besides the main entrance. An ensuite bathroom, nice... and a walk-in closet! Damn. This countess gig might not be all bad yet.

Aileen shivered. Why was it so cold? She checked the fireplace. The embers hardly smoldered, providing comfort mainly to the gray ashes around them.

Aileen looked down. Shit! She had been so spent last night she hadn't even undressed. She was still wearing the same jeans, shirt, and jacket. What a slob. At least she'd taken her boots off... The gun! Aileen patted the small of her back and, panicked, ruffled through the sheets. A sigh of relief escaped her lips when her fingers snugged the hard, cold shape under the pillow. Good girl.

She sniffed her collar. Yuck. She had to change. And a bath. Where was Marie when she was needed?

Aileen wrapped the blanket around herself and collapsed onto the bed. *Countess Aileen* had a solid sound to it. She didn't need to run anymore. To hide. To escape. To do anything! She could spend the whole day in bed, and no one would dare to object! Maybe that's what she should do. Treat herself. The last week and a half had been so mentally exhausting, the tiredness saturated her to her bones. Yes. First, send a messenger to Locksville and to Marc, then have a bath, then breakfast in bed, then—

A series of insistent knocks on the door interrupted her daydreaming. "Your Ladyship? Are you up?"

Aileen rolled her eyes and growled, "Come in!"

Parsons entered, followed by Marie. One look at his concerned frown was enough to blow off the last vestiges of Aileen's complacency. Fuck. The best-laid plans...

"What is it?" She reached under her pillow for the gun.

"My lady, scouts report a large Ithacan force advancing through our territory. It's moving fast, bypassing all villages. Looks like they're aiming straight at Watkins Glen."

"I take it, not their usual raid."

"No, my lady. This is something bigger. The scouts also spotted foreign reinforcements. Possibly mercenaries, with firearms."

Aileen rubbed her face. "This is bad, right?"

"Worse."

"That Terrence's move you were talking about yesterday, is this it?"

Parsons hesitated. "I don't think so, Your Ladyship. It is not impossible that the news had reached him already, but assembling such a force takes time. My gut tells me it's a freaky coincidence."

"Which doesn't make the danger any less real."

"No, Your Ladyship."

"So, what do we do? Advise me, Master-at-Arms."

"They'll be delayed by the snow. If we leave now, we can ambush them between Odessa and Montour Falls. The road passes through dense vegetation there. That's our chance to break them. From there on... The fight will show. If they don't turn tail, we'll make it our last stand."

"I don't like the sound of that."

"Me neither, my lady. But if we fail, nothing will protect your capital from the invading force. Every trained, able-bodied militia member will be there."

"What are we waiting for? Let's roll! Marie, get me something warm to wear, I'm freezing." No bath, then. Sucks.

"Your Ladyship will ride along?" Parsons cocked his head, and a vague hint of approval flickered in his eyes.

"Of course Your Ladyship will ride along!" Aileen spiced up her response with a generous pinch of indignation. "Did you think I'll stay behind and cower?"

The militiaman cracked a smile and bowed. "I hoped not, Your Ladyship, but didn't want to presume." He reached into a bag and produced a holster and a belt. "I thought you may find these useful."

Aileen snatched them from his hands, wrapped the belt around her waist, and holstered her gun. "That *was* presumptuous, Parsons. Thank you."

Without saying a word, he fished from the same bag two more magazines and a box of ammo, like a magician. Their eyes met. Aileen nodded.

"This should do, my lady." Marie brought a long woolen trench coat, a fur hat, a knitted scarf, and a pair of mittens.

"One slight hiccup," Aileen said, letting Marie dress her. "I can't ride."

Parsons didn't bat an eye. "I'll have horses harnessed to your stagecoach."

"*My* stagecoach?"

"Yes, my lady, the one that brought you from Buffalo."

"Oh." Maynard wouldn't be thrilled. Did he even know about her coup? *That* would rattle him, for sure. And fucking LeClaire would have a seizure! Ha! If she survived this day, she'd show the Buffs the mother of all middle fingers by signing an alliance with Rochester. *If*.

"Let's go kick some ass."

"Hurrah!" Parsons saluted.

Aileen blocked Marie's way into the stagecoach. "Where do you think *you* are going?"

"A good maid—"

"Oh, shut it." Aileen moved aside. "Your funeral."

The door on the other side creaked, opening, and Henry climbed in. He dropped onto the cushioned seat, shook the snow off his feet, and rubbed his hands under his armpits.

"What?" he asked, innocently meeting Aileen's glare.

"You too?"

"Wouldn't miss it for a fortune."

"What's the point of being a sovereign if I can't get rid of you two?"

A command sounded outside. The bench underneath jerked and shook.

Aileen's mood took a nosedive. The same coach was taking her into the unknown again. This unknown didn't look any rosier than her trip out of Buffalo.

She'd never been in a battle. Never seen real fighting, beyond a few benign brawls. Never been shot at. Jack had kept a straight face, but their odds sounded atrociously poor.

What the fuck, fate? Really? Why, why couldn't she get a single day to relax, to enjoy a win? Why did she have to roll from one crisis straight into another?

If she hadn't challenged Anna... No, if she hadn't escaped from the Hive... She would've been safe and sound, warm and secure now. Probably basking in Ajinder's tender hug, nuzzling his neck.

Aileen shivered at how distant, illusory that memory seemed. Too far away, too long ago.

A black-and-white, depressive terrain rolled outside the window under the overcast sky. A spike of hatred constricted Aileen's throat. Was this foreign land going to be her last view before she died? She didn't need this, *any* of this. The title, the responsibility, the politics. She yearned to be a nobody; a gray, invisible girl no one knew. The simple future she'd been destined to have, if her parents hadn't perished in that fire. Terrence wouldn't have had any beef with her; wouldn't want to kill her, capture her, take her to yet another prison and force her to abdicate her throne... Damn it to the Seven Hells, she hadn't even got a chance to sit on the stupid thing! And the truth was, she couldn't care less. All she wanted was for this insanity to be over with, one way or another. To go home, wherever that might be these days, and fucking *rest*.

The stagecoach stopped. Parsons climbed the steps. "We walk from here."

Aileen obeyed, her head filled with echoing emptiness. *Get it over with.*

The forest, a gloomy mix of naked deciduous trees and lofty, unapproachable conifers, greeted Aileen with a demonstrative indifference. She followed half the force led by Parsons. The second half was spreading on the opposite side of the road.

The militia took cover behind the first line of trees, stringing their bows, sticking bunches of arrows into the snowbanks, and talking in hushed tones. As if nothing out of the ordinary was happening. As if they'd made their last stand every other day.

The tree trunks provided concealment, but no protection from the vicious wind.

Marie offered Aileen the sheep skin she'd brought from the coach.

Aileen shook her head. "Give it to your father. If he freezes his fingers off, who would write the epic account of our heroic deaths?"

The historian, shaking in his inadequately thin jacket, gratefully accepted the extra layer, too frozen for snarky comments. After some awkward waddling around, Marie snuck in too, cozying up to Henry. He drew her closer without saying a word.

Aileen's cheeks itched from the pinpricks of the cold. She pulled her scarf up, covering her mouth and nose up to her eyes.

"Contact!" A wave of whispers passed down the chain of the militiamen from the easternmost flank. They dug deeper into the snow. Aileen took a knee behind a second-row tree. Her heart refused to race, numb to the danger.

A clump of people appeared on the road. A hundred? More? The tail of the column was not in sight. At least twice her militia's numbers. Yes, the Watkiners had the element of surprise and the cover, but would that be enough? She couldn't tell.

They were all going to die. All these men—and a few women—whose names she didn't know, whom she wouldn't recognize in the street. Mature veterans and fourteen-year-old kids. All of them. And for what? To keep her on the throne she'd neither asked for nor wanted? Fuck that.

"Stop!" she yelled, and waded through the snow to the road. Her cry echoed in the woods, spooking a flock of birds.

Jack's wide, uncomprehending eyes flashed in her side vision. "Lady Aileen—"

She plowed past him without slowing down. His heavy steps rustled behind.

The invading column stopped, dismounting and taking cover behind their horses. A hedgehog of Apocalypse, bristling with arrows, pikes, and glaives. A few gun muzzles followed her from its head.

She lost her footing and tumbled into the roadside snowbank. Jack's firm arms helped her up. His kind, encouraging nod stabbed her under the ribs. This man had made his peace with dying by her side. *Stay back, you fool!* Aileen pushed him into the snow and stomped forward.

She stopped in the middle of the road, facing the sole man who hadn't dismounted.

This must have been Terrence. She'd never given him much thought. Subconsciously, she'd pictured some kind of Prince Charming from the books Mom had read to her. The short, rather plump, middle-aged man with tiny eyes on a bland, pockmarked face couldn't be further from that image. To his credit, he showed no fear.

"Who are you, woman?" His voice, unexpectedly deep and sonorous, defied the wind.

Aileen forced a step forward. What did she have to lose? She was already as good as dead. She unwrapped the scarf to show her face. "Countess Aileen of Great Watkins and Odessa, Baroness... Protectress... blah-blah-blah, haven't learned all the titles yet."

Terrence's slack jaw was precious, but Aileen didn't get to marvel at it.

"Aileen?!" Several voices exclaimed in the lord's retinue. She glimpsed a beard, a smile, and a turban before a tall figure swept her off her feet and whirled her in a tight embrace.

"Aji?" she squeaked. Her heart was about to burst through her ribs. "Here?"

He carefully planted her on the ground. His lips found hers. The world blinked out of existence before whistles and catcalls brought her back. Ajinder pulled away, smiling from ear to ear, still clinging to her. Over his shoulder, she saw Bo limping closer at his top speed, and Fox brandishing a shotgun. Pinky was there too, carrying a scarily massive gun like it was a feather, and Waffles, and even Pogo. Wow. They came. They all came for her.

Aileen's vision blurred.

"Anyone cares to explain what's going on?" Terrence cut into the celebration.

Aileen delicately pushed Ajinder aside. "This is my mess to deal with." She blinked the tears off. "Don't go anywhere."

"They'll have to knock me out cold and drag me away. I am not letting you out of my sight!"

Aileen caressed his cheek and approached Terrence. He finally dismounted and waited, tapping his foot while Aileen hugged Bo and the rest of her crew along the way.

"Your Lordship?" Aileen nodded.

"Your, hm, Ladyship?" Terrence, a foot shorter than her, wrinkled his forehead. "What's your claim on this title? What happened to Anna? I don't like being confused. Please explain."

"A long story, but here's the more pressing matter. You and your force are in the center of an ambush."

"I figured as much."

The Watkins militia were peeking from behind the trees, cautious but not hiding anymore.

"We have two options." Aileen emphasized her math with the matching number of fingers, but her mitten rendered the gesture useless. "One, go for each other's throats and try to kill as many as we can. Chances are, neither you nor I survive to see the outcome, and it will take both our domains decades to recover. Two, you and I sit and talk like civilized people."

Terrence scanned the trees, his own force, and returned his attention to Aileen. "We have the numbers. And the firepower."

"Respectfully, Lord Terrence," Bo wedged into the conversation, "our firepower belongs to whichever side Aileen represents."

Terrence grinned. "I presume, this is the hostage you asked me to help rescue."

"The very same."

Aileen stared at Bo in awe. "How?"

He brushed her sleeve with a crooked, toothless smile. "A long story."

A commotion drew everyone's attention to the side of the road, where Marie and Henry floundered in a snowbank. Parsons pulled them out, one by one, and the three approached. Terrence's guards barred their way, but he waved at them to stand down.

Henry bowed. "Your Lordship."

"Historian. How come you're sober?"

"Can't afford to miss any part of this momentous occasion, Your Lordship." "And this?"

Aileen pointed. "My Master-at-Arms, Parsons. My maid."

"You brought a *maid*? To an ambush? I'll never understand women." Terrence shrugged. "Whatever. I'm a civilized man, Lady Aileen. What do you suggest?"

"We call all-clear, and order campfires to be set. Get our people hot chow and tea, wouldn't want any of them to freeze their balls off while waiting for our conversation to conclude."

Terrence chuckled. "Spoken like a true lady. I agree, frozen balls aren't helpful for the troops' morale. Shall we?"

"No dirty tricks?"

"Word of a Harmon."

Aileen checked with Bo and Ajinder. Both nodded. She shook Terrence's hand.

"You're a dangerous man, historian." Terrence sipped from his steaming mug. "I will remember that."

"As long as you're on the right side of history, Your Lordship, you've got nothing to fear." Henry's nervous chuckle betrayed the effect of the threat. He brought his hands closer to the warmth of the fire.

"Are you trying to intimidate my jester?" Aileen smiled, but let the edge in her voice convey the message. Henry was annoying, at times ridiculous, but he was *her* man.

Terrence did not bite, masterfully diverting the subject. "I would love to hear *all* of your story one day, Lady Aileen. I've got so many questions! How you wound up in Watkins, who your friends are"—he gestured at Bo and Ajinder—"and what they did to obtain a very compelling letter from Commander Nieminen himself."

Aileen would've loved to hear *that* part of the story, too. She glanced at Bo. He winked. Okay, later.

"For now," the Ithacan continued, "I need to know: how serious are you about taking over Watkins?"

"Excuse me?" Acidic irritation bubbled up in Aileen's stomach. That thin, understanding smile... He didn't know the first thing about her!

"Let's be rational. You come out of nowhere, accidentally overthrow your predecessor, whose legitimacy had been questionable at best, and—*shazam!*—you're a countess. Are you sure you want this?"

Aileen's anger flared—and died, hissing like a fire in an unequal fight against a bucket of water. Wasn't that the question she'd been asking herself all along? Not half an hour ago, she'd concluded she didn't need any of this. She hadn't planned to fill Anna's shoes, and was still sour about Henry's entrapping her. She should have been happy to unburden herself from the uninvited duties and responsibilities. Then why was she hesitating? No, this wasn't hesitation; she was offended and dismayed by the suggestion.

Aileen surveyed the faces around the campfire. Everyone's eyes were on her. Ajinder at her side, with an entirely untimely and inappropriate grin. Bo, expectant, calculating. Ithacan military commander, Reiner, tense and suspicious. Parsons, suspicious of Reiner too, but also concerned. Marie, appalled by Aileen's silence. Henry, brimming with joy at witnessing something big first-hand, generously pouring from a small metal flask into his tea. And Terrence, patiently waiting for her to say 'No.'

Aileen cleared her throat. "Yes." She projected her newly found conviction right into her counterpart's conceited face. "Yes, I am damn sure!"

And she was, she really was. Warmth spread through her chest, the best sign of a right decision.

A stray herself, she couldn't abide by the thought of abandoning the Watkiners now, when they were at a crossroads. Even if unwillingly, through Henry's deception, she had accepted the responsibility for their wellbeing. And, well, the lifestyle her new title offered was countless levels beyond what she'd ever experienced—or dreamed of. Its allure was shamefully selfish but undeniable. What drew her the most, though, with the irresistible force of gravity, was the enormity of the new challenge. She owed it to herself, to prove she *could*. That she wasn't a fraud, an impostor.

Terrence ruefully shook his head. "This complicates things. Understand, I'll never give up the dream of consolidating my father's lands."

Aileen shrugged. "Try anything, and I'll take your throne too."

A shadow rippled over the man's face. "The military option is still on the table."

"Is it?" Bo's pointed question poked a hole in the expanding bubble of hostility between Aileen and Terrence. "Pinky and his machinegun will decimate your force, Your Lordship. Ail— er, *Lady* Aileen's archers will mop up the leftovers. If she stays, we stay. That would change the power equation, wouldn't you agree?"

"Add Rochester to that equation," Aileen said before the Ithacan could respond.

Terrence licked his lips. "What do you mean?"

"Clearly, Bo has secured some sort of understanding with them. Enough to influence you. On top of that, for reasons that are irrelevant at the moment, Buffalo occupies the honorary first place on the list of my enemies. Needless to say, Anna's alliance with them is now null and void, which makes Watkins a natural Rochester ally. How do you think they'd look at their stepchildren squabbling? You may not like their slap on your wrist."

"We are at an impasse." Respect replaced animosity in Terrence's small eyes, then a flash of slyness. "What about a dynastic marriage? A perfectly peaceful solu—"

The scraping of Ajinder's knife against its sheath wiped the smile off Terrence's lips. "Forget I asked."

Aileen sighed. "Let's agree to refrain from hostile actions for, say, a year. I'll use this time to learn the local realities and history." She tilted her head toward Henry. "Then we'll meet and talk again. Deal?"

Terrence considered, sending a questioning look to Reiner. The commander bowed his head. The Lord of Ithaca looked back at Aileen. "Deal. On one condition: hand Anna over, and this isn't negotiable."

Aileen creased her brow. "Why? You want to marry *her*?"

The Ithacan did not reciprocate her feigned playfulness. "She'll be tried for the murder of my brother," he announced gravely.

"Fine." Aileen shrugged. "You—"

Marie snapped. "Your Ladish—"

Aileen silenced her with a dark glare. "Ithaca can have her. Less headache for me. I still haven't got the taste for those gruesome executions."

Terrence stood and extended his hand over the fire.

Aileen shook it. "Not sure how much weight my name carries for you, but what the Hells. You have my word, too."

She looked around. "Any more grudges I need to be aware of?"

"Reiner." Parsons cracked his knuckles. "Did you do Beaverton in?"

Reiner exchanged quick glances with Bo, and Aileen's heart sank.

The Ithacan commander rose to his feet and met Jack's belligerent stare. "Yes."

One plus one equals... Or, rather, *two minus one*. Aileen closed her eyes. A single spasm shook her body. "Who killed Tick?" she asked, unable to look away from the flames. Her dead tone snuffed all other sounds; even the rustle of the fire quieted.

"Beaverton," rasped Bo. "He caught us in the act."

Aileen pressed her palm into her face, so hard that it hurt, and pulled it down, as if wiping Tick's blood away. She exhaled sharply and forced her eyes open. "The score is settled, Parsons. Beaverton got his due."

Her Master-at-Arms squeezed his jaws and bowed.

"Other grievances? No? We're done. Take me home." She couldn't let them see her fall apart.

"Lady Aileen?" Terrence's voice behind her back stopped her in her tracks. She turned her head half-way, lending him her ear.

"Congratulations on your ascent, my lady. You'll... make a formidable ruler."

Chapter 31

Watkins Glen

October 16, 42 PE

Aileen cared nothing for comfortable seating, yet was given the proper space in the stagecoach. Others—Henry, Marie, Fox, and Bo—huddled on the opposite couch, piling up each time the vehicle hit a hump or made a turn. Waffles and Pogo shared the box with the driver out front, and Pinky, after a brief survey of his options, had climbed straight onto the roof.

And Ajinder, true to his promise to never let Aileen leave his sight again, didn't think twice before claiming the seat by her side.

But Aileen hardly paid attention to any of that.

She should have been proud. Elated. She single-handedly prevented bloodshed. Avoided the last stand. Patched, even if temporarily, the relationship with a sibling state. All in the span of a few hours since having the throne forced on her.

Not enough? Her crew came to rescue her, forging who-knew-what alliances along the way. The fact she'd taken care of her affairs pretty well on her own did not diminish the major miracle of their appearance. Bo, who'd never traveled before that fateful job, tracked her, practically in no time. How outlandish was that?

Ajinder arrived too; what they were to each other remained unclear, but his presence this far from New Kowloon hinted at his seriousness.

Any one of these events would have made the highlight of her year. Should have. Yet, all of them, combined, were not more than a spark of light against the crushing sea of blackness.

Tick. She *did* get him killed.

She'd had her suspicions since that revelation about an unidentified body in Corning on the night of the ball. The *possibility* it was his had almost driven her off the pier, to the bottom of the lake, but she'd willfully let herself get distracted. After all, it had only been a speculation, and she'd always excelled at denial. Now, the certainty of the knowledge, its *finality*, left her no escape. Maybe someday she'd overcome this all-encompassing shame, but the pain was there to stay forever. Its jagged edges would get duller. Her calloused soul would get used to being torn every waking hour. But in this moment, the agony was slicing it into pieces, cut, after cut, after cut. She deserved that, for sending Tick to his death.

So much darkness welled inside her, it splashed out, flooding the cramped space. No one spoke, not even the habitually insensitive Henry. Marie looked terrified. Fox pretended he wasn't there. Bo, always supernaturally attuned to Aileen's mood swings, observed her through half-closed eyes.

Ajinder's arm wrapped around Aileen's shoulders. A rebuke formed on the tip of her tongue, waiting to be triggered by some stupid lovey-dovey bullshit. But he said nothing, simply holding her, and the hurtful words dissolved. His touch fed the spark of light. It grew, melting the darkness, until they split her world into two, neither able to overpower the other, with her stuck in the middle. Still, Aileen's precipitous sliding toward self-hatred halted. She leaned her head to the side, touching Ajinder's hand with her cheek.

Aileen popped the door open before the stagecoach came to a complete stop in front of her *palace* and shot like a cork from a bottle. She barreled through the staircases and hallways, eager to escape the well-wishing but intolerable company; to be alone with the pain; to relish her fully merited suffering; to digest everything that had happened without being watched, questioned, or cuddled.

She didn't get to slam her suite's doors shut, lock them, and bar them. Ajinder slipped past on her heels, followed by the rest of her tiptoeing entourage.

Bo shuffled in last, dragging his leg, hauling a black tote, and huffing angrily. "Seriously? Thanks for giving me a thought! What was this race all about?"

Exasperated, Aileen turned to the window, showing them her royal backside. "Leave," she croaked. "All of you."

Not a single footstep. Bastards.

"You heard Her Ladyship." At least Parsons remembered his duties. "Out! Out!"

"Why?" Bo ignored the Master-at-Arms, addressing Aileen directly. "So you can mope and sulk? Bask in your guilt and self-pity? Not gonna let—"

"Watch your tone, little man," Parsons growled, "when talking to Her Ladyship!"

"Ah, right, Her Pouting Ladyship." Bo's mirthless chuckle hurt more than his stinging words. "Countess of insecurity, baroness of glum."

A gurgling sound made Aileen turn back. Blood rushed to Jack's face. His eyes bulged. His half-drawn sword left Bo unfazed.

"Don't mind his big mouth, Parsons." A percussive sigh shook Aileen's chest. Forcing her to give up in their arguments was Bo's specialty. "This ass is my brother."

Bo took it down a notch. "I grieve for Tick too, Leen. I was there. I *saw it happen*." He shuddered, and Aileen's heart shuddered with him. Bo balled his fists, waiting out the tremors. "Wrong place, wrong time. None of that was your fault. Leave it be."

"But if I hadn't—"

Bo winced. "I mean it, Leen. Just stop. Seriously. By the way…"

Aileen watched, speechless, as he unzipped his bag, unwrapped a thick wad of rugs, and held out an impossible glass creature.

"Careful." Bo placed it in Aileen's hand. "They're ridiculously fragile."

Aileen brought her open palm up to her eyes, letting the light play on the stained-glass surfaces. Her breath caught. The leftover darkness inside her thawed, leaving only bittersweet heartache behind. Aileen swallowed. "It's amazing."

"Is it"—Parsons approached—"from your Museum of Glass, my lady?"

Aileen reluctantly tore her gaze off the figurine. "*My* museum?"

"You're the Protectress of Corning, my lady. Part of your title."

Aileen's and Bo's eyes met. "Fuck me," she said.

"Oh, the irony." Bo shook his head. "You were contracted to steal from your future self. But that isn't all. Any idea who commissioned this job?"

"Some middleman from Buffalo," Aileen said without looking up. The creature's pull was irresistible. "They can suck their own dick for all I care."

"Nah-ah. You won't believe me when I tell you."

Annoyed by the distraction, Aileen met Bo's knowing smile. "Don't milk it."

"Shang Ka Yi."

"You're kidding me."

"And the best part is, he doesn't need them anymore. I've been dragging this bag through half the world to give these creatures to you. As your homecoming gift."

Oh, Bo. He knew her so well. Aileen pulled him into a hug. "*You're* the best homecoming gift anyone can ask for."

"Speaking of home…" Fox found the courage to jump into the conversation. "I gather you'll be setting shop here now?"

Locksville. Streeters. Another subject Aileen had pushed to the back of her mind, with everything that had been going on. "Who's in charge there? Oscar?"

Bo's indecipherable grimace could equally mean disapproval and begrudging acceptance. "He'll come around."

At her side, Ajinder added, "He's a far cry from you, but solid enough."

Aileen's eyebrows jumped up as she turned to him. "How do *you* know Oscar?"

Ajinder serenely met her disbelief. "We crossed paths in Locksville."

"Can't believe I missed *that* encounter. Glad you approve of him."

Fox grinned. "If Oscar follows Ajinder's advice, the Streeters will be fine."

Aileen traced Fox's adoring gaze. Aji? "You people are making less and less sense. We've got a lot of catching up to do. But yes, I'm kinda stuck here now. Needless to say, you all are welcome to stay, too."

Bo climbed onto her desk, dangling his feet. "You know you wouldn't be able to get rid of me even if you wanted, yes?"

Fox shrugged. "I go where Aileen goes."

Pinky saluted with a grin.

Pogo and Waffles looked at each other and nodded in unison.

Aileen couldn't contain a smile. "The crew's back together."

Parsons frowned. "What exactly will their role be?"

Aileen patted him on the shoulder. "No idea, Jack. Being on the right side of the law is refreshingly new for us all."

"Oh, my," Henry muttered from the corner. He'd been so quiet, Aileen forgot he was in the room. "Whom did I bring to power?"

"Ah, historian." Aileen gave him the stink eye. "This will enliven your chronicles, I promise. But your due punishment is still pending. Now"—she looked around—"can everyone *please* leave? Get some rest, grab lunch. Jack, see to it. I want to talk to Ajinder. Alone."

She met Bo's questioning stare. "No moping, no sulking. You win."

A flicker in his eyes. Something else was the matter. But before she could glean an insight, Bo stirred, slid off the desk, and headed straight to Marie. "Accompany me, the maid who isn't a maid."

"Ah... What?" Marie stuttered, flustered.

Bo's predatory cackle made her even less comfortable. "I know Aileen. She'd never keep a maid if she could help it. Come, tell me all about this place."

Henry and the Locksvillers followed.

Parsons paused on the brink, eying Ajinder with professional interest. Aileen waved off his concerns. "It's fine, Jack. I'm safer than I've ever been." The Master-at-Arms yielded, bowing and shutting the doors.

"You came." Aileen finally turned to Ajinder. Why was it so hot in her room? She undid her trench coat buttons.

The weight of his hands on her hips sent a shock up her spine.

"You really came."

The tip of his nose tickled hers.

"I'm sorry I didn't wait for you," she whispered.

"I shouldn't have left."

"But you came for me."

"I always will."

She touched his weather-beaten lips with hers. "Or you can never leave again."

<hr>

"This bed is a vast improvement over New Kowloon. Worth your title."

They lay across the sheets, and even stretching, Aileen's hands didn't reach the edge. She turned to her side, facing Ajinder, and grimaced. "You stink."

"Well, excuse me, Your Refined Ladyship, I've been riding fifteen hours a day to get here in time. To tell you the truth, you are quite pungent yourself. Not that I'm complaining..."

"Aren't we a pair of romantics?" Aileen sniffed her armpit and winced. "Damn. I was about to take a bath when the news of your raid arrived. Next time, I'm telling the attackers to hold off while my maid is scrubbing me."

"A bath, huh? I'd love to join you. Your maid's presence may make it... interesting." He winked.

"You're a pig, you know? You just had mind-blowing sex with the sovereign of this realm, and you dare bring up a *maid*?"

"She isn't a simple maid— Ow!" He rubbed the shoulder she punched him in.

Aileen rested her head on her elbow. "I kept my promise."

"Which one?"

"Not to sleep with my other abductors. Not that I had much say, but still."

Ajinder blinked. His unsure smile shifted into a frown. "Did any of them..."

"Well, there was this jackass here, the previous Master-at-Arms." Not exactly a pillow talk subject, but Aileen had already painted herself into a corner. She carefully controlled her face. "Tried to rape me yesterday."

In a blink, Ajinder was on his feet, with his knife unsheathed and murder in his eyes. "Where. Is. He."

Aileen slid from the bed to his side and pushed his arm down. "He's dead, Aji. I can order his body dug up, if you want to stab him some more, but I've already shot his balls off."

"Aileen..." Ajinder's knife clanked on the nightstand. He took her arms. "Are you alright? I'm so sorry. If I hadn't left—"

Aileen leaned in, so close their lips almost touched again. "Shut up, Aji. I don't want to hear any of that again. Running away was stupid, and I reaped what I sowed. LeClaire was much worse."

"LeClaire won't bother you again."

"*I* am the one who's going to bother *him*."

Ajinder's scowl softened. "That's unlikely."

"You don't think I can, or will? I'll have you know, I am not a forgiving type."

Ajinder ran his fingers through her hair. "Haven't doubted that for a second. But he's been taken care of."

"How?" Not that she didn't trust Ajinder... She *had* to know.

"We paid him a visit."

By the time Ajinder finished his story, Aileen was slack-jawed. She pulled him closer and hid her face in the side of his neck so he wouldn't see her tears. "You did all this? For me?" Her treacherous voice trembled. "Locksville, LeClaire, the jail... Then Rochester, and Ithaca..."

"Lots of people worked together to get you back. Marc, Weinberg, even Shang Ka Yi. And, of course, Bo and your crew."

"None of them stood a chance without you. Aji, I don't know what to say."

He delicately pried her head from his shoulder and waited for her wet eyes to meet his. His question was obvious; it didn't need to be put into words.

Ajinder's actions had made it clear his intentions were serious. But what about her? Aileen searched the deepest recesses of her heart, trying to call up any doubts, to discern any sign foreshadowing future abuse. She came up empty. No man was perfect, but this one, whose touch made her safe and warm, who fed her strength rather than leeching on hers, came damn close to that mark.

"Yes," she said, and nodded for emphasis. "Yes."

Ajinder squeezed her in a bear hug, extracting a crack from her spine and a squawk from her throat. "Just so we're clear," his playful whisper tickled her ear, "you've agreed to the life of a housewife, yes? Popping babies and all?"

Aileen, momentarily dumbfounded by the contrast between the solemn moment they'd had and this ridiculousness, giggled and bit his earlobe. "Your ability to have those babies is in a serious peril, Aji!"

"Uh-oh. Fine, stay the countess. What does that make me? A count?"

"Keep dreaming, mister! You'll be my, whatchamacallit, consort."

"Sounds *deliciously* dirty. Let's *consort* some more?" His hands wandered, making Aileen acutely aware of her nakedness.

"You're so twisted."

"Or we can have that bath."

"I'd love that. Let me order hot water. Put something on, I am not sharing you with anyone. Especially not with my maid."

———————

For dinner, Aileen raided Anna's wardrobe and settled on a much more modest dress than the last time, but let Marie do her hair again.

She didn't invite anyone but Bo to the dining room. Marie, despite her protestations, was left to vent to a closed door. Aileen, Ajinder and Bo could serve themselves well enough.

Between the spoonfuls of soup, Bo kept watching her and Ajinder with an oddly calm expression.

"Bo?" Aileen put her spoon down. "What's wrong?"

"Wrong? Nothing's wrong. You two look radiant. Must be great to be back together."

"Of course, it's great! And I can't tell you how happy I am to see you here, too!"

"Right."

"Aji told me about everything you've done to get me back. It's... It's insane! I know, it sounds silly to thank you for that, and I would've done the same for you, but... Thank you, Bo. You're the best! Oh, and those glass creatures, I—"

"I'm leaving, Leen."

Aileen inhaled a gob of saliva and descended into a coughing bout. Bo patiently waited.

"Why?" The word scratched her tortured throat. "Where to?"

"Home. Locksville. With what I've seen and done, I can take the Streeters to the next level. Oscar is, um, uninspired. We can do so much better. I've got connections now, everywhere from The Hive to Ithaca. Just imagine the possibilities." Bo was talking levelly.

A piece of Aileen died. Life without Bo? His jokes, his rants, his advice? His very presence by her side? It was unconscionable.

"You said I wouldn't be able to get rid of you." She wasn't haggling, only trying to make sense of Bo's absurd words.

"You won't. I'm always here for you, Leen. Just not from up close, going forward. Time for both of us to grow up."

"I... don't understand." Aileen's wrists fell limply onto the table. The dishes clinked.

"He loves you." Ajinder slowly nodded to Bo.

"I love him too!" Aileen threw her head up. How was this supposed to explain anything?

Ajinder covered her hand with his. "Not like a brother, Aileen. He's *in love* with you. It's painfully obvious. You seem to be the only one oblivious to this."

Aileen's nose and lips went cold and numb. A moment later, a wave of heat broke sweat on her forehead. She searched Bo's peaceful face for any hint of contradiction. That this was some kind of stupid, elaborate hoax. If this was true... Where was his pain? Jealousy? Anything?

Bo met her feverish attention without flinching.

Aileen closed her eyes. He'd already gone through all those phases, that's why. He'd made his peace. Aileen forced herself to look at Bo again. Her heart pounded. "Is this true?" An unnecessary question, but she needed to hear this from him.

"Of course, Leen. Since the day we met."

Aileen gasped, sobbed, and hid behind her hands. "I'm so sorry, Bo," she whispered.

"Don't be." How could he be so lighthearted? "It's all good. You're safe now, and happy with Ajinder. That's all that matters to me."

Aileen sniffed and peeked through her fingers. "I don't want to lose you."

Bo's toothless, mildly reproachful smile turned her inside out. "You can never lose me, Leen."

"Bo..."

"Shut up. Let me tell you about my ideas. You, of all people, will appreciate them."

"Ideas?"

"I should've started traveling sooner. Seeing all those places, how different yet similar they are, got me thinking. Imagine the stretch of land between Rochester and the City tied by cooperation agreements. Free trade, protected passage, mutual defense, all connected by The Station's trains and New Kowloon's ships... The Silk Road, like in the history books."

"Don't forget Shang Ka Yi's science lab," added Ajinder.

Bo considered. "Sure, if you say so. Now, we can add Finger Lakes to the list. Unless, of course, Your Ladyship objects."

"My Ladyship will consider your proposals favorably, Uncle Bo." Aileen stumbled, evaluating the name. It tasted perfectly balanced. Like something that should have been in use for a long time.

"Buffalo Union is the only thorn in my future vision's side. We can all gang up on them..."

"Wait a second." Aileen sat up. "Maynard! Fuck, I totally forgot about him."

"The trader who escorted you here?"

"The *Senior* Trader."

Bo shrugged. "Let's hear him out."

To his credit, the Buff kept his cool when Parsons brought him in. "Hello, Aileen," was all he said.

"It's Lady Aileen, or Your Ladyship," the Master-at-Arms corrected him.

"I see." Maynard looked straight at Aileen. "Am I in trouble?"

"Do you want to be in trouble, Richard?"

"I'd rather not."

"Excellent. I used to be mad at you, but it's all in the past. Your one good deed on that train has bought you my forgiveness. We're even."

"How very generous, Your Ladyship." Maynard's bow concealed his expression. If he was mocking her, he did well to hide that.

"Here's a question for you, Senior Trader." Bo cut to the chase. "How senior *are* you?"

The Buff tilted his head. "And who might *you* be, young man?"

Bo's fingers tapped on the table. "You're misreading the situation, Maynard. You're not the one asking questions here. But to get this conversation flowing, let's say I am the person who may take you back home. Depending on your usefulness and level of cooperation."

Maynard scoffed. "'Cooperation'? You mean betrayal? Forget about it."

Bo snorted. "No one needs your betrayal. In fact, we're talking about a better future for Buffalo. But by all means, go ahead and blow this chance."

The Buff lowered his eyes. "You should know that I am not welcome in Buffalo at the moment."

"What you're saying in so many vague words is that you've been exiled by LeClaire, yes?" Bo rested his chin on his hand.

"How do you... Never mind. Yes."

"Assume the Deputy Security Supervisor won't be a problem."

"Are we talking about the same LeClaire? How can he *not* be a problem?"

"Wrong question, Senior Trader. 'How can he not *be*?' would be more to the point."

Maynard opened his mouth and closed it, shaking his head. "Are you saying..."

"I am saying the probability of you ever running into him again is very low."

"Okay." The trader dragged the word over several syllables, examining Bo with fresh appreciation. "Assuming *that*, I'd be happy to return. My daughter is expecting a baby next month. Dawson will take good care of them, but I want to be there too."

"Dawson?" Ajinder straightened, paling. "Scott Dawson?"

"Yes." Maynard frowned. "Why?"

Ajinder's face sobered. "Lieutenant Dawson has died. Valiantly but unnecessarily. Sorry to bear bad news, sir."

Maynard searched around, and without asking permission, dropped into the nearest chair. "What do you want with me?"

Bo's side glance scolded Ajinder. "Are you senior enough to influence the Union's policies, without LeClaire to hamper you?"

"Yes."

"Do you have any issue with normalizing Buffalo's relationships with its neighbors?"

"No."

"That's all I needed to hear. I'm leaving for Locksville tomorrow. In your stagecoach. Can give you a ride... if you drive the damn thing."

Maynard pushed himself off the chair. "I'll be in my room. Pick me up in the morning." He nodded to Parsons to escort him out.

Sticky silence followed their steps and the closing of the door.

"Tomorrow morning, eh?" Aileen risked a quick look at Bo. He was staring at her, as if trying to memorize her image. She blushed. "Anything I can do to make you reconsider? To make you stay?"

"Leen." Bo sighed. "Don't make it any more awkward. Please."

Aileen lowered her eyes. "Take someone else with you. Anyone from the crew?"

"Think bigger. The entire Streeters organization will be my crew. And you'll need *your* people around you here. People you can trust unconditionally. But I'll ask," he hurried to agree under her pleading look.

"I know you'll bring Weinberg and Marc up to speed," said Ajinder. "May I ask you to pass a message to the Golden Dragons, too? And Jihan, if he's still at The Station."

"Sure thing."

Ajinder rose, rounded the table, and hugged Bo. "You can always count on me, brother."

"Now *you* are making this awkward. Stop this already."

Ajinder beckoned for Aileen. She hesitated only a second before joining the hug.

When the door closed behind Bo, Ajinder sat, pulled Aileen into his lap, and ruffled her hair. "He'll be fine. No, more than fine. Now, out of your shadow, he's destined for greatness. Trust me. That vision of his? I know it will work."

"But—"

"And he'll find someone who'll make him happy. While you and I are busy running this place... and making each other happy. How does that sound, my countess?"

"Mostly, like a pile of bullshit, my consort. Because we're destined for great-ness, too! But that part about making each other happy... Tell me more."

The End

2021

Afterword

If you are reading this, you likely have made it through the entire book. Yay! I cannot overstate how happy this makes me. But there's one thing that would make me even happier: if you left an honest review!

This may sound minor, merely playing to the author's ego—and it does, of course, I will not deny the obvious. But it's *so* much more than that! **Every single review counts.** Those are worth their weight... well, not in gold, being virtual, but, say, cryptocurrency. Especially for the self-published indie writers such as yours truly. The more reviews a book has, the more favorably the mysterious Amazon algorithms are going to treat it. So, if you've enjoyed this novel, please help fellow readers discover it! A nice side effect is that knowing I've done something right alleviates the inevitable author anxiety (hint: that's where your positive reviews come into play). Less positive (but constructive) reviews point out the shortcomings, ensuring each next book is even better. Rest assured, I read them all. Did I mention that every single review counts?

I appreciate your time!

Be sure to check the ***Also By*** to see my other books.

P.S. Oh, and don't forget Goodreads! https://www.goodreads.com/author/show/27317704.Alex_Andre

Find more, follow, and get in touch:
https://alexandre.ink/
https://www.facebook.com/AlexAndreWriting
https://www.instagram.com/alexandrewriting/
author@alexandre.ink

Acknowledgements

My special thanks to the early readers who took the time to go through the entire book or its parts, provided their constructive critique, and helped shape it the way it is today.

This book would not have been the same without you.

Roman, Jaime, Gennadiy, Cassandra, Lev – you know who you are, the unsung heroes!

About the Author

Alex has lived on three continents, is fluent in three languages, suffers an unhealthy interest in linguistics, and never has enough time to get to all the books on his ever-growing To Read list.

He has always appreciated select authors' ability to string words into elegant sentences and tie those sentences into intricate plots.

The E Apocrypha is his first series of novels.

Also By

LESSON NUMBER SIX
   A short story prequel (Book 0.5), providing a glimpse into the past of one of the *Lost & Found* protagonists, a year before the events of Book 1 of *The E Apocrypha*.

   Yun-mi, a young scavenger aspiring to become her clan's best Rat, is cornered.
Has she bitten more than she can chew? Had she sharpened her skills enough to survive the ambush? Or... Wait... Not everything may be what it seems.

LOST & FOUND
Book 1 of *The E Apocrypha* series
Available as an ebook, paperback, or audio book on Audible

In a world shattered by loss of technology, survivors live off the scraps of the fallen civilization.

Ambitious young scavenger **Yun-mi** is thrilled that her mentor is finally taking her trading. Events take a horrific turn when his murder leads to her being sold to slavers. Driven by her ferocious determination, Yun-mi fights against her abductor. Survival depends on aligning herself with powerful allies, yet whom can she trust in the fractured society?

His first assignment as a recruit in the religious confederation military leads **Buck** into the fabled City. The brutal reality he finds along the way destroys any fairy-tale notions he clings to. Rocked by the revelations, Buck sees all the fundamental ideas he's been raised on crumbling before his eyes. Is he truly one of the good guys? Or part of the problem plaguing the land?

As Yun-mi and Buck's paths cross, they must work together on a mission that could alter the course of history. Forced to rely on one another, can they grant their decaying world another chance? Or will Yun-mi and Buck become collateral damage?

AS & WHEN
Book 2 of *The E Apocrypha* series
Available as an ebook, paperback, or audio book on Audible

They've messed with the wrong woman. **Aileen**'s got a city to run—its shady part, in any case. Abducted and whisked away from Locksville, she refuses to be a pawn in powerful players' games. She most definitely is not a damsel in distress and needs no freakin knights in shining armor to come to her rescue. Alas, her best-laid escape plans misfire, landing her in even hotter waters far away from home. Aileen must find her footing in an unfamiliar, unforgiving society, fighting tooth and nail to survive.

Bo, Aileen's sharp and grumpy advisor, would move mountains to find her, his limp and aversion to violence be damned to the Seven Hells! He wouldn't trust anyone else with the impossible search for the most important person in his life.

Ajinder, executive protection specialist, won't tolerate his principal being taken—by someone other than himself. He is no stranger to dispensing violence and doesn't shy away from being on its receiving end. With his motivation stretching beyond pure professionalism, woe to those who question his skills and determination.

Will their grit, smarts, ruthless single-mindedness, and game-changing technology be enough to find Aileen before it's too late?

Meet familiar faces from *Lost & Found*. Return to Locksville, New Kowloon, The Station, as well as discover new corners of the world that had lost all technology.

HERE BE DRAGONS
Book 3 of *The E Apocrypha* series

Technology is power. More so, in the world where both are sparse. But would those possessing the former share the vision of the latter?

Kat, a fierce pirate with a lot to prove, disowned for insubordination and left ashore to face certain death.

Karim, an officer with demons to fight and revenge to exact, struggling with reconciling his homeland's troubling past.

Denny, a young smuggler and wannabe criminal mastermind, forced to flip to the legit side by a betrayal at the peak of his career.

The three find themselves, through a sequence of unrelated events, unwilling participants of an irrational journey beyond the edge of the known map, where be dragons. Will their skills, smarts, and sacrifice be enough to stave off the disaster and save the day? Is the day even worth saving, or is their visionary leader's obsession with technology misplaced?